Blood and Promise

FAE RISING

MIRANDA LYN

Copyright

Blood and Promise

Fae Rising

© 2020, Miranda Lyn

All rights reserved.

Cover Designer – Tairelei – www.facebook.com/Tairelei/

Copy Editor – www.penmanshipediting.com/

Proofreader – Mel Smith www.LinkedIn.com/in/melsmith42

CONTENT WARNING
Violence, Language, Sexual Situations

Also by Miranda Lyn

FAE RISING

Chaos & Destiny

Fate & Flame

Dedication

For three tiny girls that grew awfully fast. . .

CHAPTER

1

Ara

$\mathcal{I}$ had never seen a human before. No one looked at him apart from me. He merely stood at the foot of the dais, holding my attention like a moth to a flame. The chains cutting into the fragile skin at his wrists, the deep red droplets of his foreign blood falling to the glistening white floor. His soft eyes stared straight ahead, clouded with sorrow. He was able to portray more emotion by simply standing still than most fae would in the entirety of their incredibly long lives.

His tattered clothing and sandy, matted hair were a stark contrast to the rest of the king's ballroom, to the obnoxious gown that felt like it weighed a thousand pounds upon my shoulders. I studied him carefully from the quiet corner where I stood. No one touched his ornate silver tray; though, he was probably required by whoever enchanted him to hold it. Maybe for an hour, maybe for a week, maybe until he fell dead. This was the land of the fae after all. None of these folk cared about a lowly human.

After two long hours, I still held my first glass of sticky sweet wine. It was just a novelty, a small indication that I was partaking in the banquet. Everyone was expected to dance and sing and get irresponsibly drunk by

1

the end of the night. I didn't, of course. I was there to watch, learn, and answer questions later. I was always in training. I was my father's daughter before anything else.

As with all the majestic affairs of King Coro's court, I caught myself staring longingly at the open door more than I should have. I wished I could rip this terrible dress off, throw it in the trash, and go home. Maybe not in that exact order. Maybe. But the pesky invitation had come because I was Thassen's daughter, and I was not at liberty to deny the king, even if he didn't know who I was. Even if he'd never looked in my direction. I leaned my back against the cool, marbled wall and remembered that eventually time would pass, and I could leave.

"Pardon me, beauty," a high fae with pale skin and extraordinarily small eyes said as he leered uncomfortably close.

I lifted my chin in the air as I looked down on him, hoping my 'stay the hell away' face was translated into whatever drunken language he needed it to be.

It was.

The fruity smell of aged wine permeating the air was so strong, a lesser fae would be drunk from the scent alone. The tinkling of glasses mixed with the patter of feet filling the dance floor, the cheerful fiddle music so precise, one could easily get lost dancing to it forever. It had been known to happen. I shifted my eyes to the warm firelight glow from the winged tree sprites zipping through the air high above us. The trills of their laughter grated on my sensitive ears.

I looked to the corner, where a group of insufferable brownies sat huddled together. Troublemakers. We had a brownie move into our home several years ago and he wouldn't leave, no matter how much or how often we offended him. We found salt in our sugar shaker and pebbles in our shoes. He did nothing helpful and everything awful. I hated brownies. I'd have rather hung out with a boggart, and I had half a mind to interrupt whatever tomfoolery they were scheming, but I didn't want any of them to follow me home.

Scanning the oversized room, my eyes landed on Nadra in the middle of the crammed dance floor with her bright red hair swaying as she sashayed around two fae males. I would have killed for those curls, but I preferred the dark wine, auburn of my own hair. She was my only friend. An acquaintance, really, but that's the closest I had ever had to a friend.

Nadra was a faithful daughter, but she had a secret lover. Her mother, however, insisted that she find a husband. So, like me, she came to all the soirees and dances and drank and played the part so perfectly, even though most of us knew she would be stumbling home on the arm of a married male—her lover. She looked up at me and winked as if she could read my mind.

I chuckled and raised my glass in her direction.

At least one of us was enjoying ourselves.

The first invitation to a kingdom celebration or holiday is a dazzling experience that answers all the questions a childhood dreamer could imagine. The next time, it's only a pleasant evening, and after that, it's the same drunken faeries, drinking the same damn wine, prancing around to the same noisy music, as the same laughter fills the room. The monotony is deafening. And unfortunately, I had been coming for years and years.

We were celebrating Beltane. The festival started outside in the dark green grass with droves of food on brimming trays and agile servants weaving through the crowd with leaning towers of wines and spirits. Morwena, the sea queen, opened the festival with an atrocious song before we were slowly herded into the castle ballroom where, again, the servants swerved through the crowds with endless refreshments. Thank the gods the fire dancers stayed outside. I didn't think the guards were sober enough to handle rogue flames. This particular festival used to be held at the Flame Court, but the Elder King hadn't invited outsiders to his kingdom for ages.

"Have you seen him?" a harpy's high-pitched voice shouted into my ear as she nearly crashed into me with her wings.

I took a step back, trying to shake the smell of her rancid breath out of my face. "Seen who?"

She rolled her eyes and hit me in the arm. "King Autus, of course." She let her wings shimmer in the firelight, drawing out his name in an annoyingly arduous way. Too much to drink, apparently.

I stepped close to her and pointed my favorite dagger into her ribs. "Hit me one more time, and you'll never see daylight again, let alone the northern king."

She smiled a vicious smile, showing me as many razor-pointed teeth as she could manage. "Didn't your parents ever teach you not to play with knives?"

"No. They taught me how to sharpen them." I flipped the blade in my hand and held it to her throat.

She laughed and flitted away.

Fucking harpies.

At this point in the night, most of the faeries were hardly dressed, and while such a sight would have been shocking to me many years ago, it soon became expected. Normal.

As I always did to pass the time, I began to memorize the slight details other fae probably wouldn't notice—a game my father taught me as a child. The obvious things were in place: the guards of all shapes and sizes that wanted to be seen, and the ones who didn't, easily identifiable by their body language, the subtle weapons they carried, or the way they watched the crowd a little too intently. Secret messages and gossip were circling the room as a long-nosed pickpocket filled his trousers. I had pinned him with a knowing glare earlier, and he had since given me a wide berth. Thieving lutins were worse than brownies.

4

"Ara," Nadra said, stumbling up to me. "Isn't this wonderful?" She leaned in so close, I could see the pattern of freckles dusting her nose.

"Maybe a bit less of this," I said, taking the drink from her hand.

"Don't be silly." She took another glass from a passing tray and was swept back onto the crowded dance floor.

"Pardon?" A deep voice cleared his throat behind me. I jerked around to find a striking fae with broad shoulders and the most charming smile staring down at me.

"What?" I pursed my lips, narrowing my eyes.

"I'm just trying to pass." He turned his head slightly and I noticed the rugged tips of horns hidden within his curly brown hair. His hands were full of overflowing wine glasses and I was standing right in his path.

Without a word, I took a careful step back and watched as the lesser fae carried his drinks off to his companions from the north. He'd probably come as a servant to the Wind Court king.

The Marsh Court ballroom was capacious, with plenty of room for every fae who lived there. I searched for my king among the crowd. He was easy enough to find with his round belly and shining crown. I'd always thought he looked kind with his rosy cheeks and infectious smile, until I saw him murder three lesser fae servants for spilling a heaping tray of food all over the head table. Sure, he was kind. Until he wasn't.

My father said he was known for being a fair ruler, and I should thank my lucky stars I lived in his kingdom, but as I grew into an older female, I learned to make my own judgements. The Marsh Court had proven to be far less fair in recent years. It was a kingdom where middle-class high fae were still invited to the revelry—even if I didn't really want to be there—but if you looked at someone wrong, you'd be killed. Still, in some kingdoms, anyone less than high fae was a servant and would never be seen as anything else.

At the head of the room, upon a raised platform, sat four gilded thrones. One for each court. King Coro, of the Marsh Court sat in his, the largest, and next to him was Queen Morwena of the sea. The other royals were only visitors, but our king always rolled out the red carpet for them. Though, he would never be upstaged.

If kingdoms were given away for beauty, Morwena would rule them all. Most high fae were alluring, but Morwena was jaw dropping. I knew I was beautiful, but when I looked at her, I felt as appealing as a potato. Morwena's hair flowed white, like the caps of the ocean, and her eyes were as blue as glaciers, unlike the dull gray of my own. In fact, the only thing that wasn't beautiful on Morwena was her smile. When she smiled, pure evil poured from her. Something so cruel could never be beautiful. Morwena was not a fae you wanted to cross paths with. Ever. I had left the last ball covered in the blood of a lesser fae she murdered because she could hear him breathing. I was standing far too close to him when her knife flew through the room and stuck right in his throat. Pure. Evil.

In Alewyn, all faeries were not created equal. You were either high fae or lesser, there was no in-between, and gods help you if you were a lesser. The high fae, like my family, were usually tall, beautiful faeries with perfectly pointed ears and gentle features. The lesser fae were the creatures and hybrids of Alewyn: tree people and winged races, horned males and serpent ladies, and a plethora of other faeries that nightmares could hardly fathom. Though there were handsome lesser fae. The northern king had a collection of them that traveled with him. All beautiful

My eyes shifted to the open throne beside her. She was not married. Rumor had it, she would soon be betrothed to King Autus of the northern Wind Court, but that was just the talk of the folk. Nothing had been announced. A rumor was rarely spread without some truth behind it, though. How could the sea marry the wind? Surely, they were not mated. Even for the high fae, it was somewhat rare to find your mate. Royalty should wait for that kind of bond. Sometimes, I wondered if my parents were secretly mated. They adored each other to a sickening degree.

A shout across the crowded room caused my attention to snap to King Autus. I'd bet anything someone was about to die. The music paused, the dancing stopped, and the entire room fell silent. His angry roar had frozen every guest in place, and I watched as he crossed the floor to a lesser fae. Even though it was nearly summer, and our land had warm temperatures during this time of year, he still wore furs wrapped around his towering frame. It was completely unnecessary, but I decided years ago he did this to appear even larger than he was.

"Kneel," he commanded.

The small fae, who was a quarter of my own height, likely half pixie, sank to the marbled floor. Her body tremored as she panted for breath, panicking.

"I'm s-sorry my king," she whispered. "It will n-never happen again."

For the briefest of moments, she turned in my direction and our eyes locked. I held my breath, knowing the outcome. Having witnessed this far too many times, I had to look away.

"No," he answered. "It won't." Without pause, he brought the sword down on the pixie female, and her body crumbled to the hard ground.

"Autus, my dear, what's the matter?" Morwena's toneless voice called from across the great room.

He looked at the pixie's body, raised his cup in the air and said simply, "She ran out of wine to fill my cup." He dropped the glass and, as it shattered, walked away, causing the room to spring back into motion, as if we hadn't all just witnessed murder.

I watched the room to see if anyone looked even slightly bothered, but they didn't. What was a gathering of the folk without at least one death, anyway? I decided that was my cue to leave. I could never refuse an invitation to the palace, but unlike the general population, I drew the line at murder.

I stopped to take in the room one more time. The human remained a solemn statue with his tray of wine, contrasting with the fluidity of the rest of the ballroom. Just as I turned to leave, he glanced up. For the second time that night I shared a look with a doomed soul. Momentarily stunned, I gave a curt nod in his direction and walked out.

Murder. I drew the line at murder. Just because you *can* kill someone, doesn't mean you should. I couldn't worry about a human that likely wouldn't last the week. There were high fae, then lesser fae, creatures and then humans. Their lives were but a blink of time for the fae.

I called for my carriage and began the long trip home. I leaned out of the window, watching the castle fade away as we traveled through the city, avoiding the swampy marsh, until we entered the countryside, with towering trees and green grassy hills for as far as the eye could see.

I trusted my fae horse to know the way. Twice the size of standard-bred horses, his hooves kicked up just enough dirt and dust to add a soothing balance to the cool evening air. I listened to the wheels grind into the stones on the path and the pattern of the trot as he carried me home.

Just before I drifted off to sleep, I saw the face of the dead pixie in my memory. Why did I live in a world like this? Did she intentionally look at me, or was she simply searching for a single person in a crowd full of animosity who would empathize with her?

Days later, I arrived home at our simple cottage, with just a few lamp lights glowing in the windows. Traveling to the castle was such a long journey for just a few hours of lukewarm entertainment. A home in the country far away from the courtiers and hustle and bustle of the city beyond the castle was the only thing my father had ever asked of King Coro.

I unhooked Brimir from the carriage and took him to the stables. As I was brushing him down and generously feeding him pina fruit, I got that all too familiar feeling creeping up my rigid spine, like the legs of a spider, telling me that someone was watching, lurking.

I hit the ground just in time to dodge the arm coming for my neck. I swung around, keeping low, and kicked my assailant just behind the knees. His body kicked up a cloud of dust as he tumbled to the ground. Hard. I had two choices. I could run for the house, hoping I had incapacitated him enough to make it, or I could go on the offense. As I pulled the small knife from my thigh, I smirked. As if I would ever run.

He was painfully slow. I could only see the outline of his stocky body in the moonlight shining into the barn, but it was enough. I stepped into position, holding my knife loosely in my hand. The sound of him pulling his long sword from its sheath was like music to my pointed ears. I needed this. The smile on my face hadn't wavered.

Come get me, you bastard.

He lunged forward, sloppily chopping his sword.

I spun to the left, dancing behind him. As I hopped up and down on my toes, anxiously waiting for him to try again, I kept my breathing steady and focused on everything around me. There could have been more than one attacker, and I had been caught off guard before.

My assailant noticed my distraction and used it to his advantage, as he should have. It was a game, really. I could have had my knife in his chest before he took another breath, but where was the fun in that?

I doubled over as he kicked me in the stomach. Just as he was about to bring the hilt of his sword down on my head, I leaped to the side. I did *not* need that headache.

He brought his weapon back up and nicked my arm.

Damn. Broke the skin.

I charged for him, making the long blade of his sword nearly useless. Sure, he could have tried to pummel me again, but I was quick and went for the throat with my fist. As he gasped for breath, I kicked his wrist, and he dropped his sword. I swept it toward the wall with my foot and brought my knee up to his nose.

Just as I was about to connect for a second time, he called out. "Damn Ara. Are you trying to break my fucking face?"

I shoved him away as a wicked smile spread across my face. "Calm down, Huntagh. You nearly hit me with your sword's hilt, and you don't see me whining about it."

I sheathed my dagger and crossed the barn to reach for the salve we kept on the shelf. It was charmed to instantly close a small wound or heal a burn. Anything bigger than a scratch took a bit more medical attention. Next to it, I grabbed the gauze and wiped away the blood streaming down my arm, then cleaned the scrape and applied the salve wincing through the initial burn.

I struck a match, burning the gauze with my blood on it, and checked that I hadn't dripped it onto the floor, as my father had always taught me. Fae blood could be powerful, he would always say, and we should never leave it behind. I turned back to face Huntagh in his ragged farm clothes, disheveled hair and musty scent of old sweat.

"Wanna go again?" I smiled at the thought of a good spar and deflated only a little when I saw the annoyance on his face.

"Yeah . . . no thanks." He reached up and scratched the back of his head. "I've had my ass handed to me a little too much lately."

"Someone's moody."

"You could just let me win occasionally to remind me why I agree to this."

I feigned shock, bringing my hand to my chest as I walked away. "I would never insult your dignity by letting you win without a fair fight."

My parents tested and trained me often, but sparring with Huntagh, who worked on our land from time to time, had begun to lose its appeal when I knew I could beat him in my sleep. On my worst day. I guess it was better than nothing, though. I slid my knife back into its home as I crossed the lawn and made it to the front door. I paused and looked around one more time, just in case.

CHAPTER

2

Temir

*I*t didn't matter how hard the piercing wind blew. It didn't matter that I couldn't see my hand in front of my face. This was the right thing to do. Others may not have noticed, but I was that boy, cowered in the warmest corner of the freezing stables with a blanket half my body length. I would beg the breeze howling through the gaps in the walls to relent. I tossed the fur-lined blankets bundled in my arms over the tiny boy and turned to leave without speaking a word. I couldn't sleep warm in my bed knowing he was suffering, but we didn't need to make a big deal of it.

"Th-thanks, Tem," the boy whispered.

"Just keep it to yourself, kid," I grumbled and walked out.

I couldn't stand the smell of the stable. Crossing the courtyard riddled with storm-ravaged pines, I swung open the massive wooden door, imagining how I must have looked to him. A lesser fae, just like him, but with stag horns. I was allowed to walk around free, while he and nearly all the lesser fae in the Wind Court were told to keep their heads down and their hands busy. King Autus wanted them to train with the armies or cook and clean in the castle. That was it.

Why was I chosen, and they were not?

I stepped back into the stone castle and stamped the fallen snow from my boots before heading back to my rooms. Though it was nearly midnight and a storm was wreaking havoc outside, the inside of the castle still bustled with activity. The lesser fae typically cleaned through the night while the rest of the castle engaged in all manner of bedroom activities, and not necessarily in their bedrooms.

Sitting silently in my study, I leaned forward, placing my elbows on the desktop and resting my fingertips against my temples. I thought back to when I was slightly older than the boy and made the discovery that changed my entire life.

***

I had worked in the stable. I had lived in the stable. I had eaten the horses' oats just to stay alive sometimes. As a boy, I trained with a wooden sword when it was too dark to brush, feed or saddle the horses.

One day a rider came in, hunched over the front of his giant fae horse. It was saturated in blood, and I was sure the rider was dead. I was terrified. What child wouldn't be, to find a dead soldier on his hands? I wanted to run screaming, but I knew old Marte would skin me alive if I drew any attention to myself. I tied the horse up with shaky fingers, and the rider fell onto the frozen ground. He moaned so loud I screamed and darted under a tack table.

I could hear him mumble for help and I looked from the fallen high fae to the door and back, but no one came. I stayed huddled below the table for minutes, waiting. Gradually, I crawled on my hands and knees across the frozen stone floor to him, tucked my arm under him and used all my strength to roll him over. As I looked into his eyes and he stared back at me, I knew, without a doubt, he was going to die. I couldn't help him. I didn't know what to do, but I couldn't leave him. I was never allowed to step a single foot out of the stables. I was never allowed to call on a high fae, even Master Marte.

Instead, I placed my trembling hand over his gaping wound, as I had seen soldiers do in the past to stop the bleeding, and looked around for something, anything to help me, but there was nothing.

"Please don't die," I whispered. "Please don't die."

Suddenly, the world called to me. It was the first time I felt the pull of my power. All at once, I knew the male would not die. Instinctively, I just knew that if I willed it to happen, and pushed the urge to save him, I could do it. I wasn't sure what would happen to me afterward, but I could feel it in the wind. I could hear it in the trees. I had to save him.

I woke three days later in my frozen corner in the stable, half buried in straw. Master Marte was feeding the horses when I crossed the barn toward him.

"Thought you were dying over there, kid. You haven't moved in days."

"What happened?"

He huffed a breath. "Yes, indeed. What happened, Temir?"

Eyes wide at his use of my name, I stammered. "The-there was a male. And he fell from his horse and scared me. And that's all I remember, Master."

"I see." He scratched the back of his balding head. "Get these horses fed and the end stall cleaned out. I've had to come in and do your work on top of my own. A real inconvenience you've been to me these last few days. I've half a mind to keep your supper for my own belly. Best be hasty, kid."

It took me weeks to remember that I saved that high fae's life somehow. And no matter how hard I tried, I could not re-summon the power I had felt that day.

I thought I'd gotten away with it until I was beckoned by the king himself. I was a small child, a lesser fae, with no idea of who my parents were. My earliest memories were in the castle stables, raised by the hands that worked there. Being summoned by the king who kept me locked away was easily the scariest thing that had ever happened to me. While every part of my childhood was internal resentment for King Autus and the high fae children who could come and go as they pleased, having to stand before him was the very last thing I thought would ever happen.

Marte let me wash in the horse trough and, although it was chilly, it was the first bath I could ever remember having. I'd washed myself with a dirty rag every time before that. I remembered putting on the new pants and soft shirt and thinking that no matter what the king wanted, even if he killed me, I'd die happy. I couldn't remember the last time I had gotten a new shirt, if ever.

I walked to the castle barefoot with sentries surrounding me. My heart pumped in beat with their solidary steps, and I had to remind myself to blink. I wanted to look around. I wanted to run and laugh and swing my arms and spin in circles until I fell from dizziness. I couldn't believe I was actually out of the stables. The world smelled different. All I had known was dirt, mud, oats, and straw. The ceilings were so tall, and the halls were so wide, and it was better than my wildest dreams.

As we entered, I pressed my elbows into my sides and tried to make myself as small as possible. This was an entirely different world, one I had no idea where I fit into, or if I did at all. I had watched the castle out of the stable doors my entire life and imagined what it was like inside. I often practiced sword fighting with the wooden trainer Master Marte would let me borrow, pretending I might storm into this castle and tell the king he had to let me go. I realized then, in all my meekness, that would never happen.

I was brought before the king, sitting like a giant on his gigantic throne. He had furs of all sizes, shapes, and colors strewn about the floors, and sadly, I envied the stone beneath my feet. What I wouldn't have given to wrap a single fur around myself and feel what real, true warmth was. I kept my eyes to the ground as Marte had told me to do and just let the king talk. I was there to listen, Marte had said. Not to respond.

The guard beside me began to speak, and it took all my courage not to dive behind him. "Your Highness, we bring you the stable boy. He'd blow away in the wind. Are you sure this is him?"

"You dare question me, Athos? If you've brought the boy I asked for, then your job is done. Leave." He paused and shifted in his chair. "Boy, have you a name?"

I kept my head down and my mouth shut. I shook so badly I thought the room was moving with me.

"Boy, your king speaks to you. Answer," another voice commanded.

I raised my eyes slightly to see King Autus. My chin was still tucked to my chest, and again I wanted to step behind the muscled guard at my side. The king's hard, unforgiving eyes were beating down on me. I mustered all the courage I could manage and whispered, "Temir, my king."

"Speak up, dear child," the king said.

His attempt at a soothing voice had the opposite effect and my knees began to wobble.

"Temir, Your Majesty!" I shouted. I slapped both of my hands over my traitorous mouth and squeezed my eyes shut.

The king's laughter filled the entire room, and the court began to laugh with him.

"Do you recognize this male?" the king asked, pointing to a high fae with coal-colored hair and a sharp jawline.

I left my hands over my mouth and nodded to the king, locking eyes with the soldier that had fallen from his horse.

"Do you deny laying your hands on him and saving his life?" The eagerness in the king's voice was palpable, even then. Even to a child.

16

I shook my head and looked again to the floor, studying the shadow of my small horns slightly hidden within my tousled brown hair.

King Autus rose from his massive throne, walked down the few steps to me, and laid a heavy hand on my shoulder. "Look at me, Temir."

I dropped my hands and lifted my gaze to him.

"You will never spend another night in the stable. You will move to the castle and begin your training. You will be the greatest healer this world will never know. You will work for me from now until the end of time, do you understand?"

I nodded my head, unsure if I could have denied him even if I wanted to. King Autus's voice turned melodious as he spoke his next heartbreaking words. "Each of you in this room, apart from you, Temir, will hear now my call. You will not remember what Temir is able to do. You will have no memory of this meeting. When you see Temir in the halls, though he is a lesser fae, you will treat him as a high fae, no matter what your instincts tell you to think of him. You will watch over him and trust your king in all things, do you understand?"

"Yes, my king," the room replied as one and bowed.

***

I let the memory fade as I stood from my desk and walked to my bedroom. Removing my shirt, I folded it and placed it on top of my dresser, unlaced my leather boots and set them by the door. As I lay in my bed, I realized I had forgotten to leave myself a single blanket for warmth. At least the boy was warm.

CHAPTER

3

Ara

"How was it?" my inquisitive mother asked as I put away the breakfast dishes in our tidy kitchen. She had wanted to question me sooner but was kind enough to give me time to finish my breakfast. Her gentle hands remained folded behind her back as her deep brown eyes bored into me.

I shrugged. She hated that. I didn't mean to anger her, but I appreciated the occasional upper hand. "Same as always. Four guards on each side of the main door. Both outside guards carried their swords on their waists and crossbows on their backs. The outside party had all four kingdoms' guards. Twenty-seven were ours. Queen Morwena had nine guards. King Autus had only his court. One walked with a limp and another carried enough knives strapped to him you could hear them jingle when he stepped. The Elder King—"

"Use his name, Ara," my mother interrupted.

I set the stack of bowls inside the cupboard and turned to face her, pushing my shoulders back. "King Tolero had guards present but wasn't there." I paused. "Strange, don't you think?"

"Not at all. Was his son there?" She narrowed her gaze. I tried to read her expression, but she was skilled at hiding her thoughts from me. "These are important details. You must always watch and learn, Ara. Even all these years later. It's a very valuable skill to have. You—"

"You need to focus on what shouldn't be there and make note of things others may not," I said in a mocking tone. "Yes, Mother, I know. But I've never met the prince, so I'm not sure what he looks like. I didn't see the Eld—uhm . . . King Tolero's cetani sigil on anyone the rest of the night, so no, I don't believe he was there."

"So, you would rather guess than give facts?"

"No. I know that's not how we play, Mother." I dried my hands on the embroidered towel in front of me and sat down as I traced the notch in the wooden table with my fingertips. I had carved that tiny heart when I was five, right after my father gave me my first dagger. "I know for a fact I did not see the prince there, because I did not see a single face I've never seen before. Apart from one."

I dangled this piece of information before her—she was far too predictable. She would forget about the prince entirely.

She smiled, patiently waiting for me to answer the question she hadn't asked. I pursed my lips and waited for it. A small battle of wits I'd already won.

"Mhmm?" she asked.

I raised an eyebrow to her.

"Spill it, Ara," she barked.

"A human was there, Mother."

She jolted. "You're kidding." She sat down at the table, quickly folded her hands and leaned forward. "Tell me everything."

As I recalled the curious evening, she seemed just as stunned as I was last night. I had never seen a human before, but he matched the description. I explained every detail of him. "He was short, and his ears weren't pointed like ours, but rather tiny and round. Unnatural, even."

"Yes, for sure a human then. Did you see who he was with?"

"No. He just stood the whole time, exactly how I explained it. Should we ask Father?"

"Yes, we should. Just to make sure it's still safe for you to attend should you be invited back. Humans are rare and typically cause more trouble than they are worth."

I scoffed, barely holding back the eye roll. "I think we both know I'll be invited back. Summer Solstice is just around the corner. I go every year. Though, for what reason, I'm not sure."

"Ara, you can't just sit around here with your father and me all the time. Make a friend. Find a lover. Be normal."

"First of all, ew. Second, I'm as normal as I can be living with my parents. And I do have a friend. I'm going to train. Call me in for lunch?"

"One girl who you've had three conversations with isn't exactly a friend," she called as I walked out the door.

This was how it was with my parents. My father was militant. My mother followed his lead in all things, as did I. I could ask my observant father how many crystals hung from the chandelier in the smallest dining room in the kingdom, and he could have answered.

As I walked to the training area we had designed and built, I began. Lunges all the way there, stretches to follow and then sword skills until my mother called for lunch.

I was panting when I walked in, rubbing the age-old blisters on my hands. Always sure-footed, I stumbled as I saw my father sitting at the table.

"Father? Why are you home?"

I squinted slightly at my mother, and she shrugged, placing food at the table.

My father cleared his throat. "Did you not hear the horses? Did you see nothing that would indicate a person other than your mother would be here?"

"No. I didn't. I must have been too focused on training today. I'm sorry, Father."

He leaned in with a conspiratorial smirk. "Or I'm just sneaky."

As my father pulled an envelope from his chest pocket and slid it toward me on the table, my mother took her seat.

"Ara saw the strangest thing at the Beltane celebration. Didn't you, dear?" She jutted her chin for me to take over the conversation.

Instead, I pulled the invitation from the red envelope my father handed me. *Shit.* "Another? So soon?" Every part of me wanted to throw the invitation in the garbage. The ache of my workout settled into my bones as I slumped back and looked up at my father's comforting eyes.

He smiled softly and reached across the table to pat the top of my empty hand. "Cheer up, Ara. Better to be invited than left out."

I handed the invitation to my mother and angled my head to the side. "Must I go again already? This one's in four days."

Shock registered across her face as a small gasp left her. I bit the inside of my cheek to hide my smile at her dramatics.

"You must go, darling. We can never deny the palace. Your father works so hard for them. This is probably just the king's way of thanking him. After all, you are still unwed. And at your age—"

I leaped from the table and stomped out.

Of course I was *still unwed*. Faeries are cruel and scheming pricks who rarely thought of anyone but themselves. My parents raised me to think differently, to have compassion, but that also came with my father's incessant need for me to learn to defend myself. One could never be too careful. He had seen far more in his life than I had, and that's why it was so important to him. Because, if one day he didn't come back from the

Hunt, I'd be able to defend my mother and myself. That was practically the theme of my childhood.

Back to training I went, never stopping to ask why my father had come home for lunch. Probably to deliver the damn invitation I didn't want. I spent the entire next day working harder than ever with my old bow and perfecting my quiver draw with a sword in my dominant hand. Then, I had to pack and, once again, play dress up at the castle.

At some point during the two-day journey back to the palace, I found the silver lining. Maybe I'd see the human again. Curiosity and all that.

It was the end of spring, but hot as a grendel outside the day of the unexpected ball. I wore mostly sheer fabric and comfy shoes because I had no one to impress. Thankfully. Fourteen guards aligning the entrance, welcomed me. Guard number four shifted most of his weight to his left leg. An injury?

As I entered the familiar ballroom, I wasn't surprised to see it so full. Most of them looked as if they hadn't left the castle since the last time I was there. Tendrils of cascading blooms and tiny lights hung from the vaulted ceiling, giving the room the feeling of being lost in a covered garden, while the flowers perfumed the ballroom with a saccharine scent.

I looked immediately to the dais to see which royal courts we were entertaining, convinced that was all this was. Our faerie king throwing his weight around to make sure everyone knew his might. I had never talked to him, never even made eye contact with him. I'm not sure who sent the invites for palace celebrations and ridiculous fairs, but it sure wasn't him.

There he sat next to the sea queen, watching the room with a knowing eye and a pitcher full of ale in his hands. He turned to speak to one of his advisors as I continued down the stairs. Half-naked faeries danced in circles around the great room, laughing and oh-so merry. As always. Tables were set up tonight. Sitting. This was new and, honestly, so welcomed.

I pulled a chair out and my eye caught the human again. His hands were empty, and he had been granted a bath and a clean shirt. Blue like the sea. Hmm. How kind of his keeper. I watched as he walked from one side of the room to the other and then back again in a perfect, slow march, his eyes fixed straight ahead. What an odd command to give him. More so, why did no one seem even slightly intrigued by the odd behavior? Not a glace, not a whisper. Was he so below them that he warranted shunning?

I turned my gaze, just as I saw Morwena looking directly at me.

Dropping my head, I looked away. As my pulse quickened, I took deep breaths. *Why was she looking at me?* Unable to check to see if she was still staring, I twisted in my metal chair and it squeaked on the marbled floor. So. Loud. The face of the fallen pixie flashed in my memory. My skin flushed. My heart hammered in my chest. The temperature in the room became sweltering. I needed air. Now.

Slowly, I stood from my table and started toward one of the empty balconies with privacy curtains. I raised my head, expecting all eyes to be on me, but no one in the room had noticed me. Not a soul. Apart from the queen. Still, I couldn't check to see if she was still watching me. I never wished to see those fierce blue eyes ever again. Fae had died for less. I slipped outside and gasped in the night air as if I were drowning.

Tension settled in my shoulders as I leaned over the balcony railing and took deep, measured breaths, willing my rapid heartbeat to slow. Below me, lovers hid within the turns of the crowded bushes, clutching each other in all manners of passion. For a moment, I forgot my fear as I longed for something like that. The freedom that came with not giving a fuck.

"Hello you."

I whirled around in surprise, coming within inches of easily the most beautiful male I'd ever seen. The way he looked at me through emerald eyes… I thought I'd crumble, just like that. Instead, I swallowed staring at him through my lashes.

"Are you alright?"

"I'm just… yes. No. I mean yes, I'm fine. Totally fine."

He smirked though it seemed forced. Then, rubbing his hand over the dark stubble on his chin, he stepped forward, closing most of the space between us. "Couldn't stay away from the castle, I see."

Not a single word came to my addled mind. I'd just been startled half to death in a room full of a thousand people I didn't want to be around. But this wasn't his court, if it was, I would have seen him before. I narrowed my eyes, and the change in my features must have intrigued him. I had every right to stand there. I lifted my chin. My mother's game. "No," I answered, holding my ground. "You get invited, you come. That's how the process works. Choice is not a factor."

"It rarely is," he said, moving closer. The pale light of the moon turned his tanned skin into a dark hue of blue, matching the undertones of his raven hair. He raised a hand between us. "Dance with me."

As if he'd heard my thoughts, had felt my longing, he'd appeared, offering me exactly what I'd wished for. If even for just a moment. I slipped my hand into his and, as he wrapped the other around my waist, fire spread below his touch, bringing my skin to life in a way I never knew possible. Somewhere in the distant ballroom, lively faerie music played. But as we swayed, we found our own slow beat, eyes locked. He leaned closer.

"You are so beautiful." His lips were only a breath from mine.

A lethargic feeling settled upon my skin and within my bones. As if I'd drank the wine all night, allowing the edges of my vision blur, focusing only on the handsome male in front of me. I couldn't resist the urge to let the rest of the world fade away as he swept me around the balcony, never blinking as we moved.

"Who are you?" I managed.

"That is irrelevant," he breathed, tilting me backward.

He pressed his full lips to my neck and my body answered, weakening. It had been so long since I'd been in the arms of a male, I'd nearly forgotten what it felt like to be worshiped, to be pleasured. Alarms rang somewhere in the back of my mind, but I pushed them all away, allowing myself a moment of release from the tight restrictions caging my life.

A throat cleared just inside the room behind us and that was enough to break the spell. He leapt away from me setting his jaw as that fire within me faded away with the lack of his touch on my skin. He looked over my shoulder, nodding once to whoever had interrupted and took another step away.

"That was a mistake" He ran his hands through his hair, strained. "I cannot be seen with you."

"A mistake?" Rage filled my veins at the liberties I'd given him. "You approached me." Desire could turn into ire so quickly. Oh gods. He was probably married. Or had a jealous lover. "So, you *are* just like every other fae asshole on the planet."

He kept a blank face as he stared back at me, glanced over my shoulder to the ballroom, then let sheer cold hatred fill his eyes. "It's probably best to head home then, Ara." I could feel the fury pouring from him like a fountain. He was embarrassed and gods, was he mad. "Now."

A tinge of power danced within his words like the lilt of a melody. Was he trying to enchant me? More so, was he failing? Wait. He'd said my name. I'd never had magic used on me before, but only royal fae were powerful enough to try to manipulate another's mind. And only one court had a young royal. Prince Fenlas of the Flame Court.

I wasn't sure why, but his enchantment failed. Now that I knew who he was, I played along. I would take any reason to leave, especially now that I'd caught the attention of not one, but two royal fae. I waited for the fear to come, but it didn't. Only anger as I remembered his chosen word. *Mistake.*

I nodded and turned back into the open ballroom. His firm hand caressed the small of my back like fire on ice. Miraculously, I resisted the urge to gut him, balling my fists as I moved. I should have been afraid. I should have lumped him in with the other royals I'd come to know from a distance. But my mind refused, holding only fury.

No matter how loud the room was, I thought I could hear his heart pounding. Or my own, I wasn't sure. He moved around to stand between me and the guards as he dipped his chin to them and they opened the door. I wanted to be shocked, but the look of hatred he shot me prevented me from being anything but curious, and even a little intimidated, which was equal parts disarming and charming.

My thoughts created a maze of questions on my ride home. *What just happened? What would my father say?*

He'd known my name. *Why.*

CHAPTER

4

Temir

I thrummed my hands along the table as I sat quietly in King Autus's private council meeting. I didn't usually have to attend, but the unrest in the faerie kingdoms had stirred the masses—none of which was my concern—but he likely invited the wielders to remind his true council members that he had been collecting magical fae for a time such as this.

I wanted to tell him how absurd it was that he believed the other kingdoms had not done the same, but he wasn't the king from that childhood memory after I left the stable. He wasn't the kind and helpful king he would have had me believe. He would never listen. I was not invited for my opinion. I would just sit here, still and quiet, and let my mind drift to my work and my desire to tend to the herbs and plants in my personal tree nursery or the indoor gardens.

"Your Majesty," Thane began, "thank you for agreeing to call this meeting."

The ten of us sat around the long council table. It had nearly as much history as the whole of our kingdom. I considered the secrets and scheming that had happened in this cavernous, otherwise empty room, the trysts upon the table and lies swept underneath. If walls could talk, what would the stones say? I glanced around the room to the familiar faces of the council and the magical fae. Apart from Eadas with his beady eyes and hopeful expression, the rest of us sat motionless. Waiting.

There were five magical fae and five true council members. Oleonis, my mentor and a high fae with the gift of plant growth, sat to my right. His long white beard matched his hair and proved his old age. Evin, having the gift of magical detection, sat to my left.

"Get on with it, I'm not interested in sitting here all day," the king demanded.

"Yes, my king." Thane stood and made an exaggerated bow in the king's direction, his black hair tumbling forward. He might as well have licked the king's boots while he was down there. "As word has spread of your betrothal to the magnanimous Queen Morwena of the sea, the kingdom grows antsy, my king. As do I. The time has come. We need to move on the southern courts before they have time to prepare. We must call in the queen and begin preparations."

I'd like to say I was surprised, but in truth, I wasn't.

I liked Thane the least of all the council members. While my nature was to heal the hurt, the sick and the dying, his one true purpose in life was the opposite. King Autus loved him for it. Every fae in that room understood that our king was vicious and merciless, that he killed at the drop of a hat and made no apologies. He segregated the fae and treated the lessers as if they were nothing. But we also turned a blind eye, because at the end of it, we were just here for show and none of us really had a choice. Even the council had no real sway over our sovereign.

"Again?" Ragal questioned, pulling my thoughts back to the room.

Thane turned to the king's cousin and only family member on the council. He squinted his eyes at him and huffed. "And what do you know of these things? What do you know of war? What do you know of opportunity and strategy?"

"I know this." Ragal stood, placing his palms on the table and leaning in toward Thane. "You have one agenda only, and it's bloodshed. If the king doesn't keep you around for your astute ability to kiss his ass, then it's because he can always rely on you to introduce the most vicious and disgusting paths to death and bloodshed."

Thane's laughter filled the hollowed room. Knowing the king's lack of nepotism, apparently court decorum became irrelevant to him. I flicked my eyes to the king, anyway. He stared straight ahead, likely not listening to the conversation in front of him.

"I'll take that as a compliment," Thane proclaimed, clapping his hands together with a gruesome smile on his scarred face.

"It is not a compliment. What is your plan, Thane? Watch our king marry the sea queen and then conquer Alewyn? Will we kill *everyone* or just every other fae? Will we stop with the lesser fae, or will we begin to kill the high fae, also?"

"Now we're getting somewhere." Thane nodded his head to Ragal and took his seat. "Our king is the rightful High King of Alewyn. His bloodline gives him that title, or do we need to revisit the Iron Wars?"

"No. If our king is to rule the world, it must be tactical and with as little bloodshed as possible. What is a reign born of bloodshed and fear?"

"The eternal reign," Oravan, the blacksmith, contributed.

The troll, Bolgan, huffed.

"No, it isn't," Ragal said, shaking his head. "It's the reign of rebels and fated death." He turned, bowed to the king and walked out of the room.

"Anyone else?" King Autus asked with a yawn.

For a brief moment, I locked eyes with Gaea, another lesser fae in the room. An almost imperceptible nod told me she would not contribute. I looked to Oleonis, my mentor and friend, but he kept his head down and said nothing, as I would have expected of him. He reserved most judgment. As a teacher, his motto was closer to that of letting one make a mistake and learn from it, rather than teaching one to avoid the mistake altogether.

"We will not make plans of war this day, Thane." The king rose from his chair and left.

What a waste of time. As the group left their seats, I crossed the room and stopped to speak to Oleonis. "Join me in my study this afternoon? There is something I want to show you."

His kindness showed across his wrinkled face as he clasped my hand between his own. "I'll be there shortly, my boy."

"Temir, could I speak to you?" Gaea asked.

Surprised, I nodded and walked in her direction.

She placed her hand on my forearm, and for an instant, the world went dark and I was falling. And then suddenly my feet slammed into the ground as we stood outdoors, the winter wind gnashing at my face.

"You could have warned me we would be spiriting," I said timidly, rubbing the back of my neck.

She shrugged. "What's the fun in that?"

I rarely spoke to Gaea. Her confidence was nearly as intimidating as her beauty, and she and I were nothing alike. I watched her fawn-colored hair blow across her face and her delicate fingers as she tucked it away. Her cat-like eyes were the only indication she was not a high fae. Pushing myself, I held her gaze until I could take it no longer and looked away.

She smirked and bumped my shoulder with her own. "Ready to go to war, then?" She posed the question as if she were asking me if I liked the gardens.

"I'll do as the king commands. It doesn't matter if I'm ready. I can't save them all."

"I need to talk to you about Oleonis."

I knew Gaea felt close to him, and it made sense that she would want to protect him. He'd taught her how to use her magic, just as he'd taught me. I remembered him bickering on and on about how stubborn and difficult she was as a child. Knowing her now, I wondered if she did it on purpose.

"What about him?" I tucked my hands behind my back.

"Occasionally, I spirit around the castle, keeping myself hidden. Seriously, if you ever tell anyone that I'll kick your ass. Anyway, I was hopping around the castle out of boredom and overheard a conversation with the king. I think he knows something about Oleo that he isn't happy about, but I couldn't figure out what it was. He is having him watched."

I knew exactly what it was. "Why tell me and not him?"

"Because if he is hiding something and not telling me, I didn't want to force the issue. He spends enough time with you. It wouldn't be strange for you to discuss it with him. Just tell him to be careful, that's all. Something's up. I wouldn't normally say anything, but that old coot matters to me and I just need someone else to help me keep an eye on him. It's important, okay? I think it's bad, Temir."

The sincerity in her voice caught me off guard. Gaea was typically aloof and void of emotion. Not that I paid much attention, because I didn't. I cleared my throat. "I'll do my best."

"Thanks, Tem."

Without another word, she grasped my hand and we were back at the castle. She chose the stairs at the bottom of my solar as a landing pad.

I let the world stop spinning for a moment before I realized she was still holding my hand. My breath caught as I quickly dropped hers and put two stairs between us.

"See ya." She giggled and then vanished.

Later, as I sat at my desk on the opposite side of the castle waiting for Oleo to meet with me, I penned my latest experiment into my most recent medical journal. Hundreds and hundreds of journals stacked my shelves and lined the walls and the floors. I practiced medicine as a traditional healer as well as a magical one. While people were unpredictable and insatiable, my plants would never fail me. I knew exactly what would happen when I mixed the extract of juniper and mugwort with an activating agent. I spent my entire life studying as many plants as I could find, just as Oleo had taught me. I thought back to my first day in the castle as I waited for him.

***

"This way, kid," the king's soldier said as he led me through the castle. "It's going to take us a full year to get there if you don't hustle."

I couldn't help it. I dragged my feet as I peeked out the drafty windows and into the open doors. The awful king said I could stay. That I had a room and everything.

We got all the way to the end of the long hall and the soldier looked at me with a blank face as he waited. I looked up to him and back to the door several times.

"I'm sorry, sir. I don't know how to open it," I admitted quietly, looking down at the floor.

He scoffed, reached out and grabbed the protruding knob and turned it, shoving the door inward.

I stepped carefully inside, and he slammed the door behind me. My body jolted. Then I just stood there, unsure of what to do with myself in the rooms King Autus had given me. No one had given me a job or told me what to do. A long time passed until I realized I was on my own, so I took a single step forward and shoved my shaking hands into my pockets. I wasn't afraid. I jerked my posture straight and raised my chin. These were *my* rooms now. I could walk around if I wanted to. I could probably turn the knob and go back out and then come back in. I could sleep under all the covers on the real bed and I could stick my tongue out at whomever I wanted.

A gentle knock on the door startled me, and I ran for the couch in the middle of the room and hid behind it, peeking over the back as the door swung open. My heart raced inside my chest.

An old fae with two books in his hands and a beard as long as I was tall stepped into the room.

I gasped and ducked down again.

He chuckled.

I heard the click of the door shut behind him and several footsteps. I squeezed my eyes shut and hoped if I couldn't see him, then he couldn't see me. I listened to the silence for several moments until I heard him whisper, "What are we hiding from?"

I leaped out of my skin and then opened my eyes to see the old fae crouched beside me, looking over the edge of the couch toward the door. I scrambled backward and fell right on my bottom.

He chuckled again. "Are you hungry?" he asked me, as if I were a wild animal.

I nodded fervently. I guess I was.

He smiled and stood, holding his hand out for me to take.

I looked down to his wrinkled fingers and back up to his old face.

"I won't bite if you don't."

My eyes doubled in size. "How old do you have to be to get wrinkles like that?" That was the first thing I ever said to him.

He tossed his head and laughed until his belly jiggled, and I giggled because he was fat enough for his belly to jiggle. "Very old," he answered, a gleam of kindness in his eyes. "Now, about that food."

I reluctantly took his hand and let him lead me out of the rooms and back down the long hallway. I took my time again, studying the people and the sconces and the artwork along the walls. He didn't complain a single time. In fact, when I stopped to stare at a woven tapestry, he stood beside me quietly and studied it as well.

"Who are they?" I asked, pointing to the seven faces.

"This tapestry depicts the gods, Temir."

"How do you know my name?"

"The king told me. I'm to be your teacher." He looked down and squeezed my hand gently.

"Oh," was all I could say.

We continued our mission, and the closer we got to the kitchens, the more my belly grumbled as the smells tickled my nose. There were no oats here. Only delicious things covered in icing and steamy sauces. My belly rumbled, and the old fae led me to a small wooden seat in the corner.

I sat as instructed while he chatted and walked through the kitchens, filling one plate and then another. My eyes were glossed over by the time he got back to me. "Come," he said.

Hypnotized by the stack of hot food, my feet moved quicker as we walked out of the kitchens and back down the long hallway. But instead of going to the rooms I was given, we turned and went down another hall, until he motioned for me to open the door to a different room. I stepped forward, grabbed the knob and turned it, just like the guard had done. I opened the heavy door, quite satisfied with myself.

He laughed at me and nudged me into the room. Green things hung from the walls and the ceiling and it smelled divine. Not like food, but sweet, soft.

"What are those?" I asked, pointing.

He looked stricken for a second, and then he set the dishes down and moved toward one of them. "These are plants, Temir. From all over the world. I take care of them."

"Why?"

"Because plants can provide us our most basic needs. Oxygen, food, medicine. You've really never left the barn?"

I shook my head and looked to my toes.

"Come eat, Temir," he said firmly.

Never one to deny an order, I straightened my back and moved to the table. I looked up to him and his angry face. Then back to the food. "Did I do something bad?" I whispered.

"Not even a little bit," he said, ruffling the hair on my head, avoiding my budding stag horns. "What should we start with?"

"Sir?" I asked. "You mean I'm to have more than one thing?"

"You must call me Oleonis," the old fae said. "And you're to have as many things as you wish. I do recommend the buttered sausage, though. It's Cook's best."

"This one?" I asked, pointing to something random on the plate in front of me.

"That's bread," he said. "This one."

I stuck the sausage into my mouth and chewed. The flavor was nothing like horse oats. I sprang to life, shoveling all the foods into my mouth until I could hardly chew.

Oleonis said nothing. He only sat back in his seat and made sure I didn't choke to death. Once I finished my plate, he slid his across the table.

I studied him carefully. This felt like a test. One that Marte would have whipped me for. I shook my head, swallowing the final bite of my food.

"Eat, Temir. There's plenty more in the kitchens for me."

"Why is there so much food in the castle but nothing in the barn?" I reached for another sausage.

"Why, indeed." He looked away, and I was sure I'd made him sad. But eventually he turned his face back to me, and the kindness had returned. He led me back to my rooms. "Bath first, and then bed. We will begin your lessons in the morning."

"But I had a bath this morning." I grumbled. "First one ever."

"Good gods, no wonder you're still covered in soot. Come. I'll help you."

I stood shivering in the bathroom, the water dripping from me as I held the towel around my shoulders. "I'm done, sir," I called into the other room.

He entered, shook his head and pointed back to the bath. "You're still filthy. Back in."

I groaned and got back into the tub. He helped me scrub all the nooks and crannies and told me a story of dragons as he washed my hair. Again. Once we were finally done and I changed into bedtime clothes, he pulled the covers up to my chin and smiled down to me.

"Why are you so nice? No one's ever been nice to me."

"Because kindness is rare but valuable. It's also deserved. You're a good boy, Temir."

I shook my head. "Master Marte says I'm the worst boy that's ever worked in the stables." I felt my lip quiver and bit down to hide the tears.

"I'm sure that's not true. From this day forward, I never want you to consider a single thing that terrible fae has ever said to you. You have a question, you come to me." He patted my arm, and his sincerity was disarming, even to a boy.

I nodded and yawned.

He leaned down, wrapped his arms around me, and for several seconds I thought he was going to squeeze my head off.

"What was that?" I asked as he pulled away.

He looked at me funny and shook his head. "That, my boy, was your very first hug. Now get some rest. I'll see you in the morning."

I yearned for another hug. To feel the comfort of another person's gentle touch. I wouldn't ask, though. Maybe tomorrow. It took exactly five minutes after he left my rooms for me to get out of bed, and taking the top blanket with me, I snuck down the halls and knocked on his door.

He smiled down to me as I stood there in my bedtime clothes, dragging a blanket. I wasn't sure what to say. I was supposed to be tough, but I was scared.

He seemed to understand, though. He stepped to the side and welcomed me without a word. He tucked me into his own comfy bed, and I fell fast asleep really, truly warm for the very first time. I woke several times during the night to his loud, old fae snoring, but for some reason it brought me peace. I wasn't alone anymore. And somehow, I'd been rescued by the kindest, old, wrinkly fae that probably ever existed.

***

"Have you done it?" Oleonis asked, pulling me from my memories.

I looked up from my book and saw him perched in the doorway. Sneaky old fae. "I'm nearly there." I gestured to the seat in front of my desk and he sat, joining me. "I need you to work on some additional herbs for me, if you could."

I crossed the room, pouring myself a glass of wine and Oleo his favored poppyseed rum. As I placed the glass in front of him, I noticed his shaking hands. I knew what it meant. I just didn't know if I should pry.

Thinking back to my conversation with Gaea, I asked, "Has it gotten any better with our last round of treatments?"

He reached for his glass and took a long draw. "No. I'm afraid herbs won't help, nor will magic. The visions will keep coming. I just need to make sure few know of them."

"How can you control that when you have no recollection of the vision itself? What if you have a vision in a council meeting? What if the king realizes what you can do?"

"Should that happen, boy, you must look as confused as everyone else. Do you hear me? He cannot know that you have kept this secret with me."

I nodded, thinking back to the first time we realized Oleo could see into the future. It was a rare gift, but not entirely unheard of. We were working in our arboretum. His magic grew the plants at a rapid speed. He worked in the gardens to feed the kingdom, and when he had time, he humored me by helping my studies. He was always a sucker for knowledge, and I appreciated his kindred spirit. One day, as we were planting seeds for a loquat tree, he fell to the ground. I rushed to him, and he whispered of a burned female, his eyes unseeing as he foretold what was to come. As the vision faded, his confusion mixed with my surprise and I helped him to his feet.

"Did I fall, Temir?" he asked

"No, not entirely. What do you remember? Are you hurt?"

"Remember? I was putting my seeds into the soil and then you were standing over me."

"And of the female?"

"What female?"

"You spoke of an injured female. Do you truly not remember?"

"I don't."

As I examined his pupil dilation, a guard rushed in and hurried me off to my apothecary room, claiming the king had need of me. When I returned, I explained to Oleo that a high fae of the Sea Court had been mysteriously burned, just as he had said. We thought nothing of it until it happened a second time, and then a third.

"How often?" I asked, coming back to the present time.

"It's hard to say, at least once a day. There been a slight development, though, Temir. I recalled a vision this morning."

"Did you?" I took my seat. "Tell me what you remember, Oleo."

"I'm afraid, like the others, it makes no sense. I simply watched a small group of fae walking in a dense fog until they all became separated."

"Hmm," I said. "I'll add it to our journal, nonetheless. I wondered if my healing magic would change anything. Before our session begins, though, there's something I wanted to tell you."

"Yes?" He took another sip of his rum.

"Without going into too much detail, I just want you to be careful. You know the king well. You've worked in this castle for him for over three hundred years. If he learns of this ability, he will lock you away. He will not let you out of his sight. He will stop at nothing to force you to become his seer, something I know you do not want."

He nodded slowly.

"Gaea overheard a conversation and asked me to warn you. She thinks you might be in danger, and now I wonder if our king has not already learned of this."

"Temir, you know if he enchanted me, I would have no choice. I would have to do whatever he asked."

"I'm not asking you to betray the king or to deny him. I'm only asking you to be careful. Keep your mental shields strong. We decided we were going to keep this to ourselves, and now I think the court may know. You can't do it on demand, and you can't clearly recall anything of significance. What if that angered the king? What if he asked you to see into the plans of the sea queen and you were unable to do that. What would he do to you?"

"We both know the answer to that question, Tem. For now, I will keep to myself as much as I am able. It is the best I can do until we learn more about this. Shall we begin?"

He reached his arm across the table, but before I took it, I watched his face closely. No sign of concern. I closed my eyes and willed my magic forward, just as the male at my fingertips taught me so, so long ago.

CHAPTER
5

Ara

*O*nce upon a time, there was a female so old, there was not a kingdom that remembered her as a child. The old female, known as Aibell, lived so deep in an ancient forest, they said the only way to find her was to need her so desperately, your heart called her name louder than your voice ever could. Aibell . . . Aibell . . .

One day, a female sought her. She called her for weeks wandering through the forest until she came upon a glen. Her heart called for Aibell. Her mind called for Aibell. Everything that she was called for her so desperately that she knew if she lay down to die, the unborn child in her belly would call for Aibell before also dying.

Aibell . . .

The female lay on the soft grass floor of the glen, and as she wept, the sky wept, the rain chilling her to the bone. Still, her sorrow-filled voice called, "Aibell."

Aibell did not come for the female. She lay down to rest in that glen and never woke.

I woke in the carriage with my mother's favorite tale in mind. It was such a sad tale, but as the years had passed, she loved to tell this story most. Perhaps it was because it reminded her of her own mother's death upon her birth. Perhaps because she liked to remember there was always hope but nothing was ever promised.

As I neared our cottage, I started counting carriages lined outside our home. Thirteen and a few lone horses. Father had called a meeting of the Hunt. There hadn't been a meeting of the Hunt in our home since I was a child. It was probably best not to disturb them, so I quietly slipped into the house and made my way to my bedroom. I wasn't worried they would hear me. They never did. I knew which floor planks were quietest and to lift my door as I swung it open to prevent the sound it otherwise made. I didn't bother shutting it completely. The click would give me away.

I stepped lightly to my bed and fell back, letting it catch me. Watching the lazy sun move across the ceiling, I listened for the males to leave. But they didn't. I moved to the mirror and tied my long hair back in a braid, then returned to the bed. Then to my bookshelf. Then back. I was pacing, I realized. Waiting, just as my father would have done. I may have looked nothing like him, but we were so similar in action and thought. I needed his advice, but his meeting was important.

As a child, I would eavesdrop on the meetings. He always knew I was there, of course, but he also encouraged any opportunity to learn anything and everything I desired. Maybe I'd just sneak down and see if they were almost done. I lifted and slowly opened my door, taking a moment to calm my breathing. When I was seven, I learned a breath could be your biggest betrayal. I moved down the hallway, hoping that my mother was not home.

The Hunt was fascinating, but they were also cruel. It was said they rode the night sky on fae wind into the human lands. The beast that led the Hunt used magic to keep them unseen by anyone but their chosen victims. They brought death to deserving humans and escorted them to the underworld.

Even the fae could fall victim to the Wild Hunt, though it was rare. That was why my father was feared. That was why I was invited to the stupid castle. My father was not the leader of the Hunt by personal choice alone. He'd told my mother they had asked him to lead for hundreds of years, but he refused time and time again. He was a badass, and most of the males under my father looked to him as the leader, anyway. He could best any of them, and they knew it.

I slipped into the open hallway outside his office and creeped down the long corridor until I was in an adjacent room. I stepped to the wall and listened, closing my eyes and trying to picture where they were in the other room.

"I think we are done here," came a gruff male's muffled voice.

"We are done when I say we are done, Edwin," my father snapped. "It's not our job to question anything. We cannot consider this at all." I heard his chair move and the steps he took toward Edwin. "You must listen to me." My father let out an exasperated sigh and softened his voice. "We gain nothing from getting involved with any of it. It's not our job to be involved. It's not our job to do anything but exactly as the king commands."

"Why?" another voice I didn't recognize demanded. "Just tell me, after all of these damned years, why you still cower. Why don't you want to be a part of something bigger? Why shouldn't we consider her offer? Who says that King Coro is the only king who can command the Hunt, Thassen?"

"My answer is final. You are talking about treason, and I won't hear another word. Get out, all of you."

I turned and pressed my back against the wall, breathing be damned. There was only one she he could be talking about. Why did Queen Morwena want control of the Wild Hunt? As the footsteps tapered down the hall and out of the house, I was torn. Should I even mention the prince to my father now? I had been a grown fae long enough to know I didn't need him for something so simple when he was battling something so much bigger. I took a step from the wall but paused as I heard muffled whispers behind it.

"You know what will happen, don't you?"

I started at that voice. I didn't think my mother had ever joined a Wild Hunt meeting.

"You and I both know that we cannot be involved in treason," my father answered. "We can't draw attention to ourselves. To her. Do you think I like this, Vi? Any of it? I see more than most people. I know where this cursed land is headed. And now more than ever we must remain steadfast."

"What aren't you saying, Thassen?" Her voice was soft.

"We know that King Autus has always favored high fae. I look at you now, darling, with your long, slender body and your beautiful, pointed ears and cannot fault him for the love of his own image. But the suffering of the lesser fae has been so much worse these past years. I think the time is coming."

My father sounded so incredibly defeated, and it broke me on a level I didn't know existed.

"We don't live in a just world, my darling. We just don't." I heard him cross the room, moving to be nearer to my mother. "At first, it was only him. The high fae in the Wind Court are held above all others there. All fae creatures, from pixies to the naga, are servants or workhorses. It's been this way for so long, I think the common folk of the Marsh, Sea, and Fire Courts forgot to care. But, three nights ago, Morwena came to Beltane, where she accepted the marriage proposal of King Autus."

My mother's gasp hid my own.

"On that same night, she left the merfolk behind in her kingdom to ravage her own sea. They went into the homes of all sea creatures and demanded they join the military submit to servitude or die." He paused, and I squeezed my hands together, afraid of his next words. "Children, my love. She now has children training in her military camps, and we have so few precious babes. Word arrived today that she left a path of slain lesser fae through our land as she and her Sea Court traveled to King Coro's castle. She has killed in our kingdom, and so far, it looks as if he will do nothing."

I scooted down the wall to get closer so I could hear my father's tale. If Morwena was murdering fae in our kingdom, trying to steal the Hunt and marrying King Autus, something big was happening.

"Do you know what will happen?" my mother asked as I heard her stand.

"Genocide. Genocide of all the lesser fae. Worse than anything our world has ever seen. And I can only imagine the human army either she or Autus want to build. Why else would they want command of the Wild Hunt?"

Exactly. My father was a genius.

"It's so easy to sit here and say at least we are safe as high fae. At least we will not be murdered. But to truly turn our backs on the rest of Alewyn? To leave them behind and watch *them* be murdered out of cowardice is just not something I will do. You know that. I've accepted this mission from the start, and I will see it through."

Long, deep breaths in and out. I needed to still my damn heart. This was war he was talking about. This was exactly what my mother had feared for years while my father and I had trained for it.

"The world is changing," he said. "I will not let them give the Hunt to her. I will not leave Coro, when he may need us all now more than ever. I've written Tolero, but no response. He still hasn't done a thing since Efi died. No sign of Fenlas yet, either. The Flame Court is strong, but they seclude themselves. They may not even bother with this until the army sits at their doorstep after wiping out the Marsh Court entirely."

"Not bother? That isn't true, Thassen. You know Tolero. He wouldn't do that. He has too much at stake to sit back and let the world burn," my mother said.

I'd never heard them speak so informally about the Flame Court. I didn't even know my father knew that king. Other than tutoring me, he'd never mentioned him.

"All of that aside, we still have to send our daughter to the castle as often as she is requested without being able to protect her, because we do not want to raise suspicion of rebellion by simply denying an invitation. Do you know how hard it is for me to send her off each time she's summoned? I watch that carriage roll away and wonder if she will return, knowing Autus and Morwena are in attendance."

He paused, and I heard my mother take a ragged breath.

"I've gone, you know. I've followed her and secretly watched from a distance just to make sure she was safe. Because she is so much more important than any of us," he said.

"Oh, my darling," my mother's voice cracked. "She is so lucky to have you. As am I."

As I heard the soft kiss, I left the room and moved as lightly as possible through the house. I opened the door and slipped out, heading to the training arena, where I pushed the heavy sliding door open. My shoulders relaxed as I crossed the room and selected a new blade from the wall of many. I considered working on the dummy in the loft, but footwork was on the schedule this week. I scattered some powder across the floor to make the movements seamless, and dusted my hands.

It was easy to get lost in swordplay when you had an opponent. It was not so easy when you didn't. I tried running. I tried target practice. I just wasn't getting anywhere. My unsettled mind was so full of questions, I didn't know where to start, and my father, whom I would normally turn to, seemed to have his hands full. I understood it. The faerie world was far from perfect. But so was the human world.

Thousands and thousands of years ago, all fae had the ability to enchant the mind. They could trick each other into seeing things that weren't there, they could use magic to make the mind forget things or control the actions of others. Without the ability to enchant, which had faded out over the years, we weren't able to camouflage ourselves so well. Now, only the royal lines could enchant the mind, and magical fae were rare as bloodlines became diluted with time.

Some fae had other abilities, though. I'd heard the blacksmith in the Wind Court could make anything and charm it. They said King Autus had a golden knife that never missed its target. Imagine never having to practice a skill, but rather be perfect by mere possession.

His commander was said to wear a set of bangles that gave him the strength of ten males. Nadra once told me she heard the Flame Court had a high fae with the ability to disappear completely, instead of only tricking your mind into believing you couldn't see her. Mother said fae with those kinds of abilities were so rare they were highly sought after by the rulers.

Happy to be normal and not have to deal with any of that, I continued my blade work. Well, as normal as anyone raised by a commander of the Wild Hunt could be, anyway. I was a loner on my best day, and I preferred it to be that way.

"You're not shifting your weight properly for that stance, Ara. I know that sword doesn't weigh enough to prohibit your ability to lean backward. Something on your mind, dear? You're home sooner than we expected."

I turned to see my father leaning against the doorframe of our training arena. The casual way he stood, with his hand in his pocket and his head tipped against the frame, tricked my mind into believing nothing was really bothering him.

I played along, choosing my words of truth and deceit as carefully as possible. "Hey there. No, nothing on my mind. Just wanted to work on the balance with the new blade, that's all."

"Well, you won't do it correctly if you can't remember where your feet are supposed to be."

He crossed the room and pulled a sword from the wall. Not his personal sword, of course. We could never train with that one. He shifted the hilt back and forth between hands and stood before me. I knew this trick. He was doing what I was doing. Trying to take his mind off what was bothering him. I guess the apple didn't fall far from the tree.

As we sparred, he refused to hold back, and it took everything I had, and everything that male had ever taught me, to just stay on my feet. I was good, but he was better.

Later that evening, at the dinner table, my mother watched us both carefully. "Ara, why are you home so early?"

I pushed the food around my plate with my fork and said casually, "Well, I went to the castle, but the Prince of the Flame Court allowed me to leave early."

As my mother's fork hit the table, I realized I'd said something to surprise her. I looked up, and her wide eyes were staring directly into my father's. My eyes shifted between them as I replayed exactly the words I had said to them. I hadn't even mentioned the strange part.

"So, the Flame Court has indeed come to the Marsh Court?" Father asked. It was rhetorical but told me exactly where his mind was.

"And you're sure it was the prince?"

"He didn't come right out and tell me he was the prince. He wasn't wearing a crown, but his skin was tanned, and his hair was dark, and I've never seen him before." He also had the most beautiful face and heated eyes I had ever seen, and before he spoke a word, I probably would have done anything that pretty mouth asked me. I spared my parents the details. Being beautiful was not uncommon. Being an arrogant asshole wasn't, either. Unfortunately, based on my encounter, he was both.

"Let's not jump to conclusions then," Father said. "It's possible, but not certain."

My mother nodded her head and stood to leave the table. Her chocolate eyes were glued to the kitchen floor as she walked away.

We'd just had two entirely different conversations at that table. The one I was a part of, and the one I wasn't.

CHAPTER

6

Ara

$\mathcal{J}$t took ten days before I was, once again, invited to the castle. This time, it was for a luncheon for all the unwed high fae of the Marsh Court. I could see the hesitation on my father's face when I asked if I really had to go. It was still a yes, but he did tell me that I could come home as soon as it seemed appropriate to leave.

He also informed me that he wanted Huntagh to come as well. He worked on our land sometimes, but my father had used him as a guard in the past. He was also unwed, so I supposed he was also invited. I wasn't sure how great of a guard he would be, considering I could best him every day of the week. I didn't anticipate a mass murder, though, so I was sure it was just for my father's peace of mind. Which was fine, I guess.

As we arrived at the palace, I was reminded of how long the days were. We stopped in the city, so I could make a casual attempt at freshening up. We were to have lunch outside, but who knew what would happen as the evening unfolded. I was hoping to be on my way home after the meal. Maybe I could piss off the prince again or make his significant other jealous. That seemed to work well enough the last time, Not that I'd been thinking of him or anything, because I hadn't. Maybe he wouldn't even be here. One could hope. Maybe he could steal away Morwena and solve all the world's problems in one shot. I shuddered at the thought.

"Do you mind if we split up?" I asked Huntagh. "I don't think anyone else has a guard and, no offense, but I don't really see the need."

I was basically asking him to get lost, but seriously, there was a reason I didn't have many friends. I kept to myself.

He grunted and walked away.

The entire lawn was full, and as I looked around, I noticed it was mostly high fae, as the invitation depicted. There was a single long banquet table lining the grass in the castle bailey. I had to admit the centerpieces were lovely and I could never fault whoever decorated those stupid things. The massive candelabras and the cascading flowers down the entire table really were beautiful. I guess I would have enjoyed it more if there weren't so many folk here. As I realized I was going to have to sit at a table full of people I didn't care to know, I scanned the crowd for prospects. I had ditched Huntagh a little too soon, but maybe I could find Nadra.

I strolled around, hoping bright red hair would pop out at me, when I slammed right into someone. I looked up to see Prince Fenlas. Of course, because that was just my luck. I held in my breath and tried really hard not to scowl at him, reminding myself pretty was not akin to kind. I tried for a quick curtsy and apology, but the stupid annoyance on his royal face made my blood boil.

"I should have known you would be here." He actually rolled his eyes and shook his head in indignation.

"Excuse me? What the hell is your problem? I wasn't aware we've ever had the *pleasure* of meeting before you came on to me last time." I dipped the word pleasure in so much sarcasm, there was no way in Alewyn he missed the point. "So sorry I offended you by simply breathing your air space."

I turned to walk away, but he grabbed my arm. He was seething, and I wasn't even mad about it. My face was inches from his and, as he looked down into my eyes, I could feel the fire there. I'm not sure if it was his or mine, but it was thrumming all the same.

Teeth clenched, jaw set with only inches between us, he whispered, "Well, if you *have* to be here, you could at least do me the *honor* of sitting at the end of the table, so I don't have to look at you."

I jerked my arm out of his hold, and it took every bit of self-control I had not to pull my knife and put it to his throat. I'd absolutely be murdered, though, and that sounded awful.

I narrowed my eyes and hissed back, "With pleasure." Then, I turned and stomped off before he had a chance to respond with anything.

What a cruel, nasty fae he was. Still reeling, I was inclined to go back to my carriage and wait until I could go home. Instead, a lanky female high fae stepped into my path, spilling a full glass of scarlet wine down the front of my gods-damned dress.

"Oops," she said, smiling at the gaggle of girls with her as she pointed. "Looks like you'll have to go way over there, away from my prince to clean that."

She pointed, and my lip curled. I lowered my chin, glared and stepped in her direction. I didn't have to kill her, I supposed, but I could absolutely throat punch her. As her smile vanished and she realized I was about to attack, she stepped back.

Something out of the corner of my eye distracted me, and rather than hitting her, I stormed past her and kept walking until I was away from the crowd. I followed the trimmed lawn around the castle turret. Just as I thought I'd lost him, the human stepped out from a shadow along the castle wall.

"Here," he said, handing me a cloth. "For your dress, my lady."

I opened my mouth, but struggled to find the right words, so shut it. I accepted the cloth and began to pat my stained gown. "Why would you help me?"

He simply stared at me and didn't answer.

"You don't have to answer if you don't want to, I guess." I shrugged and handed the cloth back to him. "Thank you."

He continued to stare, and his eyes shifted back and forth between me and the area behind me. He was so paranoid it began to make me feel like I was being watched. I could understand why he hesitated. Why should he trust me? I turned to go but he stopped me.

"I-I've been stuck in this place for a long time now." He backed up against the wall and looked to the ground. "So long, I've lost track of the days. I've seen terrible, terrible things. But you are the first person to even acknowledge my existence." He looked up to my face again. "No one even looks at me. I'm told where to go and what to do, and occasionally allowed to rest at night or eat, but that's it. Why do you look at me when no one else will? Do you know what it feels like to be surrounded by thousands of you . . . people and begin to think you're invisible because they want you to think you are so far below them you don't even really exist anymore?"

I shook my head. "I don't, but I'm so sorry. There is nothing I can do to help you."

"I have a family, you know. Back home. I went out one night and woke here the next morning. I'm not even sure how it happened, or why." He looked at me, begging for an answer.

"I can't answer that, either, I'm afraid. Humans are so rare in Alewyn. Who brought you here?"

"I don't know." His voice was barely above a whisper. He looked behind me and I turned, seeing nothing in the open grass aside from the battlements in the distance. "There are days when I wake up and I can't remember anything from the day before. They take my memories."

"Listen, there are a few things you should know about the fae. It's not the same here as it is in your world. You must never, ever make a bargain with anyone. No matter what the prize, the price is never worth it. Don't drink the wine, and never wander off alone."

He looked in every direction but my own. I could tell he still wasn't sure if he should trust me. Hell, I wasn't sure if he should trust me.

"The thing about the iron that we tell humans, it's not true. We can touch iron all day long, so don't get any bright ideas and risk your life for it. It won't help you. Oh, and we absolutely can lie to you. In fact, lying is a sport around here. The royals can and will continue to change your memories, so never trust what you think you remember."

He scoffed. "This is the first conversation I've had in over three years, probably longer. I'm never given the chance." He looked behind me again. Then he stepped closer and whispered, "You need to be careful. I think someone is watching you."

Then he turned and jogged back into the castle. Leaving me there, jaw to the ground, wondering where to even start breaking down that threat.

Humans were odd. And slightly creepy.

Reluctantly, I returned to the banquet. I was on edge as I pulled out the last open seat at the very end of the table and slid into it. My eyes darted side to side and I bounced my knee as I fidgeted with the deer-horned silverware, pretty sure the human had shared his paranoia with me. Great. It was expected to hear prophecies of doom and death from seers of fae, not so much from a human male.

I could feel my mind racing, so I did the only thing I could think of to calm myself. Taking in slow, deep breaths of air, I willed my body to relax. I shut out the crowd and imagined I was the only one there. The tension slipped from my shoulders and slowly down my back until I fully released it. I slid my fingertips to the knife at my thigh and remembered that I was anything but weak and helpless. I opened my eyes, renewed.

The air was filled with the tinkling of glasses and soft murmuring of the faerie crowd. At least we were outside, where the voices drifted away in the breeze and no one was shouting over the echoes in the great hall. The castle gardens surrounded us. A thousand different types of flowers swayed in the soft breeze, and even during the gathering, the gnomes still worked the grounds. The intoxicating aroma of all the different blossoms was so perfectly blended into the warm air, if I were alone, I would have lain in the balmy sun and taken a nap. Closing my eyes again, I took one more deep breath and savored the fantasy.

Beyond the gardens, the castle was encompassed in marsh. They were the reason it was named the Marsh Court. The marshes could swallow you whole before you could scream for help. A tactical advantage, my father said.

Way at the other end of the table, where the high fae sat separated from the lesser, I could see the guards that lined the perimeter. That's where the royalty was seated. I couldn't tell you which royals, though. Prince Fancy Pants, for sure, and likely King Coro. That left Autus and Morwena in limbo. I hadn't noticed any sea fae, but that didn't mean she wasn't lurking about.

A hush rolled down the table and made its way to me before the fanfare began. A simple trumpet played from the closest turret by a lesser fae so small, I couldn't even see him behind the instrument. When the song reached its end, my king's voice filled my ears. A charm had amplified his words, because, although he spoke in a calm and quiet tone, I could hear him all the way back in the nosebleed section. "From the merfolk of the sea to the fauns of the northern wind, welcome to the seat of the Marsh Court. Enjoy the revelry and merriment. Come, let us toast to a day so beautiful as this."

Everyone, including myself, lifted their glasses into the air and drank. After a small sip, I placed my glass back down on the table. Lines of lesser fae poured out of the castle carrying our meal. Some winged, some on foot, but I noticed they all kept their heads tilted down as they split into two and surrounded the enormous table. As one, they lifted the domed lids and placed the silver trays onto the table. They spun and skipped away before most of the guests probably even realized they were there. It was a beautifully executed dance that few took the time to enjoy.

Before me lay a banquet of frivolity and happiness. There was nothing in the world like faerie food. As I plucked a juicy red berry from a lengthy vine and popped it into my mouth, I closed my eyes and thanked the gods of Alewyn for getting at least one thing right in this broken world. I had filled my plate with meats of the wild stag and pieces of bread smothered in honeysuckle jam before I even finished swallowing my delicious berry. Audience be damned, I had come here to eat, and I was eating.

I took a bite of the roasted boar and reached again to put more fruit onto my plate. The fatty juice from the salted meat slipped down my chin, so I wiped it away with the back of my hand. I finally paused and considered how ridiculous I must have looked, but no one seemed to notice. In fact, most of the fae beside me were just as lost in their dishes as I was. The phooka, two fae down, let out a loud moan as he scratched his long ears.

Fae were fickle and so easily offended. We were grumpy and vicious, even on our good days, but we were nothing if not predictable when it came to three simple things: food, music, and wine. There was also sex, but food trumped that for me. Even I knew a good wine when I tasted it. In fact, that's probably how the human got here. In the mortal world, one sip of faerie wine or a single bite of fae food, and you'd never see your home again.

I was three plates into absolute bliss when the servants from before came to collect the remaining food on the table and set out the cakes for dessert. I piled squares of rich chocolate fudge and lemon tarts onto a new plate and licked the sweet icing off my fingers. Leaning into the center of the table and filling my wine glass in the fountain, I took a sip and wondered if Huntagh would just roll me back to the carriage if I asked really, really nicely.

At the end of the meal, most of the guests had settled into the comfort of the cushioned chairs. A few seats down the table from me, a particularly loud guest had turned sideways in his chair, swinging his feet over the arm as he continued to eat the fruit directly from the vine. He was loudly explaining to a female across from him why he preferred sweet over sour. He had the emotional depth of a teaspoon if this was how he searched for his next romance. I needed better company. But who? A few fae had moved from the table, lounging in the grass, napping or sipping wine. A rowdy bunch in the distance danced to a troll playing the fiddle.

I slipped out of my chair and decided to try and walk off my full belly in the gardens. Stopping to smell a vibrant batch of peonies, I wondered where Huntagh had gotten off to. Technically, we had eaten dessert, and since that's what we were invited for, we could leave. I'd certainly had my fill for the day. I feigned wandering casually to take everything in, nodding and smiling to the guests as I searched faces for my *bodyguard*. He was super good at his job, obviously. I ran my fingers casually through the pool of a fountain, letting the cold water ripple around my touch. I could leave him. He evidently didn't want to be found. He could handle himself. But we did ride here together, and I'd absolutely castrate him if he ever left *me* at the castle without an easy ride home.

Noticing some of the fae working their way inside, I nonchalantly followed a few paces behind a group and kept my eyes open. It seemed as though the guard population was increasing, and I couldn't help but wonder if it was because King Coro knew the Sea Court was trying to move against him. If I knew it, he probably knew it. He would have been a fool not to quadruple his personal guard and lock himself away.

As I continued down the long, gilded hallway, I realized the company I was following had turned a while back. I was alone in the castle and not supposed to be here. So far, no one had stopped me, so I just kept walking—peeking into the slits of the open doors. I highly doubted Huntagh had found a lover so quickly.

After fifteen minutes of lurking, I decided to give up and head back outside. I was surprised I had made it so far, and although my footsteps were naturally quiet, it was only a matter of time before I would be caught by King Coro's guards.

I retraced my steps and, just before I came to the corner right before the palace doors, four guards stepped into my path with anything but understanding on their faces. I brushed my hand across the knife at my thigh and then remembered where I was. I dropped my gaze and kept my voice soft and casual. "Forgive me. I've gotten lost looking for my friend. Would you please help me?"

"Not today, princess," a scaly guard said and snagged my arm.

"Hey!" I shouted. "Let go of me." I jerked my arm out of his grip and stepped backward.

Two of the guards looked at each other, closed the gap between them and stepped toward me as one.

I moved back again and had to make a judgment call. If I took them out, or even tried, I was in the middle of the castle and would have just committed a huge crime. If I didn't, I had no idea what they were going to do with me. "What do you want?"

"It's the queen that wants ye. Fer yer pretty face, likely."

Though dressed in Marsh Court attire, they were from the Sea Court, each likely wearing a hidden charm to dwell on land—the evada pearl. Morwena must have handed those things out to her court like candy.

I let the guards take hold of me and guide me through the castle. If nothing else, I'd figure out an escape plan on the way. Memorizing each turn as we traveled the maze, I realized they were trying to confuse me. Luckily, they were dumb as trolls. I'd mastered mazes and pathfinding when I was seven. Amateurs.

I'd play the confused card all day long, but I was sure Morwena had sent for me because my father refused her. Before this, I hadn't even considered the danger of coming to the castle, but now I was kicking myself. I would have been more careful. I would have been more alert. Honestly, I would have left Huntagh behind when I couldn't find him outside. I remembered the way the sea queen looked at me. She knew exactly who I was.

Of the four guards, my best bets were with the one on the right and the one in front of me. The fae in the back had to be part giant because he could squish me like a bug. It might have been fun if it were a fair fight, but with all of them coming at me, I'd have better odds taking him out first. Logically, because he was behind me, he wasn't a good first target.

The one on the right didn't seem as sure-footed on land. He had stumbled on nothing twice on our journey through the castle. A properly placed toe and a shove would send him flying down a set of stairs. Assuming there would be at least three seconds of surprise, I could have my throwing knife in the back of the guard in front's neck before he even saw me coming, but then I'd have to deal with the big guy in the back and the angry one on the left who seemed to be a wild card. Likely, I could have taken him out with my dagger while I hit the guard in front, but that would have taken divine timing, and then I'd still have to deal with the guard behind me. I might have been able to swing around him and kick him from behind, sending him down the same stairs, but for all of this to work, I needed stairs, lucky timing and to be able to get out of the castle, leaving the dead guards behind without raising an alarm. It was possible, but I didn't like my odds.

"Keep your head down and keep moving. I don't have time to babysit an insolent child," the guard on my left scoffed.

"I'm hardly a child, and I don't particularly care about your schedule. I've done nothing wrong and I feel confident you are going to regret your actions today."

The guard from behind kicked the back of my knees, and I slammed into the floor. The taste of metal filled my mouth and, having no other options, I had to swallow down the blood. I couldn't spit it out. I jammed my tongue into the cut in my mouth and narrowed my eyes, glaring fire bolts into the guard in front of me. I should have fought them when I had the chance.

I was tossed into a small room and the door was slammed behind me. I heard the lock click, and I dragged myself up off the floor. I dusted off my dress and paced. Bringing my fingers up to my mouth, I was relieved to find the cut was solely on the inside of my mouth. It stung just the same. Immediately searching the dusty room, I realized no one had been in here for quite some time. A tiny cot sat along the wall to the left and a small window floated in the center of the wall across from it.

I crossed the tiny room in three steps and looked out the window. I brought my hand up to the sill and traced the outer frame, hoping I could get the window open. I shoved along the top. It didn't budge at all. I looked out to confirm I was on the third floor. I could see the banquet below me, which meant I was also on the west side of the castle. It seemed irrelevant, but all knowledge was helpful when it was the only thing I could focus on. I crossed back over to the door and brought my ear to the crack on the floor. Two guards were left behind.

I sat down on the hard, wooden floor, closed my eyes and imagined this was a test from my father. What would he have created for an escape? I couldn't climb out the window, I couldn't open the locked door, there was no furniture aside from the cot, so nothing to look behind for secret exits. Fortunately, I still had my weapons. Of course, they wouldn't have thought to check for those—I was just a female, after all.

I had no idea how long it would be until I was summoned and likely killed by the queen, just to spite my father. I couldn't imagine how he would react. The ability for fae to have children was so rare. Though not immortal, we lived for a long time, hundreds and sometimes thousands of years. If we could have children as often as animals, we would run out of living space and have hundreds of children before we died. Some fae never conceived a single child. The loss of me would wreck my parents' entire world. I couldn't let that happen.

I rubbed my palms together and closed my eyes, pushing away my anxiety. Clearing my mind, I knew what I had to do. I was going to have to attack them as they came into the room to get me. If I stood off to the side of the door, I could take them out one by one before they could pile into the room. The first death would be a surprise and then I'd just have to wing it and hope like hell I didn't have more than two or three guards retrieve me. I moved into position and waited. And waited. And waited.

The comfortable heat from the sun had left the room hours ago and the cool air, mixed with the evening darkness kept me on edge. Still, I waited. My back pressed against the wall, I heard the clumsy guard complain to the massive guard again.

"Watchin' this door is worse than chasin' kelpie. Don't ya s'pose if we just killed the female, the queen would be happy? Havin' one less thing to do?"

"Hrmph."

"Aw c'mon Des. I didn't even have me dinner and you know how that bothers me."

"Better just tuck in, Scal. It's going to be a long night." The deep voice of the largest guard rattled the door. "Bet her majesty has already taken someone to bed."

"Aw. Dang."

I heard the clumsy one kick at the wall and plop down. The mention of food reminded me I hadn't had dinner either. Nor did I have a decent spot to rest, even if I wanted to. The cold floor was less than inviting. The tiny cot smothered in dust and who knew what else definitely wasn't an option. I relaxed my hands and slid my back down the wall, opting for the chilly floor. I had been ready to pounce for so long, my body ached. My parents hadn't expected me home for days, so they wouldn't even know I was missing. Eventually, they would know something was wrong and come looking for me. Perhaps Morwena having no sense of urgency in dealing with me was a blessing.

I rubbed my hands together and gathered my dress under me to block the icy floor's temperature from seeping into my body. Although the window would not open, the draft on the third floor was not pleasant. I flipped my dagger back and forth in my hand as I waited. Even if the door were to open right then, I was confident I could still hit my target with almost no effort. But could I kill someone? I had been trained to. I knew exactly where to hit, how to hold my knife, how to take my knife back. I knew how to kill silently and how to kill viciously. But could my soul handle it? Could I just kill someone and walk away? Could I run? I wanted to say I couldn't. I wished I couldn't. But I could. And I would because if it came down to me or them, I would always be the one to walk away.

I watched the sun come up and I stood. Stretching my limbs and twisting my neck back and forth, I readied myself for whatever this day would bring. The slow-paced breathing from both guards outside let me know they were still asleep. I began to pace, each step lighter than the last as I wore the dust away from the floor. I considered cutting off the bottom of my dress so it would be easier to run, but my only option to get out of this castle unscathed after murdering at least two guards, was to pretend I'd stayed the night in a lover's bed and was simply heading home. No one would even bat an eyelash unless my dress was ripped to shreds.

It was humid that day. The dusty corners gathered moisture and I listened to the shuffling guards in the hall. I moved back to my position by the door, holding my knife lightly in my right hand. I tried to calm my pounding heart and listen.

The seconds turned into minutes, melting into hours. The guards had changed, and I wasn't sure who was out there. At this point, I would have killed for a drink of water. These guys were quieter than the last set. I could hear their breathing and an occasional shift of body weight, but that was it. The sun had passed the center of the sky and the shadows began to grow in the lawn. I didn't dare leave the doorway. After a full day, I began to wonder if the queen had forgotten about me, or if she even meant for them to take me at all. She was not in any rush, at least, which would be fine, if someone would have thought to at least feed me. I was nowhere near starving, but I could feel my body telling me I needed something to eat and drink.

I wasn't sure I could stay awake all night again without food. The adrenaline had long worn off and exhaustion was starting to be a real problem. I lunged toward the left and then to the right. I stretched my long fingers to the dirty ceiling and tried to bounce up and down on my toes. I had to stay alert or things could go very wrong here. Squeezing my eyes shut, I let out a silent yawn. It was dark out again, which meant I'd likely be spending another night in King Coro's castle. Did he even know he had an imprisoned fae? Probably not. I was sure that was part of the game. The queen had tried to take the Wild Hunt from King Coro and, though she was denied, she harbored the daughter of one of its commanders as a prisoner in his own castle. Yes, that definitely sounded like a game she would play. I wondered if she would tell the king just to get to him. And then I wondered if he would care.

It was getting harder to stay awake. I rubbed my temples and listened as the guards were brought dinner. Since I was not a threat to them, they had wine. I breathed in the smell of the meats and thought back to just a couple of days ago when I sat at the banquet indulging without even realizing it would be the last meal I would have for over two days.

I remained quiet as I slid to the floor once again. Arranging my dress below me, I set my knife down to stretch my stiff fingers. I'd been so quiet in that room, it was a wonder they hadn't peeked in just to make sure I hadn't found a route to escape. I closed my eyes for just a moment, my breathing slowing. I felt myself drift off to sleep, just as I heard a gasp of breath. I jumped to my feet, dagger in hand as I heard a gurgling sound and then a thump. Suddenly, the door was unlocked and then nothing. I waited. Silence filled the air. What kind of trap was this?

"You must run, now," a female voice demanded.

In an instant, I threw the heavy door open and took in the scene. My watch dogs lay on the hall floor in a puddle of their own blood. Whoever let me out had run away. I didn't let myself react as I leaped over them and dashed down the hallway, following the path I'd gone over in my mind. I slowed my run to a walk and willed my throbbing heart to calm, so as not to give myself away. I made it to the doors of the castle.

As I had in the past, I simply looked the Marsh Court guard in the eyes and asked for my carriage to be brought to me. He nodded and before I knew it, Brimir was leading me home. I'd never go back to that castle I promised myself, even if the king himself summoned me.

7

Temir

A knock at the door woke me. I had fallen asleep at my desk. Again. My hands were covered in soot and grime from the work I was doing, but I was fairly certain I had finally created an elixir to ease pain instantly with no side effects whatsoever.

"Yes?" I called, standing to wash my hands at the sink.

"It's Iva and Roe, milord."

"Is it that day already? Come in." I welcomed the two little workers into my rooms. I never let them clean anything, but I enjoyed their company all the same.

"Chess today then, Roe?" I poured him a glass of ale.

"Okay, Tem." He shuffled his stout little legs to our usual spot, sitting at the small table along the wall. He took off his cap, and Iva pulled up a seat beside him.

I handed her a glass of wine, keeping one for myself. "Thank you so much, Temir." She looked to the floor, her cheeks turning crimson as she rubbed her large nose.

"You know you don't need to thank me, Iva." I sat across from Roe, stepping over the end of his long red beard that touched the floor when he sat.

"But are you sure I can't just tidy a little while we are here? I'd rather do work for someone like you than anyone else, milord."

"No, thank you. My room is how I prefer it."

She had a small crush on me, but I just didn't feel the same. Roe was like a brother to her so he was always comfortable, but I had a hard time with females. Too unpredictable for me.

We played in silence for a while. Roe always took extra time building his moves on the board. "Have you heard about the king's betrothal?" Roe asked, setting up the pieces on the board again.

"I have."

"Everyone in the kitchens is chatting about the wedding. How much extra work there'll be to do and all the extra people that'll be coming to the castle if they do it here." He paused for a moment. "When was the last time we thanked you, Temir? For giving us this small reprieve each week. It seems we've been busier than ever."

"No need to thank me for being kind," I said, moving a pawn.

"But I do. It's not very common around here," he said, making his move.

I caught Iva staring at me for the third time and shifted uncomfortably in my chair. "How's your mother, Roe?" I inquired.

"She's well, milord. Thanks for asking. Those elixirs you send fixed her right up." He wiped his brow and spent some extra time concentrating on his next move.

"I'd like to meet her for a real evaluation one day."

"Oh, she gets nervous about coming to the castle, milord. Best to just send the medicine. We sure are lucky in having a friend like you, milord."

I knew they were grateful, but I wished they knew how desperately I just wanted to fit in somewhere. It's hard to be a lesser fae among the high fae. The castle inhabitants and most of the Wind Court believed I had an affinity similar to Oleonis. The king enchanted everyone I healed to forget it happened. Only his personal guards who summoned me when I was needed and the members of the council knew I could heal a body back to perfection from near death. I was one of the many kingdom secrets.

"Them recruiting boys—"

Iva snapped her head toward Roe and gasped, covering her hands over her mouth, eyes wide.

"What I meant was . . ." He paused to think. "Them guys that work the land for King Autus, they sure wish you'd let them do the tending to your gardens in the castle. Give them a break from shoveling snow and ice."

I ignored the odd behavior. "So they tell me every few days. I just prefer to do it myself. Keeps me busy."

"Oh, aye. I'm sure you do finer work than them, anyway."

"I bet you do, Tem," Iva said with a wine drunk smile. "I bet you do."

A firm knock at the door interrupted us. Roe and Iva leaped from the table and gathered their discarded cleaning supplies. We'd been through this before. They wouldn't have been allowed to come if they were caught. Roe gave me a nod, and I swung the door open.

"Yes?"

The king's guard informed me that I was needed. I walked back to my office, grabbed a few things I thought I might need and walked out without saying goodbye to my friends. High fae do not acknowledge the lesser fae.

I approached my healing room as the guard informed me a soldier was injured during a training exercise. As we entered, I saw a fae of the Sea Court laying on my exam table with a harpoon in his belly. "An accident?"

"Yes." He stepped out and shut the door.

I approached the table as the sea fae winced in pain. "Try not to move," I told him.

"Try having a harpoon through your gut," he retorted through gritted teeth.

"Fair enough. I'm going to give you something to ease the pain while I remove this, okay?"

"Do whatever you need to do, healer. Just do it quickly."

It was odd for the other courts to see a lesser fae in my position, but I was used to it. I wasn't sure what was worse for them, watching a lesser fae walk through that door, or having to trust him.

Pulling my newest elixir from my bag, I popped the cork and poured it into his mouth. He gurgled just a little, and I could see the instant relief across his face. He closed his eyes.

"Now, that shouldn't make you sleepy, but let me know if you start to feel sick, okay?"

"Mhmm."

I grabbed ahold of the harpoon, grateful it didn't puncture both sides, and pulled. I brought my hands to the wound and brought the magic forth, closing my eyes and willing it to stitch together each part of the fae. I felt the all too familiar heat of it working, and I heard the sea fae gasp.

"You have magic?" he asked.

"I do."

"I didn't expect that. Do you know what else is surprising to me, little deer? Why do you get to walk around the Wind Court like you're a high fae when you aren't, but the high fae of the Sea Court come, and someone just slings a harpoon at me as I'm feeding our horses?"

Accident indeed. Still, I kept my mouth shut. He would forget all of this, anyway. Even his uncommonly loose tongue.

"This is exactly why my queen will never actually marry that hideous king. She hates him. Tells anyone who'll listen in our court."

I stared, trying to keep my jaw off the floor. "She will not marry him?"

"Of course, she won't marry a land dweller. It's abhorrent. I can't believe anyone believed it would happen. Most of us have a poll to see who will figure it out first. I don't think any of you lessers are smart enough."

"But why would you tell me this?"

"I-I don't know." He crossed his brows and took a deep breath "Wh-What did you give me?"

"I've only given you a pain stabilizer." I watched him closely as I continued the healing process at my fingertips. "What is your name?"

"Egrir."

"How are you able to walk on land, Egrir?" I asked.

"With my evada pearl," he answered.

"And where do you keep your evada pearl, Egrir?" I questioned, knowing full well a sea fae would never tell a land dweller where he kept his pearl.

"It's braided into my hair," he whispered. "Please stop. Please don't ask me any more questions."

My heart rate quickened as I realized what was happening. "What is your true opinion of your queen?"

"She is a selfish witch. She will still rule the world one day. She plans to drown the world in bloodshed." He started to rise from the table, likely to run from the room, but I placed my hands on his forehead and forced him to slumber.

I opened the door to let the guard know we were ready for the king. I waited only moments until he arrived.

"He couldn't handle the pain, my liege. I've had to sedate him." Confident my pounding heart was going to betray my lie, I stepped away from the king to gather my supplies and clean the area.

He leaned down to the fae and, with the most melodic tone, said, "When you wake, you will remember nothing that has happened this entire day. You will believe you fell ill, and when you wake, you will find you are feeling much better. Do you understand? Nod."

A slight movement from Egrir and the king turned on his heel and left as quickly as he had come. Now, I was the only one in the world who knew I had accidentally created a truth serum.

CHAPTER
8

Ara

*T*hat was the longest ride home of my life. I expected my parents to be waiting by the windows when I arrived, but instead, the night was eerily still. Calm alertness melted over me as I quickly unhooked the carriage and took Brimir to the barn. I left him on the hook instead of taking him to the stall. I walked as slowly as I could around him and pulled my sword from the wall. I knew someone was in there, and there was no way in hell my father would test me after having no idea where I had been for two days. He would have heard me arrive. He should have been there.

I put my sword down and turned my back to the barn. I needed whoever it was to think I was not ready. It took only seconds before I heard the familiar crunch of gravel below boots. I spun and lifted my sword just in time to block a blow that would have taken off my head. Definitely not Huntagh this time. My assailant was much bigger than me, his eyes fierce and, clearly, he wasn't there for a good sword fight. Based on his first blow, he just wanted to take me out and be on his way. He swung his massive sword so hard, the air whistled as it whipped through the sky toward me.

I hit the ground and rolled, trying to get to his non-dominant side. I turned my hips toward him and swung. His blade was there to block. Again, I shoved and he blocked. The next time, I let myself slow. I blocked, but it was best if he thought I had no clue what I was doing. I let him push my sword toward me with the next block of his blade. He smiled and stepped in.

Perfect.

The sunlight had given me just a hint of his broken, scared face. This was certainly not his first fight. The texture of his skin was so rippled, for a moment I wasn't even sure he was high fae. I was unable to see his eyes clearly enough in the distant light, but based on his actions, he was in no way concerned that I was a threat to him. Really, I was just an inconvenience.

On his next attempt to swing, I spun to the side. I was still able to block and now I was closer to him. He lifted his sword to swing once more, but before he had a chance, I buried my dagger into his chest. Thank the gods for second weapons.

I watched as he stumbled backward. He looked to me once more and, without making a sound, lifted his sword to attack me again. Instead, he stumbled forward and fell to his knees. I reached for my dagger and yanked it out as he continued to fall. I wanted to stop and feel something, anything for taking his life.

But I didn't.

I bolted to the front door of our home and threw it open.

My home, the safest place in the world, was in shambles. Nothing was untouched. Dirt from the broken potted plants covered the wooden floor. The furniture we'd had since I was a child now lay broken and upended. Even the wallpaper was shredded.

I clutched my chest and ran a jerking hand through my knotted hair. There had been a massive fight inside—my father against who knew how many. There was blood, lots of blood, and I begged the gods to let it belong to anyone but my parents. The deafening thunder filling the demolished room was my own traitorous heartbeat.

Following the familiar path down the hall, I walked as silently as possible. The bright red blood smeared down the hallway told me it was from a fresh wound. The beads of death, staining the wooden wall, would be etched in my memory like an aged scar. As I reached the first room, I found the first body. Thankfully, it wasn't one of my parents. Anticipation swarmed around me, threatening to bring me to my knees.

Were they okay?

I still hadn't seen or heard a sign from either of them. I could only hope the guard outside wasn't leaving after finishing the job, but rather running off in fear. I turned into my father's office to find shredded papers covering the bloodstained floor and two more bodies slain by a sword. The window was broken, and the chair had an ax stuck into the back of it. My heart raced faster.

How many could my father logically beat?

Where was my mother?

I clenched my teeth and continued the most difficult walk of my life. I didn't want to call out and bring another attacker to me. If there was another one, I would prefer to catch them by surprise. I was trying so hard not to register what was happening around me as I stepped lightly through my broken house. Part of me wanted to find my parents, to whatever end, and the other part of me was so shattered at the mere thought of their deaths, I could barely take in what I was seeing. I could feel the air coming into my lungs, but it wasn't nearly enough. My heart pounded hard enough that my veins throbbed.

I turned into the room adjacent to the den and crumbled to the floor as everything I knew and loved in the entire world crashed down upon me. I crawled to my father's fallen body and laid my head on his chest as gently as I could, listening for a heartbeat. There was nothing but a pit of silence so great, I wished I could crawl into the desolation and stay there for eternity. A silent tear moved down my cheek, mourning not only the loss of the only male I've ever loved, but also life as I knew it.

He'd raised me to be much stronger than I felt in that moment. He'd given me the scars, the training, the compassion and the roaring fire within my soul. All of our memories swarmed as I listened to the sound of my own heart cracking. I thought of the tears I'd cried when I was eight and fell off my horse for the first time. He didn't hesitate to toss me right back on. Because I had to keep going. Just like now.

"Father," my broken voice whispered into his ear. "I love you so much. Please come back to me."

I couldn't stay with him here forever, no matter how badly I wanted to, so I dragged in a deep breath and leaned forward to kiss the greatest male I would ever know one final time. I pulled his sword from his hands and moved toward the door. I stopped and looked back only once. "You may always look to the past," my father would say, "but you must never stay there, my darling."

I swallowed the lump in my throat and turned away, knowing I would never be whole again.

I would never recover from this.

Two rooms left: my bedroom and my parents'. As I turned the corner toward mine, I heard shuffling toward theirs and darted down the hallway in that direction. I slammed the door open and saw a male standing over my mother.

She was bleeding, and I could see the tears falling down her beautiful face, even though his hand was over her mouth. Her eyes grew wide as she turned to me, and I could hear the muffled scream in her voice as she realized we were now *both* in trouble. This must have been the male that killed my father and now he had his filthy hands on my mother. I dropped my father's sword, knowing it was too big for me to fight with, pulled a dagger from my thigh and rotated my own sword in a circle.

My mother started kicking and lashing about. I knew she was trying to keep the male from coming for me. It's what I would have done. Instead, that motherfucker punched her in the face then looked at me and smiled as she stopped moving.

He leaped off of her and planted his feet on the floor before me. "What have we here? A little bird come to play?"

"Tweet, tweet, asshole."

I threw my dagger so fast, he didn't even have time to react. Everyone underestimated me. The knife planted into his arm, and as he reached up to pull it free, I brought my sword down, cutting the inside of his leg. Then I realized my mistake. Now he knew I was trained and he was coming for me.

This male who had killed my father had to be skilled, strong, and fast. I didn't have a plan. I blocked his sword as often as I was able. I took the tail end of a swing to my side because I didn't get back quickly enough. I had injured his arm and leg, but he also had blood pouring down his back, and I could only imagine my father left him far from unscathed. He punched me on my injured side and I gasped in pain.

I could feel the tension in my arms. While I had fought thousands of sword fights, fighting for your life was nowhere near the same. I was strong and agile, but a bigger, more experienced fighter would still kill me if I didn't come up with a plan. Quickly. He was injured, and that was my only saving grace at this point. I dodged another massive swing of his, and that's when I realized what I had to do. I still wasn't sure if it would be enough, but it was my only shot.

I jumped as far backward as I could and pulled out a throwing knife. He soared forward, and I dove to the floor, jamming the knife as hard as I could through his foot and into the floor.

He jerked his head toward me, realizing I'd just pinned him to the floor. I bet it hurt like hell.

Any other fight, this would have been the perfect time for taunting, but this wasn't a game, and I could not give him a single second to consider ripping that knife out of his foot. I vaulted off the floor and managed to get behind him. Before he could turn toward me, I snagged the necklace he wore and yanked.

As the chain snapped, the sea dweller gasped. Now he was pinned to the floor and suffocating. He ripped his foot from the floor and pivoted to face me.

Time. I just needed a bit of time and he would fall. How long could a fish go without water? A couple of minutes? What if it was already injured? I guess we would see.

He stumbled, blood pouring from his injuries as he looked down to see that I had picked up my dagger.

I spun and sliced the cleanest line across his throat, not caring that I was sprayed with blood—the blood of the male who murdered my father. My heart ached at the thought. I still watched the sea fae die without blinking.

I brought my hand to my injured side and pulled it away, sticky with blood. I crossed the room to my mother. She lay just as he had left her.

"Mother?" I whispered. "Mother, please wake up." I gently shook her shoulders and squeezed her limp hand.

Her eyes opened slowly, and she reached for my face. "Oh, my sweet, brave girl," she mumbled. "You must listen."

"Mother, no. We have to leave. What if more come? We have to go right now. You have to get up."

She lifted her other hand from her abdomen, and then it registered. She had been gravely wounded.

"No. No." I shook my head and took her hand once more. "Mother, please. You can't leave me. Father is gone and I'm all alone. Please don't leave me here. It's the queen. She's angry Father refused her, and she will come for me. Mother, please," I begged

"No. Ara, listen to m-me." She gasped for breath. "The queen sent them for another reason. You must go, you must. There is so much you don't know, so much we have not been able to tell you." She squeezed my hand and closed her eyes in pain.

"Mother!"

She opened her eyes and whispered so quietly I had to lean in to hear her.

"Aibell, find Aibell. Take my necklace and go." She coughed and closed her eyes again. "The Neverwood Lake, Ara. You must."

I knew she was saying important words. Her last bit of advice to me was to chase a tale from my childhood, though, so she had to be slipping away from reality.

"No, Mother. I won't go. I can't leave you."

I waited for her response, but there was none. Only one slow, final breath.

I leaned over her and kissed her head, trying to ignore the searing pain in my side. If I wanted to live, and that was a very big if at the moment, I had to get my wound closed. I had to get out of this cottage smothered in death and heartache. I had to leave my entire life behind.

I placed her arms onto her chest and pulled the necklace from her neck, slid it over my head and grabbed my father's sword. I poised myself in the doorway for a long time, imagining my mother was only sleeping and I hadn't been forced to kill two people tonight. Hoping my father would call out to me from the front door, announcing that he was only testing me, and everything was really going to be okay. I waited and waited for my mother's chest to rise and fall, but it did not.

I hurt from the tips of my fingers to the bottom of my shattered heart. Crossing my arms, holding onto my shoulders, I tucked my chin as I slumped into the doorway and made the most difficult decision of my entire life. I had to leave my parents. My ears began to ring. My stomach turned. My breaths grew shallow. I couldn't swallow as my throat swelled shut. I didn't know a life without my parents. Without their guidance, their laughter. Without this home. All strength left me as I crumbled to the floor. I knew what I needed to do, but I couldn't. I wasn't strong enough to leave them. But I had to. They would no longer be the ones to push me. I only had myself now.

The queen sent them for another reason, my mother had said. More may come. Would come. And I had absolutely no idea why.

I stood, stumbled to the barn and reached the shelf with salve and bandages. I cleaned the wound as best as I could. I would have to sew myself up. I had practiced but could have never been prepared for the real thing. Holding a needle above a flame for thirty seconds, I pulled it out and let the red metal return to black before threading a string into the tiny hole and lifting my face to the sky. Taking three quick deep breaths, I pinched the gash together and shoved the warm needle through my flesh. I groaned in pain and almost had to sit down, but I could feel the world pressing in on me, telling me I had to go. At this point, the needle wasn't the worst part. Pulling the thread through my skin was. I had never wished for alcohol so much in my life. Finishing up, I layered the wound in the salve and wrapped a bandage around my waist. I tossed the bloodied rags into a bowl and lit them with a match.

As the flames flickered, I looked back to my house. I had to go back in. I couldn't just leave with the clothes on my back and expect to make it to wherever I was going.

Entering my home a final time was like crushing my shredded soul below a jagged boulder. I avoided the rooms where my parents lay. I went instead to my father's office and searched for a map of Alewyn among the chaos, then to my room, the only room untouched, and changed into simple riding leathers, a loose shirt, and boots. I grabbed a blanket from my bed and reached for my lamp. I removed the lid and dumped the oil all over my bloodied dress, then went back to the hallway and took that lamp from the hook and continued to pour throughout the house, using the oil to seal away my years of memories. As I made my way outside, tears lined my eyes. I pulled Brimir from the barn and put everything I had into his pack. I had more weapons than I'd probably have need for, but I'd have to hunt, so I strapped the bow onto my back.

My heavy feet guided me once more to the cottage. I struck the match and watched the flames flicker for a moment. This was it. In one single night, my world had shattered, and I was about to seal it away with one tiny flame. I closed my eyes and tossed the match. The fire burst to life and I walked away from the only home I had ever known, my parent's final resting place, and everything I loved in this world.

As I stepped with leaden feet, I whispered the fae's farewell prayer. "Into lightness and darkness, into shadows and mist, may you rest for eternity. Over the mountains and beneath the sea, let your spirit find peace. May nature keep your soul, the wind hold your memories, the river bless your spirit, and the fire carry you away."

CHAPTER

9

Ara

I led Brimir into the thick forest north of our cottage as the heavy smell of smoke in the air turned my empty stomach. I leaned down and hugged the only living thing left in my life. My side ached with the movement. I tried not to think about my parents— of their bodies burning in their funeral pyre as I just walked away. Shutting off the flood of emotions that threatened to drown me faster than my own exhaustion, I focused only on moving in a continuous general direction until I felt I could safely stop for a few minutes and try to figure out what the hell I was going to do. Each step that fae horse took, with his massive legs and thunderous steps, caused searing pain to my side. My stitching was not as great as I'd hoped it would be, but so far, the wound wasn't bleeding, and at this point, I had to count my blessings as they came.

I pulled the map from Brimir's satchel and unrolled it on his broad back as he continued a steady pace. There was no point in trying to run with him. The forest floor was a mess of branches and rocks. I didn't need an injured horse on top of everything else. I searched the small print scattered on the map, looking for Neverwood Lake. I wasn't sure why I needed to go there, but I had to trust that my mother's dying words would lead me somewhere important. I could only hope Morwena saw the ashes of my home and assumed I had died alongside my parents. I thought she only wanted my father to lead the Hunt into her hands, but if not, then I needed to know what my mother had been trying to say.

Thankfully, it was only nearing midday. The creatures that came out at night in a faerie forest would kill me faster than the queen, but I still had to be observant. The daytime creatures could be just as lethal. I hadn't eaten or had anything to drink in days. Leading Brimir toward the blissful sound of running water, I pulled out my knife once more. I was certainly not the only thing in the dense forest that needed to drink.

I stumbled off the horse's broad back, weaker than I would have ever anticipated. I had been running on adrenaline for hours and it was wearing off. My sluggish body was just not interested in doing more than crawling into a deep hole, and as I dragged myself to the trickling water and plopped down in the cool mud, I knew I was not going to be able to get back on the horse. Physically, I was exhausted, but my injury was also getting worse.

I cupped the chilly water into my hands and slurped. I tried to pace myself, but I had never been so thirsty in my life. About three seconds after my final gulp, I realized I had drunk too much, too fast, and the coughing and retching that followed caused so much pain I could see spots and my vision started to fade. Panicking, I took in several deep breaths, knowing that if I passed out, I couldn't be sure what I'd wake up to, or if I'd wake up at all. I had to find a safe place to rest. I crawled to a fractured stump of a fallen tree and leaned against it to pull myself up. Bringing my shaking hand to my throbbing abdomen, I could feel the heat radiating off the wound.

Slowly working my way to Brimir, I tied my hand into the stirrup leathers and clicked my tongue to signal him to move. He walked without guidance, and I did my best to hold on, keep my footing and look for a safe place. Although it felt as if we had meandered for hours, I really had no idea what time it was. The thick canopy of leaves above blocked most of the sunlight. I yawned. My body wanted to shut down. Each step became a chore, my feet a thousand pounds, and I could barely force air into my lungs and keep my heavy eyes open at the same time. I couldn't even remember the last time I'd had a restful night of sleep.

In due course, we came upon a rotted hollow tree laying on the forest bed. It was my only option for shelter, but it also meant I would have to leave Brimir tied up outside. I didn't like it, but as I untied my hand from the saddle and fell to the ground, I knew I had no choice. I took the pack from his back and crawled inside the decayed tree. Death was everywhere. I plucked the blanket from the bundle and ate a piece of my horse's pina fruit. It wasn't much, but not eating couldn't be good for me either. I gently pulled at the bandage on my side, dipped my fingers into the salve tin and smothered the wound before pushing the bandage back down. Leaning my head on the pack, I closed my eyes, keeping a tight grip on the familiar knife in my hand, and sent a silent prayer for protection before I closed my eyes and the world faded away.

I woke to Brimir shoving his muzzle into the opening of the tree and snorting dirt and chipped, rotten wood all over my face. In my broken state, I had forgotten to feed him. I sat up, and my stiff body screamed in retort. I wasn't sure how many hours or days I'd slept, but my horse had gone unscathed and my exhaustion, which had piled up from the castle, had greatly subsided.

I forced myself to crawl out of the decomposing tree and dragged my pack behind me. After feeding two of the pina fruit to Brimir, I had to deny him a third piece. There were only four left and I had no idea how far I was going to have to stretch that between the two of us. Shaking off the dirty blanket, I shoved it into the pack and unlatched the front pocket to pull out the salve and bandages. The area around the gash in my side was red and the swelling was so bad, I could barely see the stitches. If I didn't find a healer, I might be in trouble. I should have done a better job making sure the thread was sterile before I used it, but it was a simple oversight. I was just trying to stay alive.

I'd never thought of dying before. Of taking my last breath or watching my parents take theirs. I'd grown up believing my father to be invincible and my mother too clever to ever be in that situation. I rubbed the ache in my chest and trudged onward, closing my mind to those painfully naive thoughts.

A map really did no good in a dense forest when I could barely tell which direction was up. The lake was northwest of my home, based on my father's map, but it was hard to tell how far. I'd have to climb a tree to get above the dense canopy, just to see which direction the sun was moving across the sky. There was no way I could climb a tree right now, though. I was happy to just be able to stand upright. Food was my only goal. I hadn't really eaten in days, and the ache in my stomach was debilitating.

Since I was unable to feed Brimir properly, I decided it was best to walk beside him instead of riding. I pulled my bow from where I'd tied it onto him and, as I drew back on the string, I cried out. The pain from my side was so severe, it felt as if I were being struck with a sword all over again. I released, knowing I wasn't going to be able to use the weapon any time soon. Apparently, no part of this would be easy.

We trudged on. I listened to the forest and the birds singing, trying to orient myself. I'd never seen so many marbled hues of green and brown. The smell of the oak trees mixed with the aroma of the fetid dirt, gnarled roots dipped in and out of the ground, hidden only by last season's fallen leaves and broken branches, and somewhere high above, I knew the sun was shining, as tiny beams of yellow light lit the forest. The rough terrain sloped up and then down, adding hill climbing to my tumultuous journey. I thought of my father as we moved. I kept my steps light and my eyes open, just as he would have instructed me.

Eventually, the hills turned into steep drops, and more and more rocks began to mark the ground. I looked at my map once more, wondering if a landmark might indicate my location, but so far, I could only see that I was still in the forest, but the clear sound of rushing water grew louder as we moved, and I was glad for it. A river was a marker on the map, but there were so many, I wasn't sure which I'd found. Still, I filled the canteen I'd emptied hours ago and let Brimir drink as long as he wanted.

Following the muddy riverbed, we came across an abandoned animal den. It was the best I'd seen for shelter for the night. I couldn't push myself too hard, knowing I still needed to find food. I left Brimir to chew at the tiny blades of grass fighting their way to the surface through the dense bed of leaves and rubble amongst the forest floor. Kneeling carefully, I covered my hands in dirt and mud and whatever else I could find, trying to mask my scent as I searched for a sapling to build a snare close to, but not right beside my camp.

When I returned, I washed my hands and face in the river and fed Brimir another fruit while I nibbled on the small handful of berries I had managed to find on our walk. The deep red stains left behind from the juices took me instantly back to that cottage. Back to the blood covering my father's body. My heart stopped; my breathing stopped. My whole world came to a crashing halt as I shook. I couldn't wipe it away fast enough.

I had to keep going.

I collected some large branches to help cover the den's open hole, and that's when I heard the quiet snap of my snare. As I slowly approached, I saw a rabbit and thanked my lucky stars I would finally have a meal. The rabbit was still very much alive and, as I took a step toward the struggling animal, I heard a large branch snap and whipped my head to the side.

Standing less than ten feet from me was a towering beast with rotting flesh and deer-shaped antlers. The knovern was known for its deer-like features, although it walked on its two back hooves. Its unnaturally long arms were covered in open, oozing sores stuffed with decaying moss—likely caused by its own razor-sharp claws. Knoverns were infamous for burying their prey alive and waiting until it had suffocated before devouring it.

I remained frozen in place. If I ran, he would spot me for sure. If I stayed very, very still, he would still smell me. He was after my rabbit though, and the not-so-sane part of my brain was telling me I would rather fight him than let him walk away with my dinner. The wound in my side, however, reminded me that I was, in fact, an idiot.

So far, there was no indication he had spotted me. I lowered myself into a crouch, watching. I held my breath as I waited for him to just take the frantic rabbit and go, but instead, he swatted it back and forth on the snare and watched as the rabbit jerked its body, trying frantically to escape.

The knovern dug a hole just below the rabbit. His long fingers made easy work of the grave digging as fresh dirt and shredded leaves flew behind him.

Brimir neighed in the distance. He sensed the nearby danger and was trying to warn me. I kept my eyes locked on the creature, hoping he didn't hear.

He did, of course. His oozing head snapped up, and he leaped away from my rabbit toward my restrained horse before I could even make a plan.

I guessed I'd just run like hell and hope I'd be able to save Brimir, who was hauling my bow and both of my swords. The only weapons I had on me were my dagger and the throwing knives I never took off. A throwing knife is no replacement for the speed of a bow, but I supposed it would have to do.

As I approached the makeshift campsite, my heart stopped as I watched my tremendous fae horse rear up onto his back legs and kick toward the knovern. He dropped my pack to the ground and continued his piercing scream and only line of defense. I aimed and threw a knife, severing the end of the reins so Brimir could run. He reared to the left and bucked at the knovern, missing entirely, but the creature did back up a few paces.

I watched from behind a tree as the knovern circled him. And then I knew. I knew this wasn't going to end well. But watching that horse die would sever the last few stitches of my broken heart, and I just couldn't let that happen. I pulled out another throwing knife and thought about everything I knew about knoverns. And then I had a plan. It was a stupid, reckless plan, but a plan.

Hoping Brimir could hold off the attacker a few precious moments more, I ran as fast as possible, still injured, back to my rabbit. After several frenzied moments, I was on my way back to the camp. Halfway there, I found a tree and as quickly and carefully as possible, hauled myself up as far as my wounded body would allow me. I would have liked to be higher, but there was no time.

I pulled the rocks from my pocket and hollered with my hands cupped around my mouth. "Hey, fucker! Over here!" I could barely see the knovern, but I knew he could hear me.

At first, I didn't think he was going to leave the guarantee of a massive meal, but curiosity got the best of him and he stopped his hurried digging and came toward my shouting. I threw a sharpened pebble in his direction and watched as he spun around, trying to figure out where it had come from. I threw the next pebble closer to the snare and the next back at him until he began to follow the trail back toward the rabbit, thinking my pebbles were noise I was making as I ran from him.

He turned back toward Brimir a few times, but as I continued to make noise and draw him away, he eventually followed. Once he was past my tree, I turned and aimed a pebble at Brimir's flank, hoping like hell he ran in the right direction. As I watched him cross the river, it took everything in my power not to climb down and join him. But I knew the knovern was still faster than I was, and if he got a chance, he would catch me and rip me to shreds. I had to wait until I heard the snap of my fresh snare and the roar of the beast.

When that roar came, it was mighty and shrill. Had I not been expecting it, I still would have run as fast as I could. I slid down the tree, ran to the camp, grabbed my things and crossed the river, knowing that snare was going to hold him for maybe two minutes. It was an annoyance more than an actual trap for anything his size, but I only needed a small window of time to get my things and cross the river.

As he charged toward us, I began to doubt everything I thought I remembered about knoverns. At least until he skidded to a stop at the edge of the flowing water he could not cross. As he realized he had been outwitted, he tilted his head back and screamed again.

It came from his core, and I decided not to stick around to see if he could find a narrow enough spot in the river to cross. I threw my bag onto Brimir's back and shoved him away.

The attack had made my stoic horse skittish. As the dark forest grew even darker, I realized we had no shelter for the night. We just had to keep going. We rushed away from the river, leaving the beast behind. The trees became close and grew so dense, Brimir and I couldn't fit through side by side. I had to pull him along as he reluctantly followed.

There was a small clearing ahead of us, so I aimed for that, knowing whatever may come, would have to get through the tangled trees first, and they would probably be loud enough, so we would have time to run. In the center of the clearing was the tiniest pond I had ever seen. I could have swum back and forth across the water in just a few minutes. Pulling the dead rabbit from my pack, I had to make a tough decision. Lighting a fire in fae forest at night is probably the worst idea I could possibly think of, but I was so hungry I didn't care.

I made the smallest fire I could, focusing mostly on creating hot coals rather than large flames. I was trying not to attract company. I skinned the rabbit and placed the meat onto the coals. When the juices ran clear and the gristle sizzled consistently, I pulled the meat off and stomped out the embers. The heavenly smell of freshly cooked rabbit meat was the only thing on my mind. It took me only minutes to finish, but already my stomach felt better.

I took a long drink from my tarnished canteen and gave Brimir the last of the pina fruit from the bag. Brushing my fingers through his coarse mane, I leaned my head to his, breathing in the familiar scent of the barn mixed with the new, foreign odor of the forest. My heart ached for home, and for the first time since I had left my parents, tears streaked down my face.

"I'm sorry I don't have a better plan, boy," I whispered as I gently rubbed his face. "Can you ever forgive me for dragging you into this?"

I didn't know where I was going. I didn't know when we would eat again. I didn't know if I could keep both of us alive in this forest. And worst of all, I didn't know how to heal my injury or my heart.

Walking to the waterside, I sat along the edge, pulling my feet to my chest. I stared at my reflection, barely recognizing the pale likeness in the water, before leaning my head down onto my knees and squeezing my eyes shut, wishing for a different reality.

Today had gotten me nowhere but almost killed. Again. I pulled my blanket over me and let sorrow sweep me away.

CHAPTER

10

Temir

I practically ran to Oleo's room to tell him what had happened. He invited me in and, through panted breaths, I explained. "I've no idea how, Oleo . . . I believe I've accidentally created something incredibly dangerous should it fall into the wrong hands. I gave a sea fae a new elixir for pain. It worked brilliantly but doubled as a truth serum."

He sat silently in his worn leather chair and thought for several moments. I studied the hundreds of plants hanging about his room while he considered the news. "You're sure?" he finally asked, his navy eyes studying my expression.

I nodded.

"Dangerous indeed, my boy." He gestured for me to sit. "You are the boy I never had and always wanted. I knew you would do great things, but now we both harbor treacherous secrets and I wonder if we would be safer away from the dangers of the palace."

He watched me closely for my reaction, and as sad as it made me, I knew I would let him down. "You know we could never leave. King Autus would never allow it."

"But if we could," he whispered, "would you join me?"

I sat back in my chair and took the deepest breath I'd ever taken in my life. War was seconds away. I understood that more now than ever. Egrir had all but shouted it from the rooftops. My very nature told me I needed to be there, to heal the wounded soldiers. If I really thought about that, I knew I'd never be able to draw a line between high fae and lesser fae. And if each lay in front of me to die, would I do as the king demanded? I would have no choice. He might enchant me if I refused.

"Yes."

He knew I would think it through. If he had brought it up to me, he had thought about it many, many times.

"And Gaea?" I asked, knowing she and Oleonis were also close.

"She would leave in a heartbeat. I'm afraid the only reason she stays behind is to watch over an old fae. She is like the wind, you know. She was never destined to remain still." His eyes glistened over as he spoke of her. It would have sparked jealousy in me as a child, but I saw his emotions for what they truly were. Love. He loved us both. Raised us. Still, the open emotion was rare.

"Have you had another vision, Oleonis?"

He hesitated long enough to spark concern. "I saw you, my son, in chains." His voice cracked as tears filled his eyes. "We must leave, Tem. If my visions can be changed, we have to try. We must get you out of here. I'm not sure why, but you are in danger. Gaea can help us. She can spirit us away from the castle. To anywhere she has been. She is hiding something from the king. She has asked me not to tell, but please ask her."

"And have you thought about where we would go?"

"Someplace warm. Someplace where the waves crash in the distance and the summer sun's fruit dries to our lips." He closed his eyes and leaned back in his chair as he continued. "A place where fae children run laughing on the beach without a care in the world. A place that feels, at last, that we are finally free of the Wind Court."

"I'll speak to Gaea. We can try to build a plan. Stay here. Stay away from the eyes of the court. The last thing we need is you having a vision of our escape in front of them. They might not believe you, but they will surely think you've gone mad."

That night, back in my room, I stood staring at the piles of medical journals lining the walls and floor. My entire life's work would be abandoned to a place where it would likely be cast out and forgotten. I'd have to leave behind the gardens and the nursery, and wherever we went, I'd have to start again. I would never be able to reference any of these books. I would only take a few, I'd decided. I knew how to make the basic things I needed, so I wouldn't drain my power anytime someone was hurt. That would have to be good enough.

I headed to the gardens to gather a small supply of herbs to begin drying them for travel, but as I opened my door, I found Gaea standing just outside.

"Well, this is awkward." She pushed past me, letting herself in. I shut the door and followed, figuring it was as good of a time as any to find out if she would be helping us leave. "You're a funny male, Tem. You know that?" Poking me in the chest, she slid her hands down my arms and pressed her chest to mine, closing the space between us.

I tried to take a step back, but she only moved with me. Surely, she felt my pounding heart.

She leaned onto the tips of her toes and brushed a golden-brown curl behind my ear. I stared into her feline eyes, not daring to breathe, as she reached her hand behind my neck and brought her nose level to mine.

"Why . . . ahem. Why am I funny?" I managed. I could smell the sweet wine on her breath, and I knew she'd hate herself tomorrow when she remembered where she had come.

She dropped her hands and walked over to my couch, plopping herself down and swinging her legs, her beautiful, long, long legs, up over the arm.

I caught myself staring and snapped my attention back to her.

"Because you're just here looking like allll of thaaat." She waved her hands wildly and gestured toward me. "And you literally don't even know it. Do you even own a mirror, Tem?"

"I'm sure I do somewhere."

"They adooooooore you. And how you're all pretty and brooding and quiet. Everyone knows, you know. About the boy. How you went three nights with no blankets because you didn't want to let anyone know you helped him. You're just . . ." She paused. "You are so good. Do you know who is not so good? Me." She answered her own question, raising her wobbly hand high in the air. "And, well, basically the rest of the population. Everyone just wants to kill everyone. It's so exhausting." She patted the seat beside her as I raised a single eyebrow. "Come sit by me, Tem."

"You're drunk."

"Who cares? Half this place is drunk most of the time, and the other half wishes they were."

"I care, Gaea." I took a step forward but caught myself.

"Of course you do, Mr. Perfect."

"Gaea, there's something I need to talk to you about."

"Tell me in the morning, Tem." She laid her head on my pillow and closed her beautiful eyes.

I waited until her breathing slowed and then gathered her in my arms and laid her in my bed. I slipped her shoes off, pulled a blanket over her, filled a glass of water, and set it on the table beside her. Shutting the door, I headed back to my study.

I stayed up the entire night, unable to shut my mind off, and when I heard her slip out the next morning, I hoped she knew I was honorable. I guess I'd have to wait until later to ask her about helping me and Oleonis leave the castle.

Ara

The warmth of the sun pouring into the clearing pulled me from the depths of sleep, and for the first time in days, I felt a new sense of purpose. I did have a destination. I just needed to figure out the journey. I ate the other half of the rabbit I had saved and led Brimir to the water's edge. This was the safest place we had found in the forest, and as much as it was going to hurt, I had to leave Brimir behind. He could eat here in the glen and drink water from the pond. I was afraid traveling together would be more dangerous for him than leaving him behind. A fae horse was no ordinary beast, and I could only hope that one day we would find each other again.

I took off his pack and removed his reins, then stood in front of him. He pushed his great muzzle over my shoulder, drawing me in closer to him. I lifted my arms up and around his massive neck, hugging him one final time. I let my heart speak to his and hoped he understood that, although he was the only thing in the world I had left, I loved him enough to let him go.

I gathered the few items I had to my name, stuffing them into the pack, and turned to see Brimir bowed down behind me as I walked away. A fae horse farewell told me he understood why I had to leave him. It didn't make it hurt any less.

I pulled the map from my satchel and marked where I thought I was. Based on the river we had crossed the day before and the tiny pond, I could see Neverwood Lake was still quite a distance. I wasn't really headed in the right direction to begin with, but at least after orienting myself, I could try to follow the map. It was challenging in a dense forest, where every damn tree looked the same, but if I went back toward the river and followed it down, it fed into the lake. I could only hope I wouldn't run into another knovern.

As I walked, I pulled back on my bowstring and released it over and over again. The wired string rubbed on my aching fingertips until they were tender and raw, but still, I continued. My side ached, but the itching told me it was slowly healing. The lack of fever or cold sweats was enough to know I had miraculously avoided infection. I just needed to get my strength back up.

Stomping through the forest, I reflected on everything that had happened, trying to build answers from the knowledge I already had. It was harder than it should have been. If my parents were keeping a massive secret from me, then likely I had been groomed from a child to believe certain things were normal. I could figure out the obvious things, the training, the testing, but the others—the planted seeds of knowledge—those were likely hidden in my childhood memories.

But maybe they weren't keeping things hidden, and the attack and mysterious rescue at the castle were not related at all to what my mother couldn't say. She could have learned something while I was away and didn't have the strength or time to tell me. It was so much easier to believe that my parents weren't liars.

For days I walked through the most monotonous and never-ending forest on the planet. I found the poorest excuses for shelter, where hours of sleep were few and far between. The pace at which my body healed was annoying at best. I couldn't go as fast as I wanted. I couldn't hunt the way I wanted. I couldn't even use my weapons the way I needed. The journey so far had brought on a few attacks from desperate, starving creatures, but after the knovern, everything else was inconsequential. Working with my bow to build strength lasted only the first day, until I realized that if I tore open my wound, I had nothing to stitch it back together with. My fae salve was running low and I only stopped to get food when I absolutely couldn't go any longer.

Snagging a branch from the ground to try to catch fish from the river I was following, used my knife to sharpen the edges while I walked. Despite my lessons in harpoon throwing, a pointy stick just wasn't the same. There were times I caught a couple of fish and times I caught nothing at all.

I only allowed myself to stop for brief moments, trying not to attract unwanted attention. I had also begun to wrap my uneaten cooked fish in leaves and store it in my pack. The good thing about that was having a cooked meal for breakfast and dinner without starting a fire. The bad thing was, well, the fish smelled horrid. The odor from a fish was so strong that running across a hungry enough animal always meant trouble.

I didn't need to look at the map again. I had memorized my path over and over and worked on the alternative route, should option one fail, and then made a backup for the backup. Being alone in a forest with nothing to do but walk as fast as my injured body would let me was grating on my nerves. I pulled out the map anyway.

Running, my fingers over my father's precious handwriting, I tried not to think about how long it had been there. I wanted to rip the sea away from the map. I didn't want to look at the islands or the symbols for the northern and southern courts. I wanted to place my fingers on the little house he had drawn for our home and somehow erase everything that had happened since Huntagh and I left for the castle.

As I sat there, hating everything about my current and past problems, a tiny rustling in the distance caught my attention. I wanted to curse the faerie forest. I wanted to curse the running river. And I wanted to curse the stinking fish that likely drew whatever or whoever straight toward me. I watched as my newest adversary grew closer and louder. Before I could even process what was happening, a tiny forest pixie with iridescent dragonfly wings and an acorn hat came tumbling out of a nest of roots raised above the forest floor and landed in a heap before me.

"You. You must helpsies. Come so fast, hurry, quick like," she said.

Pursing my lips but otherwise ignoring her, I went back to my lunch. Although pixies weren't the trickiest of fae, I had learned that in the forest, things were rarely as they seemed.

"I know you can hears me. You come helpsies, you must."

I watched out of the corner of my eye as the little creature put her hands on her hips and stomped right up to me like she was going to fight me. It was so hard to take her seriously, considering I could reach out and squish her like a bug.

"Now, you listens to me right nows." She fluttered right into my face and continued. "There will be so big bads things happen if you don't come. You mustest."

My mother always said helping a pixie would bring you good luck, but the timing was awful, and so was not being a people person. I could think of at least a thousand other things I would rather have done than consider traipsing through my version of hell following a pixie. And I'd probably have to be nice to her, and that was even worse.

"I sees you considering. What would yours mother says? Me being so teensy tiny and you being so bigsies, bully?"

I narrowed my eyes at her. "Don't say a word about my mother. Take your problems to someone else. I'm not interested."

"You must come for helpsies, Ara." She attempted to grab my hand and pull me to my feet.

"How do you know my name?" I asked, shooing her away.

"Because it's your nameses, sillies." She looked at me like I had just asked her the dumbest question she had ever heard.

I rubbed my temple. "Yes, I realize it's my name, but why do *you* know it?"

"You have to comes with me to learn the things," she said, again trying to tug on my hand.

"Come where?"

"To the place that has no names but needs the helpsies."

"Me specifically, or someone to help, little pixie?"

"Yousies, sillies. I said that already."

If nothing else, there were promised answers on the line, and that alone ensnared me. "What was my mother's name?"

"I don't knowsies, sillies. I comes for youses," she said.

"Just so we're clear. You expect me to follow you to some unknown location, for some unknown reason, because I 'mustest'? You dangle the thought of my mother in front of me like bait, and yet can't tell me a single thing? No thanks, little pixie. My schedule is full for the day. Bug off."

She stopped fluttering and sank to the forest floor, perching on a small stone in front of me. She paced back and forth on her rock, tapping her tiny fingers onto her chin. "Okaysies. I tried but can't. Ofra might be mads at me, but I thinks on all the things and can't do it. Good lucks."

"Wait," I stumbled, "did you say Ofra?"

"Uhm, yep. I dids. Ofra says you can come to pixie glen. Yousies so special to pixies."

The face of the slain, half pixie female from the ball flashed through my mind. "Lead the way."

98

CHAPTER
12

Temir

s I made my way through the familiar maze of stone castle walls, I kept my head down. The castle was buzzing. Something had happened.

"Did you hear?" a female whispered to another as I passed.

"He hasn't done a thing," another said.

"Serves them right," said another.

By the time I made it to the east side of the castle, I understood what had happened, and my stomach turned. I thought of all the lesser fae working in the castle, listening to the high fae and their righteous attitudes. Queen Morwena, our potentially future queen, had left a path of a thousand deaths through the Marsh Court.

They said King Coro had ordered a hundred lesser fae to welcome them at the shoreline. They started there. They killed one hundred lesser fae just for existing. The Red Beach, they were calling it. The sand stained red with so much blood, the sea could not or would not wash it clean. Then the death toll rose as they traveled. King Coro had yet to say a word or lift a finger.

I yanked and pulled at the delicate flowers. It didn't matter that I had spent so much time tending the pristine garden, that I would ruin half the leaves just by pulling this way. It didn't matter that I was a lesser fae enchanted to be treated as a high fae. It didn't matter that I was just like them and nothing like anyone. I couldn't be there. I couldn't save a single soul. Why had I been gifted the ability to save if I couldn't save anyone?

"So, you've heard?" Oleonis said softly, kneeling beside me on the ground.

"I've heard," I said back, harsher than I had a right to.

Oleonis placed his wilted hands over my destructive ones, and instantly I stopped yanking. He buried his hands into the soil and called his magic to regrow the plants I had destroyed. I imagined watching me destroy the garden was as hard for him as it was for me to hear of a mass murder. He loved the plants more than I did.

I bowed my head, taking a deep breath. "I'm sorry, Oleo."

"Never apologize for your nature, Temir. Never apologize for caring." He placed a comforting hand on my back.

"None of it matters, anyway. For everyone that lives, someone else dies, and it's a never-ending cycle of death. I'll never save them all. I'll never stop a war. I'll never make a damn bit of difference."

"You may not save them all, Tem, but you may save one. And that one may save another, and that one may save the world. Your magic demands you to care about living and heal the broken. Consider your own spirit, though. Look into yourself and find what needs to be healed. This should not break you but build you. Let this spark the greatest fire in you. Let this feeling, right now, drive you to do, and be better for a world that needs you."

I couldn't look into those kind eyes with the fury that nestled deep within me. "The world may need me, Oleonis. But no one knows it. And as long as no one knows it, I've done exactly as Autus planned all these years. As long as I am close, he is immortal. He has made sure he can never be killed, just by keeping me near. And if we leave, he will hunt us to the ends of the world. He will drag us back here and keep us in the dungeons, enchanting us to do every little thing he wants." I slumped my shoulders and shook my head.

"The point is, we have free will now to choose to leave. The rest we figure out along the way, son." Oleonis moved to one of his beloved plants and began pruning.

"We have free will right now only because he has allowed it. Only because he takes pleasure from knowing we actually choose him. He lets us sit in on the council meetings and gives us nice rooms. He provides space for our garden and lets us work in peace. He does all of these things because he can't fathom anyone wanting to leave if they have everything he thinks they want. If we betray that trust and he finds us, we may as well be dead."

"Then we must not be caught."

"We are going to need a very good plan. If people could just leave the court, I'd imagine we would know it. How do we know he hasn't enchanted us? How do we know he hasn't instructed us to return immediately and confess if ever we should leave? Or told us to kill ourselves? How do we know he hasn't planted demands?"

"I think he is too arrogant, but we must be sure. It's a good thing you've just discovered a truth serum."

I snapped my attention to him and shook my head. "You wish me to use it on the king? If it even worked on him, he would remember."

"No, Temir. I wish you to use it on me. If I must speak the truth, then I have to believe on some subconscious level I know what the king has enchanted me to do."

"You would trust me with every truth in your entire life? Knowing I could ask you anything I wanted, and you had to answer, no matter how much you didn't want to tell me."

He grabbed my hands. "Yes, without question."

"Shall we go to my study?"

CHAPTER

13

Ara

In the glen where wild pixies danced on the gale,

Ofra called to me.

In the glen where rainbows bowed and the wild woods hale,

Ofra called to me.

In the glen where dawn's candied dewdrops lazed in the open glade,

Ofra called to me.

In the glen where hopes and dreams would intertwine and memories never fade,

Ofra called to me.

*S*o, this is how it would be. My parents had known something. Maybe not my father, but my mother had been unquestionably hiding things. I followed that annoying little pixie in the opposite direction of where I was going for an entire gods-forsaken day. The whole way she chattered on and on, mostly nonsensical bullshit.

"Haves you ever met a hapricon? Haves you?"

"No," I answered for the millionth time, caressing my wounded abdomen.

"One times, when I was itsty bitsies teensy pixie, I comes to the forests and saws one. He was greats and giants, he was. I hid under a leaf again. Likes I did withs the huda. You remembers what I saids about the huda?"

"No," I grumbled.

"Ara is so sillies. Doesn't likes the pixie stories."

"If you tell me how you know my name, I'll pretend I do." I quirked an eyebrow at her as she flew beside my face.

"I saidsies," she said in the most exasperated way a forest pixie probably had the capacity to do. "It's your nameses, and my nameses is Esa, and we knows it because that's always beens it."

"M'kay, well . . . I can see we aren't going to get anywhere with this. How long until we get to the person that needs help? I don't have an eternity, you know."

"Oh, thanks, you finally askes. Now we can goes."

"We are going. We've been walking all day." I stopped short and glared daggers at Esa. "I've just about reached my limit on patience for one day. Where are we going?"

"To the helpsies in the pixie glens. It is heres."

Every fucking thing in Alewyn was either a trick or a puzzle. Of course I had to ask first. Because that was completely illogical.

The entire world changed. One moment, I was in a forest with no end in sight, and the next, rolling fields of wildflowers. These two worlds did not belong adjacent to one another. The cozy sun caressed my skin as I took a hesitant step toward the open meadow. I could have bathed in a thousand rose petal baths and would never smell as lovely. The breeze was so gentle, it was only a whisper, cooling the sun's embrace. The sound of flowing water called to my curiosity and drew me deeper into the pixie's glen.

"You must sleep now, Ara," a voice called out.

I'm not tired, I thought or said out loud. I couldn't remember which one. "Someone needed help," I managed to breathe.

"It was you, Ara."

I spun in a sluggish circle. "Who are you? Show yourself," I slurred.

"Sleep now, and I will tell you a story."

"I don't—" I yawned. "I don't need to sleep. I need to go."

"Hush, child of Alewyn. Let the meadow heal your outer wounds."

"Ofra?" I could feel my eyes grow heavy and my breathing slow, so I plopped down in the bed of scattered flowers and melted deeper into the rawest exhaustion I had ever felt. "My mother . . ." I closed my heavy eyes and laid down, struggling to finish my sentence. "She told me . . ." And then it was dark.

Ara, the voice echoed in my dream. *It's time to hear the story you were promised. My name, dear one, is Ofra. I am connected to the sea. I am connected to the wind. I am connected to the very ground you slumber on. I have no mate and am unable to have children of my own. Instead, I protect the children of my heart, the pixies of all shapes and sizes.*

Hundreds of years ago, I favored one pixie in particular. Her name was Rosera. From the day Rosera could carry a conversation, her only goal had been to find her one true love. Only that and nothing more. She begged and begged me to tell her the secret to leave the glen. Her heart's desire was not here with me, though it pained me so. Alewyn is a vicious world. But alas, I knew she would wither from sadness if I did not allow her to leave. So, she left.

When a pixie leaves the glen, I send a piece of myself with them. A trinket to allow them to come home. I watched from afar, hoping she would choose to come home to me, but she didn't. Instead, she found what she thought she needed and wanted. She had spent so many of her young years listening to the tales of others, she didn't realize that love isn't always as it seemed.

With love comes an incredible vulnerability that can lead to a sacrifice of self, and with it, you can lose the ability to see reason. Your heart can convince your mind that what was once abhorrent, would now be okay.

The male she found used the word love to control her like a weapon. Each day, I watched from a distance, convinced she would choose that day to come home. The manipulation from her lover became so severe that, eventually, he convinced Rosera to give him the trinket I had gifted her.

You see, he knew what she was and where she had come from. She had told him all her truths in desperation to keep him. But, he was never interested in Rosera. He thought that he could use the trinket himself and come to the glen. He thought he could burn the glen and use the ashes for trade. He hoped the ashes of the glen would heal the wounded of the world and bring him all the power and riches he wanted.

He left her the very night she put the trinket in his hand and came to the forest. As soon as she felt her bed empty, Rosera knew. She knew in her broken heart that not only had she been betrayed by someone she thought she loved, but that she had put everyone at risk. She ran to your mother, whom she had met on her journey to find a lover, and your mother dropped everything and rode to the forest with her. I could only watch, unable to manipulate the outside world.

Together, they set a trap for Rosera's traitorous lover, and he was slain at the hands of your mother and her cleverness. Rosera gathered the trinket and, just as she was about to wish herself home, she prayed to me and then dropped the trinket into your mother's hands.

She promised your mother I would call her to the pixie glen if ever she needed. Rosera remained in your world, giving your mother the gift of this one. It was the only thing she had to thank her. And so, I honored Rosera's promise and waited for your mother. The pixies of the glen love to hear the story of her unfaltering friendship. I began to watch her as well. I watched and I waited.

Finally, she called upon me. But rather than asking for her wish to be fulfilled, she bequeathed her wish to you. And now you lay slumbering in the healing meadow, no longer wounded, tired, or famished. You may stay if you like, you need only ask. Wake now, child.

I woke in the meadow feeling like I had slept a thousand years, and yet, none at all. Momentarily, I forgot where I was. I jumped to my feet, and the lack of ache in my side told me the dream was laced with truth and I had been healed. I had been healed so thoroughly, the ache from never really being full had subsided and my heart, though still broken, felt mended along with the gash in my side. I looked around and saw nothing more than the tranquil land I had entered with Esa, who was nowhere to be seen.

"Hello?" I whispered.

"Helloooooo. Welcomes to the Pixie Glen."

I circled one way and then the other, looking for any sign of another living creature. Nothing. "Uh, thanks?"

"Yous is welcome," a tiny voice called.

And then the small heads of a million pixies emerged from the flowers, the beating of their wings flapping in unison as they rose. Curiously, some of them flew closer to me. Some flew above me. Some flew around me in circles.

"She comeses!" a pixie yelled, as much as a tiny bug could yell, I suspected. Immediately, they all raced back to their hiding spots.

"Ara, welcome," the ethereal voice from my dream said.

Startled, I spun again, and there she stood. Ofra was not quite as tall as me, but as I stood before her, she still looked down at me as she hovered just above the lush green grass. Her long, slate-black hair flowed to below her waistline, and her pure white, celestial skin was a constant reminder that she was god-like and in no way someone to be angered, but apparently, I had a death wish. "Was it all true, then?"

"It was."

I exploded. "Why would my mother not save herself? Why gift me something I didn't need at the cost of her own life? Why were my parents killed? Is the queen really after me, or was it just my parents? For the love of the gods, please feel free to step in here and answer any of these questions." I began to pace. She opened her mouth to speak, but I cut her off. "I don't know who you really are. I don't know why my mother would plant your name into a poem for me to memorize rather than just saying 'Oh, hey. By the way, I'm secretly a badass and killed a male. Here's a fucking favor I earned but won't use. Don't worry darling, your whole life is a lie, but I'm sure you'll just figure that shit out as you go.' Why didn't she tell me? Did he know? Did my father know? Please don't tell me he lied, too."

I pierced her with a razor-sharp glare, and she simply smiled at me. She simply, fucking smiled.

"Not one answer then? Not one at all?"

"I kept a promise I made to your mother and healed you. I have done my part on your journey. There is nothing else that I can say. You may—"

"Just don't even bother. Send me back. I want to leave right now." I turned to look for a damn exit.

"Have you not considered staying? Is it so bad to be here, where you are safe and cared for?" she asked, her eyes empty.

"Staying? I can't stay here. I have to find Aibell. That's where my mother wanted me to go. You claimed you watched. You sat here and watched my mother die, knowing you'd promised her a favor. And for what? I would have healed. I would have been fine."

"Your mother bequeathed her call to you long before her deathbed, my dear. Until you held that necklace, I could never call upon you, but it has been your wish for nearly your entire life. It was not my choice to make, but your mother's."

I crossed my arms over my chest and planted my feet, raising my eyebrows at her.

"Very well, I'll send you home. Our paths will cross again. Then you will see that you need me just as much as we need you. You have your mother's heart and your father's fire. I expected no less." She lifted her hand and pointed behind me.

I turned to see the forest and began to walk away, but just as I was about to take a final step out of the meadow, I turned back to Ofra.

"Thank you," I mumbled, "for keeping my mother's promise. If I ever meet Rosera, I'll tell her to come home."

The first and only genuine emotion she expressed was sorrow. "I'm afraid that won't be possible. You watched her death at the hands of the northern king, Autus."

My head snapped up as I realized who Rosera was, but Ofra was gone, and with her, the pixie glen.

CHAPTER

14

Ara

Although I walked for nearly an entire day in the wrong direction following Esa, Ofra sent me right back to the riverbank where we first met. She *could* have just dropped me off at the lake I was searching for, but I guess pissing her off didn't work in my favor. She probably didn't deserve it, but I had spent days walking through that gods-forsaken forest, hurt and hungry, and when someone had come trotting along begging for help, what did I do? I just left my own needs behind and off I went. I had put that necklace on as soon as I left my mother's body. Did she think to come save me from nearly dying then? No. No she did not. So, she did deserve it.

The only good news I had was that finally, *finally,* I was able to draw my bow and my sword and hold it before me without straining. I suddenly became the hunter instead of the hunted.

Before the pixie glen, I thought I had about a day and a half left of walking, but being healed and rested I could alternate jogging and walking and possibly make it to the Neverwood Lake by nightfall. I decided I would only stop to hunt if something worthwhile crossed my path.

Otherwise, I kept going. I wasn't sure what I was going to find there, but I was hoping for shelter.

As I walked, I thought back to my mother's words. *Find Aibell*, she had said. If what I knew of Aibell was true, I'd spend forever calling upon her, and who knew if she would actually come? That didn't really feel like a solid plan to me, but I didn't have any other options.

I started thinking about all the fairytales and nursery rhymes and wondered if there were colloquialisms in my vocabulary planted for deceit and direction. Those thoughts were a dark hole. One I had to be leery of falling into. When I started to feel like my entire life was a lie, I also started to wonder if I was the only one who didn't know it. Then I questioned everyone and everything I had ever known. And by then, my mood was so dark, I didn't even notice the lake until I nearly slipped into it.

Looking around, I saw nothing. The word lake was clearly used pretty loosely. I stood before an over-sized pond. There were no cottages, no fae. It was eerily quiet for being in the middle of a fae forest.

"So, let me get this straight," I said to no one. "I come all the way here for this? Nothing?" I swung my hands into the air. "Perfect. Just perfect."

I snorted and paced. I pulled out my sword and swung it through the air as I tried to reason with the universe.

"What was I expecting? Oh, I don't know. Some help? I was expecting something, anything, to actually be in the only place I was told to go. What am I supposed to do?" I asked, trying not to sound as lost as I felt. "I can't go home." I stopped flicking my sword about. I stopped pacing. My erratic mood swung like a pendulum, and I was losing control of where it would land.

"Aibell, can you hear me?" I prayed.

And then I proceeded to scream her name at the top of my lungs until my voice was gone and my throat was raw. Nothing happened. I knew it wouldn't, but it didn't, and that was still devastating. I crumbled into a heap on the ground, setting my sword beside me. "Enough already," I whispered. "I've had enough. Aibell, please come save me from myself, if not the world."

Still, nothing happened.

I crawled to the edge of the water, and, laying on the bank, I dipped my fingers into the glass lake and watched the water ripple. I moved my hand back and forth, watching my tears fall like raindrops onto the surface, and wished I was strong enough to keep them to myself. I had never felt so vulnerable. I knew this wasn't how a warrior would act. My parents had groomed me into the perfect weapon, and here I sat, lost and crying like a child. And that was where I drew the line. I had spent these last few days feeling sorry for myself. Letting my emotions get out of control. Letting the unknown take me to places I didn't even want to go. If ever I was going to take control of my own destiny, it was going to be now.

I got to my feet, peeled off my clothes, sat everything at the bank of the water and jumped in, bathing in the silver moonlight. I let the water wash away my tears, and with it, my desperation. I needed no one, and it was time to let the universe know it.

"There you are. I was wondering when that storm would come out."

I turned to the voice, realizing I was still naked in the lake. Swimming only an arm's length from me, was a water nixie. Or at least I thought he was. I had never met a water nixie, but his giant mirrored eyes and long tentacles wading in the water below his waist suggested I was right.

"Who are you?" I inquired, swimming back to the edge of the water.

"My name is Mikal, but you have it wrong, my dear. I am not a water nixie."

Trying to keep the shock from my face I asked, "Can you read my mind?"

"I can read your mind as easily as I can read your face, dear." He jumped high out of the lake, twisted in the air and dove back into the water. His tentacles disappeared and became the tail of a fish.

I rolled my eyes. It was always a game with the fae. "Turn around," I demanded.

"Shy, little Ara?" he smirked.

"Yes. Let's go with that. Turn around."

Mikal nodded his head and turned as I stepped out of the water, keeping my eyes on him as I dressed. When I was done, he faced me once more. "You've come to ask me something," he began. "Actually, you were sent to me. The questions developed on the journey."

"I—"

He raised his scaled hand from the water to stop me. "Before you even ask, no. I am not Aibell. I will show you how to reach Aibell when we are done, because that is who you must see. But first, let me think."

"If I cou—"

"No," he said again, raising his hand.

Anger boiled in my gut, but I remembered how that came back to bite me with Ofra, so I bit the inside of my cheek and waited. And waited. And waited. Fae were rarely in a hurry. What's the rush when you have an eternity? I tapped my foot and raised my eyebrows. And waited some more.

"I see there are no holes in the ancient magic. I can say only this: who you think you are now is not the entirety of who you will be. Your mother sent you to me because I hold a message for you. She wanted you to know that no matter what you learn, she and your father loved you more than they could ever say. She wanted you to know they regretted nothing but that they couldn't be here to help you when you needed them. Trust no one. Always keep your guard up."

"So, she knew she would die?"

"She knew there was a great risk," he said, watching me so closely, I felt naked again.

"And my father also kept this secret from me?"

"Your father kept your secret. It was not by choice, but the lack of it."

"So, there is something I need to learn. I'm not just going to Aibell on my mother's whim?"

A slight nod.

"And the queen? Am I to run from her?"

"As far as the world will take you, my dear. Your story will not end when you reach Aibell, Ara. It will only begin. As a creature of the water, the vibrations of disarray reach even to me, in the middle of this world. You must be careful. I hope our paths will cross again."

"Wait!" I shouted as he plunged into the water. "How do I get to Aibell?"

She waits, he spoke into my mind, *just beyond the clearing, but so does another. Take heed, dear one. Stay here for the night and rest. You will be safe.*

CHAPTER

15

Temir

I sat across my perfectly organized desk from Oleonis, watching him carefully as I tapped my pen on the notebook in front of me.

"Bottoms up." He tilted his head back, then smacked his lips. "It's bitter."

"I'll work on that." I chuckled.

"Shall we wait a few moments to start?"

"Remember, the idea is to try to lie to me."

He nodded. "Yes, I do get the basic concept of proving a truth serum. I'm ready." He took a deep breath.

I studied those deep eyes for several minutes, looking for a sign of anything. There was nothing. "What is your name?"

"Greyford," he said matter-of-factly.

"Okay. Hmm. Let's give it another moment."

Oleonis shifted around in his seat. He twisted forward and back and then stood and quickly sat down, before standing again and lunging across the room.

I couldn't help the smile that plastered across my face at his antics.

"It may not be a truth serum, but I feel great. The pain in my back is gone entirely."

"That was its original intent, but I didn't know you had back pain, Oleo. How long?"

"Don't you go examining me now. I'm old, not broken." He lowered his chin.

"Well, that's true enough," I said, still beaming at the old coot.

"Was that a joke, Temir? I didn't know you had it in you."

Changing the subject, I asked, "What is your name?"

"Greyford Butefrous." He laughed.

"You silly old fae. I know this worked before. I just know it. What do you think is the difference between then and now?"

"Well, I think the most obvious is the fact that he is sea fae and I am a land dweller. As the plants and such from the sea work differently, it's reasonable to assume the inhabitants would react differently to the plants of the land. I'm sure with some minor tweaking or additions, it could be converted. What was the lotus to fennel ratio?"

"Equal parts. The serum does have an extract of taonia atomaria."

"Ah, sea kelp. Perhaps try finding a land equivalent to its dominant traits?"

"Precisely," I admitted, capping the flask and pulling out my journal. "I'll keep this one handy though, because I'm fairly confident it worked on the sea fae. Nothing else would explain his behavior. He was convinced I had done something."

"There's one way to find out for sure. You know, the first time may be an accident, but the second is a deliberate finding." He took his seat once more.

"I'll work on that. This will set our timeline back, though. We haven't made a plan yet, but we can't do anything until we know that we can leave, minds intact. I want to make sure we aren't going to rush out of here and regret it later, Oleo. Can you continue to avoid the court?"

"I'm in no rush, son. I've explained to the king that I am working on a project in tree growth to double the production of our weapons. I've asked not to be disturbed."

"Clever, but you spoke to the king? That's dangerous." I leaned across my desk to him.

"Through messenger only," he assured me.

Later, I sat alone in my room, reading through some herbalism studies I had written years ago. There had to be an equivalent, but there were so many options, I wasn't sure where to start. Most nights, I took my dinner alone in my room, but I needed to step away from the monotony of research and clear my thoughts. Perhaps coming back to it with a clear mind would help lead me in the right direction.

I walked through the castle, casually looking for Gaea as I went. I wasn't sure where we stood since she simply slipped out after her drunken visit, but I knew it wasn't common for her to dine in her rooms. I could feel the stares as I entered the hall. Gaea would have me believe it was because of my looks, and though she might be right, I doubted it was in the way she thought. I looked like a lesser fae, and in this court, that could get you killed. Never mind that they all had to treat me as a high fae. Never mind that my stag horns, though I painfully kept them filed down, were a constant reminder I was the exception to the rule.

Just as I turned, deciding I wasn't in the mood for social dining, Gaea sidled up beside me and bumped me with her shoulder. "Hey, Temir."

"Hello, Gaea." I dipped my chin to her.

"I'm so sorry about last night. I hope I didn't embarrass you."

"Embarrass me? Why would you think that?"

"Oh, come on, Tem. You know we avoid each other for a reason."

"We do?" I squinted my eyes and tilted my head. I knew we didn't go out of our way to spend time together, but I'd never avoided her.

Her eyes shifted away from me and then back. "Listen, when I was young, Oleo was all I had. Sure, I was jealous of the time you two had together. But now that we are grown, I would hope we can put that behind us."

"Oh. Uhm, sure. I hadn't realized."

"And last night was a mistake." She lifted a shoulder. There was the aloof fae I knew her to be. Again, her eyes shifted away and back to me, and I felt my face fall a tiny bit. "Can we try to be friends? Be cordial?"

"Gaea, I have always been cordial to you. I don't know where this is coming from."

"I *know* we don't spend any time together," she said, pinching my arm, "but maybe we could some time?" She tilted her head to the side and subtly nodded as I noticed the king's guard watching us.

"Oh right, sure. It would probably help the high council if we got along better." I finally realized what she was doing. "Shall we have dinner together?"

"Sure." She shrugged. "Just don't expect me to eat like a bird."

"Why in the world would I expect that?" We walked away from the guard and chose our seats.

"We have *got* to work on your social cues, Tem," she whispered.

I leaned into her and tried not to notice the intoxicating scent of lavender she probably bathed in. "Why are we announcing a truce between us?" I asked, truly confused.

"Because," she said, lifting her wine glass to her lips, "Oleo said you needed to talk to me, but the guards have been extra nosey and on edge lately."

"I hadn't noticed."

"Honestly, Tem. You barely notice the world around you. I, on the other hand, like to make it my business to know what's going on."

"Oleo was right. I do have something to talk to you about."

She laughed unnaturally loud and placed her hand on my arm. Speaking louder than necessary she said, "I'd be *delighted* to come to tea tomorrow."

"There is such a thing as taking it too far, you know," I whispered behind my napkin. She only laughed and batted her eyes at me. *Females.*

I noticed most of the council members sitting at the head of the table, though the king was markedly absent. He never left the castle without me, though, so I knew he was around somewhere. I hoped he wasn't planning another trip to the Marsh Court. I loathed the trips away.

"Have a nice dinner?" Thane asked, stopping me at the hall entrance.

"Well enough." I nodded, trying to push past him.

He stepped into my path and pasted his slithery smile across his face. Thane had no reason to believe I didn't like him. I'd never exchanged words with him, or even actually acknowledged him, outside of the council meetings. Though I wasn't really, I liked to think I was above him. My integrity, specifically. Which wasn't saying a lot.

"You will join me in my rooms, Temir," he stated. Not a question.

"Of course," I muttered. "Lead the way."

I noticed none of the king's guards were with him, and that was unusual. Or was it? Maybe Gaea was right and I wasn't as observant as I thought.

"I haven't seen you out in the training field lately." He ran his fingers through his hair, letting the stark-white strand blend into the rest of the black.

Small talk then.

"No. It has been a while, hasn't it? I've been busy with work."

"It is curious, Temir," he said with a sneer. "Why bother with all the medicines and plants when you could just use your magic? Time well spent elsewhere if you ask me."

"Eventually, perhaps I could teach others to use the medicines and elixirs I create. We could have healers all over." I would not be explaining to him the process and ability to exhaust magic and be helpless. This male used anything he could as a weapon. The less he knew the better.

Someday he would hunt me. It would be after we escaped, and he would enjoy every minute of it. I wasn't of the mind to help him with anything.

We stepped into his rooms, which, not surprisingly, were much, much bigger than mine. Stuffed animal carcasses lined his walls, the gaps filled with different types of weapons, and a mace lay on his coffee table like a book. What kind of person just leaves a mace hanging around? His room was cold and uninviting. There wasn't a book in sight. If your home was a reflection of your inner self, Thane's was spot on. The only thing missing was a puddle of blood, but then again, I hadn't seen every room. I doubted he kept his skeletons in his closet, but rather, displayed them like trophies next to his bed.

"Ahem," he said.

My wandering eyes shifted to his.

"I've asked you here tonight because I need a favor. It's nothing big, just a simple request," he said, leaving the room. He returned, leading a female lesser fae with a massive gash on her head.

"Good gods, Thane. What happened?" I rushed to the female.

"She fell."

I didn't believe that for a second. Though it would do me no good to argue. "You'll need to bring her to my healing room and call the king to handle her enchanting."

"Actually," he said, taking a seat, leaving the female standing, "the king has . . . a strong disdain for my extracurricular activities. You will need to heal her without him."

Stunned, I took a step backward. "You wish me to expose myself without the king's permission? It's forbidden, Thane. You know this."

I should have known. The council was sworn to secrecy without enchant, a trust game of the kings. Naturally, Thane would try to use me as his own pawn, because Thane was nothing if not predictable, and he had a sick way of trapping people.

"It is only forbidden if someone finds out." He stood and crossed the room, slowly running his fingers along a sword hanging on his wall. Then he moved to another until, finally, he pulled down a small dagger. He crossed the room to stand behind the female and brought the knife to her throat, pressing so hard, a bead of blood pooled on the flat of the blade.

The female swallowed, but otherwise remained quiet and still.

"Thane!" I took a step forward, my nostrils flaring. "Stop this nonsense. What are you doing?"

"Will you not save her, then? Will you not heal her, king be damned?"

I squeezed my eyes shut and tilted my head to the ceiling. Every single ounce of me wanted to cross the room and close the gash. I wanted to punch Thane until *he* needed to be healed. I deeply wished I didn't have to play this game.

"I will not," I said sharply and stalked out of his room. Fuming, I knew what had to be done. I had to get the hell out of the Wind Court. The northern kingdom was just not my home anymore. It was my prison.

I stormed through the castle and, when I was just outside of my rooms, I walked up to a lone sea fae and punched him right in the face. He didn't even see it coming. It was not my best moment, but as I dragged him quickly into my room, I felt no shame.

Plopping him into the chair in my sitting room and leaving his head hanging backward, I placed my hand over his forehead and called my magic to heal his broken nose. I poured the truth serum into his open mouth. I had to be really, really careful with how this played out. I needed to do a lot of things without being able to wipe his memory afterward. I gave him a small injection of a rootswart and fungus blend. His cognition and memory would be hazy at best.

"Wake." I commanded.

Instantly his eyes opened, and he stared at the ceiling. "Wheerrrrem I?" he asked, words slurring.

"I found you in the hall on the floor. It looked like you needed help. I wasn't sure where else to take you, so I brought you to my rooms," I lied.

The lying was the worst part.

"Oh," he said, rubbing the back of his neck.

"Do you remember what happened?" I asked as casually as I could.

"No," he answered.

Good.

"Is there anything I can get you? Perhaps a drink?" I kept my voice neutral.

"No. I 'ont take drinkss frim lesserss."

That could be a reluctant truth, though maybe not.

"You'll find in this court I am the exception to that rule. Please, water?"

"I prel, pref, preferl ale," he slurred again.

"It sounds as though you've had one too many tonight already."

"But I dinn drink. I'm onguard duty tonnn tight." He blinked several times, trying to clear his mind.

"I see. What are you guarding in the king's castle? I didn't see your queen here today."

"Ima guardin err soldiers. Your *king*," he mocked, flopping his hand in the air, "doesna thing when his shoulders attack ours. Though we are s'pose to be werkin togather to plans a waaarr."

Bingo. A sea fae would never speak to a lesser fae about war, or his duties. It was casual, but likely not in his control. "I see. When do you think your queen will return to us? Perhaps that will keep the northern courts at bay?"

"She kips her own agenenda, creature. I've no idea what 'er planss err. We errr waitin' fer her to gib us premison, permison," he paused, trying to get the word out correctly, "permission to fight back." His eyes widened a bit, and I hoped I hadn't pushed too far.

"If it's all the same to you, I think I'll retire for the night. Can I show you to the door?"

"No," he said and stood. He wobbled, and I grabbed him under his arm for stability. Though I wanted to just let him fall for his prejudices, I was used to them.

"Have a nice night then. Be careful in the hallways."

He nodded and stumbled out the door. I had given him a strong enough dose, if he even remembered the conversation in the morning, it would be a miracle.

I tabbed my journal with green and slid it into a tear in my bedroom mattress. Green meant the theory was proven. I hid the journal because it was the most dangerous item I owned. It was a weapon in the wrong hands. The best books always were.

Falling into bed that night, I remembered who had slept here the night before. Her scent was all over my pillow and, try as I might, I could not get her out of my head. I wanted to. She was a distraction. We couldn't afford to be distracted right now. I hadn't known Gaea to be a flirtatious female, and I couldn't recall ever seeing her with a male, actually. So, while I wanted to chalk my feelings up to her flirtatious nature, I couldn't. I also refused to accept her passes as genuine. She deserved so, so much better.

CHAPTER

16

Ara

*A*fter fishing in the large pond the next morning and eating my fill, it was time to go. With any luck, I'd be with Aibell soon. If you could consider that luck. I wasn't sure where I'd go from there, but at least I'd be where I needed to be—for now. I shoved my things into my bag and tied it below my shirt. Mikal had said someone else was waiting for me, and I wasn't going to take any chances. I strategically strapped on my weapons so I could reach anything I might need. My bow was useful at a distance, and since I didn't know what hunted me in the forest, I kept it within easy reach, while I strapped my father's sword to my back first, and then my own. I left my dagger secured to my thigh, and though I had lost a few throwing knives over the last few days, I still had two in my belt. I tied my hair up and stepped back into the forest.

It was quiet. The birds sang their tunes and the leaves rustled in the slight breeze. My skin tingled, and my fingers curled at that familiar feeling. Someone was watching. It didn't take long. I gripped the cool hilt of my sword and pulled it from my back, pivoting in a circle, looking for a pair of eyes.

Before I found them, a dagger sliced the electrified air and caught my upper arm. *Damn.*

"You missed," I hollered.

"Did I?"

I turned to see a male dressed in all black, similar to the attackers in the cottage. The sea queen sent another hunter for me. "A little warm for leather, don't you think? Gets your male bits all sticky, or so I've heard."

He glared and drew his sword. Oh, fun.

He was a decent fighter. His stance was correct, and he shifted his weight proportionately. But it became a lot harder for him to fight me after I put a knife in his throat. They just never saw that coming.

He grabbed his throat, attempting to gag around the blade until he fell in a heap on the decayed forest floor. I had to end his life quickly. I could feel my movement slow and an immense burning sensation spider through my body. Once I realized the knife he had thrown was poisoned . . . well, that just pissed me off. Males ruin everything.

I started to walk, but the blurred vision and pain made it hard. Within four paces it felt like someone had tied bricks to my feet. Within another two, I couldn't hear a thing. I felt myself hit the ground, screaming, but making no sound.

"Foolish child."

I couldn't even look around to see who spoke. It wasn't the flopping fish in leather Morwena had sent. He was never getting up. Unable to respond to the crone's voice, I closed my eyes and let the darkness take me. I liked the darkness. Even in misery. It lifted at times, giving way to hazy recollections of intangible voices in the room.

"Of all the places in the gods damn world, you chose to bring her here? They will find her. They will find her and kill her, and it will be your fault, Old One."

That voice. I knew that male's voice. How? Or did I at all? Though I tried to fight it, grasping for reality, I again drifted back to my cloud of stormy haze. The ebb and flow of my mind was difficult to follow.

"Your heart may call what your mind resists, child. Sleep. You must."

Often lucid but occasionally fleeting dreams of bloodshed and murder haunted me. I watched my parents die at the hands of the knovern, then Aibell, and finally the queen slicing my mother's throat over and over. Still, I slumbered.

"This can't be normal. She should be awake by now. Are you sure you've given her the right antidote?"

Everything and nothing. The world was there, dancing on my fingertips, yet as my mind again abandoned me, I couldn't remember a second of it. That world where a stranger caressed my soul.

"What is a garden with no water?" the old female replied.

"Don't start with me," he said as his footsteps faded away.

Hours, or days, or weeks later my dreams evolved from watching my parents die to watching them live, and that was so, so much harder to bear. It was simple things. My mother tidying the sitting room. My father brushing down Brimir. The three of us sitting around that sacred table, laughing. My mother leaning against my father's chest with his arms around her as they watched my perfect landing from the second-story loft. The two of them stealing kisses by the fire. Those beautiful, terrible memories tortured me, slowly.

"You may always look to the past, but you must never stay there, my darling." The old female whispered my father's words to me, but I don't think I wanted to listen.

I wanted to stay in my agonizing memories forever. They were harrowing, yet beautiful and full of love. Reality was not so kind to me.

"Which is weaker, girl, your will or the world?"

Each time the female spoke, I could feel the heat of her ancient magic deep within me. Calling to me. Pushing me to come forward. I refused.

"Stubborn as the mountain, I see it in you now."

I needed release from the limbo of there and gone. I knew it was time, difficult as it was, and so, the next time she came and her magic burrowed into me, I embraced it, grasped for it, pushed forward as she pulled.

"Yes, child. Follow my song."

I followed. Through the darkness, I let her lead me like a river to the ocean, until the muffled sounds became clear and the storm had passed. I opened my eyes, blinking slowly and deliberately. The blurry outline of a short, silver-haired female with unnaturally large eyes stood before me. I squeezed my eyes shut and opened them over and over again, trying to bring the world into focus.

"Are you . . ." My scratchy, dry throat failed me. I tried to swallow, but it led into a coughing fit.

She sat on the bed beside me and placed a hand on my cheek, then clicked her tongue. "Yes, dear. I am. Now sleep."

Her power jolted into me, and back to sleep I went. It was a restful, peaceful slumber, solid black and silent until I woke again. This time, I was alone. I sat up and took in the humble cottage that smelled like home. Exactly. Aibell's magic must have known. It was a comforting and equally unsettling thought. I knew it wasn't, but if I closed my eyes, it was there. All around me. I lay upon a small, unassuming bed with multiple layers of thick blankets over me. Beside me, there was a small table with a simple lamp, and next to that, a wooden chair. That was it. Ordinary.

I brought my feet to the cold floor and stood, and as the world below me tilted, I reached out a hand and knocked the lamp to the floor. I fell to my knees, hoping I hadn't broken anything. My eyelids remained heavy, but I pushed through, grabbing the stupid lamp. Using the bed to brace myself, I stood, and before I could put the candle back in and put it back on the bedside table, I felt the old female's presence before she spoke.

"Rivers and fire in a single day," she said.

"What?"

I knew my thought process was still a bit slow, but what?

"Yes."

"Okay? Aibell? Is that your name?"

"They say it is."

"My mother told me to find you. There was an attack and she died, and my father died, and all this terrible stuff happened and I talked to Mikal, who claims he isn't a water nixie, but I'm not convinced. He also told me to find you. You can answer what he couldn't answer, and I need to know what is happening. Who attacked me in the forest?" I paused, realizing I hadn't stopped for breath.

"Was it fire and rivers, then?"

"I'm sorry, what?" I squinted my eyes.

She smiled and nodded. "Water nixie, water nixie ever shall he be. Water nixie, water nixie, no says me," she taunted.

"So, he isn't a water nixie?"

"'Is' and 'was' live in the same forest."

I took a deep breath. Either I'd lost my mind, or she was losing hers. Either way, I was absolutely confused.

"Let's start over. My name is Ara." I placed my hand on my chest. She looked to my hand and back to my face. "And your name is Aibell?"

"Did you hit your head?" She slanted her head almost unnaturally.

"Wha . . . no. I just . . . I didn't—"

"You fail to make sense, child. Sit back down."

"I'm hardly a child, Aibell."

"When you are the age of the trees, everyone is a child. Even the parents of your heart were children when they last came to me."

130

"Both? Both of my parents came to you?"

"Good heavens, do sit down."

"But I—"

"Time is but a race."

I plopped down on the bed, worried I was going to lose her in her own delirium again. "Could you start from the beginning?"

"I did start at the beginning, child."

"More specifically, then? Could you tell me the story of my own beginning?"

"You are not asking the right questions."

"I don't know what questions to ask. I don't understand what happened or what is happening."

She gathered my hands into hers and closed her eyes. "Mated souls are as powerful as the sun, but not more powerful than a fated destiny. Your parents' light called to me, to offer shelter to you in need. I offer that now."

"Are you saying that it was their destiny to die?"

"No. It was your destiny to live."

I put my hands to my temple and massaged, taking deep, calming breaths.

"To heal a wound, you must let it be."

"I am here because this is where my mother told me to go. You have agreed to let me stay here because you told them you would. Is there any more to the story? Is there a reason the queen would kill my parents or take me prisoner?"

"Stories are seldom a single chapter."

We exchanged a long and awkward silence. I thought she might be done answering any questions, but finally, she spoke. "Queen Morwena's knowledge is like the water she dwells in, ever elusive and tenuous. Of the fate that befalls you, only half has been prophesied. There is a second half of the prophecy that is yours alone to acquire. I warn you now, child. Once you learn your fate, you will never unlearn it."

"Do you know my fate?" I asked, clutching my hands.

She shifted on the bed and once more grabbed my unsteady hands. Rather than saying the words aloud she spoke into my mind. *Have you heard of Alewyn's Promise?*

Shock ripped through my body like a lightning bolt straight from the heavens. I shook my head fervently. "No . . . no. You're wrong." I yanked my hands from hers as the world went silent. I stood, pacing. No, absolutely not. "Are you sure?" I asked, my voice breaking. There was no strength left in me at all.

"As the mountain."

CHAPTER 17

Temir

"Pro," Oleonis said. "If my hypothesis is correct, a person could never truly be enchanted."

"Con," I answered, leaning back in my study chair. "If the king found that out, he'd kill me for sure."

"Big con," he said, as he considered why I should pursue discovering the corrected truth serum. "Pro, if everyone knew you could force the truth, more people might naturally offer it."

"I highly doubt that. Con. If the king finds out and forces me to dish it out on his every whim, I will also have to watch fae after fae die, and I would be responsible."

"Pro," Oleo countered. "In the right hands, a truth serum could help build a trustworthy kingdom between its rulers and subjects."

"Con. We have no fair rulers, so they would just use it against one another as a weapon. Honestly, Oleonis, I need to really put some thought into this. If he found out, we would never leave. If he knew I could keep him immortal *and* sort out friend from foe, he would likely chain me to him so I could never even consider it. Imagine if he captured the Flame Court's general and forced me to give him the serum. He would know all of the secrets he needed. He would conjure the biggest bloodbath in history. I just don't think I could do it. If I never make a weapon, it can't be used against me, or you or anyone.

He sat silently, weighing my words as he stroked his beard and searched for response. "Fear will always hold you back, Temir. You can't outrun your destiny because you fear it."

"I can, and with good reason."

A knock on the door pulled us from our debate.

"We will have to finish this later, son. I've got to get back."

I guided him through my rooms and to the closed door, only to find Gaea on the other side.

"Hello, lovelies," she said, sauntering in. Perhaps she didn't actually saunter. "Oleo, I wasn't expecting you to be here." She leaned in and kissed his cheek. Her eyes genuinely lit up at seeing him.

I wanted to be surprised by her kindness, but I wasn't. Not with him. Ever.

"I'm sorry I can't stay, my girl. I've been here all morning fighting with Temir, and I need some rest." She shot daggers at me with her eyes, and though I took a step back, Oleonis only laughed. "I'm just kidding, dear. We were having an intellectual debate, that is all. I'll see you tomorrow for dinner?"

"Same as always." She leaned in to hug him.

He shuffled out of the room and, as I shut the door, Gaea's warm face turned frigid. "He. Is. Old. You can't argue with him."

"Gaea, he is older, yes, but he is not fragile. His mind is stronger than ours put together."

"Speak for yourself." She walked across the room to the wine decanter. "So, is someone going to tell me what's going on around here, or am I supposed to start guessing?"

I cleared my throat. Of course this moment was coming. The moment where I would have to tell someone other than Oleo what I had discovered. Still, I hesitated. "What has Oleonis told you?"

"Are we going to do that thing?" she asked, raising her eyebrows. "The thing where you deflect because you don't want to talk about it?"

"I'm not doing *a thing*."

"Fine, Temir." She sat, her long legs propped over the arm of the couch, taunting me. "Oleo told me he thought there was something we should talk about, but that we shouldn't make it obvious we were meeting. You're lucky I knocked."

"As opposed to . . . ?"

"I could pop in and out of your rooms faster than you'd know I was here. Using a door is inconvenient."

"Yes, I can see how it would be." I moved to lean against the chair across from her.

"Was that sarcasm? First a joke with Oleo and now sarcasm with me? What is this personal growth journey you are on?" Clearly, she and Oleonis talked about me a lot more than we talked about her.

"Gaea," I said, taking a seat. "I need to ask you a question."

"Nope. I don't answer questions. Is that it, then?"

"It's not." I rubbed my face. This was harder than I thought. "It's not all bad. It's just that Oleo . . . Well, he knows you're hiding something, but he said it wasn't his secret to tell and I should ask you about it."

"I'm sorry, what?" Her eyes narrowed on me, and the sudden chill was alarming.

I couldn't even think of a retraction. "Did I misunderstand him?" I asked, looking away. I could not hold that stare.

"You most certainly misunderstand me, Temir. My business is mine alone, and Oleonis had no right to say a thing to you about it."

"So, he can tell you about a ridiculous joke I made, but he can't tell me anything? Is that how that works?"

"Seriously? Those aren't even close to the same thing. There is one person I trust. One person in the entire gods-damned world, and even that was misplaced. My business is my business, and you can take your jokes and shove them up your—"

She spirited out of the room before she could even finish her sentence. She didn't need to though. The implication was there.

I snapped my gaping mouth shut. Of course I should have gone first. If I had told her first, maybe she would have understood. I should have thought that out. I should have made a plan.

18

Ara

"Several millennia ago, before the Iron Wars, before the many races of fae, when Alewyn was born among the stars, the creator promised a light to a king, should the world ever grow dim. A blood oath, constructed by the elven king and Alewyn, so that when the days grew darkest, there would always be the hope of life and light."

I recited Alewyn's promise in pure denial. I knew what it meant. It just couldn't be me. I didn't want to admit that it all made sense. I spiraled as my childhood raced back to me. Of course he would teach me to kill. Of course my cunning mother would find a way to plant seeds without telling me directly. How can you tell your young child that she is a gift from the creator? How could you expect her to grow into anything but what destiny planned? But then again, how could you not tell her? How could they let me discover the horrid truth this way?

When I was young, I would recite that promise as I practiced swordplay with my father, just as the kids at school would sing a nursery rhyme while skipping rope. Fae children were so rare, we had only a few kids around. They would tease me for my tales. How odd it seemed that they didn't also know them. I remembered how much it unsettled my mother to hear me recite it. I envied that promised savior who would travel the world and conquer it. The promised hero who would speak to fantastical dragons and slay evil kings. What did I know about being a savior? How could this be it for me? Could Alewyn be in such a dark place that a savior was needed?

Yes.

The lesser fae needed someone, but so did the high fae. From their own superiority complex. It had to be wrong. It had to be some other fae, some other female.

"The maze of memories cannot move the ocean, dear." Aibell pulled me grudgingly from my thoughts. She still sat upon my bed, watching me.

"You can't imagine how this feels. To learn you have lived a lie and the truth for all this time. Everything is always a game with the fae. Even my parents played the game, but with their own child, and that's the worst part." I closed my eyes and saw their faces.

"Yes, Ara, the safety and comfort of a home is a terrible thing. You will come with me. The next time I am besought. You will see then how fortunate you are, child."

"Do I have a choice in anything?" I demanded. "It seems those are few and far between these days."

"No," she answered.

"Great. What am I to do in the meantime? Shall I just pop over to the castle and make demands of King Coro while I wait?"

"No," she answered again. "You may have your tantrum, child, but once you are done, there is work to do."

"What else could I possibly have to do? Saving the world isn't enough?" I threw my hands in the air.

"Follow me." She stood and walked to the door, but I remained standing and placed my hands on my hips. She raised a single eyebrow and lowered her chin.

"Fine," I mumbled, realizing she had just won my mother's game.

We walked through the humble cottage. I didn't know what I expected, maybe shrunken heads and bags of bones, maybe a cauldron over the fire and sage burning in the corners. Instead, it was just plain. A small amber fire danced in the bricked fireplace and the seating area was covered in furs. A cup of tea sat on a side table and, to be completely honest, it was the plainest, most uninteresting room I'd ever seen. There were no personal belongings, no paintings or pottery. Just simple. I couldn't help but wonder if Aibell had intended that, or if everything was an illusion in her enchanted world of magic.

We left the cottage, and once we stepped outside, I realized I couldn't remember the last time I had seen the sun, felt its warm embrace or a gentle breeze sweep my hair away. "Aibell, how long was I asleep?"

"It has been forty-three days since I brought you from the forest."

"Forty-three?"

"Even my magic has boundaries and limits. A grain of sand buried in the seafloor travels slowly."

I rolled my eyes and continued following. She hesitated for just a moment, and though she was not looking my way, I could have sworn she knew I had done it. Bossy old hag. I had to whisper-think that one. I didn't know if she could read my thoughts. Honestly, I was pretty sure she could. So, probably whisper-thinking wasn't even a real thing. Yeah. She probably heard me. *Damn.*

We walked until we were in an open area a good distance from the house. I watched her expectantly as she stopped and turned toward me. "Place your hands in mine and close your eyes, Ara."

I could feel her foreign magic, even with my eyes shut. She was in my mind, and the pressure grew as it filled in the open space around us.

"You may open your eyes now child."

I opened my eyes and felt the breath leave my lungs as I was plunged into my past. We stood in the middle of the training arena my father and I had crafted and perfected over many years. The wall by the door held my favorite weapons. I soaked in the details: the gouge in the doorframe from a missed strike, the haystacks in the loft, the smell of oil slathered on the swords and axes, the tattered targets and discarded arrows. All of it.

"How?" I breathed.

"Your mind is an open dialogue of memories. We will start there." She looked at me with those large eyes.

"What do you mean 'start there?'"

"An old hag will show you."

Shit.

"It is simple. You will build a wall around your mind." She began.

It was a small buzzing noise at first. I tried to picture a wall—because how does one build a wall in their mind? The small buzzing noise turned into a hum. There was no question she was there now as images began to form. I shut my eyes. I could see what she was digging for. The images of my trips to the castle and my glances to the royals flashed before me. I tried and tried to lay brick after brick, imagining it was between her and me. Still, the noise grew louder.

"Thinking of a brick wall will not work," she said, her voice cold.

"Okay." I shoved my palms to my temple to try to block the sound as it grew. "What do I do?" I shouted.

"You must close me off entirely. It is not a matter of thinking of an object, but of sealing your mind away."

"I can't think at all! The noise is too loud."

"Then turn it off," she bit out.

"I'm not like you. I don't have magic."

"This is but a mind game."

"I hate games," I said, doubling over.

The noise stopped, and the peace left me gasping.

"Your mind is weak, but your potential is strong." She smiled. An evil, wicked smile.

"Mhmm, that's great. Not helpful, but great."

"Stand straight and try again," she demanded as she walked circles around me.

"No. I need a min—"

She didn't start small the next time. She simply began roaring like a troll in my brain.

I tried to imagine my mind as a tangible object. I placed my memories into a box. The noise receded slightly, but still, it penetrated, rattling my core.

"Continue," she demanded.

My box would never hold her.

"You must not shut your mind off from yourself. You must be the only keyholder to it. Again."

I tried. Mother above, I tried for that entire day. I hated the thought of someone being able to bore into my mind but keeping someone out was so much easier said than done. By evening, my mind was mush and the headache was incapacitating. Not once did I ask her to stop. Not once did I refuse. Training was in my blood, it was the essence of my upbringing, and I knew nothing worth perfecting would happen in a day.

Rummaging the cupboards later, I prepared a deer stew for dinner, practicing blocking my mind over and over while Aibell drank tea by the crackling fire. While I wanted to dislike her, I couldn't. She had promised my parents she would give me shelter. Anything else she was doing was of her own free will, and though it pained me, I was grateful. She had probably lived in her home for decades in solitude, yet here she was, sacrificing her own time and the peace of her world for me. Maybe I didn't understand everything she said, but I recognized her intent as kind, and kindness was so very rare.

Just as I was closing my eyes for the night, Aibell gently shook my shoulder. "Come, I am called."

I crawled out of bed, threw on some clothes, and followed her to the door. She pulled it open and, rather than being in a clearing in the forest, the house lined up with others on a small-town street, as if it had always been there. I looked, shocked, at Aibell, but she acted like moving the cottage was the easiest thing in the world. "I thought they had to come to the glen and beg for you?" I whispered.

"Why ever would you think that?" She walked down the stone path from the house to the sidewalk. For an old lady, she sure walked fast. "Shield your mind before you insult me, Ara. They will not see you, so keep your ears open, but your mouth shut. Look around you, child."

She was right. I hadn't noticed until I looked closely, but something terrible had happened here. The houses were decrepit. Glass from dozens of broken windows littered the yards and some doors hung off their frames. It was dark outside, but even more quiet than you would expect of a small village.

We marched only a few houses down the sidewalk before we came upon a male with skin like tree bark and a tall, thin female with colorful butterfly wings standing in their front door as if they had waited for her all day.

"Where is the child?" Aibell called without an introduction.

They said nothing but stepped to the side so Aibell could enter. I followed closely behind. We shuffled through their home that smelled of stale chimney smoke and tobacco, then down a short hallway and turned into a bedroom only big enough for the bed that sat inside of it.

"Don't leave a single detail out," Aibell demanded, sitting on the side of the bed. She leaned over and placed her hand on the forehead of the tiny fae babe lying bundled in the middle of the bed.

"It was the fae of the sea. Two nights ago, they came barreling through town. We had just gotten our little one to sleep. I heard a ruckus outside and went to see what it was. They were smashing windows and hollering, then they set Maver's barn on fire. A few of us got together to fight back, but two were killed. And that's when we realized they were going into our homes." He took a deep, ragged breath, and Aibell gestured for him to continue. "I ran as fast as I could to get here. There was one of them pinning my wife to the floor. I lost my mind, and I'm ashamed to admit I beat him until his last breath. But the babe . . ." He paused again, a tear rolling down his swollen cheek.

His wife stepped beside him and took his hand in hers. Whispering, she said, "We were hiding in the closet. The baby began to cry. I tried to feed him, to keep him quiet, but he must have heard. He threw open the closet door and grabbed him from my arms. He . . . he tossed him like a doll across the room, and then grabbed me and held me down, crawling on top of me. I screamed and screamed. More for my son than for myself, but that's when Banel came in and, well, you know the rest."

Fire licked up my spine at the account of the lesser fae. A deeply embedded fury had me shuffling through the room as I tried to picture the wretched assault.

"We are luckier than most of the others. Every family in our village lost someone close to them. My mother, Banel's brother, and his wife. So much death happened in one single night. Please help our baby. We will give you anything."

"We will do anything," the male said.

"There, there," Aibell said, turning once more to the baby.

Heartbroken for the slaughtered village, I stepped out of the room and slipped quietly down the hall until I was standing outside. Aibell didn't need me in there. I was here because she wanted me to learn, she wanted me to gain perspective, and as I looked around the suffering village, I knew she was right. Others had it so much worse. I needed to check my attitude and find a way to do better for this entire world.

As I stood on the sidewalk, a small fae child came to me and grabbed my hand. Silently, she led me down the street. Aibell must have released the spell hiding me.

"Hello," I said. "What's your name?"

"Sueni," the child whispered, looking up at me with sweet little eyes and trimmed golden hair. Her rosy cheeks glowed in the blue moonlight.

"Where are we going, Sueni?"

"You'll see," she said with a small smile.

We walked hand in hand, and I kept my head up. As difficult as it was to see all the devastation, I needed to. To remember why my destiny was so important. The closer we got to the center of the ghost town, the more blood lined the cobbled streets. The bodies must have been moved already, but clearly, this was an intentional massacre.

"There!" Sueni pointed.

Across the street from where we stood was a small group of lesser fae with a table set up outside and an older female filling bowls with soup as another handed out pieces of bread.

"It isn't much, but we have to stick together."

"Oh no, I couldn't. I've had supper. This is for your families."

"Please. Momma said it's important that we share with everyone." The young girl pulled me across the street.

I could feel the eyes on me as I went, and in that moment, I realized how I must have looked. A high fae approaching a table for food after what had happened there. I paused as the female dishing the bowls locked eyes with me. Slowly, she lifted a bowl into my hands and nodded, tilting her head to the male with the bread. "All are welcome, dear."

"Thank you. There is a couple down the road with a very hurt child. I wonder if I could take the soup to them, as I have already eaten."

"Yes, that poor family. Banel lost his brother also. It's all very sad. Please, help yourself. Sueni, be helpful."

"Yes, Momma," she said, gathering a second bowl.

We carried the soup back to Banel's house and left it on the table, then I took Sueni back to her mother because it seemed ridiculous to let a child walk around alone after the attack. After dropping her off, I wandered until I found the rest of the survivors.

There were so many bodies and so few resources, the villagers decided to make one elongated pyre instead of individual ones for each fallen male, female, and child. I carried log after log to that pyre and worked with them until the sun rose, until our fingers had blistered and our shoulders ached. We gently moved the bodies atop the pyre in silence. Then we waited.

Slowly, the surviving villagers gathered. Banel, his wife and baby came. Aibell came. Sueni and her mother came. Two lesser fae with giant wings carried a third so he could be there. I looked into the eyes of every single one of those villagers and let myself feel the depth of their collective pain. I may not have lost my parents two days ago, but I had lost them, and in that, we were kindred spirits.

We stood in a large circle. A small faun stepped forward and sang the most beautiful, haunting song I had ever heard. Her voice carried through the vast night sky. The lilt of her tender words bled into each other, and though no music played to accompany her, her single voice enraptured us all. Tears fell and sobs played the base to her melody. As her song finished, we gathered hands and prayed.

"Into lightness and darkness, into shadows and mist, may you rest for eternity. Over the mountains and beneath the sea, let your spirit find peace.

May nature keep your soul, the wind hold your memories, the river bless your spirit, and the fire carry you away."

Temir

I found myself aimlessly wandering, trying to get Gaea out of my mind. Sometimes I forgot how substantial the castle was. It was easy to forget when I locked myself away. Before I knew it, I found myself in the kitchen. The cook handed me a few tarts. I didn't even need to ask for them this time. She knew. They all did.

Stepping outside for the first time in weeks, I realized I had also forgotten how beautiful nature could be when it wasn't working hard to remind you how vicious it was. The wind didn't blow, the sun glittered on top of the remnants of yesterday's blizzard like stars in the sky, the entire castle was lit in a winter blue as the sky reflected off the snowfall, and for the briefest of moments, I forgot I hated everything about Alewyn.

Instead of walking directly to the barn, as I had originally planned, I headed for the lists to distract myself a bit more. It was swarming with more fae than usual, but I hadn't been there in so long, I had no idea what was normal anymore.

There was a clear divide between the sea fae and the northern fae, but both sides were there, as was the tension. It was odd to me. The king allowed the sea fae into the lists with his own soldiers, but perhaps he was blinded by love, and assumed they would have to work together eventually. Or perhaps he just didn't care.

Thane called out to the northern soldiers as they practiced with blunt weapons in perfect unison. This was probably a new batch of recruits. I used the term recruits loosely. I doubted anyone was there on their own free will. Free will was a foreign concept to most of us. It didn't take enchant, though, only starvation or threat of death.

"Shields!" he shouted, and the males lifted their arms. "You there," he called to the male struggling on the end. "Do you want me to come and lift that shield for you, you fucking worm?"

The lesser fae's response was so quiet, I didn't hear him.

"Down!" he shouted.

The males lowered their arms.

"About!" he shouted again.

I cringed as I watched the struggling male. He turned the wrong way, and Thane went barreling toward him. I wanted to look away, but I couldn't.

"Do you see all those fish over there?" He pointed to the sea fae.

"Sir!" the recruits replied.

"Well, we aren't fish. We don't let the weak ones thrive around here." He kicked the fae's stomach and, as he doubled over, he swung his blade up, shoving it straight through him.

I jerked forward. My first instinct was to try to heal the male. I had to ball my hands into fists over and over. I couldn't let this argument with Gaea continue. I needed to find her. I needed to apologize and say

148

everything in the right order. My secret for her secret, so we could get the hell out of here.

Stepping into the old barn, that all too familiar scent slammed into me. Dirt and manure mixed with oats and stale smoke from the small stove that was rarely lit.

The stable boy was there, standing on his tiptoes to brush a centaur's back as he stomped around dry dust and snorted. "I don't know why I even bother coming here. You'll never do it as well as the females in Volos," he said, clumping out.

Good riddance.

"Temir," the boy said, dropping the brush so he could run up to hug me.

"Hey, kid. I brought you some leftovers."

"Mmmm," he said, smelling the air. "The lemon. My favorite. Thank you."

"Don't mention it." I ruffled his blonde hair.

"I never do," he said as he scampered over to his bench and plopped down.

"Want one?" he asked, mouth full.

"No. Not today."

"The sea fae been bothering you, too?"

"No. What do you mean?" I asked, sitting next to him.

"Well . . ." He forcefully swallowed his bite. "Them sea fae been bothering the army, I heard. Thought maybe you too."

I looked down to him and my heart clenched. He was so young. Maybe five, six. There was no reason he should even know about any of this. "What makes you think the sea fae are the problem?"

"Promise you won't tell?" He blinked up at me.

"I promise."

"Sometimes when I get all my work done and after I get a head start on the next day, Master Marte lets me peek out the loft window at the soldiers."

"Yeah?"

He wiped the back of his arm across his face, missing half of the icing. "Every day our guys have been fighting with the bad guys. That's the sea fae." I nodded, urging him on. "And sometimes, they don't even live. Sometimes their guts come out of their bellies or they chop their heads right off and our guys laugh, and the bad guys get mad about it. Master Marte says maybe that will teach the bad guys to stay away, but they never do. They just keep coming back."

So, the attacks were intentional.

"Listen. Those are all bad guys down there, do you hear me? If you think for one minute one of those soldiers from either side won't take your own guts out, you're wrong. So, you just stay out of the way and do as you're told. Stop looking out the window. They'd kill you just for that."

He grabbed my arms as I stood to leave. "When will I get to come live in the castle like you did, Temir? When's it gonna be my turn?"

Absolutely gutted, I closed my eyes. That simple question knocked the wind right out of me. I hadn't considered that one day he might ask me this. That one day I would have to be the one to crush his desperate dreams. "When the world is a better place, kid."

CHAPTER
20

Ara

*T*here's something about a funeral that opens your soul to feeling raw and tender. I hadn't known a single one of those fae, but my aching heart felt like we were kin. Their solemn faces, lit solely by firelight, would stay with me always. I would think of that nearly broken baby and remember that Alewyn wasn't a kind world. It wasn't even a neutral one. It would chew you up and spit you out just for being born.

For three days, Aibell and I worked on mental shielding, barely passing a word between us. I was able to form a shield to block her constant drilling, but it would only last a minute or so. After that, she came at me with a vengeance, and my shield would shatter like glass.

"The water may rock a ship, but it is the wind that carries it."

"Yep. Got it." I nodded.

I had no clue what she was talking about, but as the days passed, I realized this was how she was. Some days, I could partially understand her sage advice, and some days, I was as lost as the creek in the woods. Her words, not mine.

She started low and slow, pushing into my mind. A gentle request. I threw up my shield and another and another as she became more and more persistent. But, this time, rather than just building layer after layer in my mind, I backtracked, growing the shield. Making it thicker and sturdier as she persisted. I had to keep my eyes shut and concentrate, but as the minutes passed and I didn't hear that familiar buzzing in my head, I wondered if it was actually, truly working. I could feel her there, a pinprick in my subconscious. I opened my eyes and looked at her. "Are you trying, or teasing me?"

"I would not waste our time, child. Let us try something new." Without warning, a ghostly arrow shot past me.

I turned in the direction it came from to see an apparition. A shadow form of myself.

"You will keep your shield up while taking on this foe. Are you ready?"

I nodded, spreading my feet and trying to think of a strategy. "How do I fight a shadow, Aibell?"

"For now, simply dodge the arrows. Don't let your emotions suppress your intelligence."

A shrieking noise pierced my jellied mind as the shadow docked an arrow. Concentrating on pushing her out of my mind while watching for the direction of the arrow's tip was challenging.

I was able to get a basic shield up, but I could still hear the high-pitched sound as I rolled to the ground and popped back up. I put up another layer and repeated. Unfortunately, this time, the agile archer realized I was just going back and forth, so while they aimed at me and I dodged, they changed direction at the last moment and shot the arrow straight at me. I barely escaped that one. And the buzzing grew louder. I couldn't do both at once. I needed to find a way to shield so that it was second nature and not something I needed to think about as I moved.

I tried dodging and then shielding, and shielding and then dodging, but unless I figured out how to do them at the same time, I was going to keep taking arrows. They didn't pierce, but they stung enough to motivate me to avoid them.

For hours we worked on this technique. Aibell never tired. Occasionally, during training sessions, she brought a book to read in the corner. Obviously, the only one challenged here was me. I persisted though. I had to believe it would eventually happen.

"Can you tell me how to shield without thinking about it?" I asked, dripping in sweat.

She looked up from her book, and the shadow disappeared. She crossed the area to stand beside me. "Take my hands. Good. Now close your eyes."

I did as she said, and she showed me an image. A glass orb rotated with glimmers of light like jewels behind cracked layer after layer. Her mind sat somewhere within as the sphere rotated.

"This is what my shield looks like. Watch it as it turns."

"There's a line in it?"

"Yes. You see, the mental shield is not something you should put up and take down over and over, but rather something you should learn to keep up at all times, Ara. You must be the only one who can get in and out of your shield. You must be able to project from your mind, just as you are able to close everything in. I've had this shield around my mind for over three thousand years. I don't take it down. I don't open it up. It's secure. If you were to push into that crack, you would find another orb within. Only I know the maze to my mind, as only you should know yours. Keep your shield up at all times."

She squeezed my hand, and I nodded in understanding.

"Do not take it down. Strengthen it as you feel it weaken. There are more fae with the ability to penetrate your mind than you know. If one single person learns of your prophecy, your journey will change forever. You must keep the secret to yourself and learn how to keep your thoughts and memories to yourself. Your mind is not weak, girl, but there are fae that could turn it to slop without trying."

That night I laid in bed and considered what Aibell had said. She was right, of course. I could never tell a soul about my prophecy. I wasn't even convinced I could come to terms with it myself. I had no immediate plans to set out on a suicide mission, anyway. How could one fae change the trajectory of hatred in this fractured world? Still, I had to believe she had her own agenda. Everyone always did.

Life with Aibell had become comfortable. My basic needs were met, and I was safe within her illusion of the world, but my foretelling had a second half to it. If the second half was anything like the first, it was important to know. I just couldn't let that go. If it was my fate, it would happen, or I would die. But not knowing was difficult to handle. Without knowing, I felt unprepared. I felt as if half of me were lying out there somewhere, and I needed to find it. It called to me every single night.

I could stay though. I had an eternity ahead of me for fulfilling prophecies and all of that. For now, Aibell and I had fallen into a rhythm and, on some level, I felt as though she genuinely cared about me. And I needed that. I just needed one damn person in the whole world to actually care. Aibell was all I had. I knew she was a powerful being and I didn't really *have* her at all, but the thought gave me comfort. Even if she was half delirious and odd most of the time.

"Shield!" she yelled from across the cottage.

I giggled and turned over in bed. Insufferable old hag.

Once upon a time, there was a faun named Ineo, and Ineo had an older brother named Riton. Since childhood, their father would give all the chores to Ineo, claiming his brother was destined for greater things and the chores would help Ineo grow big and strong.

As time passed, Ineo did all the work without a single complaint, while Riton sat around waiting for his great adventure to begin. One day, Ineo was on his way to the market and stopped to help a female with a broken carriage wheel. After he arrived home, three days after the market, a letter waited for him.

"It must be a mistake," Riton demanded. "I am destined for greatness, Ineo is only good for chores."

Soon enough, Ineo packed his bags and moved to the palace. For it was the queen who he had helped that day on the road. She hired him to come to the castle and, before long, he had traveled the world with the queen, experiencing adventure after adventure.

Riton remained at home, waiting an eternity for his adventure to find him. It never once occurred to him to find it for himself.

I awoke with my father's story on my mind. I guess my parents had given me these tales and poems and nursery rhymes for wisdom should my journey need it. I had thought about Ineo for a reason. My father was gently guiding me from my memories to not be complacent. To never get so comfortable with life that I forgot to live. Perhaps he knew I would hesitate to leave Aibell. Perhaps he knew my prophecy would scare me into submission.

"I am called, child. We must go."

I sat my tea on the table. This was only the second time Aibell had told me to join her. I was sure there would be a life lesson in it somewhere. It seemed the folk were full of those.

"You will need a coat." She pointed to the small rack in the corner.

As we stepped outside the cottage, the crystalized gusts of wind bit into my cheeks and tears stung my eyes as I tried to adjust to the frigid temperature. I should have grabbed two coats. And while I bent forward and used all my strength to take a single step through the deep snowdrifts, Aibell simply walked like we weren't in the middle of a treacherous blizzard. As the wind gnashed and ripped around me, I tried my best to keep up.

I could only see about three feet ahead; someone could have spoken, and I was sure I wouldn't have heard them. Aibell was just close enough to reach out and grab as I began to fall, the snow pulling me down. Yes, my natural instinct told me to grab an old female so I could knock her down with me. There was definitely something wrong with me. However, the minute I placed my hand on her shoulder, the wind subsided, and I was able to walk along the top of the snow instead of sinking into it. Sure, the storm raged all around us, but inside of Aibell's charm, we were untouched. For a moment, I considered letting go, because she hadn't asked me to grab her, but since she didn't complain and I had never seen a blizzard like that, I held my grip.

"It is there." She pointed to a small golden light in the distance. I wouldn't have seen it through the snow had she not pointed it out. There in the distance, like a shadow, stood a tiny home. Maybe a single bedroom and not much else. "They will see you from the start this time. I suggest empathy before reaction."

We pushed forward. I reinforced my mental shield. I had no idea what we were about to walk into, but I knew, without a doubt, we were in the Wind Court. And while Queen Morwena would gladly massacre fae from other countries, King Autus was renowned for his hatred for even those in his own territories. But my father had said Queen Morwena ordered the death of her subjects, too, so I wasn't sure which was the greater evil.

We were welcomed into the ramshackle cottage by a female who dipped her head low, keeping her antlers just above the floor. She kissed Aibell's hand then stood and grabbed the bony shoulders of a young girl with the same ivory skin and budding antlers.

"You have summoned me, child. What is your need?"

The female glanced at me and then back at Aibell. Her clear hesitation built tension in the drafty room.

156

"You are not to worry about my company unless you would prefer us to leave already?"

"No." The female jumped. "I am sorry. It's just that she is a high fae. We do not welcome them into our home."

"There will be no death today, I can assure you. Now, what is your need?" Aibell studied the room around her.

"I need you to turn my child into a high fae. I need her to look and walk and act as they do." She pushed her child forward and stepped back.

"But she is beautiful." I kneeled and stared at the girl. "Why ever would you wish to change a single hair on her?"

"Of course you wouldn't understand," she barked. "You would stand in my home and question my decisions. You with your beautiful high fae features. Never having to worry about your children. Never having to hide in your home, hoping the males traveling through would not get curious about an occupied house in the distance. You can walk down a street without fear. Tell me, what does that feel like?"

I remained silent. Sometimes silence was the only answer.

She turned back to Aibell. "Please try to understand. I think my daughter is beautiful. I just want better for her than I had. She is intelligent and kind. She works hard and practices her studies. But she has a long life ahead of her. A life where she will never have everything she deserves. A life where she will always be hated, no matter what she accomplishes."

Aibell turned to the young girl. "And what is your wish, child?"

She shrugged and looked to the floor. Her fidgety hands picked at the exposed seam of her tattered shirt.

"Have you not considered your child's desires?" Aibell stomped her wooden staff into the collapsing floor, demanding answers.

"She is a child. What does she know of how the world works? Of life and death?"

"What is your opinion?" Aibell asked, looking in my direction.

I opened my mouth and then shut it.

"You would leave the fate of my child in the hands of a high fae? That is exactly what I intended to avoid."

"Then we will leave, and you will have nothing but the cost of our calling," she said with a curt nod.

"What cost?" she spat.

"You will watch your tone," Aibell warned as the world below me shifted. This female hadn't yet learned not to piss off the old one. Aibell rarely showed me any emotion outside of annoyance and occasional sympathy. Now, the angry old hag was scary. "Everything comes with a cost. Especially when my time is wasted."

I considered this. Aibell had never once asked me for a single thing. Would she ask for something when my time with her was over? I had nothing but my weapons to give.

"What is your cost, Aibell?" she asked with a subtle tone of respect and fear.

"Your child will come with us. She will be safe and well taken care of for two days. When we return, I will consider your request."

"No. I changed my mind. You can't take her," the mother said, desperately falling to her knees and grabbing onto Aibell's skirts. "Please, she is all I have."

"You have called me here of your own free will. We will return in two days with your answer. While we are gone, you will think about the way you have treated my guest and ask yourself if your daughter will be treated the same by her friends, by her kin. There are two sides to every coin, but yours has the same face. You complain of prejudice, yet you grow it in your own home."

Without another word, we were gone. In the blink of an eye, we stood back in Aibell's cottage. I looked into the eyes of the child, but rather than fear, she seemed . . . curious? I kneeled to the girl and took her hands. "What is your name?"

"T-Tian," she answered.

"Well, Tian, my name is Ara, and I don't want you to feel afraid. You are safe here. I would never hurt you, and Aibell wouldn't either. I promise she does everything for a very important reason, okay?"

"But my mother says folks like you are the problem." She reached up to brush the point of my ear. "She says you would have me killed."

"Your mother is wise. It is important that you are careful of others like me, but you must not be hateful. I, personally, would never hurt you."

She leaned in and whispered, "Is there food here?"

"Of course there is food here. What do you like?" I dropped her hands and sat back.

"Cheese." She giggled and brought her fingers up to cover her tiny mouth. "Is there cheese?"

"Let me see what I can find."

We spent two full days with Tian. She loved to play with the farm animals, which hadn't been there until she came. She loved to snack and play in the enchanted garden. She did all the things you would hope a free child could do. But before we took her home, I needed to know.

"Do you want to be a high fae, Tian?" I asked as we threw stones into the new pond.

"Why? What do you want me to do, Ara?"

"I want you to do whatever you really, truly want."

"I think you are the most beautiful person in the whole world. But I want to look like my mother. I want to look like me. I don't want to look like you. Miss Aibell says I should always be proud of my reflection no matter what anyone says. That sounded very nice to me. Do you think Aibell will do what Mother asks anyway?"

"I really don't know, Tian. Let's worry about it tomorrow."

CHAPTER

21

Temir

"I'm sorry," I said, standing at Gaea's door.

"For?" She stood with her arms crossed leaning against the frame.

"I'm sorry for trying to pry information from you by arguing rather than explaining my own secret first."

She moved aside and let me into her rooms. The size seemed comparable to mine, with a sitting room. I looked around, avoiding eye contact, and noticed that her rooms felt a lot colder and more unwelcoming than I had anticipated. I didn't decorate my rooms as Oleo had, but I had personal things. My books, some plants I liked to keep close and my chess board were enough. From here, I couldn't see anything that said this was not just a guest room. As far as I knew, Gaea had lived here for over half of her life.

She cleared her throat. She didn't appreciate my wandering eyes. Noted. "Is this something we need privacy for?" she asked.

I nodded, and she took a step forward and placed her hand on mine. In a breath, we were gone. I opened my ears before my eyes and heard the waves crashing in the distance as foreign birds cawed. Her magic was wondrous. To be gone in an instant when my end goal was simply to leave.

"I'm listening," she said.

"You're sure the sea doesn't have ears?"

"The sea has plenty of ears, but Morwena has murdered the fae that lived around this island. It is safe for us."

"Let me start from the beginning." I put my hands behind my back and paced back and forth, making deep tracks in the golden sand as I explained to her Oleo's new ability, the truth serum I'd potentially found, Morwena's inevitable plan to deny Autus marriage, the sea fae targeting at the hands of the northern soldiers, and the overall hostility growing like invasive weeds in a vegetable garden. "We have to leave, Gaea. You, Oleonis, and I. We need to get out. To a safe place they can never find us. Where they can't use us anymore. The problem is . . . Well, there are a lot of problems at this point. We can't just walk out. They'd hunt us down and lock us up before we got to the next town."

"That's why you need me?" she asked neutrally.

"Yes. I mean, no. Not exactly." I dug my boot in the sand, watching it pour over the worn toe as I lifted it. "What I mean is, Oleo would never leave you behind. We need you because we wouldn't want to do it without you, but I suspect there is more to it than that because Oleo insisted we talk. I'm not trying to pry or force you to share anything. I simply wanted to tell you everything and let that decision be yours, as I should have done in the first place."

"You know this is absolutely crazy, right? For starters, I can only take us to a place if I've actually been there before, so we are still limited on where we are able to go. King Autus keeps me very close. The only reason I'm able to bring you here is because I did for a meeting he had ages ago.

He didn't even let me get out of the ship because he thought that would keep me from being able to come back."

"And yet you did."

She leaned down, grabbed a handful of the sand and sifted it between her fingers. She looked out to the water, and her eyes followed the gentle waves. "I leave at night sometimes and walk or swim to new places to stretch my reach. I never get far, but a little bit at a time takes me farther and farther away from him."

"There's a chance that he has enchanted us and we don't know it. Potentially, we will make an honest attempt to leave and it won't work the way we hope. Oleonis thinks the truth serum will expose those mind alterations, but we won't know until we try."

"But you don't even have it yet, so why bother?"

"That's what Oleo and I were arguing about the other day before you came. If I scrap the whole thing right now, it won't matter." I lifted my shoulders.

"But think of the good, Temir. Think of what that could mean in the right hands."

"But are there *right hands*? I've met King Coro and Queen Morwena. Even King Tolero many years ago. I can't believe they or Autus would ever be the right hands. King Tolero has potential, but only in the unknown. It's not just that though. Imagine if there were a bunch of lesser fae that all stood together against the cruelty in this world. Imagine if we could be a part of something like that."

"I'm not sure I want to change the world. I really just want to escape it." She sat in the sand at the edge of the water.

I sat beside her and watched wave after wave come, reaching for us but never quite meeting our feet.

"I blackmailed Oravan," she said quietly.

"You what? Why? How?"

"Several years ago, I heard him in the castle having a conversation. He was talking about leaving to go to work for King Coro. Apparently, they approached him with a bargain. As soon as the person left, I stopped him and told him I had heard everything. He begged me not to tell the king. He thought if Autus knew he was considering leaving, he would have him and his family killed before he could do so. I told him if he made something for me, I'd keep his secret." She sighed. "I wouldn't have told, but I needed the trinket."

"And did he?" I pried.

"He did. He made something more powerful than the king, in a way. I wear a charm that prevents me from being enchanted by the king."

My breath caught in the back of my throat. I didn't even know that was possible.

"I collect information for the king more often than I travel for him, and I'm good at it. But I knew he was erasing my memory because the more frequently I spied in other courts, the more I had blank spots in my mind. Things didn't make sense and, at first, I thought I was losing it until I realized what was happening." She plucked a small stick out of the damp sand and began to write her name as she continued. "In some ways, it's nice to have a choice, but I have to act like a loyal servant. He has forced me to do things I wish I could have said no to. And now I can never forget them."

"Do you have a desire to leave?" I asked, sifting the cold sand through my fingers.

"The first memory I have is trying to leave this place. I tried so many times, but he could always find me. The only reason I haven't left now that I'm older and could probably manage it is because Oleonis is all I have. If I left, I would have nothing and nowhere to go."

"Then I guess we can find somewhere to go together. The three of us."

She leaned into me and laid her head on my shoulder, her brown hair falling down my chest. "Sometimes it takes every ounce of my will just to go back. And I only do it because I know I can leave again."

"Until this moment right here," I said, leaning my head onto hers, "I wouldn't have understood what that felt like."

We stayed like that for a while before she stood, grabbed my hands and pulled me to my feet. "The council meeting is in less than ten minutes. We'd better get back." She took my hand, and those feline eyes locked onto mine for one fleeting second. And then I was back in my room and she was gone entirely.

I tried not to look at her the entire council meeting. We would have never passed glances before, so we couldn't start now. Everyone in this room was far too observant.

"You'll excuse Oleonis' absence. He is working on a project for me and must not be disturbed." The king pressed his palms onto the table and leaned forward, narrowing his eyes as he stared at his chosen council and magic wielders.

I saw Gaea's barely perceptible shift, and I knew to hear the king even say his name made her skin crawl. He may have been the older mentor, but she was now, and would always be, the one to protect him. She had already sacrificed nearly her entire life to stay here, just to be with him. Not that I could blame her. I would never leave him either.

"As you all know, I am soon to be wed. And while I'm sure that is exciting news for some, I would hope everyone in this room understands what that means. I'm not simply taking an ally or making temporary plans. Once we are wed, it is forever. We will conquer the entire world together. I'm not interested in making peace. I don't want a truce with the southerners. I want them all to bow before me. I don't care if they respect me, but they will fear me."

"Hear, hear," several council members cried, lifting glasses into the air. They smiled as if he had just announced a ball, not a war.

"Our troops are ready, my king," Thane said, eager as ever.

"They aren't. Not really. How can anyone truly be ready for war? The Marsh Court more than doubles our size, and I don't think the Sea Court will close that gap. Not to mention the Flame Court. Do we even know how many they have anymore? When was the last time we even considered them?" Ragal asked, looking to his cousin.

The king stood. The room did as well. "We have time. We will not be hasty, but instead plan," he said, meeting eyes with Thane. "But it is happening."

The next thing I knew I was walking out of the room and back to my own. I let myself in and locked the door behind me. As I turned back around, Gaea stood in my sitting room. "Mother of the Gods, you should announce yourself." I clutched my chest. "You've nearly startled me to death."

"Don't be a baby, this is important."

"What's wrong?" I stepped toward her.

"What do you remember from the council meeting?" She analyzed me cautiously.

"The whole announcement and that's it. Why?"

"Because the king did something I've never seen him do before. He enchanted the entire council and the magic wielders. He announced the war just as you remember, and then he used enchant. He told everyone to watch the sea fae closely because he didn't trust them but didn't want anyone to remember why they were doing it. He told us to report suspicious behavior directly to him. Then he told us we were all to report for personal orders from him as he called us. He said that anything said in the council room from that point forward would never be able to leave the room. Everyone is now bound to keep everything secret." She took a step toward me and brought her hand up to run her fingers through her silky hair. "You have to do it, Temir. You have to make the truth serum, and we have to get out of here. Not to just escape, but to find someone better. Somewhere better. And we need to do it quickly."

"Is it possible that you could get Oravan to make you two more charms for enchanting. If Oleonis and I both had one, we would at least be safe. If he questions us now, we won't be able to resist him."

"I'll work on it. How far are you into getting your formula right?"

"I'm not sure. It's simply one ingredient I think I need to replace, but I don't have many people to actually test it on. The last test, well, it did and didn't go quite as planned."

"Could you test it on me?" she asked, her flirtatious gaze locked on mine.

"Gaea, no. If I give you the truth serum, there is nothing you could hide from me. I could ask you anything, and you would have to answer me."

"We have to start trusting each other. That's the only way any of us are getting out of here alive." She took a step toward me, placed her hands on my arms and looked up.

I'd never noticed how much smaller she was. I looked away, unable to help myself.

"I want to trust you, Temir, and I want you to trust me."

I didn't have words. This little fireball held me completely captivated. I could only remember to breathe. Breathing was good. She reached up, tucking that loose curl behind my ear again. She was making a habit of that. Breathe, I reminded myself. "I do trust you," I managed.

She smiled and slid her fingers behind my neck, interlocking them.

I placed my hands on her tiny waist and leaned down to her, breathing in her scent as it sashayed through me, just as she did. The world around us stood still.

"I think I'll kiss you now," she whispered.

"Are you sure?" I pulled back just slightly, searching her eyes for regret but only finding a wild abandon, a hopeless hunger intertwined with my own desperate need.

There was no impending war; there was nothing but her and I in that one distended moment. The fearless female who would run away with me. Gathering her hair, her face, her entire frame, I drew her into me, closing the miles between our lips, and claimed her.

She pulled away and laughed. The most beautiful sound I'd ever heard. "I sure hope that's not your idea of procrastinating."

"I thought that was your idea?" I teased.

"Come on, Tem." She grabbed my hand and pulled me into the study. "So, how does this work? Do you use your magic, or is it actually something I drink or what?"

"Well, it's a little bit of both," I said, shutting the door. "There is magic in the making of the serum, mixed with some herbs and such, but essentially, you just drink the serum." I crossed the room and pulled a vial with a new formula from the shelf. I had mixed it in with my regular medicines, so anyone looking wouldn't find a thing. I pulled the top from it and handed it to her.

Our fingers brushed each other, and her eyes snapped to mine.

"You don't have to."

"I want to," she said firmly.

"Fair warning, Oleo thinks it's bitter."

"He tried it?"

"Oh, yes. You'll have to ask him about Greyford Butefrous." I chuckled.

"I will." She laughed.

She tipped the vial and drank every last drop. "Wow, he was not kidding. That's awful." She coughed into the crook of her arm.

I jumped up and poured her a glass of wine. She drank the entire thing in one gulp. "What color is the sky?" I asked.

"Purple," she answered.

I looked out the window just to make sure.

Damn.

"You don't think it's my barrier charm do you?" She twisted the ring on her finger as I returned to my seat.

"No. This is molecular. It has nothing to do with enchantment magic. You could take it off, to be sure." She slipped the ring from her finger and set it carefully on the desk. "What color is the sky?"

"Purple." She sighed. "You'll get there, Tem. Just give it some more time."

CHAPTER

22

Ara

*W*hat are two days when you can live for an eternity? They are gone in the blink of an eye, and while they would never change the world, Tian's visit had changed mine.

"Shall we go?" I asked Aibell as I helped Tian into her furs.

Aibell knew. She had brought Tian here for a reason. I didn't know the extent of her power, but on some level, she knew I had made up my mind. If Tian could so bravely be herself, no matter what she knew the world would throw at her, I didn't have the right to cower either. I didn't get to hide in Aibell's paradise and let the broken world rot around me. Perhaps that was the lesson she taught, having learned from leaving her own world behind, the importance of returning. It was time to go.

Moments later we stood back in Tian's shabby home.

"Oh, my darling girl." Tian's mother wept as she gathered her into her arms. "How I have missed you. Are you well?" She pushed her daughter to arm's length and examined her from head to foot before pulling her back into her arms.

Tian only giggled and let her mother sob. "I'm fine, Mother. Really. Aibell had lots of cheese, and she had a real live chicken, Mother. And Ara, she's my friend. She's not so bad once you get to know her. Honest."

"So, you've decided then?" the female asked, looking only at Aibell.

"I've not. Ara has, and I will honor her decision."

I'm not sure when I decided anything, but I nodded all the same. I knew what I hoped Aibell would choose.

The female looked down at me, the disdain was present but distant.

"I'd like to start by telling you how much we truly enjoyed Tian these last couple of days. She is exactly the joy you said she was." I walked to Tian and grabbed her small hand in mine. "I understand your fear more than you know. I wish the world didn't work the way it did, but your daughter is kind and brave and had she told me she wanted to change, I would have supported that. She doesn't. She knows what this world has to offer her, and she still chooses the life you gave her. She is proud of it, and I hope you will be one day, as well."

Her mother said nothing, but I could see the heavy tears she held back.

I wanted to change my mind so badly, but for Tian, I just couldn't do it. "She will remain as she is. She will choose her own destiny. She will be able to call Aibell one time in the future, and if she chooses to change, she can. But it is and will remain her choice alone."

"She will die. You speak of her joy and bravery. None of those will matter when she is ash in the wind. Please," she said, taking a step toward me. "She doesn't understand. You don't understand."

"The decision has been made." Aibell turned to Tian. "If ever you should need me, call on me, just as I taught you. I will come one time. I will grant you a single wish, and that, child, is a gift from your mother."

"Please," her mother whispered.

We were gone just as quickly as we had come. We were barely back to Aibell's enchanted cottage when she faced me. "Choosing someone's future is like holding a thorny bush, yes? You'll likely cut yourself no matter which way you turn but choosing your own is like holding the tail of an imoogi. You can never really escape what is destined to happen, no matter how hard you hold on. You're better off just letting go."

"I've been here too long. You're starting to make sense. I thought I could stay here. For a while. Until life seemed a bit more bearable. But I think I'm only lying to myself. It's never going to get easier. If I just sit around, waiting for something to happen, I'm wasting my own time. This world really is damaged. That's why I'm here. I don't think I can hide from that anymore. I have to go. I have to figure out what my purpose is."

"When will you go?" she asked, leaning her staff against the wall beside the door. This had always been her plan. To show me I couldn't stay.

"I don't have anything to pack. Today is as good as any other day, I guess. I know you've done far more for me than you ever promised my parents, and I'm so thankful. I will miss you more than you will likely miss me."

"Without a doubt."

I smiled and shook my head.

"You are ready, though, child."

"Am I?" I asked desperately. "I'm certainly not heading out to kill anyone or save them, no matter what my fate says will happen. With half of the prophecy missing, I just need to find the person that knows. The person that gave the original prophecy, or someone that can help me. That's all I'm after. I can worry about the rest later."

"A wise decision. The journey will be difficult, though. Not even I can give you the answers you seek. You must seek out Nealla."

"You know, I really want to stand here and tell you that Nealla isn't real but based on how the past few months have been going for me, of course I would have to find someone of legend and nightmares and not the bread maker in Tresa or the jeweler in Fron."

"Of course," she said.

Apparently, she still didn't appreciate my humor.

"So, any idea where to start?" I asked.

"You must start from the beginning. Naturally."

"Naturally. Thanks for all that intuitive advice. It's so helpful." I knew sarcasm was likely the only language she didn't speak.

"You are welcome, child." She reached forward, and I felt the warmth from her withered hands as she tapped my mother's necklace. "So pretty." She paused and held me at arm's length. "Mental shields up at all times, yes?"

"Yes."

"What was once normal will now catch the eye. Trust yourself, protect yourself always."

"No more poisoned arrows?"

"Poisoned arrows will be the least of your worries," she said, shaking her finger at me.

"Oh, fun!"

"Gather your things, child. Take this cloak."

I strapped all my weapons on for the first time in a long time. The load was heavier than I remembered, and I looked back wondering how I had managed to wander through the forest injured and carry everything. My thoughts shifted to Brimir, and I let that heartache in for just a moment, before walking out of the room that healed my body and spirit.

"Aibell, I need one final favor from you. Something I would only trust you with."

"Yes. I will hold it for you. It will come to you if ever you need it."

"Thank you." I handed her my father's sword. It aggrieved me to part with it, but I knew it would be safe here, and I didn't know where my journey would take me.

"Seek the spine with no bones. The keeper of tales and knowledge. The only thing left when memories fade."

"Aibell, must you send me off with a riddle? Can't you just tell me where to go?"

"No. Now go save your world."

My world . . . not hers.

I blinked, and she was gone. So was her cottage and everything around. Standing just outside of a small town, I realized I was entirely and completely alone with nothing but a riddle, a bag, and my weapons. Emptying the contents of said bag, I examined what I had. My blanket was there, as were some strips of dried meat, a loaf of bread, my flask, Tian's favorite cheese and a few coins at the bottom. Not much.

The long cloak camouflaged most of my weapons, though there was no way to hide my bow and quiver. I walked the gravel roads of the small Marsh Court town trying to figure out why, of all places, Aibell sent me here. But I had learned that the old female did nothing without good reason. I just needed to find whatever was here for me.

The town was simple enough. Uncomplicated. A few scattered homes here and there and, in the center, a few merchants and a local tavern with a broken inn sign hanging above.

The heavy door creaked as I walked in, and all eyes turned to me. I kept my hood high, my face sunken in shadow, taking in as many details as I could while working myself to the back corner of the crud and dust-settled room. The reek of the place was nauseating. It smelled like the ale-soaked tables had rotted for a decade in the sun before they dragged them inside and let inches of dirt and grime grow before they used them.

"What'll it be?" the local tavern girl asked as I slipped into a wobbly chair in the back.

I didn't have much coin, but I had to believe I had enough to cover a simple tab in a dodgy pub. Still, I kept my hands near my knives. "What kind of meat is in your stew?"

"We're s'pose to say rabbit. Truth is, I don't know. Can't say I've seen many rabbits around here. It's fresh and the best thing on the menu, though."

"I guess that'll do. Your room still open for the night?"

"I'll have to check with Gren. He keeps track of all that. Just the stew then?"

I nodded and pulled my hood farther forward to keep my face hidden. Apart from the server and myself, there wasn't another female in sight. The two males sitting closest to the door were probably armed more than I was. A shifty eyed male sitting next to the broken window watched the other female a little too closely. Those were the least of my concerns, though. Two tables down, a high fae with a knife handle showing just slightly below his cloak was arguing with a lesser fae at the table beside him.

"Honest, sir," the lesser fae with goat horns said. "It was an accident. Here, let me help." He dropped to his knees to help dry the spilled wine.

Two things were always guaranteed in a tavern, drunk fae and fighting.

The high fae stood from his table, grabbed the lesser fae by the shoulders and shoved him across the bar and into the table with the males I knew were carrying a load of weapons.

They stood abruptly. They were also lesser fae, but nearly twice the size of the high fae. Part troll, maybe?

The victim stood slowly, backing away with his palms up. "Please, I didn't mean any harm. I just got a little carried away is all."

"Keep your trash to yourself," one of the two troll males said to the high fae across the room.

"Or what?" he sneered.

Obviously, his superiority was clouding his judgment, or he was just plain stupid. I turned to see the tavern girl walking toward me with the stew I had ordered as the two males leaped across the tavern at the high fae, who effectively pulled his knife.

Nearly all the drunken patrons vaulted from their seats, eager to jump in. I stayed in my comfortable dark corner and watched as fists flew, glasses broke, one guy and two chairs were thrown through the air.

Before long, a burly lesser fae came running out from the back. Panting, but still quick. His presence alone stopped about half the drunken brawlers. As he walked through the tables slamming people back into their seats and scolding the familiar faces, I noticed the tavern girl never made it to my table. The shifty eyed male had gone missing as well.

Just perfect.

Standing, I made my way through the ruckus to where I had last seen her. Noticing the spilled bowl of fresh stew close to an outside door, I slipped out and looked around. Nothing. But then there was a small whimper and, following the sound around the building, I found exactly what I thought I would.

I pressed my knife into the back of the male, and he froze. "Let her go."

"Who the fuck are you?" he grunted.

"Social hour is over. Let her go." I pressed the blade harder.

He shrieked but released the girl. She fell to the ground and sobbed while pulling her top back up.

"Now get lost and stay there."

"I don't think so," he said, stepping away. He pulled a small blade out of a pocket and slashed it through the air toward me. Careless.

176

Drunk fighters could be dangerous, but I had to laugh. I folded my arms across my chest as the girl frantically scooted backward toward the building. "Listen, I'm trying to give you a chance to not be an idiot. Believe me, you want to take it."

"The girl and I were just having fun, and you had to come and ruin it. Maybe after I'm done with her, we can have a little fun of our own, hmm?"

I rolled my eyes and spun the dagger in my hand. "I'd rather not."

He slashed his knife again. I avoided it entirely and cracked him in the face with my elbow. Blood poured from his nose, and he doubled over in pain, dropping his dinky knife.

"Done so soon? I thought you'd have a little more than that in you. Pain tolerance the size of your dick?"

He yelled and leaped toward me. I stepped to the left and kicked him into the side of the building, where he didn't get back up.

I put my blades away and walked over to the girl. "You alright?"

"Who *are* you?"

I had to think on my feet. If the queen was after me, she knew my name. "Name's Lilleth." I stuck out my hand and helped her to her feet.

"Thank you so much for helping. He's been here the last three nights watching me. Gren said I was being paranoid, but I knew I wasn't."

"Males will never understand a female's intuition. Let's leave the trash in the alley."

We made our way back into the tavern, where I slipped back into my seat. It seemed the fight had died down, though there were a few busted-up fae.

"Here's a new bowl of stew, and I brought you a glass of wine. Gren said the room's yours if you want it. On the house for tonight." She set the room key beside the stew.

"Thanks." I dipped my chin taking the wine.

No clue why they called it wine. It tasted like water they'd poured in a room next to someone thinking about grapes. I slid it across the table, leaving a distinct track in the dust and lifted my spoon to the meat concoction in front of me. I took a few quick breaths and shoved the spoon into my mouth. Surprisingly, it was delicious. I heartily took another bite and another and then dipped my roll into the sauce, letting it soak in the peppery flavor. Gods, I loved food.

The meal was gone before I knew it and, half satiated, I left a few coins on the table and headed up the stairs. The room was small but cleaner than the tavern, and even though I locked the door behind me, I still slid the chair beneath the handle. I washed my face in the small basin and sat on the springy mattress.

It would do, I guess.

There was a light knock on the door. I stepped toward my weapons, but otherwise ignored it.

Again, a knock.

"I've brought you something, my lady. It's not much, but it's what I have."

I moved the chair and opened the door. The tavern maid held a folded gown for sleeping and a tray with an assortment of small desserts. I took the items and nodded my thanks.

"Is there anything else I can get for you?"

"Not unless you know what a spine with no bones is," I mumbled.

"Sounds like a book to me." She shrugged.

Exactly. A book.

"Listen, next time some eager drunken fool grabs you, scream like hell no matter what they threaten, and if they cover your mouth, kick them where it counts and run."

"Gren usually watches over me well enough."

"Well enough isn't good enough."

She nodded and turned away.

Shutting the door and sliding the chair back, I tossed the nightgown aside. There was no way in hell I was wearing that scratchy thing. I devoured the sugary desserts, though. And then remembered the only place I was likely to find a book about Nealla. Absolutely the last place I ever wanted to go. The royal library. In Coro's castle.

CHAPTER

23

Temir

*E*verything was different. Before, I wasn't sure Gaea and I intentionally saw each other, but now I looked for her in the halls, hoped to see her at dinner—which I had been attending more often—and I avoided the subject of her more than ever to Oleonis.

"Do you suppose there is something in the cyprus extract that might be similar to the taonia atomaria? I could break it down on a molecular level to see," Oleo offered.

"No, I've tried that." We sat working in the dirt of the tree nursery. Sometimes it felt as though we were in a humid forest rather than Autus's stone castle. If only. Perhaps that was why we came.

The trees were more difficult to work with because of their size, of course but I had tried every other flower, herb and even weed I had access to. Oleonis concentrated on using his magic to grow the saplings we were working with, while I did extractions for samples. Fortunately, we were always alone when we worked in the indoor gardens and nurseries. We did have a few hands that handled simple things, like weeding and watering from time to time, but mostly we preferred to do the dirty work ourselves. Oleonis could grow a plant from seed to an aged tree in a day if he expended all his magic but using up a lot of magic in one day could put you to sleep for two, so we took our time and worked at a steady pace.

"Have you talked to Gaea about the plans?" he asked.

"I've mentioned the basics only. We haven't come up with anything solid because we need to finish this first, obviously." I ducked my head and tried to keep the guilt off my face. Gaea was like his daughter, and I'm not sure how he would feel knowing everything. "There is something we should talk about, though." I hoped to move the conversation in a different direction.

He faced me but didn't stop his work.

"The high council had another meeting and requested the magic wielders again. The king announced the war officially, and then he enchanted the entire room. Basically, we are all watching the sea fae for unusual behavior. He also said he would be calling on us for personal orders and swore the whole room to absolute secrecy. Which means he didn't think he had it to begin with, and that is a problem. He has never shown concern of loyalty from his council or wielders."

"And you know this because Gaea finally told you of her charm?" He pulled his hands from the fresh dirt.

"Yes."

"Perhaps we should arrange—" he stopped abruptly and straightened his spine.

I dropped the crumbled soil in my hands and rushed over to him, knowing exactly what was happening. "Oleo, are you here with me?" I contemplated using my healing magic, but I didn't know how our magics would collide, and since we had not studied prophesying or done any testing yet on Oleo, I didn't want to make anything worse.

"The water . . . I can't," he whispered.

"Tell me what you see."

I wasn't sure if he could hear me. I laid my hand on his shoulder and shook gently. "Come back to me, Oleonis. It isn't real."

"It is real. She is there in the water. No one can find her, but she is there. The cuffs."

"Who is in the water?"

"The girl. The one he hunts."

"Can you see anything else around you? What else do you see?"

"Only darkness."

He coughed as if he were drowning, and instinctively I reached for him, calling my magic forward to search for an illness or injury. There were certainly times when I felt I couldn't control the urge to heal, but to have someone in my arms resisting the pull was impossible. As I let the ebb and flow of magic grow and move, I learned several things. Trying to interrupt this occurrence was not going to happen. Oleonis had his mental shield in place, as most of us were taught to do, but his was glowing. I had seen his mental shield several times, but never had I seen one glow.

Sending my magic to simply feel the light and try to determine its origin, which was essentially the first step of healing magic, resulted in shutting me out. I tried to go back in, concentrating hard enough to form sweat on my brow, but I was again denied access by the illuminated orb around his shield. I checked over the rest of his body and took the liberty of healing some pulled muscles, but there was nothing else I could do other than wait for him to come out of it.

I laid him gently on the floor and rushed to get him a glass of water. By the time I was back, he was sitting up again, clutching his head and blinking rapidly. "Are you okay?"

"I am. And I remember it again," he said shakily.

I handed him the glass of water and sat beside him. "Tell me what you remember."

"It was a female that I have seen before. Not in life, but another vision. I only remember that she was not a sea fae but was trapped in the water somehow and that people were trying to find her but couldn't."

"You said 'the one he hunts.' Do you know what you meant?"

"Hmm." He paused. "I don't know."

"And you're sure it isn't anyone that you know?"

"She has a depth of magic I think I would remember."

"Well, I guess we make a note of it and worry about it later. Do you have your book? The one you've been writing your visions in?"

"I decided not to write them down."

"Why?" I asked, surprised. "We document everything."

"I didn't want to leave proof of the foretelling around for someone to find."

"But what if your visions are relevant later?" I rubbed the fresh dirt from my hands.

"I'll have to just remember them."

"Okay. If that is your decision. I've got a meeting with Gaea this afternoon. Can I walk you back to your rooms?" I stood and extended my hand to him.

He grasped it and pulled himself to his feet. We both did our best to shake the fresh dirt from our clothing. "If you don't mind. The visions are coming so frequently now, I'd hate to be in the halls by myself."

"Not at all."

After walking him to his rooms, I headed to mine to wash up. I could clean my hands a hundred times over and they would still smell of soil and a hundred herbs. I would probably always have dirt below my fingernails and grass stains on my trousers, but I had never considered them until now. No matter how I tried to control them, she was at the end of every train of thought I had. Gaea was a distraction, for sure. I just wasn't sure how to deal with it. I'd never battled between brain and heart before. I'd only considered my brain, and that told me I needed some space from her. Hearts were funny, though. They never cared for the brain's sound reason. Only romantic whims and distracted thoughts of desire.

I sat in my chair and waited for her to spirit in. She was late. I adjusted my shirt and shut the book I was reading. My mind wouldn't let me focus on anything but her. Something was wrong. I stood from the chair and folded my hands behind my back and began to pace. Maybe she decided we had taken it too far and she wasn't ready. Maybe she had been caught blackmailing the blacksmith. Oh Gods, I didn't know how I would save her if that happened.

Telling myself to relax, I poured a glass of wine and, just as I put the decanter back, she came. I felt her before I heard her.

"Better make it two."

I filled the second glass as she sat on the couch. "Everything okay?" I asked, trying to mask my concern.

"Yes. Sorry I'm late. I had to run some errands for the king. I had an idea."

"You did?" I handed the glass to her and waited.

"Yes, but you have to sit next to me in order to hear it."

"I'm listening," I said, sitting beside her.

She twisted so she could lean her back into me, and I begged my beating heart not to give me away. She took a large drink of her wine and I took an even larger one. "You're having trouble finding plants that will work, and I have access to a lot more than you do. I have a couple of places in mind that we should pop over to and explore."

"Really? That's a fantastic idea!"

"It's been known to happen from time to time." She laughed. "Come on, let's get out of this stuffy ass castle."

184

"I'm all yours." I smiled.

Surprise lit her face and she stood, grabbing my hand. "Well, in that case, we'd better take the whole wine bottle." She wiggled her eyebrows, and we did just that.

Before long, we were standing in a place like nothing I'd seen before. It was incredibly hot, and sand stretched as far as I could see, with a few sparse plants here and there, but nothing significant.

"This is the southern desert. I've only been here once, and I haven't come back to expand my distance, but I thought it would be something completely opposite to what we have at home. Do you see anything that might work?"

"Well, it's hard to say." I shrugged. "I guess we'll just collect some samples from each plant we find and then move on."

"Just let me know if you get too hot and we can spirit home for a bit and then come back, or we can try some other place."

I squeezed her hand and pulled her into a lingering hug. "Thank you, Gaea."

"You can thank me properly later. Let's get what we need and get out of here."

I nodded, not quite knowing how to respond to her brazen suggestion. We walked a bit and Gaea drank while I collected small flowers and slivers of the prickly cactus. I thought about collecting seeds from the cactus itself so Oleonis could grow one for us, but we wouldn't have the proper habitat for a desert and, unless I had plans of staying, it would be a waste of time.

"I think I've gotten everything I can from this spot, should we try something else? Maybe something a bit more tropical, which might be closely related to the plant I'm trying to match?"

"I know just the place."

We left the desert behind for sandy shores. Unlike the last beach we went to, this one had a deep tropical forest behind it. The waves crashed behind us, and we were surrounded by the sweet smell of fruit trees. Before, the sun had beaten down on us unforgivingly, but now it was a kind and soft warmth.

"How's this?" she asked, slipping off her shoes.

"Perfect."

It was so hard to think of work and everything I needed to get done at home when I was here with her and we were all alone. She let the white foam from the gentle waves circle her feet as she walked down the warm beach, leaving footprints behind for the ocean to steal away. Finally, I sat my collected items down and took my shoes off as well. I jogged over to her and grabbed her hand.

She looked over at me with those perfect feline eyes, and just when I thought she may stop, she squeezed my hand and ran into the water, dragging me behind her.

I wanted to be mad that all my clothes were soaked, but as we tumbled into the water and the waves pushed us back up the beach, I could only laugh.

She splashed water into my face then jumped up and ran away. I caught her by the waist and pulled us both back into the water.

"Truce, truce!" She giggled with the most beautiful smile I had ever seen.

"Didn't Oleo teach you that splashing isn't nice?" A goofy grin spread across my face.

"No," she answered, shoving the water at me again.

Completely soaked and still wearing all of my clothes, I stalked toward her. I pulled my shirt up over my head and tossed it onto the dry sand.

She watched me with a predatory gaze. Her clothes were already tight, but now that she was also soaked, they left little to the imagination. She gradually slid her hands up my chest.

I was pretty sure I wasn't breathing at this point, but the devil was in the details, and I didn't care. I grabbed her and lifted her up to me and, as she brought her smooth lips to mine, I closed my eyes and prayed to the Gods this wasn't a dream. She was the calm and the storm. She was everything I never deserved, and as my soul met hers, I had to remind myself that our entire reality was much more serious than this one moment allowed.

"I wish we could just stay," she whispered against my swollen lips.

"Me too." I hugged her body to mine. "Soon, though, I promise. I will find a way for us all to leave and be together. I would do anything to have that with you." I stared deep into her eyes, not daring to blink.

They filled with unshed tears, and she pulled me closer, resting her chin on my shoulder as I held her waist with one hand and her backside with the other while carrying her back to the shore. We laid on the beach with absolutely no space between us, and I propped my head up under my hand. She intertwined her legs with mine and placed her hand back on my chest.

"What's wrong?"

"We wasted so much time apart, Temir. And now we don't know what the future holds, and the only thing I can think of is how much time we could have had together had we even tried."

"We have forever, Gaea. This is only our beginning."

"We have only borrowed time unless we come up with a really good plan, and soon."

"We can talk about it if you want to. Making a plan?" I held her closely.

"I've thought it through, and I'm not sure what to do. The only places I've really been are places the king knows of, and he knows that. He does that on purpose. I do know of some caves I have seen, but if I were him, that's the first place I would look. And right now, we can't do anything until you figure out this formula."

"It will happen, though. Can you think of any place he has taken you only one time? Someplace that you went to long ago? Perhaps we are better off doing that."

"The only place I can think of is one that would be difficult for us. We wouldn't have much food or shelter." She trailed her fingers casually across my chest.

"We will have Oleonis, though, and I have seeds packed. We may live off fruit, but as long as he is there, he can grow food as we need it. And I can hunt. I'm a fair fisher, as well. Oleonis can also grow trees or bushes for shelter. We can make it work. Our biggest hurdle is choosing a place that we can travel quickly from and isn't too treacherous for Oleo to walk." I rolled to the side.

"I'll try to do some more thinking and spiriting at night to expand my reach. The desert is so far it would take him weeks or even months coming straight at us to even get there, and by then we could be someplace else, but it's not a good option for travel. It's very hot during the day, but it's also very cold at night and water is sparse. We will have to have water. Plus, we have to avoid other fae in that kingdom. I've heard they are lethal there. Raised since birth to fight like champions. All of them."

"Yes, good point. I'll let you think about it and we can talk about options the next time we can sneak away."

She leaned in and kissed me once more. It wasn't passionate or desperate. It was a simple kiss for a simple moment, and I knew from that moment on, I would always be only what she needed me to be, and nothing else in the world mattered.

CHAPTER

24

Ara

*T*here's a legend told to keep babies in their bed and children from going out in the night. A story no one has the right to tell, not really. It speaks of a cloaked creature that hunts in the darkness and has been passed down so many times that no one knows fact from fiction anymore. Because Nealla hasn't been seen in centuries, and likely because anyone who has seen her has not lived to tell the tale. Alewyn creates the monsters of your nightmares for sport, but none such as this.

A long, long time ago, before the sun and moon, before the stars glittered across the night sky, Alewyn was lost to obsidian. From that darkness rose a creature, a hunter. She stormed through the evernight searching for something. Someone. If ever you should see the shadow that haunts the eventide, say your prayers to the gods.

Nealla rides the breath of nature on a beast of rot and sinew. She claims the lives of her victims by drawing out their immortal soul then steals their memories, leaving them a shell of a person. Her beast devours what's left before they disappear into the mist of night once more.

I left the tavern behind the next morning and made it to the next town by nightfall. I knew traveling the King's Road east would eventually take me to Coro's castle. I knew each of the towns along the way from my lessons with my parents, but on foot, I had no idea how long it would take me to get there.

Small towns in the central court were so similar, telling one from the other took a special skillset. Originally, I had thought to go around the village and continue my journey, but I didn't want to be caught on the King's Road at nighttime. Again, I searched for an inn, but as the sun began to set, a clamor of voices drew me into the village center, where I found twinkling lights strung through the square and folk dancing to lively music. I kept my hood up and casually wandered the outskirts of the revelry.

"You there!" a drunken male shouted. "Who are you?"

I opened my mouth, and no sooner did I get a syllable out then he stormed right past me to another male in the crowd. Relieved, I helped myself to the piled food at the long table, distant, but acting as if I belonged while I watched the fae dance and sing. That's when I saw him. *Friberg.* Extremely tall and giant nose. As if he had walked straight out of my memories.

He had worked for my father for many years, and as his voice carried through the crowd, I meandered in his general direction, trying to decide if I wanted to reveal myself. As I drew closer, I heard him speaking with another high fae in the crowd.

"That little shit. Doart means absolutely nothing to me. He's as good as dead by this time tomorrow."

The threat perked my attention. I'd never particularly cared for Friberg, but I also had never known him to be cruel. People were rarely themselves when others were watching.

"The task is simple, then. Kill him and take his body to the queen's sentries. Do that, and you're in."

190

"And where exactly are the queen's sentries?"

"There is a hut just past Grower's Pointe. They stay there from time to time, so no one bothers them."

"Consider it done," Friberg said, walking away.

In my opinion, one wouldn't stand in the middle of a busy crowd and declare to kill someone unless he thought he was invincible. Why in the world would a male think that unless he considered the fae he was planning to kill so far below him no one would even care? Which told me two things. One, Friberg had just committed to killing a lesser fae. And two, I needed to figure out who Doart was.

If I was smart, I wouldn't get involved, but I wasn't feeling particularly intelligent that day, and the faces of Tian, Sueni, and that poor baby rushed into my mind. If the queen's sentries played a part in this, then likely Doart was an unfortunately innocent target.

Before I could do anything, I had to find a place to stay for the night. The inn was easy enough to find, but it cost half my coins, and it physically pained me to let those go. I had no idea how I was going to make it the rest of the way.

The single room was small, but good enough. I paced the floors, searching, until I found a loose floorboard. It worked for hiding my sword, but I'd have to leave the bow behind. I didn't need it, but there were likely more tiny thieves with sticky fingers in Alewyn than there were honest people. I jammed a chair under the doorknob after, locking it for good measure, and hopped out the window, sliding it shut behind me. I was only two stories up, so the climb down was easy.

The local tavern was almost identical in stench to the one from the previous village, but this time, instead of hiding in the back, I sat at the bar and waited to be served. The room wasn't nearly as full as my last experience, but I assumed it was because the majority of the town was in the square.

The barkeep was noticeably ignoring me. He leaned onto the bar and continued an exasperating conversation with two patrons at the opposite end. I reluctantly took out a coin and slammed it on the sticky counter. He lifted his chin to me but didn't bother making his way down.

"I'm looking for someone named Doart. Do you know him?"

Being able to read an expression more clearly than a verbal answer was an art form. He knew him—I knew he did by those neutral eyes and tight lips—but he shook his head, no. I'm a high fae asking a lesser fae for information on another lesser fae. Of course, he would play dumb.

"Listen, I'm not trying to cause problems. The opposite, in fact. I think he might be in trouble. I'm trying to help him."

Still, he shook his head and turned back to his conversation. *Fine*.

I picked up my coin, left the tavern and made my way back to the crowd of fae. I'd just have to be observant. I watched for old Friberg, keeping my distance from him. He sat at a table with several other high fae males watching the ladies twirl and dance with curly ribbons as the high-pitched fiddle played in the background. He was consistently served drinks by lesser fae. I watched for any form of animosity between him and another, but he barely spoke to anyone, barely took his eyes off the females. The town's dance continued long into the night, and I was just about to give up when Friberg stood, nodded farewell to a few fae, grabbed a female from the dancing girls and slipped away.

I followed, keeping my footsteps silent and balanced between the deepest shadows of buildings. Close enough to see him without being seen. He let himself into what I presumed was his home, pulling the drunken female behind him. I watched as his shadow crossed the first window and then the second.

They had no servants come in or out, so that option was dead. I guess Doart was on his own. I dragged my feet back to the inn, trying to remember anything I could about Friberg, but nothing stuck out. He wasn't a leader in the Hunt or anything significant from my recollection.

Scaling the building, I made it back into my room and with a little push, slid the window back up and let myself in. The crisp night air was getting cooler, and I considered sleeping with the window open. I didn't need any flying visitors, though, so I locked it behind me and pulled the curtains closed.

I began to unbutton my cloak when my eye caught a folded piece of paper below the chair I had jammed in front of the door.

Overheard your conversation with Mgee. You can find Doart working in the smith's hut at sunup. Don't expect a warm welcome.

A friend

Last I checked, I didn't have any friends. But since I was this far into it, I would follow through and see if I could find the little bugger in the morning.

It wasn't hard. Though the village was quiet and dark and the air still crisp in the early morning, my fae senses easily locked onto that distinct stench of coal dust and molten iron. It predictably mixed with the distant sound of an anvil being struck repeatedly.

I didn't bother announcing myself. If the note was any indication, I wouldn't be well-received, anyway. There was a large, hairy lesser fae beating the glowing end of a steel rod as sweat poured down his scarred face. He didn't see or hear me as I came in. I considered him for all of three seconds and realized if Friberg was going to be assigned a target, it probably wasn't going to be the biggest guy in town.

The guy in the back, though, that was definitely him. He was just a scrawny lesser fae with tiny white wings tucked in behind his back.

"You Doart?" I asked, pulling my cloak hood back to reveal my face. I figured if he was in trouble and skittish, hiding in shadow was no better than revealing myself as a high fae. At least this way, I was being honest from the start.

"I don't know why you high fae think you have the right to storm around here and expect the rest of us to just bend over. Far as Doart goes, never heard of him. Get lost."

"Oh. That's too bad." I pulled out a dagger and ran my hands over the custom embedded designs. "I heard he was in trouble, and I was just trying to help him out."

"What's it to you?" he asked, narrowing his gaze but watching my capering hands intently.

"It's nothing to me." I shrugged, putting the knife back into its holder. I turned to walk away and got all of two steps before he stopped me.

"Wait," he called.

I pivoted, raising an eyebrow.

"Let's hear it then."

"I only wanted to let Doart know that I overheard Friberg talking about killing him last night, that's all."

"Fine, fine. It's me, I'm Doart."

"I know," I called over my shoulder as I walked out. "Good luck."

I heard the hammer clang to the floor as he rushed out to follow me. "What did I do to him?"

"I've no idea. Just the messenger here."

He quickened his pace until he was beside me. "Please, I don't know what to do. I didn't do anything to him. You have to help me," he begged.

"First of all, I don't *have* to do anything. Second, what makes you think I can?"

He stepped in front of me, bringing us both to a halt. "I have a family. Please. I'll pay you. Friberg's son wanted to work at the shop and we hired him on for a few days, but it wasn't a good fit for 'em. He burned himself pretty bad and Tig made me fire him. It's his shop, ya know, and I need

194

to keep my job. I had to fire the boy, but I did it real nice. Even offered to teach him on the side if he wanted."

Damn, a nice guy. Now I had to get involved. Plus, I needed the coin. "That's it? No other meetings with him or confrontations that would piss him off?"

"No." He squeezed the bridge of his nose and kicked the dirt road. "Friberg's been talking to those other high fae soldiers that's been in and out of town lately. A few of the guys were talking about it. I don't notice much, I guess, but that's all I know. Here." He pulled a small bag of coins from his pocket and held it out to me. "It's all I've got, but my family will starve if I die."

"You can pay me when I've actually done something. Go back to your job and stay there. Don't talk to anyone. Don't leave until I tell you to. Watch the door better than you were this morning, and for the love of the gods, don't you dare try to sneak out, or I'll kill you myself."

"O-Okay," he stumbled, heading back toward the shop.

Despite it still being early morning, a gray mist had rolled in, cloaking the sun that would have otherwise begun to rise and, as I perched on a nearby roof watching, the moisture seeped through my clothes and chilled me to the bone. Still, I waited. From this vantage point, I could see Friberg's house and watch three out of the four sides of Doart's location.

I assumed it wouldn't be long, and I was right. Killing someone in broad daylight was just asinine. I'm sure Friberg wasn't really concerned about a punishment for killing a lesser fae, but Doart had friends somewhere, and they would be the bigger issue.

Friberg walked right out of his front door, knife in hand, and stormed toward the blacksmith's hut.

Showtime.

I hopped down and decided rather than interceding him close to the shop, I'd keep him farther north, where it seemed relatively quiet because there were fewer homes along the path. That was about as far as my plan took me. I didn't plan on killing him, maybe maiming if I had to, but I had two deaths on my hands now, and that was two more than I ever wanted.

"Going somewhere?" I stepped around a corner directly in front of him.

"Fuck off," he said, attempting to storm passed me.

"Mmmm. No, thanks." I pulled my sword free and held it to his throat before he even saw me move.

He stopped so fast, his feet slid out from under him and down he went, carelessly dropping his knife just out of reach. I stepped over him, a foot to each side of his shoulders while keeping the tip of my blade at his throat.

"I've seen your face before. Who are you?"

"You know, I'm not really in the mood for introductions. Let's skip to the point here." I leaned forward, pushing the tip of my sword just a little harder into his throat. "Why do the queen's guards want Doart dead?"

"How the hell should I know?" He grunted.

"Ah, ah, ah, you tell the truth now, Friberg."

He squirmed with his feet, but as I stood above him, he really could do nothing unless he wanted to grab the honed edge of my blade. He didn't. I leaned an infinitesimal amount and, judging by his wide eyes, he felt every bit of it.

"They don't." He gasped as the tip broke his skin then paused, realizing he wouldn't be able to speak without impaling himself.

"We talked about the lying thing, remember? You're to drop the body at the hut past Grower's Pointe. Why?" I pulled back only far enough for him to answer.

"Stupid bitch," he spat.

"Let's be logical here, Friggy. Mind if I call you Friggy? No? Okay, great. I'm holding the pointy end of a very sharp weapon against your jugular, and you're lying on your back like a kitten in the road. Now, I don't claim to be an all-knowing fae, but simple reason tells me you probably shouldn't piss off the lady with the sword."

I waited for a retort. Nothing.

"Oh, good. We are learning today! So, answer the question.

He pursed his mouth shut and slightly shook his head.

"I was really hoping it wasn't going to come to this." I pulled the sword back and kicked him in the face hard enough to hear the crack echo off an adjacent wall. I kneeled as he groaned, moving his hands up to his face. I pulled my dagger out and jammed the handle just hard enough into his groin for him to cry out. "Next time I use the other side, got it?"

He frantically nodded, his hands filling with blood from his broken nose.

"Tilt your head back, you idiot."

He began choking on his own blood while still gasping from the pain in his crotch.

I held my dagger to his bobbing throat and whispered in his ear. "I've got all day. I'm in no rush. You keep avoiding my questions, and I'm going to draw the biggest crowd I can manage and let them all watch while I kick your ass from here to the moon. That's your problem, isn't it? You don't give a shit about Doart. That he has a family. You want someone to notice you. You work for the Hunt and hate that no one ever even glances in your direction next to the others."

"The queen does," he gagged, "ten times better . . . than Coro." He turned his face to the side and spat out the mouthful of the blood he couldn't talk around. "She doesn't give a shit about Doart. She sent a message that I could take over once the Hunt is hers. Just have to kill a lesser first and show proof I'm not a sympathizer."

"Why does she want to take over the Hunt?"

"I don't fucking know. I don't even care. Coro is shit, and she wants everything that belongs to him, Hunt included."

"So, who picked Doart as a target, you or her sea fae?"

"He's got it coming to him. Firing my son. Why should a lesser have that right?"

"Now, see, I notice you used the present tense, and that's just not going to work for me. In your opinion, he *had* it coming to him. But you're going to have a change of heart, got it?"

He didn't respond. Fire and ice played across his expression like a dance.

"Don't make me do something I really don't want to have to do." I dangled my knife above his crotch and let it sway back and forth for dramatics. He pressed his lips together. "I knew you'd see it my way. Now pop on up and head home, Friggy. Get something cold for your face." I stepped away from him and watched as he slowly rolled to the side and tried to haul himself up. I walked over and picked up the knife he had brought. "Promise to be a good boy and leave the lesser fae out of your power struggle?"

He held his hand out for the knife like he expected me to give it to him.

"I thought we were learning today?" I tucked the knife into my belt.

"Fuck you."

"We've really got to work on your vocabulary skills, Friggy. See ya around." I turned to walk away, knowing I was testing him. He thought I didn't know he had another knife in his belt. Even though I just handed his ass to him, he still assumed I was an idiot. I faced him again just as the knife left his hand. I dodged it easily. His aim was atrocious. I flung his own knife at him and turned away as he fell to the ground. "I really didn't want to have to do that." I sighed.

As the misty rain transformed into a dense fog, I made my way back to the inn. I wondered how many times I'd be able to go in through the window before someone alerted the innkeeper. I guess we'd find out.

CHAPTER

25

Temir

"Oh, I've seen this beauty before." Oleo held up the small pink flower we'd collected from the desert. "It was worn by another beauty. I was a young lad just starting to work for my father's business and he had to travel for work. I had planned to stay behind and run the shop for him, but he insisted I come along and learn how to sell to the southerners." He leaned against the massive tree trunk we sat under having a small lunch in the middle of our workday. "A lovely female was wearing this flower in her hair. I remember watching her from across the market as she filled a bucket of water in the fountain and sang the most captivating song about the sea." He twirled the flower between his aged fingers.

I didn't dare interrupt his memories, especially the happy ones. His recollections were the basis of my childhood bedtime stories. They were the escape from deep-rooted childhood fears and the comfort of lonely, wild boys.

"She took a liking to me, too, and I went down to visit her from time to time. She always sang that song to me and told me pretty stories of her dreams for her own future." His eyes were distant for a long time. Finally, he cleared his throat and sat the flower in the sample box.

"What happened to her?"

"I'd gone south for another visit and filled the desert with wildflowers in hopes of capturing her heart. It was the grandest gesture a poor merchant could ever make. But I had no idea Autus's grandfather was traveling at that time. Naturally, when he discovered wildflowers in a field of sand and scorching sun, he hunted me down and captured me, ripping me away from my beloved and my father."

"You've never told me that story before, Oleo."

"Yes, well, I hate the sad ending."

An hour of sorrow passed in the blink of an eye as we both imagined what his life would have been like without the unfortunate capture. It doesn't matter if you're high fae if you're also magical.

I cleared my throat. "I believe we will find our solution in the hornwort," I finally said.

"How so?" he asked.

"The seaweed has no vascular tissue. It's basically algae. If I focus on the way it releases gases, the hornwort would be the most similar. It's subtropical, but also has no vascular tissue."

"Ah. What's your extraction rate?" he inquired, letting the emotions melt into the air like vapors.

"It's slow and steady. I'll have to find some time to go back to collect more samples if this is it. The stems are small and I'm getting only a few drops per sample. Gaea has been away for over a week, so I haven't been able to go back for more." I stretched my aching muscles from the hours of work.

"Sounds like you may be on the right track all the same." He took a long drink of wine. "Are you nervous about your meeting with the king today?"

"I am. Anyone that wasn't would be a fool."

"Try to circle around the truth instead of directly lying if he asks about anything he shouldn't know. He knows you to be a loyal servant, so he likely won't press too hard."

"If he enchants me, your vision will come to life."

"Even in enchant, you still have the ability to circle the truth if you are careful."

"I can't recall being enchanted at the council meeting, or ever. How will I know what I say or how I'm saying it?"

"We will pray to the gods and be hopeful, come what may, my boy."

"Will you see him also?" I leaned forward to study his meticulous expression.

"He has not yet called upon me. I'm sure eventually my turn will come. Let us hope we are gone before that happens."

Later, I stood before the mirror in my room. My meeting was under an hour away and I couldn't put this part off any longer. I held the hoof rasp in my hand and let my fury build. My self-degradation in this manner was only possible deep in emotional despair, so I played memories of the bloodthirsty king over and over again in my mind.

I watched him murder for pleasure, forcing me to stand there and observe. I watched him rape a female barely older than a child to teach her father a lesson. I watched Thane slice the throat of that fae in his room. I dug up memory after sordid memory of proof that King Autus was the last male that should ever have endless power, and then I watched myself blindly serve him. Answer his every call. Heal who he told me to and let the others die. I sat idly by and watched him rip the world apart. I was no better than he was. A greater male would have found a way to escape long ago.

I took in a sharp breath, tilted my head, and frantically filed down the visible horns on my head. The pain was vast, but the hatred for myself was far worse. I watched the dust fall and, with it, my dignity. I was not a worthy fae. I was less than. I would always be less than because no matter what good I created, I'd supported the corrupt and broken. Angry tears stung my eyes as I continued to file, hating myself more than I could ever hate anyone else. Hating the thought of ever touching Gaea again, knowing my hands were not clean and she deserved a better male.

It hurt. Gods, it hurt the closer I got to my head. I had gotten much better at it, but occasionally the file would slip and cut into my scalp. I was always able to heal it away, but I'd never use a numbing agent on the horns. I wanted to feel every second of my desecration. I wanted to remind myself that even though they made eye contact with me and allowed me to walk beside them, I was not, nor would I ever be, their equal. I had no honor.

I fell to my knees, grinding the file into my horns. Tilting my head back, I roared to the heavens. The pain was so powerful. There was no way to hide the horns aside from this. The floor was covered in shavings as my hands shook from agony and despair. This was the reality of my life as a lesser fae living amongst the high fae. I had to wonder if Gaea hated herself as much as I did, but it seemed she did better with numbing herself to all emotions. I couldn't fault her for it.

I dragged myself from the floor and rinsed in the basin on the dresser. I healed the cuts on my head and dressed in my nicest attire. Emotionally, I was lost, but none of that mattered when the king called.

I stood behind the great hall doors with my hands clasped tightly behind my back. A nervous habit, I supposed. I squeezed my knuckles and willed my heart to slow. Two months ago, I could have stood in this spot confidently and unwavering, but so much had changed, and if things went poorly, I'd spend tonight in the dungeons. I didn't think King Autus would kill me just yet. At this point, he would only learn that the three of us intended to run away but had no means or plan to do so. He would also learn Gaea had been betraying him, though, and I just couldn't let that happen. Nor could I let him find out that Oleonis was a seer. I changed my mind. He could actually learn a lot today, and maybe he *would* kill me.

I forced my tense shoulders to relax and tried to exude annoyance rather than fear. The king understood fear like a second language, but annoyance would be unexpected and hopefully distracting.

The king's guards opened the doors, and as I entered the expansive room, I kept my eyes low and my pace brisk. I counted my unsteady breaths and begged the Gods that listened to keep him from enchanting me. Once I reached the dais, I took a knee and held it firm until he addressed me directly. There were soft murmurs in the room. He would allow a crowd to watch my interrogation disguised as a simple meeting.

"Rise, Temir," the king called, his voice echoing.

I stood and placed my hands behind my back once more. "You have called upon me, my king. How may I be of service?" For the first time, I allowed my eyes to shift from side to side, taking in the familiar room.

Rows of court fae sat watching the exchange.

The king turned to Eadas, his sniveling advisor, and whispered something to him. He bent over the king and they exchanged words back and forth until, finally, the king held his hand up to stop him. "Leave us," he commanded the room.

Without hesitation, the king's court rose from their favored seats and filed out. Some watched me closely as they passed, and some acted as if I were not standing there at all.

I wasn't sure which I preferred, but it wasn't doing much for my nerves. Still, I stood immobile as a statue waiting for what was to come. Begging my thundering heart not to give me away. The king walked down

204

the steps to stand in front of me. Our eyes locked for only a brief second until I dropped mine to the ground. This was not a pissing contest. I was his to command, and he damn well knew it. I rubbed at my knuckles still held behind my back, trying to steady myself.

Without warning, I felt her. I knew she was there and gone before anyone would have suspected her presence, though it stayed with me. Empowered me. Gaea had just saved us all.

I felt the cold ring she had slipped onto my finger just as the king's melodious voice rang out.

"You will answer all questions honestly and directly. You will say everything you don't want to tell me, and you will tell no one what is asked of you, Temir. Nod your head if you understand."

It was odd. I knew I didn't have to do as he told me. I could feel the ring's magic bite into my finger as I slowly nodded my head and kept my eyes to the floor.

"Good." He slapped me on the back. "Walk with me, Temir." The king carried himself like a twenty-foot giant. I supposed that came with the job title, but he had mastered it all the same. He adjusted the crown atop his head and shifted the piles of furs on his shoulders before taking a deep breath. "I believe I have always been more than fair to you, a lesser fae treated as a high fae in the castle. Do you agree?"

I tried to suppress any emotion as we talked. If I was truly forced to answer his questions, I would have no feelings of doing it. I had seen the king's enchantment work on others thousands of times. I wanted to eliminate emotion. That is what he would expect to see. "Yes, my king."

"Is there anything you've been hiding from myself or the council?"

"Yes, my king," I answered, voice flat.

He paused and looked back at me. "What is it?"

"Thane called upon me several nights ago and asked me to heal a female without your permission. He had no intention of telling you.

Though I didn't come to you myself, I also did not heal the female." A small thing would be more believable than nothing at all.

"And why did you decide not to tell me?"

"I didn't think the question alone warranted disclosure, my king. I did not heal the female, and I also didn't think you would care for the life of the female, anyway. No rules were broken, and I know you have been busy with your betrothal and planning for war."

"Quite right," he answered. "I have had you tested, Temir. You passed. The events in Thane's room were concocted by my own hands to see if you would break the rules. It pleases me that you would not, but I must ask why you wouldn't heal the lesser fae."

I knew the answer he wanted, and it destroyed me to give it to him. "She was only a lesser fae. She is not important to us."

He only nodded as we walked for a few more paces. "Is anyone close to you hiding something?"

"No," I answered firmly, hopefully not too quickly.

"Let me rephrase that question. Is anyone close to you hiding something from me, specifically?"

"Not that I am aware of, my king," I answered, keeping just behind him as he walked.

He let out a big breath and we walked in silence for several long moments. I watched the dust flecks move in the rays of the sun filling the room. I watched the texture of the carpets change as we stepped on them. I watched anything I could but the king. I kept my eyes carefully locked on a speck of dirt on the clean floor as he stepped in front of me to watch my blank face. "Would you ever betray me? Would you even consider it?"

I thought about this question longer than I probably should have. The simple answer would be no, but what would he believe? What would be an honest answer that he would expect?

206

"I would only betray you if it meant saving you in the long term. I have never considered otherwise, nor will I."

"What do you mean?" he asked, his face hardening.

"Only that I can never predict the future. I would never betray you unless your life depended on it. In the end, I will always remain your loyal servant."

"I see," he replied. "So, you mean to say, if I asked you not to heal me, you would do it anyway to be sure I could live forever."

"Exactly that, my king."

"Do you believe Oleonis is acting strangely?"

Even to hear his name from the king's lips caused me to pause. I hoped he thought it was because I was sifting through memories. "No, my king. I have not witnessed any odd behavior."

"He seems to be more withdrawn and distant. What can you tell me of this? What is he planning?"

"To my knowledge, he is working very hard on your weapon production. Just today we were discussing where to make additional space in the nursery for the additional saplings we planned to grow. I know using his magic at the rate he is makes him quite tired, so likely that is why he seems withdrawn. He wants only to serve you, my king. As do I."

"It's come to my attention that you have been spending additional time with Gaea. Can you explain this?"

My heart stopped. I thought we had been so careful, but the king's eyes were everywhere. People were watching even if they didn't know it. People would sell their own secrets for favor with the king. "She is a beautiful female. Who can blame me?" I hoped that was the right answer.

He chuckled until his entire body shook with laughter. "I never knew you had it in you, Temir. Finally, you have tasted that sweet honey. A beautiful female indeed." He laughed again.

I'd never wanted to slice someone from neck to navel more than in this moment. I had to conceal my emotions away. She was so much more than he could ever know, and his filthy comment sickened me.

"I am glad I never have to worry about you, Temir. You've been loyal since the day I plucked you from the stables and saved your life. You are released from my enchant. You will not remember any of this conversation."

"Yes, my king."

"Thank you for meeting with me today, Temir. I have a simple question for you and then you may return to your work." He wanted to create a separate reality for me. He wanted me to believe whatever his next question was his only question. "Do you believe we can win this war, Temir? Do you have any ideas on how we should?"

"I believe we can win this war, my king." I added expression back into my voice. "I'm no general, but I believe in you and have faith that you will find a way, as you always do."

"Very good, Temir. You are dismissed."

I dipped my head and as he walked back to the throne. I turned and walked briskly out of the hall.

I opened my door just as Gaea rushed across the room and slammed into me. "Oh my gods, Temir. Did I make it in time? I was so worried. Are you okay?" Her voice broke.

I fell to my knees and wrapped my arms around her waist holding her. "You saved us all."

She dropped to the furs on the floor and lifted my face with her hands. "I'm so sorry I wasn't here sooner. The king has me traveling with Thane all over the place, but Oleo was able to get word to me that you were being questioned. I couldn't get here any sooner."

"It's okay. It's all going to be okay. I promise." I pulled her closer and breathed in her scent of wild lavender. She grounded me and sent me soaring all at the same time. Her beautiful cat eyes pierced straight through me, and I had to look away. "How did you manage it?" I pulled the ring from my finger and held it out to her.

"It's yours to keep. That's all that matters."

"The king knows something is going on with Oleonis. He questioned why we were spending more time together. I had to tell him I thought you were beautiful. I'm sorry. I didn't mean to betray anything we have together, but I knew it was the only way I could appease him without the whole truth. And he is going to test you. He is going to try to make you break the rules and see if you will. You need to be so careful right now, especially with Thane. We all do."

She brought her nose to mine and whispered, "I don't care if he knows. I don't care if anyone knows. As long as you're fine and we are fine, I don't care about anything else."

"I don't deserve you. I shouldn't hold you so close. I know I'm not good enough, but I've never wanted anything so badly in my entire life."

"Stop. You are the best person I have ever met. You are good and kind and everything this world needs. You're everything I need," she said.

"I wish that were true."

She ran her careful fingers through my wavy hair and inhaled a sharp breath. "Where are your horns?"

I looked into her eyes, broken and ashamed.

"You didn't," she gasped. "Temir, how could you?"

"I can't change who I am. I can't be what everyone wants me to be all the time. I am not a lesser fae and I am not a high fae. I am nothing. My horns are only a reminder to everyone else that I am worthless."

Again, she lifted my chin, and I watched the tears stream down her face. She only shook her head as her silent tears turned into sobs. A part of me shattered watching her cry. Knowing I had caused her pain. We sat on the floor, knees together, riding a wave of emotions. Me, a broken male and her, nearly perfect, learning more about me than she probably ever wanted to know.

"I'm sorry," I whispered. "I'm sorry I hurt you."

"No." She shook her head. "You didn't hurt me. You hurt you. I just don't understand. How could you ever think you are worthless? How?"

"I walk down the halls and see the way they look at me. They loathe me, even though they are enchanted to forget who and what I am. The lesser fae hate me for my immunity to the discrimination that haunts them and the high fae for the same thing. No one wants me here. Don't you feel the same? Don't you look at them and feel it?" I reached for her hand.

"I know someone is out there holding their breath, waiting for me to fail, Temir. I just make sure they suffocate. Their thoughts are their own problem. I hope they look at me and see the smile I put on and hate me more for it. I hope their hatred drives them mad. You are beautiful. Your horns do not make you lesser, Temir. They make you greater. They make you better than all of them."

Another sacred tear fell down her face, and I reached up and brushed it away with my fingers.

"Promise me you will never do this again. Promise me. If you let them win like this, things will never change. They need to see us. They need to understand us. They need to know that we aren't going anywhere, and we aren't going to hide who and what we are."

I crushed her to me again and held her close. Her heart beat to the same rhythm as mine. I knew she believed she was right, but the world wasn't as black and white as she would hope it to be. They hated her just as much as me, and she may turn a blind eye, but I had lived so many long years in hiding, how could I ever escape that? I knew one day soon, I'd disappoint her for my opinion, and if it was even possible, I despised myself even more for it.

CHAPTER

26

Ara

*A*fter sitting in the inn for half a day, I figured word of Friberg's body had spread like wildfire and I could finally leave without raising too much suspicion. No one had seen me slip out this morning and, even if they did, no one could prove a thing. Friberg was killed with his own knife.

I found Doart exactly where I had left him. Perhaps slightly paler and more respectful than before, but otherwise unscathed.

"I see you listened and stayed put to secure your alibi. As far as anyone knows, you were working all morning. Because you were."

"You killed him."

Not a question.

There was a pang of guilt deep within me about that. I hadn't wanted to. I'd never been the type of fae to sit back and think of taking anyone's life. It wasn't like murder amongst the fae was rare. In fact, it was the opposite, but it didn't sit well with me. I would have rather saved him than killed him, but he would have never let me walk away. I looked to the side, hiding the shame on my face. "And? He would have killed you. What's the difference?"

"It's just . . . you're high fae. And you killed another high fae for the protection of a lesser fae. It's just not done that way."

"Not every high fae would see you dead, Doart. Don't let the actions of some speak for the masses. I protected an innocent male, race aside, and that's how it should be."

"Here's your coin." He held the pouch out.

I grabbed it and dumped the coins in my hand. There were only sixteen coins, but I placed eight back in the bag and handed it to him.

"No, please, miss. You must take them all. I'm grateful, I am."

"You also have a family, Doart."

"I know a guy," he said. "He lives in Rocsbrew, just down the King's Road. He is having some trouble with his boss. You could help him. Make some more coins. He's come to Erast a couple of times asking around for someone. I can give you his name?"

I considered this. Did I really want to go down this road? On one hand, Aibell had sent me to the last town for a reason, and now here I was again, helping the lesser fae, which seemed to align with her own vocation. If I was really going to do this, it should be my choice. I had to eat, though. And each town brought me closer to the castle. A few coins here and there as I traveled would cover the cost, though it might not help me stay under the radar if I went around killing everyone as I traveled through.

"I'm not a killer for hire."

"No, of course not," he stated, taking a step back, thinking he'd offended me. "He's never said anything about killing. Might just be worth looking into."

"Alright, I'll think about it. What's his name?"

"His name's Wrate. He works for a high fae who owns most of the town. I can set you up a ride. Tig's got a delivery to Rocs that's s'pose to leave later today."

***

Rocsbrew was a bit bigger than Erast, and there seemed to be more than just a handful of high fae around. I had the delivery driver drop me off at the home of an elder fae who made shoes and rented a spare room from time to time. She was short and so were her sentences, but she let me have the room, nonetheless. Her small cottage had a circular front door and low ceilings, reminding me of Aibell's home.

The room was quite a bit nicer than the last two places I'd stayed. There were no loose floorboards to hide weapons in, but there were plenty of good places in the room if one knew where to look. The gaudy floral-patterned window coverings matched the enormous rug draped across the floor. There wasn't a speck of dust in the whole room, but I'd wager she hadn't opened a window in this old, creaky house for over a century. The air was so stale, I could feel the weight of it entering and exiting my lungs.

As opposed to the other places, I had a private bathing room, and with it came the likely reason the room was so expensive, a giant clawfoot bathtub. I would have paid triple. I hadn't been in my room for more than two minutes before I filled that bath with the hottest water I could stand, and as the steam filled the room and poured into the bedroom, I added way too many drops of the rosewood oil I found on the sleek countertop.

As instructed, I called for the elder female, and she took my clothing to wash while I dipped my toes into the scorching water and moaned in ecstasy. I let myself sink ever so slowly into the bath and begged the water to melt my stress away. With my eyes closed and my head leaning against the inside wall, I remembered for a moment what pure bliss felt like. The life of a poor traveler was certainly not for the faint of heart. Eventually, the water turned cold. I considered just refilling and starting over, but my wrinkled skin protested, and I knew I needed to get on with my plan if I was going to accomplish anything that day. I stepped from the bath, and as the droplets of water left trails down my skin, I dried my long hair and took a moment to appreciate the simple luxury.

I pulled out the elaborate gown Doart had helped me acquire from the dressmaker in Erast. For the first time in a long time, I let myself look into the mirror. Although I wasn't the same person I was the last time I had bothered, I still saw a little bit of her in there. Letting my auburn hair fall down my back, I adjusted my mother's necklace and took a final deep breath before heading for the door. I hadn't been this female in a long time, but if there was ever a way to draw a male out, this was it.

After a bit of direction from the elder fae, I made my way toward the market and roamed. I stopped only at the most expensive shops and took an exorbitant amount of time at the jeweler's.

"Oh yes, that one is especially lovely with your smoky eyes." He shoved a mirror in my face.

"Yes, it is quite lovely. It's just not quite big enough, though. Are you sure this is all you have?"

"But, miss, that one is the size of your palm. Anything larger would tip you over."

"Yes, I'll need to think about it. I'm just passing through and staying at Betha's. Do you know where that is?" I asked, leaning into the counter.

"I do, my lady."

"Please send a messenger in the morning and I'll let you know my answer. I've been spending money all day and I'm quite tired now."

"Yes, ma'am. I'll have a boy there in the morning. Please, can I walk you back?"

"Oh no, I'm sure you have more important things to do than follow a young, lonely widow around. Thank you for the offer," I said, patting his hand.

I almost felt bad. Almost. He had spent several hours with me and then watched me amble out without a single item. He was a persistent little guy, though, and if I had more than a handful of coins to my name, I probably would have spent a real fortune. It didn't matter, though. The bait was set.

Just as I had hoped, by the time I made it back to Betha's, there was already a messenger waiting for me. A greedy male could never pass up a wealthy young widow. "My lady." The lesser fae lowered his head. "I've come to ask you to dinner for my employer."

My eyes shifted to Betha, and she sat rocking in the corner of the room, brushing circles into a leather boot sitting in her lap. Amusement and confusion crossed her face, but she remained quiet all the same.

"And just who is your employer?" I asked, adjusting my dress nonchalantly.

"So, you really are new then?"

"Obviously." I waved my hand around. "I've rented a room. I'm not interested in meeting your employer. Have a nice evening."

"No, please. He won't be happy if I come back without you. He is used to getting what he wants."

"And you think that is going to encourage me? What's your name?"

"My name isn't important. I'm just a nobody. It's Rodalf you should be asking about. That's his name."

"I'll have your name, or I won't even consider it."

"My name is Wrate, my lady," he said, bowing his head.

I held my blank expression. "If you'll allow me to change, I'll accompany you on one condition?"

"Okay?"

"Miss Betha here mentioned earlier that she would like to visit her son in Tresa, but she hasn't an escort. Would your employer make such arrangements for her?"

Again, my eyes met hers, but she remained quiet.

"Well, I'd have to check with him, of course. That's a long ride from here."

"Okay then. You have a chat with your boss, and if he agrees to help her, then I will to meet with him."

"Oh, no. He asked me to bring you tonight, Miss . . . I'm sorry, I didn't catch your name?"

"My name is Lilleth, but no. I'm not really concerned with your boss's demands. You'll ask him and we will see what tomorrow brings. Have a lovely evening, Mr. Wrate." I turned and left him at the door. I went to the room I was staying in and waited. Within moments there was a firm knock at the door.

"I don't recall telling you I had a son in Tresa. Nor did I ever ask to see him."

"I noticed the letter on your desk and thought it might be a lovely gesture," I said a little too sweetly.

Her knowing eyes told me she knew I wasn't telling the whole story, but how could she refuse?

"I could call after him if you'd rather not go? His employer did seem awfully eager to meet me for some reason. I was hoping the expense of the trip would grant me a few more days in your beautiful home."

"Clever little thing, aren't you?" she asked, walking out. "You should stay away from Rodalf, girl. Trust me. He collects pretty girls like you for sport."

"I'm counting on that," I mumbled. I changed out of the dress and back into the clothes that had been placed at the end of my bed. I strapped a few weapons on for comfort and saw myself out the window. No need to get Betha involved in this.

It only took me a few minutes to catch up to Wrate. I had hoped his reluctance to deliver bad news to his boss would slow him down a bit. "So, now that we have been formally introduced, how about telling me what's going on with Rodalf that you need taken care of?" I said, jogging up beside him.

Pure shock registered all over his face. "I don't know what you're talking about," he said, steps faltering.

"Doart told me you'd say that. Here." I handed him the note Doart had written and, despite his reluctance to take it, he opened the letter. His eyes lifted from the page to me and back to the letter several times. "But this can't be right. How are you going to help me?"

"Let's start with the basics. I don't work for free. You either agree to pay, or you don't and Rodalf is none the wiser."

"There is nothing too great. I will pay whatever you ask."

"Tell me why."

"Rodalf is awful. He's a high fae who started off by blackmailing lesser fae. He would promise them big riches to do his dirty work and then threaten to expose them if they wouldn't continue working for him. He's acquired houses, businesses, even females, like this. The entire village lives in constant fear of him, because if he can't blackmail them, then he sends out his lackeys to put pressure on people until everyone is doing exactly as he wants. There are few in Rocs that are even happy anymore. And it's not just the lesser fae. It's the high fae, too. Something's got to happen. There's a pool of money me and the boys have been collecting to find someone who can run him out of town." He slowed his pace, and I matched it.

"Let me see what I can do. Here are the rules. Unless we are alone, you know me to be a wealthy widow, got it? You go back to him tonight with the proposition of providing transport for Betha. You don't tell anyone else, and you don't do anything else unless I personally tell you to. You're to meet me here after I return home from meeting him, understood?"

"Yes. Although, when I go back without you tonight, he will probably have my head."

"You just tell him that being at the jeweler today reminded me too much of my late husband, and you couldn't force a distraught female to meet another male."

"Okay, yeah. I could probably pass that off. As long as you'll see him tomorrow?"

"Oh, I'll see him tomorrow. Just as soon as he agrees to my bargain. And don't worry, he will." I smirked. Males were nothing if not predictable. Especially this kind.

The next morning, as expected, there were two messengers, one from the jeweler and one from Rodalf.

"Please do tell your boss I absolutely adored that emerald necklace, but I worry what others would think of a lady purchasing it for herself. I'll have to pass this time. And you," I said, turning to Rodalf's messenger, "please let your employer know that I accept the terms of his note and I will see him for dinner. As long as I can find something suitable to wear, of course."

"Yes, my lady," they said in unison and bolted out of the door.

"What kind of web are you weaving, girl?" Betha asked. "I keep to myself and don't need any trouble."

"Not to worry, I'm simply securing a ride for you to visit your son."

"I bet you are." She turned back to stitch the sole onto the new shoe she'd been working on. "And next time, just use the front door instead of the window."

By lunch, there was another knock on the door. Rodalf's messenger. He carried a large box and a lopsided smile as he wandered through the empty house and plopped his cargo onto my freshly made bed. He then withdrew a small note from his pocket, handed it to me, and let himself out.

Looking forward to our dinner. A small gift for a beautiful female.

-R

218

I opened the box and drew the long, sequined gown from it, laying it gently across the bed next to the shoe box. I took out the smaller package and had to laugh as I opened it to find the emerald necklace inside. It really did look good with my gray eyes, though it matched a certain prince's exactly.

Two entryway doors led to the foyer. Approximately twenty-five feet until the hall began, and sixteen doors lined each side. A servant had let me in and instructed me to wait in the dining room as Rodalf finished his meeting. I memorized every detail as I followed her brisk pace to the dining hall. I expected a maze, but it was far less complicated. Though grand, the home was fairly similar in layout to my old house, yet the air was musty and stale. Unfortunately, most of the doors were closed, but I could pinpoint my position standing outside the home, and that had to count for something.

"If you'll just wait here, my lady." The servant pulled a chair from the table and gestured for me to take it.

"Actually, the ride was a little rougher than I had expected." I lifted my fingers to my tousled hair. "Do you mind pointing me toward a room I can freshen up in?"

I knew she was annoyed, but she was probably also being blackmailed by Rodalf and didn't particularly care what I did, so long as it didn't interfere with her.

"Yes, my lady," she said, walking out of the room.

Again, I followed her until we were two doors down from the dining room.

"You may use this room to freshen up. Please see yourself back to the dining room when you are finished. I must go check in with the cook about your meal."

I knew kindness from a high fae would raise more alarm than disdain, so I simply turned my nose up and walked into the room she indicated. I closed the door behind me and did a quick scan. The room was small and clean, so it wouldn't have anything useful inside. Still, I crossed the window and unlocked it, carefully opening it to see if it would be silent. It was. I shut the window and relocked it, counted to ten and opened the door. The servant was gone.

I stepped as lightly as possible through the bland hall, checking for unlocked doors and listening for quiet voices behind them. I didn't have time to pick the locks without being caught, and the few rooms I managed to get into were mostly bare. A few bedrooms here and there, but that was about it. The lord of blackmail was turning into the lord of boring.

I went back to the dining hall and took my seat just in time for Rodalf to walk in.

"My beautiful lady, I am so sorry to keep you waiting."

I stood as the overweight high fae approached. He kept his beard long, and as he took my hand and placed his disgusting lips to my fingers, I plastered the best smile I could manage on my face. "Thank you for inviting me, my lord. The jewelry and gown you sent are just beautiful."

"Not nearly as beautiful as you, my sweet. Please," he said, gesturing to a chair behind me, "let us have wine."

It was strange to play a role, but it was more so knowing the person across from you was also playing a role. Nothing in this conversation would be easy. I just had to hope I could keep the sarcasm from my face. The lack of eye-rolling would be the hardest part.

"I must ask, why did you invite me tonight?"

He snapped his fingers into the air until the servant from before entered the room. "Fill these glasses. What good are you if you can't do your job?"

"Yes, my lord. I'm sorry, my lord."

"This is your third and final apology this week, do you understand?" He slammed his palm onto the table.

"Yes, my lord." She filled the glasses and scurried out of the room.

220

"I can never find good help these days."

I cleared my throat and lifted my drink. "Cheers to better servants. They must exist somewhere."

He laughed and raised his glass in return. "Now, back to your question. I make it my job to know when beautiful females come to town without proper security. You must be careful out there. It's a dangerous world for a female to travel alone. Do tell, where is your husband?"

A dangerous world indeed, prick.

"I'm so sorry, I thought your servant told you. My husband tragically lost his life to a group of lesser fae. I am now widowed and left alone in life." I lifted the cloth napkin from the table and dabbed the corner of my dry eyes.

"Were you mated?" he asked, as if he were checking the weather.

"We were not." I answered the questions just as he would hope. Of course, if I had a dead husband and we were mated, I would likely die of a broken heart long before he could get his hands on my inherited fortune.

"My servant has told me you've asked for transport for the female that owns the home you are staying in. The shoemaker, is it? It's a bold request of a stranger, don't you think?"

I smiled as sweet as honeysuckle and batted my long eyelashes at him. I stood from my chair and let my hips swing as I crossed the room to sit on the edge of the polished table and took his leathery hand. "Oh, you must understand, Master Randalf."

"It's Rodalf," he said with a grunt. "Please, continue."

I stroked his fat fingers and swallowed the bile rising in my throat. "Miss Betha is the sweetest little old lady, and she misses her son dearly. My husband would have seen her there himself, had he been alive. After your messenger told me how wonderful you were, I just had to make sure you were also a male of your word. I'm so, so glad you are." I stood from the table and walked back to my seat. "I'm not sure how I could even thank you."

The show was disgusting and over the top, but I played my hand and watched him fold.

"I'm happy to oblige, love. I will have my driver ready for the trip in two days' time."

"Oh no, you must let me take her myself. I would feel so much better knowing she arrived safely. I'm sorry to say it, but your driver was a bit careless on my journey here." He'd kill him for sure with that knowledge. I'd have to make sure the driver escaped tonight.

"I'm sorry that happened. I'll have a word with him. Are you sure you want to go alone? Just the two of you? It seems an awfully long journey for two simple females."

My cheeks flushed, and I hoped he thought it was from embarrassment and not the utter rage that ignited inside of me. *Fucking Randalf.* "I'll be sure to leave my fortune behind, so I don't attract unwanted thieves. That sounds like a good plan, wouldn't you agree?"

"Indeed," he answered behind a large smile.

A little too large.

He drove me home himself that night, and it took all of my will power not to slap his ugly face when he held my hand as we rode. Fortunately, the ride was quick and Miss Lilleth was shy and proper. He was certainly annoyed, but that was the only pleasure I had the entire evening. Denying him a kiss as I escaped the prison of his covered carriage.

I waited for him to disappear and, like clockwork, Wrate stepped out from the shadows. "How did it go?" he asked.

I finally got to roll my eyes. "He'll be gone by the end of the week. I have a bit of a plan, but I need to get into his house tomorrow, and I need you to make sure he isn't there when I do it. Can you arrange that?"

"He will be at the tavern tomorrow for three hours beginning at noon. He spends time there every week collecting his rents. Will that be enough?"

"Perfect. Make sure he stays there. You're to unlock but leave the window shut in the third bedroom on the north side of the hallway. Also, you need to get the driver out of town tonight before he gets back. He will die otherwise."

He nodded and turned away into the night.

I walked into Betha's house using the front door and, though she lifted an eyebrow in question, I shook my head and went back to my room. The less she knew, the better.

The next morning, I watched from a distance as Wrate himself drove Rodalf to the tavern. I hoped he was able to sneak the driver away. I watched the house for half an hour more as several servants also left. I wasn't sure how many were left at home, but I could only hope Wrate arranged for most of them to have other jobs.

I followed the outside of the house until I came to the window I needed, slid it open with the same ease as last night and climbed into the house. The home was undeniably silent. I soundlessly made my way down the hallway. Starting on the left side, I checked the doors, keeping my eyes and ears open. They were easy enough to get unlocked with a hairpin. The first room was completely bare. No furniture, only drapes covering the window. As I walked in farther, I noticed the bloodstains on the floor and quickly realized what this room was used for. I backed out as quickly as I had entered and continued down the empty hall.

The next several rooms were similar. A simple guest room with nothing. However, when I got to the fourth, I saw the disheveled desk in the middle of the most elaborate room in the house. The office was more like a library, with towers of leather books crammed into the wooden shelves. The room smelled of paper and glue and was once again nothing I would have expected to find from the male who treated people's lives like card games. I searched the stacked papers on the desk for anything of importance. Most of them had names and schedules of random things, but nothing of use. I tugged on the center desk drawer and wasn't surprised to find it locked. Kneeling, I pulled the hairpin out again and wiggled it inside the keyhole, once again grateful for my father's persistent lessons.

Just as the lock clicked, I heard a distant voice and froze. Footsteps pounded down the hallway. I dove under the desk and made myself as small as possible as I pulled a knife out and waited.

"You're sure it's in the office?" a female voice said.

"Yes. Hurry before he comes back. I'll watch the hall."

"What exactly does it look like?" she called, stepping into the room.

I held my breath and listened.

"It's a book. That's all I know. Has everything," the male replied.

"You know if we get caught, we are dead," she said as she slowly crossed the room.

"We ain't getting caught, and if we don't do it, we are dead anyway. You saw what happened to Reni. Hurry up."

"Why do I have to find it?"

"I'm the brawn, you're the brains."

"I'm the brawn and the brains," she mumbled, shuffling through the bookshelf.

I listened carefully as she searched through the stately room. I hoped she wasn't looking for whatever I was looking for, but more than that, I hoped I didn't have to knock her and the brawn out cold. She searched the room for an eternity, and she hadn't even gotten to the desk yet when the male called from the hall.

"I think I see someone coming down the drive, Ygret. Let's go."

"But I haven't found it yet," she hissed.

"Time's up. That's the boss's buggy."

224

"Shit." She hurried out of the room and locked the door behind her.

Fuck.

As quickly as I could, I crawled out from under the desk and slid the freshly unlocked drawer open. I hoped like hell the black, leather-bound book inside was something important. I crammed it down my shirt and bolted across the room. A paper scroll pinned on the crowded corkboard by the door caught my eye, and I snagged it. I unlocked the door as noiselessly as possible and listened for anything coming down the hall. In the silence, I sprinted for the room I had entered in and launched myself out the open window. I pulled it shut, cursing Wrate for his terrible information, and squatted in the bush, hoping not to be seen.

Eventually, I made my way back to the shoemaker's home, and after locking myself in the room, pulled out the only two items I had found, hoping they would be enough. I thought about why I had agreed to this. I wasn't a vigilante. Sure, I needed the money, but I also had bigger fish to fry. I needed to get to the castle, and this was only slowing me down. I meant to be here for a night, maybe two. This was taking a lot longer. Tomorrow would be a big day, though, perhaps the final day, and then I could move on.

I opened the black book and realized this was probably what the female was looking for. It was full of page after page of notes in rugged handwriting. Names were listed in columns, and beside them were deeds that had been done. Everything from rape, to murder, to thievery filled the pages. And if that wasn't enough, the notes I pulled from the board made this mission ten times more dangerous and ten times more likely to succeed. It was probably the one thing he should have locked into his desk. Fortunately for me, powerful fae tended to become careless.

Before the sun rose the next morning, just as planned, the carriage was delivered to Betha's house and we began our lengthy trip to Tresa. We sat in silence until just before we made it to the smallest village I'd seen.

"I suppose you'll be joining me for my visit then?"

"No. I'll drop you at your son's house and be back at supper so we can hope to be back in Rocsbrew before dark."

We arrived, and I helped her down from the cart. I unhooked it, leaving it behind and mounted the horse.

"What are you scheming, girl?"

I could only shake my head and answer, "Something really stupid."

I had planned to get the shoemaker out of town because if things went wrong, I'd hate for her to be caught in the middle of it. Upon last night's findings, though, the plans changed, and I had to ride like hell to make it back in time for this all to work out. I'd need the stars to align tonight.

CHAPTER 27

Temir

The thunderous banging on my door yanked me from my dreamless slumber. I opened one eye and then the other. It was still nighttime, which meant someone needed my magic. I hurled my blankets off, dressed as quickly as I could and grabbed my bag while the frantic shouting outside of my locked door grew louder.

"You are needed," was all the king's guard said before turning and all but running down the hall.

I kept pace with him. I didn't need an escort. I had spent many hours traveling between my rooms and the solar. This was how we did it, though. I'd admit, this seemed a bit more urgent than any other time I could recall.

"There is a wounded council member," the guard panted as he hustled down the hallway.

"Who?"

"We weren't informed. Only saw someone carried in as the king yelled to retrieve you. We must hurry."

We jogged as we navigated the long corridors. For many years, I had asked to have the space moved closer to my rooms, but King Autus had always said it's easier for me to come to the wounded than the wounded come to me. I wondered if he regretted that now.

I slammed the door open and looked around. I expected it to be full of concerned fae. I thought half the council would be here by now, but aside from me and whoever was wrapped up on my worktable, the room was unnervingly empty. I took a step forward, steadying myself. I had to remember that Oleonis and Gaea were not council members.

"Ragal?" I asked, pulling down the fabric covering him. "Mother above," I gasped. "What in the world happened?" I peeled back the blood-soaked bandages, and even I had to turn my face away. He was still, so terribly still. I burrowed into my power as I removed layer after layer of shredded fabric. He looked as if he had been torn to pieces with handfuls of knives his entrails poured out of him, he was white as a fresh blanket of winter snow, and someone had wrapped him up hastily and brought him in. I wasn't sure if I could save him.

His pulse was low and slow.

I grabbed a knife and cut off the remaining sticky material he was wearing. He laid bare as the day he was born on the flat table and, as I placed my hands on him, I knew nothing in this would be guaranteed. This was going to nearly drain me. I concentrated on pacing my magic as I pulled all the way from the bottom of the pit and, as slowly as possible, threaded Ragal back together. I pushed and pulled my magic through him. I had to start on a molecular level, then build to blood cells, then nerves, then bone and finally tissue.

"Come on, Ragal," I whispered. Feeling faint, I drew a chair up to sit, never taking a hand off of him. Deeper and deeper I pushed, willing my magic to stretch as far as possible. It was running dangerously low, and the shallower that pit became, the more concerned I grew.

I could feel the sweat beading on my forehead, the heat growing in my ears. I was getting closer and closer to draining myself. The edge was dangerous. If I gave every last drop, I would save his life but end mine. The last drop of a fae's magic was pure and powerful, but could only be given in exchange for your own life. When I was younger, I wasn't as familiar with the expanse of my own magic. I nearly killed myself trying to heal too many in one day. Oleonis never let me forget that lesson, and I'd never gotten close to the last drop again. Until today.

The room spun, but still I pushed. I could visibly see him healing. Red welts began to show where deep gashes had been hours ago. He hadn't moved, hadn't made a sound and no color had returned to his pallid flesh.

Healing magic wasn't like other magic. It had to come from a place of purity and precision. Precision was like a dance, moving from one diminutive section of the body to another without pushing too far or too fast. I watched that last drop of magic coming closer as I worked. I felt it taunting me, as it always did, but rarely had I felt the desire to use it as I did now.

The edges of the room blurred and swayed, and my body shook with the effort to remain upright. My own self-loathing built a bridge between myself and that final drop, calling me to end it all. It would be so easy. Months ago, it might have felt like a considerable solution, but now, everything was different. I had to keep reminding myself of that as that drop inched closer and closer toward me.

And then I saw her lovely face and those mesmerizing eyes that could stop a beating heart. That was it for me. I pulled my trembling hands from Ragal and swayed in my chair. He took as much as I could give him, and as I reached my hand to feel his pulse, the room went dark.

"Temir?" Gaea called.

I felt my body shaking and reluctantly opened my eyes. I was laying in my bed in my own rooms as the most beautiful creature stood above me with her arms crossed, eyebrow raised and scowling.

"What did you do?"

I shook my head and rubbed my weary eyes. "My job."

"How close were you, Temir? Do you even know what day it is?"

"It was close. How is he?"

"He has not woken, but he lives. They found you both in your healing room and brought you here."

"Both of us?" I asked, trying to sit up.

"Yes. They brought a cot in for him, and he is in your study." She sat on the side of the bed.

"Why would they move him here?"

"I might have forced them to." She shrugged.

"How long has it been?" I asked.

"Three days since he was found."

"Do they know what happened to him?"

"No one will say a thing. I've been spiriting my way around the castle, trying to learn anything, but everyone is silent." She paused. "Are you okay?" She bit her bottom lip and, for the first time, worry showed through.

I tugged her into a lying position in the bed, rolling to my side so we were nose to nose. "I'm better now."

She scrunched her face. "Let's just stay in bed."

I flung the blanket over her, and she nuzzled into my chest. As much as I wanted to lay there and stare at her, I closed my eyes and fell back asleep.

"Temir?" she whispered.

"Mmmmm."

"I think your new roommate is awake."

"Five more minutes," I groaned, pulling her closer.

She giggled and pulled away. "We've been asleep for hours. You need to go check on him."

"Yes, Mother." I sighed, sitting up. "I take that back, you're too pretty to be anyone's mother." I brought her fingers to my mouth and kissed them. "I'll be back in ten minutes, don't go anywhere."

"I'm coming with you," she insisted, crawling out of bed.

I opened the door to my study and, sure enough, Ragal sat bewildered on a folding cot, rubbing his temples and blinking his eyes repeatedly. "Where am I?" he asked.

I crossed the room and checked his pulse as I answered. "You're in my rooms, Ragal. You were injured and I healed you, but it took a lot of magic and I had to rest. Gaea had you brought here. Probably to make sure that whoever got to you the first time wouldn't chance a second time. How do you feel?"

"Like I rolled around in a nettle field and then took a bath in acid. You?"

"I'm fine now. Do you remember what happened?"

Gaea handed him a glass of water, and I watched to make sure he didn't choke as he swallowed.

"My memory is hazy." He squeezed his eyes shut and rubbed his temples.

"Take your time, Ragal. We are in no rush here." I wished I had my truth serum worked out. Surely his subconscious remembered.

"I just can't believe it." He rubbed his head.

"What is it?"

"I need your word that I can trust you, Temir. I've not known you to be a liar or a disloyal fae. Can the two of you keep this between us, while we try to figure out what happened?"

Gaea crossed the room and took my hand, nodding to Ragal. I squeezed and nodded back.

"I have royal blood. Many don't know this, but the king's enchanting doesn't work well on me. Things become fuzzy, and it's rare when the memory comes back. The king can make people see things that aren't there, and he can force people to forget. He puts a mask over reality, and those that don't have royal blood don't know the difference. I can usually put the pieces together and puzzle it out."

"Perhaps we can help if you tell us what you do remember."

"Autus . . . Uh, King Autus asked me to travel with Thane to The Bog. He said there's a gryla living there that might have something he's looking for. He thought the royal blood might be able to persuade her to part with whatever it was. I guess I didn't realize he meant literally my blood."

"He sent you to The Bog? Why would you ever agree to go there? It's so dangerous," Gaea said.

"I know it is, but there are no choices where the king is concerned. Thane was there as well to help keep the peace. But rather than helping me," he paused, rubbing his temples again, "something happened. We were on our way back, and that's when it all gets fuzzy."

"But how could you have gotten back to the castle in time if you were attacked in The Bog. You would have had to travel for days?" Gaea asked.

"I don't know. I know we left on horseback and it was just me and Thane. The journey took a week. He was odd the entire way. He kept talking about the war and the king and—" He stopped mid-sentence and locked eyes with me. "He's going to put you all through a test."

"We already know that. He's been making the rounds for the last few weeks." Gaea gave me a look that reminded me to keep my mouth shut. "One of the servants let it slip that Thane was bragging about the king's dirty work," I added quickly, trying to cover my tracks. I was terrible at this.

"As if it isn't all dirty," Gaea mumbled.

"No. It's more than that. It's Oleonis. He thinks something is going on with him. More so than the others. Thane was obsessing over it. He doesn't believe anything. You have to watch over him. Something is up."

Gaea went on defense immediately. "Oleonis is helping the king build archery weapons and extra fuel for the blacksmith's fire. He is barely sleeping from working so many hours."

"I understand. I'm just telling you to watch out for him."

"I'm always watching out for him," she answered.

I took a step forward to move between them. "Can you remember nothing else of The Bog? Anything at all that was said by Thane or the gryla?"

"We were to demand her presence at the castle. The king summoned her and, like it or not, The Bog is in his territory. She is his subject."

Gaea snorted behind me, and I had to give her the same look she had given me earlier. "What?" she asked. "Telling a gryla what to do is like cutting the wings from a wyvern. You'll only piss them off before losing your head."

"But she didn't protest. She agreed, almost eagerly, to come. We were half a day's ride from the castle, maybe a little farther, when I'm not sure what really happened." He closed his eyes and shook his head. "It's like Thane was provoking her. But why would anyone provoke any creature from The Bog?"

"You'll never make sense of anything Thane does. He's crazy," she said.

"The next thing I can remember is being here."

"I had to heal you. You were completely shredded open. It makes sense that it would be from a gryla. I thought someone tied you up and sliced you across the stomach repeatedly. It was a terrible set of wounds."

"Thank you, Temir. Really. I am in your debt."

"What will you do?" Gaea asked him.

"What can I do? What can any of us do? I suppose I'll leave this room and pretend like nothing happened. I know that's what is expected of me."

"Then I suppose you should keep your guard up also," I advised.

"I guess so." He slowly heaved himself off the small cot.

I sprung forward to help steady him as he swayed. "Easy. Shall we call for a meal before you go? Just to make sure you can keep it down?"

"No, no. I'll be fine. I need to get to my rooms."

"Let me help you," Gaea offered.

"As you wish." He held a shaky hand out to her.

She reached out and touched him, and they were gone instantly. I hoped the landing wasn't too jarring for him. Within minutes she was back again. "We have to go see Oleo right now," she said.

"Can you take us directly to his rooms?" I didn't want anyone knowing we were there. Not a single fae.

"I can, but he hates it when I pop in unannounced."

"You can blame me."

"Remember you said that," she said, reaching her hand out.

I lifted her fingers to my mouth, and she paused for a wink before whisking us away.

CHAPTER

28

Ara

I picked Betha up sooner than she probably would have liked, but we had to get home faster than we had traveled coming in. Thankfully, I had swapped horses outside of Erast in order to make it.

"I see you've made it back in one piece," she said as she climbed up beside me.

"Let's hope I'm still in one piece by the end of the night."

She said nothing and looked forward as I urged the horse to a quick pace.

When I dropped her off at home, and before I could leave, she stopped me. "Have you got all your weapons?" She gave me a knowing stare.

I nodded and continued down the path. Rather than going directly to Rodalf's house, I went north and stopped just below the crest of the hill so I could watch without being seen.

Within moments, several horses trotted down the lengthy drive, carrying four large male fae dressed in black and armed to the teeth. I watched as they charged into the home and hoped like hell Wrate followed my instructions exactly. I held my breath until I saw the shadows of the males cross the office window, and then I waited until, over an hour later, the sea fae stormed back out of the house and disappeared into the night.

The house was still and silent as I made my descent of the hill and creeped my way to it. The full moon lit the gravel pathway, and though instinct pulled me toward the darkness, I knew it wouldn't matter. My plan either went perfectly well, or it went absolutely awry and I'd have to deal with the consequences.

The door hadn't been shut behind the fae as they left. I softly pushed on it and a small squeak had me holding my breath again. I walked down the hallway and directly to the office, where I found Rodalf laying on the floor in his own piss and blood. For a moment, I thought he might be dead, but his gargled moan gave way to his rasping breaths, and I kneeled beside him in the moonlit room. "How's it hanging?"

He groaned once more and rolled to his side to look at me. "You?"

"Yep. Just little ol' me."

"Why?" he creaked.

"Well, let me tell you a story. Do you mind if I sit?" I sat in the leather-wrapped chair behind the desk. "Once upon a time there was a bad, bad male." I placed my hand to the side of my mouth and loudly whispered, "That's you." I paused for dramatic effect. "The bad male took advantage of too many fae for far too long, and after meeting an absolutely beautiful female—that's me—all of his life choices caught up to him in one single night. You see, when I had originally heard of what you were doing to these people, I thought I'd steal your little black book of shame and use it against you, just as you did to the fae of Rocsbrew.

"However, on my way out the door, I found your secret treasure. I had no idea at the time, of course, but after reading your notes over and over again, I discovered your other dirty secret. You've been plotting against the sea queen for ages, and with the northern king no less. I've spent some time at the castle. I recognized some of the names. I don't even want to consider why the northern king would plot against his betrothed, but her sentries were sure happy to look into it. Looks like they weren't too happy with you. How's the head?" I leaned over the desk.

He turned to the side and vomited.

"Here's what you're going to do," I said, standing. "You're going to pack up one teensy, tiny little bag of absolute essentials and disappear. You don't get to take a single dime with you. Traveling when you are poor sucks, believe me. But let's just call it a journey of personal enrichment. That sounds nice, huh?"

He attempted to sit up and swayed from the motion.

"I'll just wait here while you pack. Wouldn't want you breaking the rules, after all." I sat back down at the desk and plopped my feet atop it.

Eventually, he made it to his feet. "Ygret," he called.

"Oh no, no. Don't bother asking for help. For starters, none of those fae work for you anymore, and also, they hate you. Shocking, I know. The house is empty. I made arrangements for them to be long gone this evening. Better get moving."

He tried to pull himself up by the edge of the desk, but after a few moments, he gave up and crawled down the hallway.

I wanted to be sympathetic, but forced myself to remember how many times I read the word rape in his damn book. How many times I read the words kill and murder? This was a sick, sick male, and while ultimately he got to live, this shame would stain him for a long time.

He was standing by the time he made it back to the office.

I stood and pulled his packed bag from his shaking hands, dumped it onto his large desk and removed the pouch of coins he had stashed inside a wadded-up pair of trousers. I slammed the hilt of my knife into the hand he had resting on the desk.

He fell to his knees.

"You don't get to cheat this time. You don't get to take advantage of a single person. You don't get to break the rules because you think you are better or above anyone else. I have eyes and ears across this entire planet, and if I ever hear word of you on the wind, I'll hunt you down and kill you myself. I'll take my time and peel layer after layer of skin from your rotten bones. This is not a game, but if it was, you lose."

"I-I'm sorry," he stumbled. "Please let me stay. I swear I'll never touch another person. I'll do anything."

"You will not stay here. You will not remind these people every day of what you've done to them. You will leave and never come back."

He nodded and gathered his bag, walking to the door. "How did you know?" he asked. "How did you know they wouldn't kill me?"

I shrugged. "I didn't."

***

Later, Wrate and I stood in front of Betha's house. "I still don't understand how you managed it all. How'd you get the queen's guards here?"

"It was a team effort." I held out the emerald necklace for him. "You'll need to have this delivered to Doart in Tresa. He put himself in a very dangerous position to deliver a message to the queen's guards. Likely, he and his family will also need a place to stay so they don't go looking for him."

"I'll ride there personally tomorrow to get them and bring them here. We have a vacant house to fill now, after all. Here's your pay." He tossed me a large bag of coins. "My wife has asked me to invite you to dinner. We don't have much, but she insists."

"Doesn't sound like I have a choice, then." I smirked.

"She rarely leaves anyone with a choice these days." He beamed. "I'll see you tonight. It's not too hard to find. You just follow the main road east out of town. You'll ride into the hills for a bit and find the moss-covered cottage on the south side of the road."

"Sounds easy enough."

Laid on my rented bed in Betha's home, I replayed the events from the long day. I knew asking Doart to deliver a message to four sea fae that would have killed him for pleasure was asking a lot. I was glad he talked the large blacksmith into joining him for safety. Still, I worried about him. Not only was he successful, but he traded horses with me so I could make it back in time. I hoped whatever payment he received in Rocsbrew combined with whatever he could get from the necklace would be enough.

I considered dinner with Wrate and realized that while these lesser fae asked me for help, I needed them to succeed just as much. And working as a team, side by side, felt more like winning than watching Rodalf run off in the middle of the night with his proverbial tail between his legs.

I changed for dinner with Wrate's family. He was careful to mention they didn't have much, so while I changed into my simple leathers and riding boots, I slipped off my mother's necklace. I wanted to go to dinner on their terms and show them all that not every high fae wanted to rub superiority in their faces. Some of us just needed a good meal and a sincere conversation. I still wore my knives, though. I hadn't completely lost my mind.

"Are you sure you don't want to come along?" I asked Betha again, standing at the front door of her home. "I don't think they would mind."

"Would you just go and leave an old fae in peace?"

"Okay," I surrendered.

I mounted the standard horse I borrowed from Doart and made a mental note to leave him with Wrate before I left for the next town. I sped through the rolling hills and the massive ones, just as Wrate said I would. The beauty of dusk and the vivid colors painted across the unabashed sky, struck me. I couldn't remember the last time I remembered to look for beauty in this fractured world. And then I was reminded why I never got to do that anymore.

From behind a hill, I saw a head pop up and duck quickly enough that an untrained eye would have never seen it. A hint of light from the setting sun glared off the tip of a weapon, and I drove my heels into the side of the horse. I was likely too far away from the stalker for an accurate shot with a bow or the throw of a knife, so I dashed behind a hill and leaped from the horse. I quickly tied him to a tree and bolted in the opposite direction, hoping to draw whoever it was away from him. I needed that horse, damn it.

It seemed I was back to the life I knew in the forest. Running for cover and questioning who the hell was chasing me. I circled around to where I had last seen him and, though I couldn't see him now, I could hear him, but that only worked to my advantage. If I couldn't see him, he couldn't see me, and I was far quieter. I backed myself into a small cave on the side of the hill and watched for him to come into sight. His tromps were getting closer, and it was only a matter of minutes before he appeared, and I realized who he was.

I wasn't sure if he was one of the queen's sentries from last night's attack or just another of her sea fae roaming the countryside, killing innocent lesser fae as he traveled, but either way, I'd spent the last of my stored patience on Rodalf and needed a good fight to blow off the steam.

I pressed my back against the jagged wall and listened as his footsteps grew louder and slower. He was searching for me. I turned and tossed a pebble deep into the cave, hoping he'd think I was running away.

The idiot charged full speed right past me and stopped just before the cave was completely dark. His black leather pinned him as another of the hunters that kept popping up. I stepped out from the wall and kicked him right between the legs from behind. Without hesitation, I followed by jamming my foot into the pit of his knee. He fell forward. I was behind him with two blades before he could even turn. I brought one to his neck and stabbed the other into his shoulder, before holding him upright as he wailed in pain. I gave him no time for a reaction as I used my free hand to snag the rope from his belt and slip it around his neck.

"Looking for someone?" I taunted.

"No. Found her," he grunted.

"Listen, I'd love to stay and play, but I've got a dinner to get to."

He bucked, realizing too late what was about to happen. I tossed the knife I was holding to his throat, grabbed the second end of the rope and pulled like hell. It took all my strength to hold on as he stood from the ground and swung me back and forth, feet hanging.

A normal fae would pass out after maybe twenty seconds, but this son of a bitch seemed to be half whale and was going to take longer. He dug his fingers into the rope and rasped as he slammed my back into the wall.

I felt a rock cut into my spine and the wind knock from my lungs. The rope slipped a bit, but still, I managed to hold on. He began to waver on his feet, and I only hoped I outlasted him.

He moved again toward the wall, but before he could shove me into it again, I jumped as high as I possibly could over the top of him and twisted in the air, tightening the rope. The momentum from my landing pulled him face-first into the hard ground. I put my boot between his shoulder blades and pulled until he stopped moving, then removed the rope and kneeled to make sure he was still alive. I had questions for him. I didn't have anything to actually tie him to, so instead, I left him on his stomach and tied his hands to his feet, pulling the rope between his legs so if he woke up and decided to move too much, his prick would hurt as much as his pride. That was a win-win in my opinion.

"See ya later, sweetums," I called back as I picked up the knife I had tossed and left the cave.

He wasn't awake yet, but it was the thought that counted. I found my borrowed horse where I left him and continued toward Wrate's house.

"My goodness dear, what in the world happened to you?" his wife asked when I stepped inside the humble home filled with patchwork furniture covered in handmade quilts.

"The horse got spooked and threw me. I'm fine," I lied.

"Well, please do come in. I've got a lovely roast duck ready for you."

Wrate only shrugged as I walked past him and to the dining room table. There were several fae there to join us. None I recognized.

"You've become a bit of a celebrity around here," Wrate's wife said.

She went around the table introducing all of the lesser fae. Her name was Red and she wore a red polka dot dress and a stained apron tied around her plump waist. I noticed Wrate tended to stay within a few feet of her no matter where she stood in the room. Mates.

"Please, do have a seat. I'm just about ready," she said, looking pointedly at Wrate.

He hustled behind me and pulled my seat out.

I put my fingers on his wrist to stop him. "Please, you don't need to do that. I'm no one special. I just helped someone that needed it."

"But don't you see," the fae with leaves in her hair peeped, "that is special."

"But it shouldn't be." I took my seat.

There was a pause, and everyone looked to me to carry on the conversation.

"I heard the Court of Wind and Sea are to be united in marriage," a guest said from down the table. "I can't decide if it's incredibly romantic or incredibly dangerous."

"It's most definitely dangerous to anyone living south of the Dregan mountains," I answered. "This divide of the lesser and higher fae in the Marsh Court has been orchestrated by the northern kingdom. I'd bet my last coin on it. How much easier will it be for them to tear through the Marsh Court when we are already doing half the damage ourselves?"

"I hadn't thought of it like that," Wrate said.

"Everyone needs to start seeing beyond themselves and really look at the power in the kingdom. It's like a magic trick. They cause a distraction with their left hand so you can't see the trick in the right hand."

"How did you learn it all?" The little boy at the table leaned on his elbows to peek at me.

"Learn what?"

"To kill the bad guys," he answered so nonchalantly, it startled me.

My eyes doubled in size, and I looked to the adults in the room. They all shifted forward, watching me. I wasn't entirely sure how to answer that direct question. "The short answer is I learned from my father. But I never wanted to kill anyone. I still don't. If I went around killing people because I thought my actions were justified, I'd be exactly the same as they are. I don't want to be like that, and I hope you'll grow up to feel the same way. The only way to fix the future is to change what we are doing now and let go of the past."

Someone down the table scoffed, and all eyes turned to him. "We aren't doing anything. We are living, and that's the problem with you high fae. You don't want us to live."

I opened my mouth to counter, but could say nothing.

"Not much you can preach about on that, is there girl? Sure, you come into town and run off one male. You didn't even do it alone. You still needed a lesser fae in Erast. And from what I heard, you made him do the most dangerous part. Didn't want to risk your own life, princess?"

"Now wait just a minute," Wrate intervened. "I've been looking for someone to help get rid of Rodalf for years. Not one person has even come to try. Lilleth here came to the village and he was gone in three days' time. How in Alewyn could you fault her for that?"

I cringed at my false name.

"It's awfully easy to sit up there and talk down to us about what we need to be doing when most of us don't have a choice in any of it. My brother wasn't protesting, he wasn't even arguing when he was killed by a high fae because he dropped a plate while serving them. You say we need to watch both hands, but you forget yourself. We also have to watch the boot that will come for us either way."

I placed my hands in my lap as the guests began to twitch in their seats. "I didn't mean to offend anyone. I just mean that glorifying the death of an enemy is also shameful. We are fae. Higher, lesser, green, blue, square, round, whatever, we are meant to live forever. No, we aren't immortal, but time will never conquer us. We are our own enemy. I mean only to stop the trajectory of prejudice any way that I can."

"You can't sit here and lecture us on killing when you've killed before. Left a fae dead in the streets for money, didn't you?" He leaned forward to watch me closely.

I stiffened my posture. "I tried to let him live. It came down to him or me, and there really was no choice in that. And not that I have to justify myself to you or anyone, but I've got my own problems, and I needed the money to get to where I am going. I took eight coins in exchange for saving an innocent male who tried to do the right thing. I won't apologize for that." My muscles became tight and my posture stiffened as I stared that fae in the eyes.

"You sound just like the rest of the high fae. No, you won't apologize for anything. You say your father taught you how to murder? He wasted his time. He should have been teaching you how to go to the castle and spread your legs like the rest of the high whores."

Half the table gasped, and the other stared at me, waiting for a reaction. They knew I could be dangerous. They just didn't know how dangerous. I felt fire in my blood and lightning in my soul. I absolutely

244

would not prove him right, no matter how much I wanted to in that moment. I clutched the table.

"Rupert!" Red shrieked bursting into the room from the kitchen. "Get the hell out of my house and don't even think about coming back here. Miss Lilleth is a guest, and you will watch your mouth in this home." She came stomping from the kitchen, grabbed him by his elongated ear and pulled him to the front door. "Your mother would be ashamed to hear you speak to a lady like that."

He locked eyes with me and shoved the door open. "Too bad she isn't here to witness it. She was also killed at the hands of your kind," he spat scornfully and walked out.

"Lilleth, I am sorry, dear. He hasn't been the same since his mother died."

I released my death grip from the table. "There is something I want you all to know. Opinions like those are poison. I won't stop helping innocent fae because one fae throws a fit. If I have to choose between killing or being killed . . . Well, you can guess which one I'll pick. If I must choose between saving a high fae or a lesser fae, it will always come down to right and wrong only." I turned to Red. "I'm sorry for ruining your dinner."

"Ruined? No. Now there is just more to go around."

I left their home earlier than they probably would have liked. Dinner was incredible and, someday, I'd return just to eat at that table again, but for now, I had a sea fae tied up in a cave, and after the words from Rupert, he probably wasn't going to like our next conversation. I was still reeling and as I made my way back to the cave, that tension built inside of me.

The cave entrance was quiet, and everything was pitch back.

"Here fishy, fishy, fishy." My voice echoed from deep within the cave, and with it came a grunt. "Didn't get rope burn on your little wee wee, did you?" I took a step forward and kicked my foot, trying to feel for him in the dark.

245

"Go to hell," he said.

He had to be only feet from me. I took another step forward. I could fight in the dark, but why choose that? This guy was a monster. "Listen, I've had a terrible night. Some guy was being a total asshole at dinner and I just don't feel like dealing with you right now."

"Stand there long enough and you'll have more than me to deal with, little witch."

"See, at this point, I don't think I really have to deal with you at all. I could just leave you here forever. You technically wouldn't die, you'd just be starving and alone for eternity. That could be fun, I guess? It's not my thing, but to each their own."

"They will never stop hunting you. As long as she wills it, it will be done."

"Oh, code lingo. I like it." I tapped my finger to my mouth for a moment. "You be Blackhawk and I'll be . . . Deathrider." I creeped farther into the cave and continued my sweeping until I kicked him. Hopefully in the face, but it was hard to tell. "There you are, Blackhawk."

I kneeled and reached a hand out. He was still stomach down, so I grabbed onto the ropes where his hands and feet were tied together and pulled him toward the door. He didn't budge at all. "Blackhawk, what did you eat for lunch? You need to diet, buddy. Less salmon, more kelp."

"Untie me and I'll get right on that."

"Ah ah ah. 'Untie me, *Deathrider*.' We had a pact."

"How the fuck did I get tied up by a child?" he asked trying to roll to the side.

I kept my grip firm. "Just got lucky, I guess. Care to tell me why you were hunting along the King's Road?"

"I'm not telling you shit."

I reached up and shoved my fist into the shoulder I had stabbed earlier. "I think you'll change your mind eventually." I placed the tip of my knife against him. "You realize it's pitch black in this cave and I have no idea what I'm stabbing right now, right?"

He remained silent, so I pushed the blade in. I felt it break the skin, and though he inhaled a deep breath, he still said nothing.

"Tell me why you were on the road."

Nothing.

I pushed farther.

He called out in pain but didn't answer.

I pulled the knife out as slowly as possible and jammed it back in. "Tell me," I demanded.

"I'll tell you something. Your father was a real pain in my ass and I'm glad he's dead. I only wish I could have been there to watch him die. I would have fucked your mother before she died, too."

I felt the fury from earlier crash through me again, and I jammed my knife into him. He definitely knew who I was, he knew what had happened to my parents and I doubted he just got lucky coming upon me on the road. He knew I was going to be there. "How did you know I'd be on the road?" I twisted the knife.

Fun time was over.

He panted, and I reached up and squeezed his shoulder again. He said nothing. I stood and kicked him in the face.

"How the fuck do you know who I am?"

He gurgled.

I grabbed hold of the twisted ropes and pulled him toward the cave opening again. It wasn't pretty, and it took longer than it should have, but eventually, I had him in the moonlight. I wanted to look into his eyes before I killed him. I noted the thin trail of blood. It wasn't enough. It would never be enough. "How do you know who I am?" I demanded.

Silence.

I jammed my knife into his side. "Why were you on the road?" I grabbed his inky hair and yanked it backward, lifting his face to the sky. "How do you know who I am?" I screamed.

His hair burst into flames in my fingers, and I wasn't sure who was more surprised, him or me.

"There's a charm," he roared. "Make it stop."

I couldn't even if I wanted to, but I jerked my hand away. "What do you mean there's a charm?"

Again, he was silent.

I grabbed his arm. "What do you mean?" I yelled.

His arm became pulverized below my grip, and he shrieked. "Okay. Okay. No more magic. Please, no more magic."

I pretended like I was controlling it, though internally I was panicking. "You'll answer all my questions, or I'll burn you alive right here and now."

"I don't know why the queen is hunting you. I only know that she sent several of my soldiers to your house to kidnap you after she learned you escaped the castle. They beat you home, and rather than waiting for you, they killed your parents and set your house on fire. Everyone knew the queen hated your father for refusing her, so they thought that would be enough. We all thought she only kidnapped you to get to him. To make him hand over the Hunt."

My father had always made me take the long route home. Now I knew why. I'd never be found on it. But the charm, the vision of Aibell touching the necklace I'd always worn, flashed through my mind. She could have told me. Crazy old hag. "Why does she want the Hunt?"

"I don't know," he grated. "It's not my business. I go where I'm told."

"And you were told to find me?"

"You've been hidden to us since your escape, and suddenly tonight I could sense your location."

248

"How?"

He was silent for several moments. I was sure he wasn't going to answer, but he did. "I also have magic. I am able to find lost things."

"Have you been staying at Grower's Pointe?"

"Yes, but we had information that brought us to Rocsbrew last night. We camped outside of town and discussed moving on or going back to Erast when I sensed you were near."

"What did you mean by charm?"

He hesitated, realizing he was giving me way more information than he should.

I grabbed his leg. That was enough motivation.

"No, stop, please. You had to have a charm to hide yourself from me."

I did. I just didn't realize it. "Are there more like you? Hunters?"

He didn't answer.

I placed my hand on him again. Still, he didn't answer. I tried to imagine a fire, but nothing happened. I had to resort back to the old-fashioned form of torture. I put my knife to his throat. "Answer," I scowled.

That was where he drew the line, apparently. He wouldn't give up his brethren. "You can't control it, can you?" he asked.

Control it? I didn't even know it existed five minutes ago.

He attempted some broken form of a laugh, but the knife didn't leave him much room for humor. "You land dwellers are all so worried about the sea fae, you have no idea what's coming for you from the north. Go ahead and kill me, Ara. It won't change a thing."

"I don't need your permission. I don't want your threats. I just want to know what the hell is going on."

"Well, it looks like the queen knew you had magic and intends on collecting you. That's what the royalty loves the most."

"I'm not available."

"Neither was I."

"Tell me if there are others like you."

He went still and silent.

"Answer," I demanded, pressing the blade until I knew he was bleeding.

"I'll hunt you until the day I die," he sneered. "You won't even have to worry about the others. You are mine."

"I am no one's." I ripped the blade across his throat and shoved him to the ground. Things just got a lot more interesting. Magic or no magic, I needed to get back to my mother's necklace as fast as possible.

CHAPTER 29

Temir

"What in Alewyn are you doing in my bedroom? And unannounced, at that," Oleonis asked.

"We need to talk right away. Will anyone be able to hear us, Oleo?" Gaea asked.

"No, of course not. You know that," he answered.

"It's that important." I followed. "I'm not sure if you know, but a council member was gravely injured. It was Ragal, and he nearly drained me while I was trying to heal him."

"Tem—"

"I know. I know. It wasn't intentional and I was able to stop. That's not the problem. Apparently, the king isn't able to enchant him as thoroughly as he would like. And Ragal had a little bit of information we didn't. I told you that Thane is checking everyone's loyalty. Well, apparently the king, or at least Thane, thinks something is different with you, and from what we gathered, to an obsessive degree."

"I see," Oleonis said, sitting back on the edge of his bed, analyzing as always.

"There's more," Gaea said, giving me an apologetic look.

Puzzled, I gestured for her to continue.

"The king had me spiriting Thane through Alewyn searching for something. Before you ask, he wouldn't tell me what, but while we were gone, he asked me to take him to The Bog. I doubted the king had asked him to go there, so I refused."

"What?" I nearly shouted. "You mean—"

"I don't know. It could have been me instead of Ragal, but I've been to The Bog before and I know it's dangerous. As soon as I refused, he let it go and didn't bring it up again. Maybe that was my test."

"Or maybe Thane has a separate agenda from the king?" Oleo said.

"The only thing Thane wants is bloodshed," she answered.

I hadn't moved. Hadn't breathed. I saw red. Pure, unadulterated red slowly pouring over my body.

"Temir?" Gaea whispered, stepping forward to put a hand on my arm.

"It could have been you," I said behind clenched teeth.

"But it wasn't. I'm smarter than that."

Numb, I turned to the door. "I'll kill him."

"You can't, Temir. Stop, you can't."

"I can and I will."

"Temir!" Oleo shouted, pulling me from my rage. "Stop this at once. You're smarter than this. Think. I'm not saying you can't, but not like this. If you're going to best him, you're going to have to do it on your own terms and not his. Don't play his game, Temir. You will lose."

"There's more," Gaea whispered.

My head snapped to her and my heart stopped. I didn't think I could hear anymore without completely losing it. I saw Ragal laying on that bed and then it was her and I knew. I would have given her that last drop. I would have died to save her, and I hadn't even had the chance to love her. "Say it," I demanded

"I think whatever the king is searching for, it's very bad."

"I could have guessed that," Oleo said, not taking his eyes from me.

"No, I mean the end of the world bad."

"Explain," Oleo demanded.

She crossed the room and took my hand, shifting the immunity ring. "I went back to Oravan and asked for this one and one more for Oleo. I had a whole plan in place to acquire both, but he didn't fight me. Didn't protest or anything. He took this from his own hand and placed it in mine, promising to make another. I've never noticed him wearing it, but I'm sure he also knows the king is using enchantment on the council now. He said the king has ordered him to make something he didn't think he could morally commit to. He didn't directly say it, but I think he is also planning on running."

"That would leave only Evin," Oleo said.

"If the king loses four of the five magical fae he has, I can't imagine what he would do," Gaea responded.

"He would turn the world inside out searching for us, for sure," I answered.

"What do we do from here?" Gaea asked.

"We leave. With or without the serum, we have to take that chance."

"We will not," Oleonis barked. "Suppose the king has enthralled me to kill any accomplice if I ever try to leave."

"Well, so far you haven't tried," I answered.

"Everything to this point is hypothetical, which I think would stall the enchantment from direct action. The moment a plan is in place, everything may change. Or the moment we follow through. I'm not willing to take that risk. We need the serum more now than ever."

"I can't do it, Oleo. I've tried a thousand plants and more. It's not the same. Perhaps nothing exists."

He took a moment, and then his eyes grew wide and understanding lit his face.

"Exactly, Temir," he said.

"Exactly, what?" I asked.

"It doesn't exist. All this time we have been trying to replace the taonia atomaria with something else we can find naturally, but what if the substitute does not exist?"

"I don't understand," Gaea said.

"You're right," I said in understanding. "We have to molecularly build the substitute ourselves and then harvest it. It doesn't exist."

"Again. Still lost," Gaea said, crossing her arms.

"We have been trying to find a similar plant to substitute the active plant that works on the sea fae," I explained. "Oleo is suggesting that we have to actually create a new species of plant with the same molecular build as the one that we know works."

"Could you do that?" she asked.

"I think so," I said. "It would take some time, but I think it can be done. We would only need to cross-pollinate the seaweed with a similar plant species. It would be like starting back at square one, but it's something we haven't tried yet."

She looked between Oleo and me and said, "Why are we just standing around then?"

"I've got a few ideas," Oleo said, tapping his chin. "Leave it to me for now, Tem, and I'll let you know when I think I've got something."

I nodded, knowing he would be more successful with plant origins than I would. "Gaea, shall we leave him to it?"

She crossed the room and hugged Oleonis, wishing him luck, and then spirited us back to my rooms.

"Are you okay?" she asked, holding onto me still.

"I'm fine."

"I should have told you about Thane earlier, I'm sorry. I didn't think it mattered, and then there wasn't time."

"I'm not mad at you, only for you," I answered, pulling her to me.

A knock at the door drew us apart instantly. "It's Iva and Roe, my lord."

"Damn."

"We have eternity, Temir. It's okay."

"Eternity is looking shorter and shorter as the days go by." I opened the door.

Roe's eyes swept the room before he spoke. "Sorry for the interruption, shall we come back later for your cleaning?" he asked, shifting his eyes to Gaea and back to me.

"Tomorrow, then?" I asked, raising an eyebrow to him.

"As you wish, my lord," he said with a bow.

"Oh, wait," Iva chimed in. She looked to Gaea. "Forgive me, my lord," she said, bowing as well. "We were told to deliver this to you." She handed me a folded paper with the king's sigil pressed into a wax seal.

"From whom?" I asked.

"Everyone is getting 'em, milord," Roe said, forgetting himself. His eyes went wide, and he bowed again.

It would have been comical had it not been so sad. I imagined there were few places in the castle he truly could be himself. A trait we shared, I supposed.

"Thank you," I said, taking the paper and shutting the door. I looked to Gaea, who only smirked at me and shook her head. "What?" I asked, smiling.

"Your room hasn't been thoroughly cleaned in ages, Temir."

My eyes swept the paper. "We play chess." I shrugged.

"Just when I thought you couldn't get any better, you surprise even me." She laughed.

"Will you join me, then?" I held the invitation out to her.

She snatched it from my hand and read out loud. "The honor of your presence is hereby requested at the Wind Court by his majesty, King Autus of the northern courts. Blah, blah, blah six days' time, blah, blah, blah . . . masquerade, dinner . . . blah, blah, blah." She handed the invitation back and smiled. "Should we coordinate outfits and everything?" she teased, taking a step toward me.

"If you wish," I answered.

"And will you buy me flowers and dance all night?" Another step.

"If you wish."

"And will you walk me properly to my door and kiss me goodnight?" Another step.

"If you wish," I chuckled.

"And if I want you to stay?" She wrapped her arms around me and looked up.

"If you wish," I whispered. I leaned down and kissed her softly. She reached up and threaded her fingers through my disheveled hair. The sensation enraptured me. I could feel myself growing harder as she purred. I slid my hands under her and lifted her from the floor, then carried her into the bedroom.

She threw her head back and laughed as I tossed her on to the bed. I crawled over the top of her, dragging my nose up her body as I inched my way to her neck. She moaned and bucked as I kissed just below her ear and pressed my body into hers.

My eyes rolled as pleasure surged through me. I lifted my weight up off her, and she slipped her hands under my shirt. Though I wanted to feel the full force of her skin on mine, she barely touched me as she moved her gentle fingers up and down my body. I lifted my head to the sky and let a grumble escape as she laughed.

"My sweet, Temir," she said, pushing the curl of hair from my eyes. She kissed me again softly.

All these months of stolen kisses and deliberate touching had been building to this one moment. I never knew it was possible to want something or someone so badly. I pulled back, searching her eyes for an answer. I needed it to be her choice. I was reaching the threshold, and if we pushed any closer, I'd never be able to stop myself from taking her.

She leaned up to my ear, whispered, "Wear something blue," and spirited away.

I fell into the empty bed and buried my face into the pillows, refusing to scream. That little devil did that on purpose, distracting me from my earlier rage. I knew there was only one place I'd be able to work off the steam, though, and if she found out, she wouldn't like it.

"It's been a while." Thane smiled, tossing me the waster.

I juggled the wooden sword between my hands and tried my best to keep the contempt off my face. Oleo was right. Thane would murder me in hand-to-hand combat. I'd have to plan his death accordingly.

"You!" he called across the pit. "Grab a sword."

A lesser fae, matching me in size, did as he was told and crossed the yard to stand before me.

"Until someone taps out!" Thane roared, excitement booming.

I stepped forward, holding my hand out to shake before the match. The other fae only spat and readied his weapon. A small crowd gathered, a few of them laughing. We exchanged blows and blocks, and while I was able to hold my own, I was also quickly reminded how long it had been since I'd stepped foot in the training arena. I was out of shape and my reflexes were slower than I would have liked. I used to spend ages down here after I moved into the castle, but slowly, I'd stopped coming.

"Is that all you've got?" the fae jeered.

I didn't respond, only pressed forward, causing him to lose his footing for a moment. The growing crowd gasped as he stumbled backward. Instead of accepting his mistake, he used it to his advantage and slammed his fist into my face while I was waiting for him to right himself. Again, the crowd cheered.

"Tell me, pretty Temir, whose dick do you have to suck to sleep in the castle with the fancy bitches?"

I held my tongue. I could feel my icy rage growing. I pushed forward, landing strike after strike with my practice sword.

"Swords down," Thane called from the side.

Of course, he didn't want to see me best any of his trained males. I tossed my sword down and raised my fists. The other fae slammed his sword into my gut before throwing it. I doubled over and he kneed me in the face. Blood poured from my nose, but I ignored it and swung, slamming my fist into the side of his face.

"I saw your girlfriend the other day," he said, spitting blood into the dirt. "I'd love to crawl between those legs and show her what a real male feels like. I bet she moans louder than a manticore."

He was trying to get a reaction out of me, and it was working. He thought he could distract me, but my anger only streamlined my blows. I struck him again in the face and, as he stumbled backward, I kicked him in the chest.

"Does she?" he stammered. "Does she like the taste of the king's cum in your mouth when you kiss her? Does she like it as much as she likes it fresh from his cock?"

The world spun, and I lost all control. I flew across the arena and slammed into him, knocking him to the ground. He laughed as I punched him over and over again. I couldn't see his face through the blood that covered it and, as I continued to strike, he began to choke on it.

"Get up you fucking pansy," Thane called.

He didn't, though. His haggard coughing turned to gasping, and suddenly I realized if I didn't help him, he would choke to death. I leaped off him and tried to roll him to the side.

"Leave him," Thane said from above me.

"But he's choking," I said, still trying to roll him.

"Let him," he hissed, moving closer.

"I can't, I didn't mean to—"

"I said let him, Temir. The king won't save you now. Oleonis won't save you. You will have this death on your hands forever, all because you couldn't handle a little jeering." He leaned down so he was closer.

"No," I said, shaking my head. "I won't just let him die."

"Then you would reveal your power to everyone here?"

"If he could just roll over," I said, reaching for him.

Instantly there was the cold steel of a sword pressed to my throat, and as I sat on my knees in the frozen dirt, listening to that fae die, I realized I actually hated Thane more than I hated myself. He had me and he knew it. I wouldn't use my power, and he wouldn't let me touch the male otherwise. Why the fuck had I wanted to come down here, anyway? I stood and walked away, leaving that fae to die for no reason at all.

CHAPTER

30

Ara

Magic. Actual magic. Aibell knew. She had to know. But rather than teaching me anything about it, I got mental shielding and shadow training. I had a serious bone to pick with that old hag the next time I saw her. If I ever saw her again.

"There's a note on your dresser. Messenger didn't leave a name."

I felt bad. Betha didn't need to be in the middle of any of this, and if people were leaving notes for me at her home, then I had made it too obvious I was here. I knew what the note would say, though. It was probably another lesser fae in trouble and offering coins for rewards. I didn't want to even consider it after everything that had happened at dinner and then after. But how could I not help someone who likely couldn't help themselves?

"Thank you, Betha. I'll be leaving in the morning. Hopefully, everyone will stop bothering you once I'm gone."

"Hopefully," she answered.

I smiled and went to my room, tossed my cloak onto the bed, glanced at the white envelope on the dresser and decided to take a bath instead. I needed to move on from Betha's, and that meant leaving this gift from the heavens behind. I filled the blessed bath with oils and soaked for a long, long time. Eventually, the water turned cold and I had to drain and refill it. My eyes were tired, but my mind would not slow down. I tried and tried to make the fire come again, but it wouldn't. But was it fire? Because I'd crushed his arm with no flame at all.

I had no clue what I was doing. I closed my eyes and pictured the magic, just as I had with the mental shield. Nothing happened. It was pointless. Either someone would have to teach me, or I would just keep it a secret and take it to my grave.

After leaving the bathroom and drying my hair, I lifted the note from the dresser. If I didn't open it, I wouldn't feel compelled to help someone. I still had a choice here. But as I remembered the conversation I'd overheard my parents having, I knew I had to read it.

It's so easy to sit here and say at least we are safe as high fae. At least we will not be murdered. But to truly turn our backs on the rest of Alewyn? To leave them behind and watch them be murdered out of cowardice is just not something I will do.

My father's honorable words echoed back and forth in my head. If he wouldn't do it at the expense of his own life, then I wouldn't either. Based on the story of my mother and the pixie, I knew she would make the same decision. I ripped the envelope open and pulled out the neatly folded sheet of paper.

Come to Hythe. It is a matter of life and death. I've heard you can help with high fae. I have a job for you.

-D

Before I even considered that, I had a few loose ends I needed to tie up in Rocsbrew. I decided to get a full, comfortable night's sleep and figure everything out in the morning. Who knew when I'd have a nice bed to sleep in again?

I wanted to leave the posh gown behind and take only the essentials, but it might come in handy to have something other than riding clothes and a hooded cloak. I had to roll it up and cram it into my pack, but at least it fit. Unlike the shoes that I left on my bed for Betha. She wouldn't wear them, but perhaps she could sell them.

"Thanks for the room," I told her as I walked to the door.

"Cost is double next time," she said, smiling as I walked out.

I think I liked her. I wasn't sure if she liked me, but we understood each other. She didn't fuss or interfere, she didn't poke her nose in, and she seemed to always know more than she let on.

I let myself into Rodalf's old house and confirmed no one had been back since he left. I figured looters would have had their way through here yesterday, but likely many fae were still worried he'd just come right back. If I were smart, I'd dig around for more of his money, but eventually someone who really needed it would probably find it, and that wasn't why I had come, anyway. I scanned the books in his office one by one. He had many of them about the human world and several on the history of Alewyn. It was a respectable collection, and probably harder to leave behind than anything else, but he didn't have what I needed most. Nothing on magic or magical creatures.

The market came to Rocsbrew once every few weeks according to Red, and before I left town, I thought I'd look for a bigger pack and maybe a decent change of clothes. Something that didn't involve evening wear. The streets were lined with eager vendors that traveled from town to town selling their wares out of ramshackle carts and trolleys: Farmers with chickens and gardeners with fruit from all over Alewyn.

A rotund clockmaker stood on the corner twisting his long mustache as he studied a lesser fae female with leaves growing in her hair and bells on her layers of clothes. She ignored him, watching me closely as I slipped into the shadows of my hood and tried to slide by.

"A coin for your fortune, dear," she said, grabbing my forearm before I could squeeze past.

"Not interested." I yanked my arm free.

"It's dark," she rasped, likely thinking she would intrigue me.

"I know," I sneered and walked away.

My future probably was dark. I was destined to save a world I despised from itself. It didn't sound like a very bright future at all, in fact, and I certainly wasn't going to lay myself bare before some stranger. She may be a fraud, but then she might not be, and that would have been dangerous for us both.

"Real leather!" someone called through the crowd of people.

"Half off!" another shouted.

I was tempted to abandon my plan for shopping and just start walking when a group of whispering voices caught my attention.

"They say she transforms into a dragon and eats the high fae."

"Did she kill him, too?"

"She doesn't eat or sleep, she just travels around Alewyn killing them."

"They say she wouldn't even take the money."

"I heard her eyes turned red and she summoned a demon from hell to scare Rodalf away."

Well, that was true enough, I guess. Word spreads like wildfire on market day in any town, but when you liberate an entire oppressed village, apparently it becomes the epitome of gossip. I didn't want to do anything to draw the queen or her sentries to me, but as far as I could tell, no one had put the two things together.

I walked farther from the chattering females and found a stand with leather satchels and buckled suitcases.

"Ah, that's a nice one there," the merchant said about the slender pack I'd lifted from the metal cart.

"How much?"

"Ten coins"

"I've killed a male for less," I answered, rolling my eyes and putting the bag back on the cart.

He laughed as if I were joking. "Four. Four coins!" he yelled as I walked away.

I turned back to him. "One coin, and I don't tell the guy three stalls down that you are stealing from him."

"I don't know what you're talking about," he claimed.

"Oh, I think you do." I shifted my eyes to the greedy boy in the back of his stall.

"Fine, here. One coin. Just keep it between us."

I flipped a coin to him and took it. I'd watched that boy stop at several stalls before I saw him lining his deep pockets. It paid to be observant.

I found some decent clothing to put into the bag at a reasonable price and purchased a few dried portions of meat and fruit for my journey too. Overall, it was a successful trip. If nothing else, now I knew how "D" found me. Chattering old fae treated small talk like currency, and people were poor. It was a matter of life and death, the note had said, so I headed out of town. I wasn't committed to helping, but I'd look into it. I didn't have a clue how to find "D," but I was sure if I made a grand enough entrance, he'd find me.

The King's Road was quiet. For two days I traveled on foot, stopping only when I could find cover to rest. I could have bought Wrate's horse. I could have probably demanded it, but it wouldn't have quickened the journey much unless I ran him, and I wasn't in a hurry. The exercise was good for me, and some part of me felt like I deserved to walk for leaving

Brimir behind. Each time a squealing cart passed and smothered me in a cloud of dirt, I reconsidered.

By the afternoon of the second day, I could see Hythe on the distant horizon, and I was surprised to see a bustling city similar to Hrundel. I had heard of Hythe in my studies, but never realized the size of it. As I got closer, the sounds of the city created a boisterous ambiance of cart wheels squeaking in tune with the resounding thud of horses stomping up and down the roads, murmurings of a thousand fae voices carried away on the wind, and with them, the banging of the blacksmith's mallet in the distance. A clock tower chimed, but as I walked deeper into the city, the call of desperate merchants selling their goods drowned out all the other sounds.

The smell of freshly baked bread led me into the city, and I wished I had the willpower to resist, but instead, I purchased two loaves and some rhubarb and honey jam. I strolled through the packed streets at a lazy pace, watching the occasional hurried patron try to hustle through the crowds of the languid fae. Lovers hid in the shadows of the alleys and strange guards stood at attention with observing eyes. A quiet song filled the air as a bard sang on the street corner in front of a small glass jar with only a few coins inside of it.

"Is there an inn nearby?" I asked a female holding a small child. I watched the babe's eyes and realized this was the only young fae I had seen in the city so far. She looked at me startled and hid her child away.

"Why should I answer to you?" she quipped, looking me over.

I forgot myself. A high fae, cloaked and questionable. "You shouldn't," I answered, dipping my head. I walked past her.

She called back. "Two blocks down and on the right, above the Weaver's," she said, jutting her chin in the direction I was to go.

I thanked her and continued down the street. The closer I got to the castle, the worse the divide between lesser and high fae became. I could not let myself forget that.

The inn was where she had said, and I secured a room above a shop where they braided rugs and silks and intricate baskets. My mother would have loved the Weaver's knotted creations. She was a serpent female, a naga, and the way she watched me was unnerving. The way she slithered through her shop more so.

The room was simple, with a shared bath for all the guests I didn't bother with. I washed my face in my room, instead, and changed into the fresh set of clothing I purchased in Rocsbrew before.

Sighing as I left, I realized there was no way I would be able to find "D," and I imagined they knew that before asking me to come here. The lively city was not quite the size of Hrundel, but certainly still large enough to disappear in. I decided I'd make my way to the tavern, have dinner and continue my journey westward in the morning.

I followed the line of drunks stumbling through the streets until I could smell the sweetness of spiced wine and bitter ale. I left my hood in place and found the only open seat in a local tavern.

"What'll you have?" a barely clothed barmaid asked me.

"What's on the dinner menu?"

"Don't serve food here, darlin'," she said.

"I'll just have whatever the spiced wine is then," I replied.

She didn't even acknowledge my order, just turned to the next table and leaned too far down for the male patron to focus and repeated the process.

Classy.

Before the wine I ordered even made it back, a whelpa slid into the opposite seat at my table. His tentacle-like fingers slithered on the table and he watched me with yellow eyes.

"Not interested," I said.

"Not selling anything," he answered with a jeer.

I raised an eyebrow and waited for him to explain himself, but instead, he raised a hand and called the waitress back over.

She slid an arm around his neck and plopped into his lap. "Tavi, I haven't seen you in weeks, lover. How are you?"

I swallowed the bile burning my throat and looked away as his tentacles crawled up her flushed skin.

"Busy as always, dear. Bring us a round, would you?"

"Of course."

She left the table, and I adjusted my hood while tilting my head to the side. "Do you need something?"

"You're shorter than I thought you would be."

"Ah," I said. "I'm assuming you know who "D" is then?"

"He's my boss. He had eyes all over the city waiting for a cloaked stranger to arrive."

"I see. And how did he know I would even come?"

"Everyone does what he says," he answered.

"One of those, then." I took the glass of wine from the busty female and sipped.

"You'll meet with him tonight and start your job tomorrow."

"Oh, will I?" I dug my fingers into the cushion below me. "Your boss is awfully fucking bold to be commanding me. No one gets to ask for my help and then start telling me what I will and won't be doing. He will come and apologize for this ridiculous behavior and then he will explain what he needs. Then," I said, leaning forward, "I alone will decide what I will agree to do. There is no other option here. If I haven't seen him by morning, I'll assume he changed his mind. Now, if you'll excuse me," I said, standing from the table. "I'll take my leave."

The lesser fae followed me out and called after me, but I didn't give a pixie's ass what he wanted or needed. I was already annoyed, and I hadn't even met the fae who wanted to hire me.

I stormed through the winding streets of Hythe and kept my eyes on the lingering fae. Why was common courtesy such a foreign concept? My shitty mood was more erratic than normal, but I chalked it up to a long day of traveling and tried not to slam my door as I made it to the rented room. I was in the process of packing my weapons, having decided to leave that night, when a ruckus down the hall was followed by an obnoxious banging on my door.

"If you won't tell me which room, I'll just wake everyone!"

I flipped the polished knife in my hand and threw my door open, lightning in my veins. What was with the fae of this damn city?

"Never mind," the towering high fae before me called over his shoulder. "I've found her." He smiled and took a step to force himself into my room.

I pressed my knife into his gut and leveled eyes with him. "Going somewhere?"

"So, the rumors are true, then." He reached to pull my cloak down.

I grabbed his hand and twisted, and then kneed him in the groin.

He groaned and went to one knee. I made eye contact with the Weaver standing behind him. A dangerous smile crossed her face, and she dipped her head in a slow bow, eyes locked with mine in understanding.

"I'm sorry, miss," the Weaver said. "He didn't listen when I asked him to wait at the door."

"Don't worry about it. I can handle him from here. I'm sorry he has caused such a disturbance." I glared down at the still-smiling male. He could have been beautiful, if not for his demeanor.

"May I come in?" he asked from the floor.

I stepped aside, and he used the doorknob to pull himself up with a grunt. I played with the slender blade of my knife as he stepped into the room. I leaned my back against the closed door and crossed my arms over my chest.

"I'm going to go out on a limb here and assume you are the mysterious "D"?"

"Devi, at your service, my lady." He bowed low and grandiose.

I tapped my fingers against my arms as I waited for him to stand upright. "I don't speak flattery. Did you come here to apologize then?"

"I have. Shall I take one knee or two, my beauty?"

"You could take a hike," I answered.

"Oh, ho. Your humor is only surpassed by your ravishing fervor."

I opened the door. "Get out."

He looked at me like I had grown three heads. "I'm sorry?"

"Yes, you are. Now leave."

"But I've not had a chance to explain."

"Oh, you've had a chance, you just chose to be a pig, instead," I said, challenging his tone.

"Fine, I'll skip to the point then," he said, standing.

"Finally." I pushed the door shut and gave him a blank stare as I crossed my arms and tapped my toe on the wooden floorboards.

"I need your help." He sat on the edge of my bed.

"This might surprise you, but I assumed that based on the life or death letter I received in Rocsbrew. Let's start there. How did you find me?"

"I make it my job to find interesting people."

"No. We aren't doing the thing where you dance around my questions. Answer. How did you find me?"

He gave me a glassy eyed look. "There was a fae traveling through Erast who heard of another left dead in the streets. Then, I got news of Rodalf's disappearance. We had worked together before. Terrible male. I know a fae who lives in Roscbrew, so I sent a message to him to deliver to the liberator. And here you are."

"I'm not a liberator. I just did the right thing. What exactly is it that you want from me?"

"Ah, yes. I'd like you to kill a high fae here in Hythe."

"Just like that? You just want me to walk up to someone and kill them? Why?"

"I'll pay you five times more than your highest paying job," he said, standing again, all business.

"Why?"

"I don't see how that's relevant. I'm willing to pay you a handsome fee to do a job that you have done in the past. Is that not enough information?"

I shook my head. "I am not an assassin."

"A warden, then?"

"Of sorts."

"This particular fae is creating unnecessary competition with my trade business. His name is Norst. Before you make your decision, ask around and see what the lesser fae think of him. Then, you'll see that he is evil."

"And what would they say of you, Devi?"

"Oh, I don't know." He smirked. "That I am devilishly handsome and perform miracles in the bedroom." He looked about the room. "You wouldn't need to ask around to find that out, though." He stepped closer, pressing me into the door. His solid body against mine caused a heated reaction I wasn't expecting. He leaned into my neck and breathed, "I could show you."

For the briefest of moments, I lost myself in the sugar-coated desire he was emanating. I slid my hand up to his chest and moved my fingertips along his smooth jawline. Until that moment, I hadn't realized how truly alone I had been. How desperate I was for genuine attention. Genuine attraction. I stood in the middle of a city that didn't know or care about me. A world that didn't care about me. But this male with his dark, hooded eyes and perfect smile saw me. I wanted to let go.

He brought his strong hands to my waist and slid them up my ribcage. His thumb gently stroking the bottom of my breast, conducting the orchestra of my body as he moved. It was so, so good. I had never wanted to forget myself so badly. The heat between my legs began to build and my breath fell short of my thirsting lungs.

"Let me show you," he whispered.

The vibration from his voice sent a shiver down my back. I stared into his eyes and reluctantly pulled myself away. "I'll consider your offer," I said, softer than I wanted to.

"Both, I hope," he said casually. "You can find me—"

I held up a hand to stop him. "If I need to find you, I will. Don't hold your breath."

"I'd hold anything for you." He walked out of the room and left me standing there, stunned.

My body had betrayed me. A pretty fae smile had sent reasoning out the window. I squeezed my eyes shut and shook my head.

Focus.

I waited only a few moments before discreetly following him out the door. I tracked him down the streets, keeping far enough behind that he wouldn't know I was close. It was easy enough to keep to the shadows and alleyways as he weaved through the city. His body still called to mine as I followed him to a tavern but waited outside.

If I considered myself a liberator at all, it was for the lesser fae, those who suffered day in and day out. Not the privileged high fae, and certainly not for a cocky, albeit gorgeous fae that probably hadn't known suffering in his entire life.

I mentally thanked Aibell for the cloak that kept me somewhat safe from the chill that had settled in the night's air. I tried to summon that magic again somehow, but it didn't work. I started to count the crumbling bricks on the dilapidated face of the old tavern when, finally, he came stumbling out of the building with not one, but two females under his arms. They swayed through the streets laughing as he sang a bawdy tune about a naked mermaid.

Thank the gods I had seen reason earlier. He was the stereotypical high fae, and I wanted to stab my own eyes out for not realizing it sooner. He disappeared into a decent-sized home with both females, and I decided that I had seen enough. I'd investigate Norst, for no reason other than curiosity at this point, but I wouldn't be killing one high fae for another. If history had taught me anything, the rich high fae was always the bad guy. I had a deep, genuine desire pressed into me by the guiding hands of my loving parents to help the lesser fae, and truly just the less fortunate. Devi just didn't fit the mold.

CHAPTER

31

Temir

She had stayed away all week. I never stopped thinking of the fae in the lists, and her absence only made it worse. By day three, I was going mad and had to confide in Oleo. He only laughed at me and advised me to be patient with her. *She is like the wind*, he reminded me. Nothing was easy when it came to Gaea, though.

I stood before Oleonis in my rooms as Iva fussed around, helping me dress properly. He placed his steady hands on my shoulders and smiled.

"Enjoy these moments, son. I've found in life that the good ones are always so few and far between."

"It seems foolish that a fae could die at my hands only days ago, and now I am dressing for a ball like his life meant nothing."

"No." Oleo stopped me. "That fae's life meant everything to someone, and you'll do well to take that lesson with you, Temir. You made a poor choice, putting yourself in the lists with Thane in control. Choices out of anger rarely end well."

I looked to the floor.

"But you are not to blame, and I'll hear no more of this from you, do you understand? You're a good male, Temir. You would never have chosen that outcome, and that's what makes you different. That's what matters most. Come." He walked toward the window.

I followed him and looked out.

"The sun will set on this day, whether you will it or not. It will rise tomorrow on a new day and you will once again start anew. The decisions you made in the past will not stop the sun or the moon or the stars from their dance across the sky. You must always move on, son. Hard as it may be. Now, let that moment pass and come back to this one. There's a beauty waiting for you."

"You've seen her?"

"Of course. You weren't the only one that needed the sage advice from an old fae today," he chuckled, the twinkle in his eyes shining brightly.

"Is she . . . is she well?" I tugged on the sleeves and adjusted the collar.

"Better than." He smiled as his eyes traveled a million miles away.

"Best I get finished here, then," I said.

He patted me on the back and left the room. "Be gentle with her, Temir," he called over his shoulder. "She deserves nothing less."

I looked back out the frosted window and tried to steady my erratic nerves.

"Dashing as you are, you've done it up wrong," Iva said, fretting over the ties at the cuff of my sleeve.

The sleeves were long, and when I tried to tie the delicate strings to conceal my chest, Iva swatted my hand away and told me to leave it open. I felt like a fool, but I had to believe she knew more about this than I did.

"Where's Roe?"

"He is, uhm . . ." She paused, carefully thinking her words through. "He is out today, my lord."

I thought back to the last few conversations we had together. He'd been here yesterday and slipped up again. It didn't take a genius to figure out what was going on. I only hoped he was more careful with his words with others than he had been with me. Although, I didn't think he spoke to anyone else. He was playing a dangerous game. One I didn't dare mention to anyone.

"You've got your flowers, then?" Iva asked, changing the subject. I gave her a look, and she blushed. "Of course you do. You'll need to bend for this next part. I can't reach."

"Thank you, Iva," I said as I took a knee.

She firmly tied the onyx mask on. I knew a panther was a bold choice, and as I looked at myself in the mirror, I debated leaving the room at all.

"She'll be the luckiest one at the ball," Iva said breathily.

"If she shows up at all," I grumbled.

"Not to worry, my lord. She will be there. Females can be fickle, but a handsome male is hard to resist." She had that doe-eyed look in her eyes again.

"I'm to meet her at dinner. I should go."

"Oh yes, quite so."

I entered, lost in the drove of fae who walked about the room paying no attention to the world around them. A thousand glowing lights hung from the vaulted ceiling, reflecting their warmth onto the shimmering ballroom floor. The entire room was lined in crystal sculptures, as if we were standing in the middle of a frozen ocean. The assortment of masks was unnerving. All these fae spent their lives hating the creatures they now pretended to be. I squeezed my fists open and shut, searching for Gaea amongst the crowd, but I had no idea what she would be wearing. Her note said I would know it was her when I saw her.

The side-by-side thrones explained why the room was full and decorated so much more elaborately than usual. The sea queen was here somewhere, and her court likely joined her. I kept my shoulders tucked in and my chin to the floor as I worked my way through the people, searching for those eyes. I collided with several fae as I wandered the still-filling room as the stifling minutes passed.

Maybe she had changed her mind and wasn't coming. Maybe I had pushed too hard the last time we were together and scared her. Standing there like a fool holding the flowers Oleo and I had grown just for her, I watched the door intently, debating if I should leave.

But then she was there.

I saw her standing at the door before she saw me. I couldn't breathe. Couldn't even move. Every part of me wanted to be the male who would storm across the packed room, wrap my arms around her, and declare her mine to every fae from here to the southern courts. Her white, fur-lined gown plunged down the middle and hugged her body so tightly, it was a second skin. I'd never been so jealous of fabric in my entire life. Her captivating eyes were circled in kohl and, behind her mask, she wore her face painted like a beautiful doe. The crowd parted around her as she walked. If it was not for the gown alone, the stark white antlers atop her soft faun hair was more than enough.

My heart thundered in my chest as her eyes finally found mine. Anger like I had never known heaved through me as I watched each male she passed let their wandering eyes feast on her. I straightened my stance and pushed my shoulders back as everyone watched her cross the room to me.

I shoved the flowers in her face awkwardly, and she laughed.

"I believe your jaw is on the floor, Temir," she whispered.

I could only nod, taking her in.

She took the bundled flowers and tucked her delicate hand into mine, breaking the spell as she pulled me to the long table in the center of the adjacent room. "I've missed you," she said as two lesser fae pulled the chairs from the table and we sat.

"Beautiful," was all I could manage.

She giggled and leaned her head on my shoulder. "Worth the wait, then?"

"A million times over," I answered, unable to take my eyes from hers.

I'm sure dinner was served at some point. I think I even ate a bit. Before I knew it, we were shuffled back into the ballroom and the dance began.

"You've been awfully quiet," Gaea said.

"Rough week," I answered.

"It was hard to stay away from you, but I wanted that moment. The one where you looked at me across the room and forgot the entire world surrounded us. Where, for once in your life, you forgot who you were and stood taller."

"You picked the stag," I said, reaching for her horns.

"And it's beautiful on me and repugnant on you?"

"A sack would be beautiful on you, Gaea."

"I'll consider that next time." She smiled.

Though I'd never actually danced at a ball, I spent the evening with the most beautiful creature in my arms and would have spent eternity on that dance floor. The later into the evening it got, the heavier handed we became with each other, as the heat from the lovers around us filled the room. I stole kiss after kiss, and though the room was filled with prospects, her eyes behind that furred mask barely left mine. If this was falling in love, I'd sooner die than save myself from the landing.

"Tem?" she asked, searching my face.

"Huh?"

She laughed. "I asked if you wanted to grab something to drink. My feet are killing me."

"Oh," I said, shaking the thoughts from my mind. "Yes. Of course."

We moved to the edges of the crowded dance floor, where I grabbed two overflowing glasses from a silver tray. I handed one to her and raised mine in her direction. "To you, my little doe. May every day be only better than this one with you."

She tried to hide her grin behind her glass. "And to you, my kitty cat. Because the only thing sexier than horns are those furry ears."

I finished my glass, grabbed her hand, and pulled her to the row of high-back chairs lined in the back of the sweltering room. I lifted her long legs into my lap and slipped the shoes from her feet, then pushed a small bit of magic into her as I massaged. She leaned her head back and moaned, and that was it for me. I lifted her up and carried her across the room, audience be damned.

"What in the world are you doing, Temir?" She laughed.

"You can't look like that and make those noises and expect me to sit there like a good boy."

"Kitty," she corrected.

I narrowed my gaze and growled at her. Her laugh was infectious, and she was the only thing in the world that existed to me.

Until the screaming began.

A fight had broken out between a sea fae and a northern high fae. There was too much chaos to figure out what exactly had started it, but as the king called my name, it didn't take a genius to figure out what was about to happen.

Gaea spirited us across the room, and instantly my hands were on the sea fae bleeding out onto the crowded ballroom floor.

"No one will leave this room," the king called with enchantment in his voice, though I noted the tension.

"You will all remain exactly where you stand," the queen's siren song followed, much more powerful than Autus.

I locked eyes with Gaea, and she nodded once. She wanted me to understand, and I did. I only hoped no one else in the frozen room saw her movement. I closed my eyes and let magic build around me. The sea fae had a knife in his chest, and he was not moving.

"Autus," Morwena snipped. "Call off your minion before I do it for you."

She was talking about me, but I needed to concentrate.

"Relax, my love," he answered. "Our dear boy has a rather remarkable talent. Let him work."

The gasps around the room were expected. Most of the northern fae had witnessed this before, though none of them remembered it. I pushed and pushed until I was able to pull the knife free. The sea fae gasped in response, and I worked to seal his punctured heart. I could feel the sweat beading on my lip. The tremble in my hands. But, at last, his chest rose.

"It is done, your grace," I said, bracing myself.

His gruff voice rang throughout the crowded room as he sang, "Whatever you remember of the last few moments did not happen. There was no injury here tonight. You did not witness a magical healer and you will all return to the ball, because nothing has happened."

"You are released," Morwena followed.

Gaea helped me to my feet and spirited us to my rooms before I realized we were moving. "Are you okay?"

"I'm fine," I answered. "Just a little drained. He was injured pretty badly."

"Should I go?" she asked.

"Not in a hundred lifetimes would I ever say yes to that."

"Let me get you something to drink."

"I'm fine," I said, walking to the sink to wash the sea fae's blood from my hands. I scrubbed until my skin burned from the pressure.

"It's gone, Temir." She lifted my hands from the water. "It's gone."

I pulled her to my chest and held her close. I hated the blood the most. "Is this the part where I walk you to your door and kiss you goodnight?"

"No," she answered. "This is the part where I want to stay." She reached up and pulled the antlers free from her head, dropping them into a nearby chair. She pulled off my mask, and I gently stroked her painted cheeks. "Come," she said, leading me to the washroom, ever the vixen.

She turned on the water to the bath and, as steam clouded the room, she gathered the hem of my shirt in her hands and lifted, tossing it to the floor, but before she could continue, I stopped her.

"Let me?" I asked, searching her eyes.

She smiled and gently nodded.

I grabbed her by the waist and lifted her to the cool counter, leaning in to kiss her neck as I gently pulled one strap of her dress down and then the other. My fingers shook, whether from anticipation or nerves, I wasn't sure, but still, I continued. The soft skin of her breast was everything I knew it would be.

"Is this okay?" I whispered into her ear.

"Mmmm," she responded, tilting her head back against the mirror to give me further access to her long, tender neck. That simple sound sent a message straight through my body, and I instantly hardened. I gently grazed my teeth along her collarbone. The salt and sweat mixing with her smell—that gods-damn lavender—nearly sent me over the edge.

I crushed her mouth to mine as she kicked off her shoes. My fingertips found their way to her inner thigh. It could have been the steam, it could have been the heat, it could have been her, but I had to pull back. Just slightly, enough to catch my ragged breath.

"Don't stop, Temir," she panted with swollen lips and hungry eyes. "Please."

I couldn't stop. If I did, I'd die of need for her. I moved my hands up farther, finding her wet with desire. I pressed my thumb into her core, and she made a throaty noise of encouragement, so I moved to the floor and trailed kisses up her legs. She locked eyes with me and, as I pressed my ravenous mouth to her, tasting her, she did not look away, only scooted forward on the counter so she could spread her legs further, lacing her fingers into my hair.

My skin hummed, and the primal need built as she moved against my tongue. I reached up, massaging her as I continued, and that was her undoing. She shattered into a million pieces, and the sultry noises she made were almost unbearable.

For moments, she held me back, letting the euphoria settle in her entire body. Finally, she sat up on the counter, unfastened my belt and let my pants fall to the floor. I stepped out of them, and she pulled me to her. I lifted her from the counter, wrapping her legs around me, and she slowly sank down, taking all of me into her. She rested her arms onto my shoulders and pushed herself up and back down as I held her waist.

At first, we were frantic, but then I wanted to stop. Not for lack of pleasure, but because I could feel the moment coming to an end a lot sooner than I wanted. I halted her movement, holding her steady. Both hearts pounding and both breathless. I pressed my forehead to hers. She fit around me perfectly, and as she brought her lips to mine in understanding, I finally let go of all doubt and all uncertainty about who we were together and what that meant to me. I finally had a person.

"You are mine, Gaea. From now until my last breath."

She nodded and whispered, "And you are mine, Temir. You are mine."

I stepped into the steamy bath and laid back, still deep within her. The flowing water lapped the sides of the bath and splashed over the sides as she moved on top of me again. I leaned my head back over the lip of the bath and once again felt myself building toward release. Her soaked body moved in a perfect cadence to my need. Closer and closer, I inched until she moaned, and I began to pulse inside of her just as I felt her tighten around me. I sat up, letting the water fall from my sensitive body as I held her close, exploding as her own orgasm ripped through her.

Later, we were naked in bed, legs intertwined and still exchanging deep passionate kisses when, without warning, a tumultuous banging on the door filled the room.

"I'd curse the heavens if I didn't owe them thanks," I said, kissing the top of Gaea's head before dragging myself out of bed. "I'll be back as soon as possible."

"I'll be here." She smiled.

For a moment, I paused, living in that single moment, but then as I dressed, shouting filled the hall.

I swung my door open and Ragal stood before me, hands covered in blood. Before I could say a word, he stopped me.

"It isn't mine, it's Oleonis."

And then we were running.

Ara

"**B**e careful the watchers," another fae whispered.

It was an anthem. Over and over fae warned, 'Be careful the watchers.'

I kept my hood high and queried the lesser fae that would talk. Most wouldn't, but occasionally the cloak didn't turn them away. I imagined it was difficult to tell if I was a lesser or high fae when you couldn't see my face. The general consensus was that no one liked Norst, but equally, no one liked Devi. Except for a curvy female I met in the alley, but it didn't take a genius to know why she sang his praises. By nightfall, the only thing I'd learned was that the scariest thing in Hythe wasn't either of the fae I had come for, but instead the watchers. So, rather than spending another night tracking Devi or searching for Norst, I climbed to a tiled rooftop and tracked the ones everyone warned me of.

They were easy to spot in the crowd. Most were rigid and cloaked but all had observant eyes and carried weapons. They wore matching dove-colored cloaks and strangely woven belts tied to their waists. A warning.

As the night grew colder, fae disappeared into their homes or the taverns, until no one but the watchers remained on the lamp-lit streets.

Occasionally someone would walk by, oftentimes crossing the street to walk opposite of them, even if it meant crossing several times to one side and then back to the other. Eventually, one small fae stumbled down the street, clearly intoxicated. He had neither the awareness nor the caution of the others, and they circled him.

I kept my body flat against the rooftop as they knocked out the fae and dragged him down the open street. I watched until they were just about out of sight. But before I jumped up to follow, I caught movement out of the corner of my eye. I shifted ever so slightly to see three figures on the rooftops as well, following the watchers. I stayed low as I followed both sets of figures. None of them were observant enough to realize they were being followed. Thank the gods.

The watchers disappeared into a large, dilapidated building. The fae that followed gathered close by on an adjacent rooftop. Nothing was happening with the fae who entered the building, so I couldn't bust in and save the captured fae without a plan, but since it didn't look like they were going anywhere, I scrambled to follow the other set of figures as they made their way back across the city rooftops. I thought at first they were there to liberate the stolen fae, but as they leaped down to the street and let themselves into Devi's house, everything became far more complicated.

"What do you mean 'before you?'" I heard Devi ask as I flattened my back against the wall of his home.

"They were faster, my lord," someone answered.

"That's the third and final time this week. You either get me another one or go back and retrieve that one."

"But, my lord—" another said.

"Don't," Devi demanded.

"Yes, my lord."

Two of the three figures exited Devi's house, and I followed them back to the warehouse. At this point, observing was all I could do, so again, I found a rooftop to lay low and watch.

Eventually, they left, one limping, but dragging the kidnapped fae behind them. I really thought they were going to free him. That all the things I'd heard about Devi were wrong, a persona he built. But no. As the lesser fae scrambled to get away from them, they began kicking him over and over in the street. Eventually, he stopped moving, and again, he was dragged off into the night.

Poor lesser fae.

They took him to a smaller building closer to Devi's house. I waited and watched until, finally, I decided no one was making any more moves in the game and I headed back to my room. I had so many more questions than answers at this point, but I knew two things for sure. Devi was definitely a bad guy, and if Norst was his enemy, he was either the good guy, or he was in charge of the watchers and both were in the business of kidnapping the lesser fae.

About halfway through the night, I bolted upright in my bed, remembering something haunting that Devi had said to me.

This particular fae is creating unnecessary competition with my trade business.

If Devi is in the business of kidnapping the lesser fae and trading them, and Norst was creating competition, the lesser fae in Hythe were in far more danger than I had realized. I had to think of a plan, and fast.

As I walked downstairs and through the Weaver's shop, she handed me a letter. I was really starting to hate letters.

Meet me at the bridge.

Norst

At least Norst had the decency to use his name.

"Any idea where the bridge is?" I asked the naga, assuming she had read the note.

"It's on the north side of town, past the market. He's trouble, you know," she stated cautiously, having no clue of my agenda. She swayed back and forth, the lower half of her body scaled and unable to be still.

"I know," I answered. "I'm not, though, and I'm taking care of it," I said, walking out.

A bony high fae with broad shoulders and long black hair stood facing the glassy water as I approached the bridge. "I wasn't sure if you'd come," he called.

"I don't like being summoned, if that's what you mean," I answered.

"My apologies."

"What do you want?" I halted and jammed my hands onto my hips.

"I'd like to double the offer that has been made to you."

"How do you know an offer has even been made?" I kept my body taught, ready to fight should the need arise. I hadn't seen a single watcher, though.

"Most of Devi's males report to me."

Did not see that coming.

"I don't want any part of this whole mess. I don't know why you two have it out for each other, and I don't particularly care," I lied, "but if you so much as think of calling on me again, I'll chop your balls off and feed them to the fish down there, got it?"

"Triple, then," he said as he walked toward me.

I tapped my finger on my chin and let the silence permeate. "I'll think about it," I lied again. I turned my back on him and walked away, keeping my fae ears open, expecting a weapon to come flying at me. Instead, he just let me go.

I had the makings of a plan put together, but before I could do anything, I had to free the captive fae. More so, I had to make it look like Norst did it. I couldn't just leave them to whatever ministrations Devi had planned, but I also wanted no eyes on me until I could set my plan into motion.

I went back to the Weaver's and had a long talk with her about how the next few days might go. She agreed to help and let me choose the rope I would need from her shop. Once again, I witnessed a lesser fae put her trust in a high fae even though her gut probably told her not to.

I crossed the town again in full daylight, hoping I didn't draw too much attention as I made my way to the street where I had seen the most watchers. It was the same as the day before. They stood, weapons concealed, watching the crowds flow through the winding streets of Hythe. I examined them fully and finally picked my unfortunate target. The one that couldn't keep his eyes off the females as they passed.

"Excuse me," I said, sidling up to him. "I'm so sorry to bother you, but I wondered if you could help me?" I batted my lengthy eyelashes and jutted my exposed chest in his direction.

His eyes didn't even touch my face. "I'm busy," he barely managed.

"I'm sure you are, dear. But I've just gotten myself locked out. It's just in that little street there, you see." I pointed to the questionably desolate alleyway.

His eyes lit with desire and he didn't hesitate to follow me. Fool.

The minute we were out of sight from most of the crowd, he grabbed me from behind and pulled the hem of my slinky gown up. I let him think he had caught me until he got the dress high enough to show the matching knives strapped to my thigh. He paused for only a second, but that was long enough. I yanked one free and jammed it into his leg. I knew he wouldn't call out. He had left his post after all. Norst would probably have him killed for that alone.

He swung wildly at me. I avoided the blows, and eventually he pulled the knife from his thigh.

"Took you long enough," I said.

"Who the hell are you?"

"How many females have you raped in the alleyways?"

"Plenty, including you by the time we are finished here."

"Mmm, I doubt that," I said. "I'm really glad you confessed, though. It will make me feel better about this next bit." I slammed my foot into his wounded thigh and then elbowed him in the face. I yanked on the brass buttons at his neck and, as his cloak fell free from his stocky shoulders, I kicked it to the side.

He barely noticed, panting as his face turned red with rage.

"You have a vein popping out of your forehead, just there." I pointed with my knife. "Did you know you could do that?"

"I'm going to kill you. Then I'm going to fuck your limp body. Then I'm going to cut you into tiny pieces and feed you to my pet narb."

"I've got a pretty tight schedule today. I'm not sure I can squeeze you in."

He charged at me like an idiot, and just as he was in range, I dropped to the ground and buried my knife into his stomach.

He fell forward and crashed into the brick building behind me. Panting.

I ripped my knife free and wiped it on his pants as I waited for him to die.

The shock of taking a life hadn't lessened since the first time, but I wasn't lying when I said his confession made it easier. I knew he had to die for my plan to work. Otherwise, he'd talk before the pieces could fall into place. I snagged the discarded cloak and tossed it around my shoulders. Luckily, it was not covered in his blood. It smelled horrid, though. Thank goodness I didn't need to keep it for long.

I crossed the city once more, noting that the fae avoided me. Which meant I was well concealed as I made my way toward Devi's home wearing his rival's cloak. I met the Weaver in the alleyway and changed into my regular clothes, handing her the trollop's garments I'd worn. We were silent, only making eye contact as I took the rope from her and she threw the cloak over my shoulders once more. Nodding to her, she disappeared into the crowd, taking my gown with her. I placed the Weaver's rope on the outside of the cloak, just as the watchers had worn it. An exact match.

I waited until long after sunset and then crossed the muggy street to the small building. Though I listened intently, only silence filled the air. Hoping I wasn't too late, I banged on the door.

"Who is it?" a male's voice called.

I didn't answer, only knocked again.

"I said who is it?" he called louder.

The third time I knocked, the door flew open. Before he even had a moment to register what was happening, I punched him in the throat, cutting off his airways. I shoved him back into the building and slammed the door behind me.

I was careful not to let my face show as I took in the details of the dank room. It was small, with a dirt floor and one light swinging from the low ceiling. My stomach turned as I took in the sides of the room lined with lesser fae locked into wire cages.

There was only one guard. I tied him to his chair with the Weaver's rope, the one identical to the one the watchers wore. Careful evidence I would leave behind. Within minutes, gagging him with his own belt, I shoved him into the corner so he could not see the cages or the door. I pulled the keys from his belt, and he squirmed in his chair in protest.

I unlocked all of the cages and, rather than running for their freedom, the lesser fae all backed to the walls far away from me. I pulled my hood down and pressed my fingers to my lips, hoping they would understand I was not actually a watcher. I held my hand out to one of them, and they shook their head, pulling back more.

I couldn't speak. If I did and the restrained guard heard my voice, the gig was up. I went cage to cage, but no one would come out.

Finally, at the last cage, a young fae was brave enough to step toward me. I gestured toward the door and then to my wrist as if to say time was running out. He understood and hesitantly left the building. All eyes were on the door until he came back into view and waved his hands at the captive lesser fae. As one, they ran. Scattering in all directions as soon as they left the building, aside from the one that chose to trust me first. He waited for me outside.

I pointed to the shadowed alleyway I had met the Weaver in, and he nodded in understanding. I removed the heavy cloak and tossed it inside, shut the door to the building, and walked across the street.

"You're not a watcher," he stated.

"No, I'm not."

"And you don't work for Devi?"

"Definitely not," I answered

"Then why did you free us?" he asked, leaning his shoulder against the brick wall of the adjacent building.

"Because fae are not animals." I lifted my chin and pushed my shoulders back.

"But you're high fae?"

"I'm aware." I raised an eyebrow to him.

"You're the one, then. The one they've been talking about."

I shrugged. "Any idea who they intended to trade you to?"

"They weren't trading us. They were selling us." He shook his head and looked to the ground. Ashamed of the words.

"To whom?"

"Depends on who pays more, I guess. I heard some guys went as far as the northern kingdom."

"You have to be more careful. Stay away from the watchers."

"I'm going south," he claimed. "It's better down there."

"Good luck to you, then," I answered.

"Same to you."

I lurked across the dangerous city, opened the door to the Weaver's shop, and she followed me up to my room. "You know the plan for the next three days?"

"It will be done," she answered, handing me the gown.

I nodded, and she left the room. I think I liked her.

Temir

*U*nsurprisingly, Gaea beat us to Oleo's limp body, seemingly discarded in the marble hallway. While we ran all the way there, she dressed and spirited. I couldn't imagine where her mind was, because I couldn't make sense of my own. I dropped to the floor beside him, ignoring my own reflection in the sea of his blood, and shoved the entire world away as I called my magic forward.

I was already feeling the void of power from healing the sea fae in the ballroom earlier. I laid my hands on him, and the shock of his pain ripped through me, leaving me gasping. I remained steady as I funneled the healing from my frozen fingertips and into his lifeless body. I tried not to let myself look for the inevitable end of the magic as it moved. I sifted through it, trying to direct it into the most important parts first, but his heart was not beating, and that made the flow of my magic stall. I pushed the light through him and gently caressed each chamber of his heart, willing them to work again.

Slowly, I began to seal the open wounds down his body. A beating heart would only cause more blood loss, but his lungs and other organs needed attention, too. The only part of him not torn to smithereens was his mind.

Somewhere, a million miles away, a female was screaming, and voices murmured into the endless night. I was not there, though, only here with my father, begging him to live, to come back to me. A world without Oleonis was not an option. I felt my own veins pulse and pure fear rack my incoherent body. Tremors drowned me as I held him and gasped for air.

I never once looked at Oleonis and saw him for the high fae that he was. He never acted like he was more than me, more than anyone. He would always be the exception to the rule of prejudice in Alewyn. He would always be proof that this world really could be peaceful.

I moved his long white hair from his closed eyes and let my unsteady hands trail down the cavernous wrinkles in his beautiful face. I never knew how old Oleonis was, but fae aged so slowly, I knew the world was losing one of the oldest fae that had ever lived. His life was the span of a thousand lives in one.

Time was an anomaly, as lost in the darkness as I was. I tried, gods damn it, I tried to keep myself focused on the medical aspect of my task, but I just couldn't do it. I couldn't look at the male below my hands and not think of the time he dragged me from the training yard bloody and bruised and taught me how to plant my first herb. I couldn't protect myself from the childhood memory of his laughter as we sat picking fresh berries from the bushes he grew, fingers and faces stained every shade of blue. The heartbeat of a child more precious to him than the demands of a tyrant king.

They say when someone is dying their entire life flashes before their eyes, but alas, his life played before my own. The day he held my hand as a boy and I felt love for the first time in my life. The day he smiled a real smile at me, simply because of something I said. The day he patted me on the back and told me he was proud. A word I'd never before heard in my entire existence.

This male, for all his flaws, was the embodiment of perfection, and as that last drop of magic came closer and closer, my eyes filled with burning tears as a cavernous ache grew within my chest.

Oleonis was everything the world should be. He was good and he cared more than anyone I had ever met. He saved me from myself time and time again. He never let me forget where I came from. He also never held it against me. He loved me in a raw and real way that I never deserved.

And that's when I knew. I could never walk away from his body. I would never stand on a pier and watch his funeral pyre. I'd never look into those feline eyes and be able to explain away my failure. Life with me would never fill the hole she would be left with at the loss of Oleonis.

If not for him, then I'd give my final drop for her. I mourned the life I would never have with Gaea. Tears fell for the fae I'd never save and the world that would suffer at the hands of the king. I mourned for the stable boy who would never again be given a thought in the middle of a freezing night. For Iva and Roe, who would never step foot into the room of a fae and be offered a simple game of chess. There was no question, there was not a single ounce of me that would hold back from trading my senseless existence for the life of a male who would bring her so much happiness.

I let my shaken hands slide from his still body to the polished floor and looked up, finally taking in the chaos in the hall, though it all moved in slow motion. The crowd had grown, but the sound was still mute to me.

Ragal held Gaea back by the waist as she screamed and pushed against him. Her eyes met mine, and she fell to the floor, knowing what my tears meant. "No, NOOO. Temir!" she yelled through the ringing in my ears, directly to my tattered soul.

294

I dropped my chin and put my hands back to his chest. I called forth that final bead of power. It caressed me, glowing with a powerful light as I called it forward with closed eyes and pushed, sending with it all my love to the only fae who should never die.

In my next breath, I was thrown from Oleo's broken body, still holding that final drop of magic. I looked up to see Thane's face inches from mine.

"Didn't you hear your king? He said stop."

I didn't hear the king; in fact, I hadn't realized he was there at all. "I can't hear anything above the screaming." I huffed, shoving him off of me though I was empty inside. I stood and faced first Gaea sobbing on the floor, and then turned to the king.

"Don't make me enchant you, Temir," he snarled. "That last drop is mine and no one else's. You cannot and will not save him. Go back to your bed."

He turned, enchanted the crowd to forget me, once again, and walked away, leaving Thane to guard the body. Not from the onlookers, but from me. I pulled myself to standing and looked to Gaea, but rather than acknowledge me, she simply spirited away and left me standing shattered in the castle full of blood and void of honor.

I couldn't go back to my rooms. I couldn't look at the bed and feel her absence and know I couldn't save him—not for me, not for her, not for anyone. I stormed off to the gardens. The only place I knew I'd feel him, even in his death.

I opened the door and stumbled as I took in the sight before me. I didn't know what had happened to Oleo, but he must have known his end was coming. I tried to catch my breath as I took in the room. We had just harvested the kingdom's last round of fruit and vegetables, so the last time I was here, only days before, it was fresh dirt, waiting to be seeded. Now, however, the entire room was filled to the brim with a flower I had never seen before. The cerulean blue flower's familiar scent encased the entire room, and the stalks stood from floor to ceiling and then cascaded back to the ground. The sight was staggering. Oleonis' final goodbye. He had created a flower he believed would complete the serum and set us free.

I moved to the ivy-covered wall, slid down it, tilted my head back and wept. Nothing in my life had been fair. I wasn't sure why I had expected fate to hand me anything different.

"To you, my little doe. May every day be only better than this one with you."

I had said those words to her. I could never take them back, and now looking back, I realized I spoke the greatest loss into existence. I buried my fingers into the dirt and begged and pleaded with the universe to take back this entire day. Though, only hours ago it felt like a lifetime when he said his final words to me. Did he know then?

"The sun will set on this day, whether you will it or not. It will rise tomorrow on a new day and you will once again start anew. The decisions you made in the past will not stop the sun or the moon or the stars from their dance across the sky. You must always move on, son. Hard as it may be."

He absolutely knew, and I was that much more devastated for it. I spent the night awake and mourning the loss of my mentor. Somewhere in the middle of it all, I grabbed a pair of sheers and began chopping down the overabundance of Oleonis' last gift. I snipped and hacked with fervor. I saved all the seeds I could in a pouch and lost myself in the work.

By the time the lazy sun had risen, the room was nothing but shredded leaves and piles of fertilized dirt. I walked to Oleonis' rooms, hoping to clear it of anything the king might have wanted to get his hands on, but two sentries stood outside of his doors. I walked right past them as if I hadn't noticed and continued on to my own rooms. I stood outside the closed door for several moments, knowing what I would feel when I entered. Not her, but the absence of her, and though I needed her now more than ever, I knew she wouldn't be there. By now, she was likely half a world away, lost in her own memories of the old fae she loved as much as I did, and I hated that I couldn't be there with her. But I couldn't save him, and I knew she would never forgive me for that.

Whatever had sparked and flowed through us after the ball was carried away with Oleo's death, and she would never look at me the same. I had failed her. Irrevocably.

CHAPTER

34

Ara

hree days later, I peeked from the window of my room as the Weaver welcomed Devi's minion into the shop. I held my breath and waited for the banging on my door that never came. Eventually, he left, and I made a mental check of step one.

I waited long into the afternoon. Perhaps I had overestimated Norst's desire for a monopoly in his disgusting trade business. I fiddled with the curtains and made the bed several times before resuming my father's infamous pacing. We only had a few hours left until I'd have to come up with a plan B.

A soft knock pulled me from my impatience.

I cracked the door open, and the Weaver held a tray for me. "I thought you'd like lunch while you waited."

I took the tray from her and set it on the bed. "How did the first meeting go?"

"Just as you thought. Devi doesn't want to wait any longer for you to accept the job. I told the messenger that you were gone and the rest of what you said to tell him. He seemed eager to get back to his boss."

"I bet he did. Norst seems to be taking his time. You'll need to be careful with the watcher that will likely come. Keep yourself removed from it. Only say what I told you. No emotion."

"I understand, but I can take care of myself." She bowed her head and slithered out.

I didn't doubt that. All of the pieces had to fall exactly where I had aligned them, or all hell would break loose. It probably would anyway, but at least I was trying for organized chaos.

By late afternoon, I had begun rethinking my steps, when finally, a watcher entered the quiet shop below. An empty feeling filled the pit of my stomach as I listened for any disturbance beneath me. I told the Weaver if she thought she was in danger to scream for me and I would come, but only silence filled the heavy tension in the air. I peeked through the dusty window and watched that familiar gray cloak move back down the crowded street.

Exhaling, I opened my door and walked down the creaking stairs. The snake portion of the Weaver's body was wound tighter than her coiled baskets, so I waited in the stairwell for her to calm herself. "What did he say?" I asked cautiously.

"The watchers are pigs," she answered, chin high.

"I've gathered that. Did he take the bait?" I picked up a heavy rope and moved my fingers down the coarse fibers as I waited for her answer.

"I believe he did, schemer. How long do you have, then?"

I looked out of the shop window, examining the vibrant sky. "Two hours at most."

"You'd better get moving. The cart is in the back."

I tossed the rope, scurried up the stairs two at a time, and grabbed every weapon I owned, my cloak and the discarded necklace from the counter. I headed out of the building, mounted the readied horse, and soared down the streets and out of Hythe, watching for the landmarks the naga had described, and, soon enough, I was in place.

The truth was, half of my plan was dependent on my buddy Blackhawk's omission. Either way, I was going to have to kill again today. Only the timing would determine how many fae.

I jumped from the horse and into the seemingly sealed cart in the back. I watched from the gap in the wooden slats as the sun kissed the horizon and, somewhere in the distance, my fae ears finally heard a sound. I wasn't sure who would arrive first, but so long as it wasn't everyone at the same time, I was ready. The Weaver had told me repeatedly how dangerous and foolish my plan was, and as I counted the twelve watchers storming toward me, weapons out, I knew she was right. Better the watchers first than Devi's males, though. They had a score to settle, but I supposed Norst did also.

"Is this it, then?" Norst shouted. "It doesn't look like a load of lesser fae to me."

"The naga said several fae would be guarding the cart until the lessers arrived. Then they were to transport them south to safety."

"Remind me again why we listened to the Weaver, a lesser fae?" he asked.

"Because, my lord, she only gave up the information to save her own life."

"Well, where are they, then?" he snapped.

"'Tis only sunset, my lord. The Weaver said midnight. Perhaps the cart is ready but our company has not yet arrived?"

"Obviously, our company has not arrived, you idiot," he spat. "If they see us standing here, they will run. Go hide yourselves."

It was messy, but it worked. The Weaver told me she would convince them, and miraculously, she had.

"Going somewhere with my cargo?" a familiar voice called in the distance.

"There's nothing here that belongs to you, Devi," Norst answered.

His guards moved into a tight line beside him as Devi and his larger group of minions approached. They pulled their swords and, as Devi stopped, several of his companions continued walking until they joined the watchers and faced back toward their former employer. The treacherous playing field now evenly matched. Approximately twenty-eight fae with weapons stood ready to fight.

"A little too convenient, don't you think?" Norst said, tilting his head to the side. "That we would both meet here, outside of town, on the word of a girl known for saving the lesser fae?"

"As far as I'm concerned, she did what I asked her to do," Devi answered, sweeping his long sword before him. "I want to get rid of you, and here you are, delivered on a silver platter. Perhaps after what you cost me, I should tip her."

"You're a fool, Devi."

"I know." He drew his sword.

And that was precisely when all hell broke loose.

I looked back and forth to my mother's necklace several times, wondering and waiting. The fae outside continued their blood bath while I remained inside the cart, waiting for the final moment. Would they come? I had given them three days, more than enough time on horseback. Did the queen have more trackers, or was it just the one, then? This was the only time I'd let myself test the power of that necklace. Eventually, the clash of metal and shouting grew quieter, and I peeked out again, just in time to see Devi shove his sword into Norst's chest and push him to the bloodied ground. Only five males remained standing.

"Come out, come out wherever you are," Devi called into the vacant night.

Again, I looked back to the discarded necklace. I really thought the queen's hunters would come to join the fray. At least now I knew. I slipped it over my head and put my hand up to shove open the cart door. I'd never taken on five at once. They may be tired and some injured, but five was still a lot. I'd rather fight them out in the open than cornered in a box, though. I stepped out and dropped two males with my throwing knives before Devi could finish whatever quip he had prepared for my arrival.

He lowered his chin and leveled his gaze to me. "Get her," he growled.

Two left. Only two males, then it was just him.

I reached for another knife and threw it.

The larger male on the right dodged and leaped for me. The impact knocked me back and my head slammed into the ground as the edges of the world began to fade while the smaller fae stepped in, kicking me in my stomach repeatedly. The larger fae slammed his fist into my face, and the sound of Devi's manic laughter was the last thing I heard before I passed out.

I was every bit the fool the Weaver had said I was.

The jostling of the tiny cart and crunching of pebbles below heavy wheels brought me back sometime later. I brought my hand to my head and winced. I heard a cheery, whistled tune from the driver up front, and could only imagine Devi having the time of his life up there. I seriously hated that fucker. From what I could tell, most of his entourage had either betrayed him, died or both, but onward he drove, not a care in the Gods damn world. I peeked one eyelid open and then another. I was alone in the cart. I guessed he was taking me back to town, which meant I had minutes to act or I'd have a much harder time escaping.

They had taken most of my weapons but hadn't accounted for the ones I'd strapped into the cart. I wouldn't be going far without getting my sword back, though. I took the blade out from below the cart bench and slipped it between the slats of wood, unlatching the hook. I kicked the door open, and complete shock registered on the faces of the two fae walking behind the cart.

I jumped at the smaller fae, tackling him to the ground, and jammed my knife into him, then snatched my sword back as I rolled away, keeping the larger one from grabbing me. I held my sword before me and moved my feet into the position my father had drilled into me as a child.

He ran at me, thinking the move from before would work twice. It didn't.

I heard Devi call the horse to halt, and I knew this was going from bad to worse.

I kept my eyes on the large fae until Devi came into view. He said nothing, only drawing his sword. He held his hand up for his guard to stand down, and he did so, reluctantly.

I swung my sword in a circle, loosening my grip.

"Aw, sweetie. And here I thought I'd live out all my fantasies tying you up at home. There's still time, you know."

"Hard pass."

He lunged for me.

I dipped to the side. My elbow connected with his crooked nose. His guard stepped forward, but again, he thrust an arm out. I didn't want to play. This wasn't a game, and even if I could beat Devi, I probably wasn't going to take down the behemoth behind him. I moved to the side and then back again as he tracked my deliberate steps. His eyes flicked to mine as I looked before I stepped. I knew that move. He thought he could read me. I looked left, stepped right and buried my sword into him. I shoved him forward and let him fall to the ground.

"No!" the other fae yelled, stomping toward me.

He pulled his own sword and swung. He was by far the stronger of us, and though I was likely quicker, I was sluggish from the earlier blow to the head. I kept up the best I could but took more hits than I would have liked. The vibration of his sword crashing into mine resonated through my entire body, and I slowed as I fell to a knee and pushed myself back to standing. I blocked him again, but again, I fell. I felt the final blow coming.

He rose above me and took a deep breath.

The fates had told me I was a savior, but they had gotten it wrong.

He lifted his great sword high above his head, blocking the moon from my view. I closed my eyes and waited, but it didn't come. Instead, there was a crash. I opened my eyes to see the Weaver in the distance lowering a weapon I had never seen before.

She moved through the grass like water rippling in a pond until she reached me. "You are an idiot." She grabbed me from under the arm and helped me to stand.

"I know," I grunted. I looked back to the fallen fae. "Is he dead?"

"Probably." She shrugged. "We've got bigger problems back in Hythe, though. We need to get back."

"I need to clean this first. Have you got anything to make a flame?" I asked, seeing my blood on the ground.

She handed me a flint from her satchel.

I made quick work of it and then we were off, moving as quickly as we could back to town, guided by the milky light of the full moon. When we got there, we didn't go back to her store. "What are we doing?"

"The shop has visitors."

My eyes enlarged in understanding, and she nodded. I brought my fingers to the necklace. "How long have they been there?"

"They showed up shortly after you left. I didn't let them in. I crawled out the back and came straight for you."

"Where are we now?" I asked, watching the buildings of the city pass us by.

"At the rebellion's meetinghouse."

"The rebellion?"

"You'll see." She moved off the cart and headed to the alleyway behind the run-down building she had parked beside. "Put your cloak hood up," she whispered.

I did as I was told, and she knocked three times on the door, paused and knocked two more times, then paused and knocked four.

A screen slid open and then shut again just before the metal door clicked a few times and she let herself in, beckoning me to follow. The old building was completely dark inside. As run down as it was, it was no surprise there was no lights. I had to put my hands out in front of me as we moved through shrouded darkness.

The soft tones of several voices echoed in the room ahead. "She is here," someone called.

"Can you see her?" another said.

"Move over."

"This is a terrible idea."

"How do we know it's her?"

The room gasped in unison as the Weaver crossed the threshold into the pale light.

I followed closely behind and kept my hood up.

"The rumors are true!" the Weaver called. "She is here. She is high fae, and if any of you move against her, you will answer to me. Is that understood?"

Several lesser fae nodded and some verbally agreed.

"You may lower your hood," she said, turning to me.

I didn't want to. I wanted to bolt out of that building and never look back. I knew what this was, and I couldn't be a part of it. But I already was, wasn't I? Accidently, I had joined the rebellion. I stepped forward and gently pulled my hood back. I knew my face looked atrocious. I'd been beaten to a pulp and knocked out only hours before.

"Is it her?" they whispered.

"It's her!" someone shouted from the back. The brave young fae that first fled the cages moved to the front of the stunned room. "This is the high fae that freed us that night."

"I thought you were going south," I said, still studying the faces in the room as they watched me.

"I am," he answered.

"Have a seat, Wilo," the Weaver instructed.

His back stiffened and he backed into the crowd.

Her story was far longer than I had given her credit for.

"Did you really kill a high fae?" someone asked from the back of the room.

"Please, if you would all wait just a moment." The Weaver slid toward me and leaned in. "Tell them only what you wish them to know. You do not have to answer their questions."

"Why did you bring me here?"

"Because they needed to see you, just as you needed to see them." She turned to the crowd of lesser fae. "We are the oppressed. We are the shunned. We are the murdered, and the beaten, and the raped. We are the abandoned. We are the fae's rebellion. The Marsh Court used to be safe, but King Coro does nothing as the poisonous hatred grows like invasive weeds. The Wind Court has always placed us as servants and nothing more. The Sea Court waters are filled with the blood of our brothers and the Flame Court remains the only sanctuary left. But we cannot all flee to the south. These are our homes. This is where our families are. This is where we belong, and we have the right to be here."

"And what do you want from me?" I asked.

"You are rare. The rebellion has followed your story: first with the death of the high fae in Erast, then the justice of Rodalf, and now we have you to thank for freeing thirty-two fae and for the death of Devi." She paused, letting the news spread over the room. "And Norst, and every one of his watchers."

"But you must know I didn't do any of that alone. I never planned for any of that to happen until there was no choice but the right one."

"And that is why you are here. We ask nothing of you. The rebellion is recruiting across all kingdoms of Alewyn. The rebels of Hythe are small in number, but we are indebted to you all the same. You will stay the night here and regain your strength, and tomorrow we will deal with the trouble at the shop."

A lofty fae with branches for arms came into the dark room and whispered something to her. She nodded and turned back to me. "The queen's sea fae remain in the store. We have eyes on them."

I paused, realizing the enormity of that statement. The key players on the board had always been the royal families. Everything was changing.

"What is your name?" someone called.

Instantly, the Weaver coiled and snapped in the direction of the question. "You will not ask that of her. In ancient times, there was power in names. Just as you do not know my name, you will not know hers. Now you must all go back to your homes. In pairs out the back door. The watchers are gone, but the danger is not. Go with caution."

I stood in awe of her and her extraordinary command of the room as it emptied. I had absolutely no idea Alewyn had a growing rebellion, and that only spoke to their leader's secrets, whoever they were, and the fae who kept them. This changed everything and nothing at the same time. At least I knew in my journey to fulfill my destiny, I was not alone. Even though, when the time came, I probably would be.

She led me to a tiny room with a plain mattress tossed on the floor, handed me a blanket and left without saying another word, which I appreciated. I needed a silent moment to process everything from the entire day. And I still had to figure out what I was going to do about the sea fae squatting in the Weaver's store. It hadn't gone to plan for sure. I thought if there were still fae tracking me, they would show up to where I was in that moment, I hadn't guessed that when they had to travel so far, they wouldn't have a precise location. They would only be able to track me to where the magic or whatever they used was strongest. And likely, where I hid above the Weaver's shop for days drew them right there. Obviously, they stayed, waiting for me to return.

The next morning, we stood across the quiet street, watching through broken glass panels as her wares laid about the ransacked store. I had tossed and turned all night on the broken springs of the borrowed mattress. I wanted to complain, but seeing the devastation of her lifelong work, I kept my thoughts to myself.

"There are only two inside," she said.

"Do we know if any more have been seen? There were four in Rocsbrew, and I killed one of them." Her mouth fell open, and I smiled. "Your rebellion doesn't know everything, Weaver."

She only smiled back and tilted her head toward her shop. "Five coins say I can take that one out from here."

"I've got six that says I can take the guy in the back before you can hit the guy in the front." I pulled my final throwing knife from my belt, and we exchanged grins. I dipped my knife into the opaque jar she held.

"Deal." She laughed. In unison we moved, dropping the sea fae before they knew what hit them.

Naga venom, who knew?

CHAPTER 35

Temir

I stood on the swaying dock, alone and cold, watching Oleonis' funeral pyre drift down the turbulent river and out into the open sea. Color had been drained from the world as an icy fog settled low to the ground, the thick air matching the sharpened lump in my throat and the unrelenting tension in my chest. My entire body trembled, but I would not let anyone see my shameful tears.

She hadn't come. I hadn't seen her in three days. I'd heard she was drowning herself in wine and tears. I didn't know how to reach her. I couldn't knock on her door. I couldn't look into her face and know what to say. Instead, I gave her space and time, oceans of it. I'd never felt so alone in my life, not even as a boy when I had absolutely no one. I'd had Oleo's wisdom at my fingertips for so long, I didn't know what to do without him.

The icy wind pelted me and snow stuck to my lashes. Only King Autus had been there, along with a few castle servants, to handle the pyre. He recited the funeral poem, lit the fire, and walked away before it was even pushed into the water. He didn't look at me as he passed. I mourned alone, and I would forever do so, the weight of my broken heart a million pounds.

"Temir?" a small voice called from behind me.

I turned to see silvery blonde hair and piercing blue eyes staring up at me sadly. "What in the gods' names are you doing out of the barn? They will kill you."

"I know and I don't care." He slipped his small hand into mine and stood beside me, silently watching the flames drift into the distance.

I faced the water, hiding the tear that rolled down my cheek, and he squeezed my fingers in solidarity. I stood there with that boy until the pyre was long gone and the tears had frozen. He sniffled occasionally, but otherwise only offered me his presence. A boy with more understanding and compassion than an entire kingdom. I watched the wind blow through his hair as he stood tall, observing the curious waves in the tousled water as he remained beside me. My heart caved as I realized the first time this boy had ever seen the river was as it carried away one of the last good fae.

I put myself in the boy's shoes and realized he was already stronger than I'd ever be. I would have never dreamed of leaving the stable. The beginning of my life started in that barn. I thought back to the times I'd been beaten for not completing a task on time. I thought of the days I would go without meals. I remembered sharing the water with the horses because I was only allowed a small sip sometimes. I thought about the boy's fragile fingers in mine and remembered the belly aches from eating the horse's dried oats.

Then, I remembered the day I was pulled from the barn and thrust into Oleo's hands. And Oleonis, rather than scowling, complaining or mistreating me, embraced me. It was the first hug of my life. I remembered the protection he provided me. He took in a half-starved, wild boy and loved him anyway. Flawed as I was, he still smiled when we talked and laughed as I grew. Oleonis was always so much more than a high fae. He was the best father and mentor anyone would ever have. And he was taken from me.

And then it hit me. It slammed into me like the weight of a thousand books. I was to the boy what Oleonis had been to me. That's when I knew the fractured world had to change. It wasn't for me, it wasn't for Gaea or my love for her, it was for him. The child who would suffer a lifetime if someone didn't do something about it. I knew what my first step had to be. I knelt down and pulled him into my open arms.

He squirmed, just as I had when Oleo hugged me. "What are you doing?"

"It's a hug. Come, boy. You'll catch your death in this cold."

He said nothing, only sidled up next to me as we traipsed back to the barn, leaving a trail of footprints in the crisp snow.

"Where exactly have you been, you little maggot?" Master Marte demanded.

I held my hand up to stop him. "He was with me. I needed some help and thought he was right for the job."

"Well, I don't give a damn what you wanted. He is not to leave the barn, and you should know that more than anyone."

"Yes, Marte, I do."

"Get in here before I chop your ears off, boy."

He left my side and ran into the barn. Marte grabbed the whip from the tack board.

"I don't think so." I snatched it from his hands.

"Don't even think about telling me how to run this stable, Temir. That boy is mine to do with as I please, and he broke the rules. Now he will be punished."

Before I even realized what I was doing, I snapped the leather whip across Marte's hardened face.

"What in the . . . ?" He staggered back and brought his fingers to his broken skin. Bright red blood poured down his face.

"That boy is a *child*. A *rare* fae. From this point forward, you will do better, Marte, or I will kill you myself. You will light that gods damn wood stove and keep it lit so that he may be warm. You will feed him twice a day and three times every holiday. You will offer him new clothing that fits, and you will let him leave this barn or so help me, I'll burn this fucking building to the ground. And do you think for one minute the king will care? Do you think he will listen to you over me? I am his prized possession, and you are a thorn in his backside. He hates the way you complain about every single thing that happens around here. You're lucky you still have a job, and I'm done playing this game with you. You haunt my childhood memories. You let me suffer. You will not do the same to him or any boy that follows." I wrapped the whip around my hand. "Understood?"

"Y-yes my lord." He shook.

"Now, get him a proper meal, coat, and more blankets."

"Yes, my lord."

I stormed away, taking that damn whip with me. I'd had enough. I had sat back and warned Oleonis, but never took any actions to save him until the last moment. I'd never do that again. He believed in me, she believed in me, so maybe it was time to start believing in myself. I tossed and turned in my bed that night as a roaring fire was lit within me.

***

The next day, I slaved away in my solar, perfecting the extract from Oleonis' flower. He'd made an entire harvest of the plant, and if it didn't work, I wasn't sure what I'd do next. The day was long and tedious, but by the end, I had more than enough for several vials of the serum.

Later, I sat across the chessboard from Iva and Roe.

"You're sure it's okay, milord?" Roe asked for the hundredth time.

"The funeral was only yesterday, Temir. We can come back another time," Iva added.

"I'm sure. I could use the company," I said, trying to remain calm. I hated what I was about to do, but it was the best option I had. I only hoped they'd forgive me. "Ale today, Roe?" I held a full glass out toward him.

"Oh yes, milord. Been a long week indeed." He finished the glass in one gulp, and I guiltily handed Iva her glass of wine.

She sipped on hers, and I waited. Watched. They seemed normal so far.

"How was the funeral then?"

"Roe!" Iva gasped, slapping him on the arm.

"It's fine. The funeral was just that. A funeral."

"I've always hated them myself," he said, standing to refill his glass. "They only have them for high fae, you know. Us lessers aren't worth a pile of sticks and a spark."

"Roe!" Iva shouted. "What in Alewyn has gotten into you?"

"Oh Iva, you know it's true. They'd sooner dig a hole and toss us all away like the garbage we take out."

I had to believe it was working, but I needed to be sure. I had to ask him the one question that had been burning in my mind. "When did you join the rebellion, Roe?"

They both jerked, and I simply sat, waiting for my answer.

"Months ago, milord." He covered his mouth with his hands and looked to Iva. "I don't—I'm not sure why I said that," he told her.

"How did you know?" she asked.

"Roe's all but spelled it out to me the last few times we've spoken. The recruiters, the elixirs for his ill mother, his odd behavior, loose tongue. I could go on. When do you meet next?" I asked, my face neutral and voice bland. I didn't want to alarm him, only collect answers.

"There's a meeting in two weeks," he whispered.

"Where?" I asked, setting up the chess board.

"In the tunnels," Iva said.

"The castle tunnels? Those haven't been used in ages."

"They have, milord," Roe said, turning red.

"So, the rebellion meets right under the king's nose, and he has no idea?"

"He doesn't," he bit out.

"What is happening?" Iva asked.

"I hope one day you will both forgive me. I've created a serum that forces the truth. Oleonis helped me." The impact of saying his name out loud still hollowed me.

"But I thought we were friends," Iva whispered, tears rolling down her powdered cheeks.

"We are still friends, Iva. Your secret is safe with me. I assure you."

"Why didn't you just ask us, Temir?" She sniffled.

I stood and began to pace. "I had to know it was working without giving any preface. I apologize to you both. You're my only friends, and I didn't want to punch someone like the last time."

"We're your only friends?" Iva asked.

"Of course you are." I stopped, facing her. "As you will continue to be?"

"Aye, milord. We are," Roe answered. "And now you know about the rebellion."

"Is that everything, then?" I sat back down in my chair and looked at nothing.

"It is," Iva confirmed.

"I read a lot. History would prove that a rebellion was imminent. Still, I didn't know for sure until today." I didn't look at them. Only watched the potential future play out a thousand different ways in my muddled mind. It hardly ever worked out for a rebellion. "I have to go," I said, standing. "Stay as long as you'd like. There's more ale in the cabinet, Roe. Drink the red vial on the table to null the serum." I stormed out of my rooms and down the hall, weaving my way through the castle, and made it to Gaea's door before I'd even thought about what I should say.

I knocked.

"Go away," she slurred.

Good, at least she was here.

"We need to talk," I said.

She was silent for a long time, and just when I thought she wouldn't answer at all, I heard the lock click on the opposite side of the door, and she pulled it open. She walked back into her rooms and I followed her, shutting the door behind me.

We stood there, studying each other for minutes.

I had so much to say, but nothing came to me. "I'm sorry," I said, watching those eyes.

She didn't respond, only watched me, swaying.

"Can we sit?" I asked. I knew she'd been drinking. I just didn't know if she'd been eating or sleeping.

She turned and slowly lowered herself to the couch. I sat in the chair across from her, watching the tears well up in her eyes as she held me in her gaze. "I didn't think I had any tears left," she said, wiping them off her cheeks.

"Gaea, he wouldn't—"

"Stop!" she snapped, eyes burning. "Don't come in here and look at me like that, Temir. I'll never move on. My heart will never mend. I'll never look at you and not see him." She paused, taking in a deep shaky breath. "It may have been Oleonis that died, but he took everything good in me with him. He took every good thing this world has ever created with him. Don't sit here and wonder when I'll get over it. I never will, and if you can, well, then you never loved the male that raised us as much as he deserved. He deserved better than you, better than me. Hell, he deserved better than anything in this whole fucking prison. But then we never deserved him, either, so at least that was fair." She broke down entirely, laying on the deep cushions of her upholstered couch and sobbing into the pillow.

Her words hurt me, but I think they hurt her more. I crossed the room and kneeled beside her, rubbing her back as she cried, wishing I could heal the emotional wounds as easily as the physical ones. "We can leave," I whispered. "We can go away from all of this."

"We can never leave, Temir," she scolded me. "It's all just a fucking cat and mouse game to him. You know he killed him. If not by his own hands, then by demand. Do you think that fae in the ballroom was a coincidence? He knew he needed to drain you enough that you couldn't save Oleo. And he wanted to show you off to that ugly bitch, knowing he couldn't enchant you from her mind. You're a part of his twisted game, and we're stuck here with that repulsive monster, and there's nothing either of us can do about it."

"Gaea, please."

"Just go, Temir. Go back to your perfect world and keep playing the loyal servant. I don't want to see you right now. I thought I did, but I just can't do it."

I stood, stricken, and walked out.

CHAPTER

36

Ara

*O*nce upon a time, in another world, in another lifetime, those with magic were called the Theondaras. In that world, the Theondaras were hunted like wild animals. The inhabitants believed magic came from the darkness of one's soul. The darker the soul, the greater the gift of magic. Reign was a Theondara tasked with hiding within the ranks of the hunters' military. A lowly foot soldier with a deadly secret.

As her magic grew more and more powerful, she found it harder and harder to keep hidden, buried deep within the enemies' borders. She had grown knowing the Theondaras to be a cunning and ruthless sort, and she struggled to keep her need for the blood of her enemies at bay.

Until, one day, she realized she could do more than report to the coven leaders. She carefully planned and schemed to turn the hunters' heads while she escorted a lost Theondara across their camp. Word spread among the Theondara that she could deceive the hunters right under their noses. Slowly, she built a life balancing the duties of her job as a foot soldier and the dangerous game of saving her sisters, one deception at a time.

Eventually, she was called to a meeting of the coven leaders. A very rare occurrence among the Theondara. But rather than honoring her and her daily sacrifices, they shamed her and cast her out, claiming she had grown too close to the enemies. With nowhere to go and no reason to return to where she had come from, she went to her home from centuries past, before she knew she was a Theondara, before she slipped into the ranks of the hunters, before she knew she had a greater purpose in life.

She chose not to be complacent. Helping the occasional Theondara was not enough for her. As her magic grew, so did her desire to save not one, not two, but all the Theondaras. They had cast her away, but she never stopped believing in them, in herself. Doing small things for the good of a few was the easier choice but choosing to do great things with immense personal sacrifice for the good of all was how Reign eventually conquered the world.

I laid on my bed above the Weaver's store sorting through the scattered memories of my beloved parents and their colorful stories embedded in my mind for life lessons. The simple knowledge of the rebellion changed more for me than it probably should have. Reign was always one of my favorite heroines as a child. My mother told me many, many stories of her and her life, and now I understood why. I couldn't continue this way. I needed to do things on a grander scale or not at all. But unlike Reign, I needed to be selfish first.

I never wanted to be a vigilante. My goal was always to find the second half of my prophecy. The only way to move forward, whether it pushed me toward a fate I detested or not, was to find a way inside the castle library and obtain the mysterious book about Nealla.

I know that's what Aibell was trying to tell me. The bedtime story I was told of Aibell was only a version of the truth, and I could only hope that Nealla's real story would be the same. Because my deepest, most frantic desire had nothing to do with lesser fae or high fae. It wasn't about finding love or saving a broken world. I wanted her to tell me that they had gotten it wrong. That I was not a savior. I was not chosen. For I

318

certainly didn't feel chosen. Guided and trained by my parents, yes. But not chosen.

It was that simple, and yet not simple at all. To have a prophecy as a fae was a great honor. But I still wondered how this prophecy came to light, and why my parents accepted it as truth. Did they know it was only half?

As I laid there, I realized my list of questions outnumbered the list of answers, and the only way to change that was to seek out Nealla and hope like hell I didn't die in the process.

"I hope you can understand why I have to go," I said to the Weaver sometime later.

"If ever you need help, look for this symbol and tell them the Weaver sent you." She handed me the ripped corner of a piece of wrinkled paper with a phoenix emblem drawn into it.

I put it in my pocket, thanked her and left Hythe. I liked her. We were similar in so many ways. My heart recognized the fire in hers, and I hoped I would see her again. One day.

If the weather remained decent and if I didn't stop, except to sleep and find food, the trip would take nine days. I did stop, though. Because I'd never be strong enough to travel past my home, ashes it may be, and keep my eyes forward. I'd gathered wildflowers as I walked and dropped them on dead soil where a beautiful, large cottage once stood. I thought maybe, when I stood there, I would feel them close to me, but nothing had changed. My parents were gone, and I had to move on.

I reached Hrundel on day ten of traveling. I avoided all the towns along the way. I only had the beginnings of a plan to get into the castle, but I knew the first thing I needed to do was find an ally. And since I really only knew one person who lived in Hrundel, I reluctantly made my way through the maze of buildings to the seamstress's shop.

"Eeeeeeeeeek! Ara, my darling, how are you?" Nadra bounded up to me as I entered.

It was strange to finally hear my real name again. I'd also forgotten how much energy Nadra had. She filled the entire room with it. I wanted to smile. I wanted to hug her back. But as I stood there, arms down while she squeezed the breath from me, I realized that I was really just so, so tired, and the lemons in my life weren't turning themselves into lemonade anytime soon.

"Hey, Nadra," I managed.

"How's it going, girl? It's been ages. Oh my goodness, you poor thing. I heard about your parents. Are you okay? Do you want some lunch? Good gods, Ara, why do you smell like a pig pen?" She scrunched her freckled face and took a step back.

Sometimes not having a bath was a blessing, I guess.

"It's been a rough couple of months, Nadra. How are you?"

"Same as ever." She grabbed my hand and pulled me through her mother's shop, stepping over yards of discarded fabric, took a jar full of buttons from a chair and tossed it to the side like it was nothing, gesturing for me to sit. "So, what's going on?" She leaned forward, forgetting to blink.

"Well . . ." I took a deep breath. "I need to get into the castle. Specifically, the library."

She shook her head, her curls shuddering with the movement, and clicked her tongue against her teeth. "No can do. The king has shut out all visitors who aren't members of his court. I don't know if you've heard, but apparently, the lesser fae are, like, dangerous or something."

"Nadra, don't say that. The lesser fae are no more dangerous than the high fae. You know that."

She didn't respond. Instead, she reached to the side and picked up a loose spool of thread and began winding it tight again.

"Listen, even if I could get into the castle, I can't wear this," I said, patting my leg and letting the dust float in the air.

"Seriously gross," Nadra responded. "I'm sure I can get my mother to work something out with you. See that gown over there?" She pointed to a curvaceous mannequin in the corner wearing a sheer fabric with tiny emblems of lace sewn in. "That gown will make any fae who wears it instantly beautiful. And that one?" She pointed to another mannequin. "That coat can make you sing like a canary with perfect pitch."

"Are you telling me your mother has magic?" I breathed.

"Mmhmm. Didn't you know?" she asked, tilting her head to the side.

"No. No, I hadn't realized."

"She makes special things for King Coro sometimes. One time," she said, leaning in to whisper, "Mother crafted him a wristband that made him a better lover." She wiggled her eyebrows at me, and I couldn't help but laugh. "Shall I get her for you?" she asked.

"Would you mind?"

"No. I'm not sure what she'll agree to make for you, but it doesn't hurt to ask. Be right back." She hopped out of her chair and flitted up the narrow stairs.

I stood and fidgeted with the feathered hem of an unfinished gown. I was standing in the messiest store I'd ever seen. Nadra's mom was wildly successful, but equally eccentric, and clearly didn't care for tidiness. As I waited for them to come down the stairs, I cleared a path on the floor, before I realized what I was doing. I stacked bolts of fabric on top of each other and picked up the buttons scattered across the floor.

"Shall I wait a little longer, dear? Another five minutes and you'll have the place sparkling like new."

I sat the jar on the table and faced her. "I'd probably need closer to twenty," I answered.

She laughed, cascading down the stairs in her ruffled dress like she was swimming on top of water, the folds of her gown flowing behind her.

"It's lovely to see you, Ara." She grabbed me by my arms and planted a kiss on each of my cheeks while I tried to remember her name.

I wasn't sure I'd ever really met Nadra's mother. Possibly in passing, but you'd think we were longtime friends by her intimate reaction. I suddenly remembered why I didn't like people. At all. But she had been a friend of my father's.

"Nadra tells me you are in need of clothes." She looked me up and down. "I see she wasn't mistaken."

I'd never been shy, but I felt naked before her, and the need to cross my arms, hiding myself, burned in me. I was embarrassed. "These are the best I've got, and I need to get into the castle."

"On invitation or otherwise?" she asked.

"Otherwise," I answered, not meeting her gaze.

"I see. And do you have means of payment, Ara?"

"I've got a little bit of coin if you could just provide me a clean shirt and pants. Or launder the extra set I have."

"Oh no, no dear. You'll never make it into the castle in simple leathers. You'll need something far grander."

"I only have a few coins left," I answered.

"No problem, dear. I've got a different type of payment in mind. Go to that shelf there and grab the blue fabric from the middle of the stack."

I wiped my dirty hands on my filthy pants before lifting the silky fabric she requested. I handed the bolt to her and waited.

She lifted it high into the air and examined it as if she had never seen it before. "I've woven my magic into this fabric. Can you see it in the light, dear?"

The word magic heightened all my senses, and while every fiber of my being wanted to ask her about her magic, I chose not to raise any unnecessary questions, and kept my mouth shut.

"It's just there," she said, pointing to a glimmering section.

"I see it."

"Can you guess what that fabric does?"

"No."

"It has the ability to make the wearer vanish as long as they are not physically touched."

I sucked in a sharp breath as she locked eyes with mine. "This will do."

She set the fabric down on top of a pile of other fabrics. "I'll make a deal with you, Ara. I will create the gown you desire. I will help you get into the castle. On one condition."

"Yes?"

"I don't want your coins. My daughter is in love with a married male. She thinks I do not know it, but how could I not? If you agree to use whatever means necessary to separate them for good, then I am in your debt until the gown is finished."

"How would I even do that?"

"That is now your problem to solve. It is time for my daughter to find her mate, if she should be so blessed, and marry. Do we have a deal?"

What choice did I have really? "It's a deal," I said more hesitantly than I'd wanted.

"You may stay here in the shop if you'd like." She started shuffling through her scattered coils of yarn.

"No," I accidentally shouted. And then more softly, said, "No, thank you. I've already made plans at the inn just down the road." I hadn't, but I'd figure that out later.

"I see," she said. "Well, at least take a bath before you go back out in public. You smell horrid. Have Nadra find you something more decent to wear. Nadra!" she called.

"Yes, Mother?" she answered from the top of the stairs.

"Ara will not be staying, but please start a bath for her. And get out the good oils and hair balms. She's going to need them. All of them."

37

Temir

I sat in the stuffy air of the council meeting room letting the dread melt over me like molten lava. I knew what was to come, the official announcement of Oleonis' death. She was there, sitting across from me, her strained eyes glued to the polished floor. We waited only for the king.

Beside me, Ragal thrummed his hands along the tabletop, while next to him, Thane picked at his nails with a knife. Tension filled the room, sucking the air out. I shook my leg impatiently as we waited. This day, of all days, the king would choose to keep us waiting, knowing how much it would hurt us to sit here next to that empty chair and remain silent.

Eadas whistled as he shuffled through the stack of papers beside him, and I'd never wanted to cram a knife down someone's cheery throat so badly. I let myself look at her for only a second. Her head stayed down, and she began to rock back and forth, measuring her breathing. I hated that I couldn't save her from this. I hated that she didn't have a choice and would have to sit through this reminder of what happened.

We sat there for over an hour before the king stormed in. At that point, the tension had grown so great, it was palpable. He threw his fur over the back of his chair and plopped down, swinging his feet up onto the table. His nonchalance would have bothered me more had he not crumbled Eadas's stupid papers in the process.

"I'm sure by now you all know why we are here." He snapped his fingers, and two lesser fae skittered into the room, bowing. He pointed at the empty chair.

They each grabbed a side of it and let the damn thing screech across the entire damn floor as they dragged it out in the most unceremonious way possible. I looked to Gaea again, and our eyes locked for an eternity, and yet half of a second. Again, she looked to the floor.

"It saddens me to officially announce the unfortunate passing of our beloved Oleonis," the king announced in a flat and unemotional voice.

"For shit's sake, the guy grew plants. Who cares?" Thane said.

Ragal and I shared a glance. This silence filled the air before Gaea snapped and flew across the barrier of the ancient table, screaming to the heavens. Her arms flew wildly and she connected with Thane's face several times. "Don't you dare talk about him. Don't even say his name, you bastard. I'll kill you! Do you hear me? I'll fucking kill you."

Ragal and I were out of our seats, and he pulled Thane back and grabbed the knife from his hands, while I rounded the table and wrapped my arms around Gaea's waist.

"Don't you touch me, Temir. Don't fucking touch me!" she screamed.

"Get her the hell out of here, Temir," the king demanded.

I hauled her toward the door. Her arms and legs kicked wildly, but still, I managed. "Take us to the beach, Gaea. Take us to the beach."

She pushed against me, but I held on to her. I pushed her back against the wall and grabbed her wrists lifting them above her head. Our noses were inches apart.

"Let me go, Temir," she hissed.

"No." She was broken. Absolutely broken and I couldn't save her. I could hear the heartache behind her rage. The devastation. When she'd flown across the table, she embodied everything I'd loved about her. The passion and the fire. If I could take it away, even for a moment so she could take a single full breath from her own despair, I would.

"I can't use my magic. I won't."

"You have to. We need to get out of here right now. Do you think the king is going to let that go? Do you think he isn't going to have a problem with your devotion to Oleo? Take us, now."

"I don't give a shit what that monster thinks," she growled.

"You have to get us out of here before that meeting ends. Either I'm dragging you to my rooms, or you're taking us somewhere safe, but we are leaving. Right now."

Her eyes shifted between mine. Somewhere, deep within her, she knew I was right. "Fine," she agreed, and then we were gone.

The moment the soggy sand was below me, I let go and took a few steps back. She stormed away. I stood still, watching her. Giving her the space to process whatever she needed to. She paused, watching the white-capped waves crash into the jagged cliffs along the foreign island for what felt like hours. The angry winds flew through her long hair as if she orchestrated the weather to match her grief-stricken mood. Then, she crumbled to the ground and hopelessly sobbed. My heart cracked.

She wanted to be strong. To be angry and rage. But beneath that, when it came to him, she was just a child, rescued by an old fae with a giant heart and I knew the thought of living an eternity without him shredded her to pieces. I knew because I felt exactly the same.

I took a step toward her and froze. She didn't want me there. She didn't want me to touch her. She didn't even want to look at me. I sat on the beach, turning my back to her so I didn't have to watch her cry. I just couldn't. Her sorrow consumed her, and I could do nothing but wait. The sun moved across the sky and the temperature dropped with it. What was once an airy gust off the turbulent ocean was now a cold, wet chill.

"Temir?" Her voice was raw.

I looked to her, and then back to the ocean. I had no idea what I could even say to her.

"I'm sorry," she said, sitting beside me in the cold, damp sand. She laid her head on my shoulder.

I took a deep breath. I knew we were scarred beyond repair, but I didn't know what that meant for either of us. "What can I do?" I asked gently.

"There's nothing anyone can do."

I nodded. "I'm sorry your heart hurts."

She drew in a shaking breath. "What do you think the king will do when we go back?"

"He will only watch you closer, Gaea. You'll just have to keep your guard up. If he thought Oleonis was hiding something, he'll probably think you are now. And you know Thane isn't going to let that go."

"I hope he doesn't," she answered fiercely.

"I know you don't want to run away now. I know you're scared. But there's something I've been waiting to tell you."

"What?" she asked.

I reached into my pocket and pulled out the flower, holding it out to her. "It was Oleo's final gift to us."

She reached out and took the delicate petals into her slender hands. A fresh tear streamed down her face as she brought the tiny flower to her nose and breathed it in. "Why does it smell like him?" Her voice broke, and as she tried to hold it in, her chin quivered.

"I think he knew, Gaea. I think he had a vision and knew he was going to die, so he did the last thing he could do to try to free us."

"But why didn't he tell us?" she cried.

"I don't think it would have changed anything," I answered.

She twirled the little blue flower in her fingers and then held it up to the moonlight. "What should we call the flower, Tem?"

I shrugged. "I don't know. Why don't you name it," I said, nudging her with my shoulder.

"Let's call it leo. After him."

"Are you sure?"

She smiled and smelled the flower again, closing her eyes as a light breath shuddered through her slender frame. "I'm sure."

"Are you cold?" I wrapped my arms around her.

"I'm not ready, Temir. My heart is not ready."

"I know. When you are ready, Gaea. I'll be here."

"I know," she answered.

"Should we go back now?"

She lifted a shoulder and let the smile fade from her beautiful face. "Now or never."

"I wish never was a real option," I said, standing up. I held my hand out to her and pulled her to her feet. She shook off the dampened sand with one hand and held tight to mine with the other.

At this point, it was the little things. Small pieces of normalcy that showed me she was still in there somewhere.

We spirited back to the castle and stood outside of my rooms. I tried not to let it bother me that she didn't take me inside. That she didn't want to be in my rooms. I knew she regretted our night together. She thought she could have saved him if she wasn't with me. I just never realized everything about me would push her away.

She was gone without saying goodbye, and that stung. Instead of going in, I made my way back down to the lists. Making sure Thane was nowhere to be found, probably still reeling from Gaea's attack, I grabbed a bow and began shooting. I was always terrible at archery, but there was only one way to improve, and that wasn't by sitting around sulking. For hours I practiced, building painful blisters and ignoring them. Letting one pain attempt to replace the other.

As soon as I couldn't pull on that string one more time, I placed the worn bow back onto the heavy rack, picked up a practice sword and swung it at the training dummy as it rocked on its shoddy wooden stand. I started with the perfect technique. I watched my footing closely and jabbed and aimed. Eventually, I stopped caring about perfection and just swung harder and harder, until I didn't care about the swing and just continued to jam my sword into the dummy over and over and over again. I pictured Thane's face—strike. The king's face—strike. Her tears—strike. Her wails—strike. Oleonis' crimson blood pooled on the castle floor—strike, strike, strike.

I fell to the cold, muddy ground, covered in sludge, and threw the damn sword away, heaving. Sweat dripped down my face like heavy raindrops. I didn't care. I stood up, lifted the dummy, and tossed it across the empty yard. I hated everyone. Everything. It was all broken. I stormed across the yard and told myself I wouldn't look up to her window. I wouldn't ache to see her. But then I did it anyway, and she was there. Watching me. My steps faltered for only a moment, and then I dropped my gaze and stomped back to my tainted rooms. Within minutes someone was knocking.

"Mother above, leave me alone!" I hollered.

"It's me, milord," Roe called.

I didn't care if it was the king himself, but Roe had never come to my rooms out of schedule, which probably meant something was wrong. I thrust the door open and stared down at him. I was fuming. It wasn't his fault, but the anger had settled into my bones. "Yes?"

"S-sorry, milord. Shall I come back?" He pulled the hat from his head and wrung it in his hands.

"What? No," I said more softly. "Come in, Roe. I'm sorry. It's been a long day."

"Thank you," he answered, shuffling in.

"Ale?"

"Got anything stronger?"

"I do, and I think I'll join you." I poured the dark brown liquor into two shallow glasses and shoved some books to the crowded floor so we could sit on the couch.

"Iva would be more than happy to clean the rooms for you, Tem."

"It wouldn't change anything," I mumbled.

"I'm sorry?" he asked, bringing his ear closer to me.

"It's nothing, Roe." I sipped my drink. "What can I help you with?"

"Well, they sent me, milord," he answered.

"Who did?"

"The rebellion, Tem. They got eyes everywhere, see. And they saw you in the lists just now. They said I was supposed to ask you to come to the next meeting."

"Trust me, Roe. They didn't see anything worthy of recruiting happening out there."

"I know," he said with a wide smile. "But you were madder 'n a makara and they said that had to count for something. Will you come, milord?"

"I can't join your rebellion, Roe. I promised I would keep it a secret and I will. But I can't. It will only draw more attention to them. I can't explain it, you just have to trust me." My voice was flat as I leaned back in my chair and stared out the frosted window.

"You could just come to a meeting and hear what they have to say? Then decide."

"I'll think about it, but that's the best I can offer."

"I'll take it," he said, throwing his drink back.

I did the same and let the burn consume me. I'd prefer anything over the throbbing ache in my chest. "Game of chess?" I offered.

"I can't stay. I've got to find Iva. Let me know if you change your mind."

He left the room and I stood, stretching. Again, a knock on the door. I thought it was Roe, forgetting something, so I pulled the door open. My jaw dropped.

"May I come in?" Gaea stood small, flashing me a smile that didn't reach her eyes.

"Are . . . are you sure?" I asked, taking a step back.

"I need to know something," she said.

I stepped to the side, and she walked carefully into my rooms. I watched as she stopped moving. Stopped breathing. I circled her to find her eyes were squeezed shut and a tear had already fallen.

She held up a hand. "Just give me a moment, Temir." She looked toward the bedroom and turned away.

I wanted so badly to believe it was because that's where she was when she heard Ragal at the door, and it had nothing to do with what we had been doing while Oleo was murdered. She slowly opened her eyes and swallowed.

"I need to know the truth. I want to know what the king has enchanted away from my memories. If you have the flowers, then you have the serum, right?"

I nodded.

"Have you tested it? Does it work?" she asked, her voice strained.

Again, I nodded.

"To your study, then?" She looked between me and the bedroom door several times, twisting the metal ring on her finger. She would have to walk through the memory-filled bedroom to get to the study.

"I can bring it out here, Gaea. You can wait on the couch."

"No," she said firmly. "It's just a doorway." She straightened her back and walked through, not looking toward the bathing room, keeping a space between her and the bed.

I had to remind myself it wasn't personal. She was hurting, and though it was probably misdirected, who was I to judge? I'd had my moment out in the lists. She only needed time. She deserved that time.

We sat in my study, me behind the desk and her in front of it. I had a bouquet of the leo flowers sitting on the desk, and the room was filled with his scent.

She buried her face into the flowers and breathed as deeply as she could. "It's like he is here," she whispered. "If I close my eyes, it's like I can feel him."

"I have already planted a fresh crop of leo flowers. They will need time to grow, but you're welcome to take these if you'd like."

"Are you sure?" she asked, stretching toward the fragrant flowers.

"I'd give you the world if I could. Please, take them."

"Thank you." She reached across the desk and squeezed my hand. "I don't deserve you. Shall we start?"

"You do realize if we do this, you won't be able to hold anything back. I can ask you anything in the world and you'll have to answer."

"I trust you. I can't love you the way you want me to right now, but I trust you completely. I'm sure."

I removed the heavy chain from below my shirt and lifted the key at the end above my head. I unlocked the desk drawer and pulled out two petite glass vials, setting them between us.

"You will be coherent the entire time, just not in control of your answers. This vial," I said, pointing toward the blue, "will force the truth from you. This one," I said, pointing to the red, "is the counter serum. It will dissolve the blue from your system. Tell me first, though." I lifted the blue vial. "If we learn you can reveal the king's enchantment, does it change anything for you? Will you leave with me?"

"Someday." She looked at me with those enchanting eyes.

"I'll take that." I smiled, holding it out for her to take.

"Cheers, Tem," she said, and took the contents in one swallow.

CHAPTER

38

Ara

he modest inn was nothing special, but it did have a private bath. Though I had been given an invasive and thorough treatment, which included Nadra's mother looking over my naked body and clicking her judgey little tongue at me, I'd happily escaped, bathed, waxed and fully groomed. It didn't matter that I was going to my room and straight to bed. They had insisted, at one point calling me a filthy animal. I'd never felt cleaner in my life, though, so I guessed it was worth the deliberate torture.

I sent a message for Nadra to meet me the next day. I wasn't sure if I should tell her what her mother had asked of me or not, but I also didn't have a clue how to drive a wedge between her and her married lover. What did I know about love, anyway? I hated people most days. I loathed the very idea of falling in love. I never wanted to be mated.

"So . . ." she said, picking at the lint on the floral printed curtains like she didn't live in fabric hell. "What shall we do today?"

"I need to take my weapons to be sharpened."

She looked at me like I had slapped her. "For goodness sake, Ara. We are not barbarians. What on Alewyn do you even need a weapon for."

"Nadra," I answered, trying to keep the condescending tone from my voice. "You yourself told me there's a problem with the lesser fae."

"I don't see what that has to do with you or me."

I clenched my jaw and gave up. "Nothing, Nadra. Come with me to drop off the weapons, and then perhaps we can take a picnic in the park." I was navigating in the dark here, but that seemed like something a high fae from the city might do.

She scoffed.

I'd guessed wrong. "Listen, we can do whatever you want to do, Nadra. I just need to do this one thing first."

"Fine, but then we should take lunch with Linnie and the other girls. Maybe we can stop at the jewelers on our way back."

I hid my face and slouched. I absolutely did not want to have lunch with the girls, nor did I want to go shopping. So, of course, I agreed, trying to keep my eye on the prize. The more I knew about Nadra, the likelier I was to find a way to end her relationship. I needed that gown to get in and out of the castle so I could leave this hell hole and never come back.

Before I knew it, we were sitting around a raised table in the swanky gardens behind Linnie's opulent cottage. Piles and piles of baked tarts and scones sat atop elegant, gold-lined dishes as beads of sweat dripped down my neck. While I felt like a pig, the rest of the females fanned themselves, looking ever the portraits of grace.

I avoided the stares from the other females and sat in silence, staring at the plethora of tantalizing sweets along the decorated table. Why in the world would they set these out here, taunting me, if no one was going to even touch them? I dabbed my chest with the napkin and tugged up on Nadra's borrowed gown.

"Don't you think so, too?" one of the females asked.

Nadra bumped my shoulder, and my head snapped up. "I'm sorry, what?"

Several of the ladies giggled.

"I was just mentioning how handsome the prince is. Don't you agree?"

I tried not to puke. "Oh, sure. Sure." I nodded, trying to fit in.

"Don't tell me you haven't seen him yet. He's been staying at the castle for ages now."

"Oh no, I've seen him. We've had several little chats, he and I," I said, forcing a smile.

"Wait, you've spoken to him?" Linnie asked, leaning in.

"Mmmhmm."

"What's he like? Really?" she asked.

"I don't know. Bossy? Angry and bossy."

She sat back and gave a curt nod. "I should hope so. He's to take over the Flame Court someday."

"Riiiiight." I nodded.

Obviously.

"Ara, darling. Nadra tells us you're from the country, just like my Huntagh. Do tell us what country life is like," one of the other females chirped.

"Huntagh?"

"Oh yes," she flipped her hand forward to show the silver band. "We were married only weeks ago. We met at the king's luncheon months ago. It was love at first sight. But do tell about the country life." She pulled her hand to her chest.

So that's where he had gotten off to. I'd doubted he'd ever find someone.

"Uhm." I shrugged. "I guess it's like living in the city?" I wasn't sure what to say. I couldn't very well tell her I'd spent hours everyday training in a fighting arena before my parents were murdered and I decided to go around killing asshole high fae.

"Oh, come now, it must be so very different," another chimed in.

I eyed the blueberry muffin as the icing dripped to the cloth-covered table. "Well, I guess we have chores. We have to keep the animals fed."

"Oh, it sounds so dreamy."

Unable to hold myself back any longer, I snatched the muffin and dropped it to my plate, adding three more to top it off.

"And, do you still live with your parents, Ara?" Linnie asked.

I shoved the entire muffin in my mouth and said, "They're dead."

Two ladies gasped, and Nadra kicked me from below the table, laughing loudly and awkwardly.

I looked at her and shrugged, cramming in a lemon tart once my mouth had the room. "What?" I mumbled.

Needless to say, she dragged me out of the lunch as quickly as she could, and I almost felt bad for embarrassing her. My father had introduced us years ago, but we had never really spent any time together. Apparently, she didn't know me as well as she thought she did.

"Remind me to never do that again," she grumbled.

"I need to go pick up my weapons and get back to the inn. Since we did lunch your way today, maybe we could do dinner my way tomorrow."

"And what exactly is your way?" she asked, scrunching up her face in disgust at the thought.

"Let's go to the tavern and have drinks."

"Okay, yeah, I could do that." She smiled.

"Forgiven?" I asked.

"I guess," she said, walking away.

***

Later, I sat alone in a crowded tavern, grateful to be out of the stifling dress and hiding within the shadows of my hood once again. I ordered the roast lamb and savored every minute of it without Nadra there to judge me. I'd let my two-drink maximum rule slide and was on my third glass when the door opened, and I nearly spit my drink across the pub.

He strode in like he owned the place, scanning the crowd, the surfaces, even the floor. Prince Fenlas had two males with him, both as tan as he was and both a little rough around the edges. The messy blond haired high fae with a boyish grin ordered drinks and pulled out a deck of playing cards, while the other, with dark hair pulled back and covered in tattoos, sat stoic, his large hand thrumming along the table as he surveyed the crowd.

I leaned against the cool back of the metal chair and cast a furtive glance at the captivating prince. For several moments, he was calm. Still. Like bated silence. A lingering breath. It was probably the wine talking, but sweet baby boggarts he was gorgeous. Broad chest, towering frame, a shadow of a beard across his sharp jaw, and those charming, forest-green eyes that weakened me. I had to kick myself to be released from the spell. Beautiful, yes. Asshole, yes. One thousand times, yes.

I looked away and soaked my buttered biscuit in the savory gravy, jamming it in my mouth. I wanted to ignore them. I did, but they laughed loud and often, and it seemed the entire place was enraptured by him and his crew.

"Hey, Kive. How's the wife?" he called across the bar with his perfect smile.

The male raised his glass in the prince's direction and answered, "Probably still trying to find me."

The entire place erupted into laughter, and I couldn't help but join them.

"How's your father, Fen?" another called.

He smiled and answered, "Probably still trying to find me."

Again, the tavern filled with laughter, and I realized not only did he frequent the place, he actually took the time to get to know the fae here. I hadn't expected that. His eyes shifted around the room frequently, almost uncomfortably, as he searched for something. He mumbled to his friends often and he spoke aloud to them, and I had to believe they were having two different conversations, though he seemed to be enjoying himself. They were analyzing the room without everyone knowing it and for a moment I smirked as I saw my father in those fleeting movements.

The low trill of the bells over the door rang out again, and a high fae with pale hair and stocky shoulders stumbled in. His face was slightly familiar, though I couldn't place him. He had his arm wrapped around a curvy female dressed in scarlet, and the bar grew quieter as they entered. They found an empty seat, and the fae could hardly keep his hands off the female while the bar girl tried to take his order.

Not long after they walked in, the door chimed again and a group of four, clad in black, walked in. The place was nearly full. I imagined this type of crowd in a small town would be the tavern owner's dream.

The four high fae sat at the table beside mine, and though one eyed me, they kept to themselves. I noted the weapons. In the entire room, Prince Fenlas and his crew each had at least two that I had counted. One female in the corner had a knife strapped to her belt and one older fae several tables down wore a sword. But all four of these males were armed to the teeth and radiating trouble.

The volume of chatter in the room reduced by half, and I watched as the prince's friends changed their demeanor. They became rigid in their seats and remained quiet. Several of the fae in the crowd looked between the two groups of males, waiting for something. Some of them even got up and left, patting the prince on the shoulder or shaking his hand before they walked out. The tavern swelled with tension.

The murmur of voices was just enough to mask the conversation happening beside me from the majority of the room. Not from me, though.

My hearing was impeccable, and they were close. I kept my head down and listened.

"You're sure?" one asked.

"Yes, he said two lessers."

"What time?" another asked, taking a drink of his amber ale.

"Whatever time this hell hole closes."

"We'll wait in the alley, then. Shouldn't take long."

My evening just got interesting.

The males stayed quiet the rest of the night and, at some point, the prince and his friends left, not quite as cheerful as they had been when they entered. I slipped out shortly after them and crawled through the darkest shadows in the dingy alley, waiting. Water dripped from a nearby gutter hanging by a rusted nail. An overflowing bin of trash left a repugnant stench in the humid air, and my skin tingled. My twitchy fingers were ready.

I heard the distant sound of a bird's cry high above and then another answer from the top of a separate building. I knew those weren't birds, and it couldn't be from the high fae in the tavern because they hadn't left yet. I decided to stick to the darkness and wait, keeping my hands steady, though my heart pounded. The last time I tried to fight several males at once, it barely worked out in my favor. I wasn't injured this time, though, so I relied on that as I tried to come up with a plan.

Before long, two lesser fae rounded the corner, just as the male in black had said. They leaned in and whispered back and forth, totally unaware of the dangerous world around them. Shortly after, the four large fae from the tavern stalked behind them. I waited longer than I wanted to. The high fae quickly closed the gap and snatched the lesser fae. Just as I was about to step out and chuck my throwing knife, a dark figure dropped from above, and then another and another. Within minutes, the four high fae were lying on the ground, the lesser fae were running off down the alley, and the three that had come were standing there like they'd just taken tea with the king.

"Damn, Fen, you always take the easy ones."

"That guy would have eaten you for breakfast, Kai." He laughed.

"Well, I am tasty," he answered.

"How the fuck would you know that?" another asked.

"Your mom told me," he answered and bolted down the alley, laughing.

The other chased after him, and the prince followed, though just before he rounded the corner, a gentle breeze blew through the side street and stopped him dead in his tracks. He turned toward me and I swear he saw me. His face was cold and beautiful, lit by only the silver moon in the darkened sky. After several lengthy seconds, he turned and walked away.

I stepped out of my hiding spot only when I knew they were gone. I had definitely just witnessed the prince of the Flame Court take out Marsh Court high fae before they could kill or kidnap a couple of lessers. What did that even mean?

I walked back to the room I'd rented for the week and prayed I could get out of Hrundel sooner rather than later. I didn't want to get involved in anything that had to do with the prince.

I bathed for the second night in a row and, as I trailed my fingers through the tepid water of the bath, let myself think of him anyway. The way he towered above me and always had heat behind his vicious stare. The way his full lips curled when he smiled. The way he commanded a room and ignored the females who fawned over him.

I watched his hands kill a male, and whether it meant I was demented or not, I imagined those skilled hands on me. Softly stroking me. I moved my hand into the space between my legs and thought of those green eyes until I was panting with need for him. I hated myself for this almost as much as I hated him, and still, I moved my fingers until the orgasm hit me.

There was definitely something wrong with me.

Temir

"*J* don't feel anything," Gaea said.

"I don't think you will feel it. Let's start with something easy. Try to lie to me. What is my name?"

"T—" She opened and closed her mouth. She tried to fight it, but still, she answered. "Temir." Her mouth fell open.

"You're sure you want me to continue?"

"Yes and no," she answered. "I want to know the truth, but that doesn't mean I'm not afraid of it."

"When was the last time the king successfully enchanted you?" I asked.

"Three years ago." She looked away, letting the memory play.

"Can you remember what it was?"

She paused for a long time and then finally answered. "He asked me to take him to meet with Morwena and then removed the memory. I remember it now," she said in awe. "It was not a big deal. I'm not sure why he enchanted the memory from me."

"Probably because he was hiding that he and the sea queen have been scheming a lot longer than they want anyone to know."

"That makes sense," she agreed. "Let's go back a lot further."

"Can you think of them on your own?"

"No," she answered truthfully. "You have to directly ask me something, I believe."

"Has the king given you any demands should you try to escape?"

"No," she answered.

"Has the king enchanted you to betray anyone that would help you escape?"

"No."

"Has the king given you orders about helping others escape?" I rubbed my coarse knuckles as I waited.

"No," she answered.

I could see the sturdy hesitation in her eyes, and I waited. We had the answers we needed to leave, but would she truly ever leave with me now? I wanted to ask so badly, but the truth scared me more than a lie.

She stood and reached into her pocket. "I want you to ask me this." She pulled out a slip of paper and slid it across the table. I opened the note and read it.

"No," I answered.

"Please. I need to know," she said, closing her eyes and taking in a calming breath.

"Has the king . . ." My voice shook. If I thought she would never recover from Oleo's death, this would tip the scales. "I can't do it, Gaea. Even if you could handle this truth, I couldn't." I set the paper on the desk.

"If it were you, wouldn't you want to know?" she asked.

I picked it up and crumbled it in my hands. "Has the king ever enchanted you to forget seducing him or anyone else?"

"Yes," she whispered as tears began to slide down her lovely cheeks.

"Who?" I demanded. "When?" I stood from my desk and began to pace furiously. "Actually, no, don't answer that. Don't tell me. Take the red serum, Gaea." I didn't even wait for her to do it. I slammed my hand into the door and charged out.

I knew the king was a piece of shit. I knew he was a murderer. I knew he had raped females. I thought I knew all of the skeletons in his endless closet, so I don't know why I was shocked to hear this one, but I was. He always pampered his prized magical fae. Had always boasted about the lives he provided us and the privileges we had. And it was all a disgusting lie. He had ruined all of us, and the worst part was, he made us forget about it. He had used her.

"Tem?" she said from the open doorway.

"No!" I roared at her. "I didn't want to fucking ask you. I didn't want to know. How could he, Gaea? How could he?" I crossed the room and wrapped my arms around her, shaking as she silently wept in my arms. Those giant tears felt like fuel to my burning heart. "I'm so sorry, my love. I'm so, so sorry that happened to you."

"I'm going to kill him. Somehow," she whispered into my ear as she hugged me back.

"It's probably going to take more than just me and you to kill the king."

She shook her head.

I held her shoulders and pulled away from her so I could see her face.

"Thane," she mouthed.

The entire world erupted into flames. My body went numb. I let go of her and stepped away. I couldn't process it. My mind absolutely refused.

I shook my head. I waited for her to take it back. To say anything contrary to what she had indicated.

"Go back to your rooms and stay there. Make sure someone knows you are there."

"No, Temir. You can't. It wasn't like that. He only touched me."

"Was it your choice, Gaea?" My nostrils flared.

"No," she said, making herself small, avoiding my eyes.

I'd never made it outside so fast. I hoped he would be there. That prick lived and breathed for the blood of others, and I'd make him drown in his own. "Thane!" I yelled.

The crystalized wind gusts ripped through the arctic air, and the snow blew so heavily, I knew only a crazy person would be outside in a northern blizzard. He was exactly that, though.

"Thane!" I screamed again, storming through the open lists.

He sat alone in a sheltered corner, sharpening a blade like a gods damn maniac. He looked up just in time for me to slam my solid fist across his face. He didn't even hesitate. He launched himself from the bench at me and we tumbled to the frozen ground. His bracelets rattled in my ear, and I remembered too late that Oravan, the blacksmith, had gifted him the strength of ten males. We exchanged blow after blow, rolling around on the ground. His solid hits breaking bones with each connection. He grabbed my neck and squeezed as his own eyes bulged.

"What the hell is your problem, Temir?" He smashed my head into the ground. "Did you finally decide you weren't worth a shit, either? Now that the old fuck is gone, you want me to end your pointless life?"

I tried to gasp for air, but there was nothing. Dots crossed my vision and my throat began to burn. I slammed my elbow into his face to break the hold. His grip loosened. I filled my burning lungs desperately. Hitting him in the gut, I shoved him off me. He rolled. I scrambled over the top of him.

"You touched her." The pounding in my ears was deafening.

He laughed, a little at first and then it grew into a full-bodied laugh. "Of course I did. Just remember every time you touch that lithe little body, I was there first. She liked it, too. Probably more than she likes it with you. Does she still whimper?"

I reached beside me, grabbed a muddy rock from the ground and smashed it across his face. I felt him jerk, a sharp pain in my side, and then the spread of warmth. He had stabbed me, leaving the knife embedded in my gut. Blood poured. My vision went dark, and the only thing I could think of was killing him. I wanted to rip the life from him. I wanted to break every bone in his body. For Gaea. For Oleonis. For myself. I struck his face again.

He pulled the knife from my side then jammed it back in.

I fell to the ground, panting. The pain was immeasurable.

He yanked the knife out again, stood and kicked me in the open gash.

I cried out.

He laughed again, got down on his knees beside me, and leaned in close. "Did you really think you could come here and kill me, Temir? And now, once you're dead, I'm going to make it my personal mission to take her on every surface of that castle, whether she wants it or not. And I'll make sure to tell her it's your fault for angering me."

Adrenaline coursed through me as he spat. I reached up and grabbed his throat. I had a secret. One I hadn't even told Oleo, though I thought he might have guessed it long ago. My power ripped from me and, without a second's warning, Thane crumbled to the ground. Not only was I a healer . . . I was a killer. I'd fought against it, denying I would ever have the strength to use it. But Thane deserved nothing less.

It had happened accidentally once when I was a child. Oleonis made me pick berries from a thick bush full of thorns. I hated that job and whined to him that I didn't want to do it. He insisted, and I obeyed. I plucked berries for hours, trying so hard to avoid the thorns, but inevitably, one pricked me. In a burst of rage, I jammed my hand into the roots of the plant and killed it. I was so worried Oleonis would think me a bad person, I dug up the bush and burned it. He never asked about it and I never told him. I was devastated to find out I carried a gift of life and of death. I'd never used it on purpose and I never would again. Thane may have deserved it, but I would not play a god in this broken world.

I brought my trembling hands to my wounded side and, as my power coursed through me, I felt instant relief. I began to stand when suddenly Gaea was beside me and then we were gone.

I fell as we landed in my rooms, grunting as she sprinted to my closet.

She yanked out a clean shirt and tossed it to me. "I've never hated you and been so proud of you as I am right now," she said, pulling my shirt above my head. "Get dressed quickly."

"Did you watch?" I asked.

"I couldn't see through the storm. I waited as long as I could and then spirited, thinking I would have to save you. And then he was dead and you weren't. How?"

I grunted again, pulling down on the clean shirt. "Oleonis told me I'd have to beat him on my terms and not his, so that's what I did. What are we doing?" I asked, standing. I was still sore from the knife wound. It was healed, but the phantom pains were still there.

She grabbed my hand and we spirited away again, landing in the hall. "We have been together this entire day. Do you hear me, Temir? You need to make sure everyone sees you at dinner. Laugh, make a scene, brood, do whatever you want, but you were never in the lists. The king will kill you without a second thought if he knows you killed his commander."

At least one of us was smart today.

"Don't make a scene. They don't deserve it and wouldn't believe it," I said quietly. I took her hand in mine and walked into the dining hall.

We made a few comments to fae who sat at the table beside us. Before dinner was served, the king walked in. I straightened, and Gaea rested her hand on my leg under the table. I felt that familiar anger settle over me as I looked at him. He had forced her into that situation and made her forget. He had used her. He saw me looking and walked straight over.

"My king," I said, bowing my head, swallowing back my burning rage.

I wanted to do it again. The dark magic calling to me was terrifying. I knew I should never feed that ravenous power. It would never work on the king, anyway. My power could never be used against a king or queen. Their magic was stronger. I just had to keep reminding myself of that as he stood there, inches away, staring at me.

"Since when do you take dinner in the hall?"

"Gaea thought I should leave my rooms and get some fresh air, my king."

"Did she now?" he asked, looking at her more critically than me.

She bowed gracefully and pasted on a cheerful smile. "It's time we moved on, my king. We have a world to conquer, and we won't accomplish anything sitting around crying over things we can't change."

I knew she didn't mean it.

"Quite right," he said, smiling. "I'm glad to have you both back. Enjoy your dinner."

We looked at each other as he walked away, and I could feel her claws digging into my thigh.

After dinner, I walked Gaea to her room. There was still an awkward distance between us, but we had moved miles that day. I didn't stay and I didn't hold the lack of affection against her.

I had one more thing to do before I went to bed.

"You sent for me, milord?" Roe asked, standing in my rooms, hat pressed to his chest.

"I accept your invitation. Just tell me where to be and when to be there."

CHAPTER

40

Ara

"I thought we said dinner," I grumbled, letting a way too cheerful Nadra into my room before the sun had completely risen.

"We did say dinner," she said, shoving arms full of fabric at me. "I thought we could do dinner after lunch."

"Well, yes, that is the general order." I rolled my eyes and dropped the gowns onto the only chair in the rented room. I moaned and stomped back to my uncomfortable bed, pulled the covers back and slipped back in, throwing the blankets over my head.

"Oh, no you don't." Nadra ripped the blankets off me and sucked away all the cozy warmth I had spent the entire night cultivating.

I took a deep breath and slowly let it out. "Remind me why we're friends again?"

"Don't be silly," she said, walking into my washroom. "Is this all you have for soaps?" She held the remnants of the single bar of soap I had brought from Betha's.

"I travel light," I said, trying to hide my growing temper behind a smile.

"Don't be such a banshee. We have things to do today."

I flicked my gaze to the ceiling.

"Ara!" Nadra chastised. "That is not becoming of a lady."

"I'm not a lady, Nadra. I'm barely alive at this time in the morning. I promise I'll do whatever you want today if you just let me sleep for a couple more hours."

"Mmm. No. Rise and shine, princess." She threw open the dusty curtains, and I smirked.

"See? The sun isn't even out yet."

"I know. But from up here, I bet it's pretty when it does come out."

Though she tested every ounce of patience I had, I knew I needed to suck it up and give her the time she needed. I had to figure out how I was going to accomplish her mother's task if I wanted any chance of infiltrating the castle. "Fine, you win. What exactly are we doing today?"

She crossed the room and sat beside me on the bed. She reached out a hand, lifted the ends of my hair and recoiled, then shuddered in case I missed the first sign of disgust. "Shopping. We have to do something about this." She gestured to all of me.

"My hair is fine," I said, pulling away, "and I don't have the coins for shopping."

She reached into the leather bag she wore and pulled out a bag of coins, dropping it onto the bed. "This should cover it," she said, smiling.

"Nadra, no."

"Listen. I rarely ever have a chance to just hang out with someone for an entire day and do whatever I want. Mother has me working in the shop at all hours just to keep me from Odir. I know she knows about him. I need a break. Just, please come?"

"Fine." I sighed. "But we are not playing dress-up."

"Oh, come on, Ara. Pretty please? I brought some options." She pointed at the pile of clothes.

I narrowed my eyes at her, lowered my chin and firmly said, "No."

So, naturally, an hour later I had tried on everything she had brought while she judged me. Spinning me from side to side and pinching the fabric at my waist and hips, she decided nothing would work.

"Let's go get this hair sorted out, and then we will stop at the shop after lunch to find something better."

They say patience is a virtue. I didn't need virtues. I didn't want them. I'd happily travel around with no morals and no decency just to avoid the girliest day of my entire existence.

"Oh my," the groomer or whatever he was called said, tsking every few minutes as he examined me from all angles. He got his fingers stuck in my long, thick hair several times.

I looked at the mirror and realized they were all right. I was a mess. Traveling across the Marsh Court had not been kind to me. It was so hard to think about being pretty when I'd killed people, when I knew others were dying for no reason, and it felt ridiculous to sit here and consider pampering was actually a thought in the world when I knew much bigger things were happening.

Again, I had to keep my eye on the end game. I needed that gown. I needed to get into the castle, find my book and get the hell out of here. The process sucked, but it was the only way. Could I have scaled the castle walls, snuck through the palace, walked into the library, found my book hidden among millions and snuck back out? Maybe. But the odds weren't great, and this would make it so much easier. If I could just get through this day.

So, I sucked it up and let them fuss and tug and pull and poke and prod until I stood back in my rooms with my waist cinched tight, my hair gleaming and smoothed, and my cheeks rosy. If I leaned over, my breasts would fall straight out of the front of the dress, and if I took too wide of a step, I was pretty sure my ass would show. The slit was high and the midnight blue dress, though beautiful, was nothing I would have ever worn.

"Don't you think, Ara?" Nadra said, pulling me from my thoughts.

"Huh?"

"King Autus," she answered, fanning herself. "Isn't he just so dreamy. The way he walks around the room in those furs and his beautiful, vicious smile. I'd marry him in an instant."

"Ew. You do realize his vicious smile is because he is *actually* vicious, right? I don't think we've ever gone an entire dance without him killing a lesser fae for something ridiculous."

"Oh, I know. But if we fell in love . . ." She sighed. "He'd do anything for me. Even be kinder if I asked."

"Doubtful," I answered, shoving a piece of cheese from our lunch tray into my mouth.

"Ara, honey, you have to stop taking life so seriously. Let a girl dream."

I'd forgotten fae still dreamed.

"Which tavern are we going to for dinner and drinks?" she asked.

"East End?" I answered, fidgeting with the dress again.

"Oh, I love that place. Everyone is always so friendly."

"You've been?"

"Oh honey, I've probably got a running tab in every tavern in Hrundel."

"Of course you do," I said, smiling. "Ready to go?"

"Yes!" She leaped out of her seat. She leaned into the mirror and pinched her cheeks a few times, then pushed her chest up a little higher.

I couldn't help but laugh as she wiggled her eyebrows at me and sauntered out the door.

Everything was different from the night before. Then, I could hide in the folds of my cloak, but this time, I was practically naked. Several of the males in the room watched us as we found a table. My eyes darted through the rugged tavern looking for danger, while Nadra didn't even seem to notice.

"Tell me about Odir," I prompted, hoping I had waited long enough to bring him up.

"Oh, honey," she said, fanning herself. "He is perfection. You've seen him before. Remember the masquerade at the castle for All Fool's day?"

"Everyone had masks on." I laughed.

"Yes, but his mask string broke and he had to walk around like a lesser fae because he was the only one that didn't have a mask."

I drew my head back and raised my eyebrows as I remembered his face.

"Yes, that's him," she said with a smile. "I knew you couldn't forget him. He's so handsome."

"Indeed," I said, hiding my expression behind my drink.

I convinced myself the prince and his lackeys wouldn't come to the same tavern two nights in a row, but as the door opened and they shuffled in, I shrank as much as possible in my worn seat and hoped he didn't see me. He knew me, somehow. Had said my name all those months ago and never left me alone when I was near.

"Sweet baby boggarts, Ara," Nadra said, grabbing my arm. "Look who just walked in. Wait, don't look. Seriously, look."

I rolled into myself a little farther and turned my back more to him.

Nadra gave me a weird look and nudged me. "He's coming this way," she practically squealed.

"What?" I shrieked.

She tried to smile naturally as her eyes began to glow. "He's looking at you," she said behind her teeth. "Turn around."

I could feel the burning of his gaze on my bare back as I slowly turned to face him.

"Hello, you," he said, glaring at me.

The baritone of his sultry voice resonated so deeply within me, I shivered as it traveled through my body. I tried not to think of that moment in the bath, of what the thought of him did to me. My cheeks flushed anyway, and I hated myself. Aibell flashed through my mind, and I did a quick check of my mental shields. Who knew what or who he kept for company?

"Prince Fenlas," I said, pulling my glass to my lips and smirking. I bet he wanted me to stand and curtsy. I didn't. I looked to Nadra and had to bite my lip to keep from laughing. Her jaw was on the floor, and I didn't think she had blinked since he walked in.

"Slumming it in the local taverns?" he asked, leering at me like a wild beast watches its prey. He looked at my chest, and I felt him falter.

He didn't want me to see it, but I did. I leaned forward, putting my elbows on the table. "Something like that," I answered, smiling oh so sweetly at him.

He cursed under his breath, and his face turned red with anger. He looked around the room and back to me.

"Is there a problem?" I asked.

He began to reach for me. I slid my hand below the table, resting it on the knife strapped to my thigh. Before he got too far, his friends grabbed him.

"Nope, no problem here, beautiful," one of them said, tugging him backward.

His head snapped to the tattooed fae who spoke, and I thought for sure he was going to kill him. Instead, the fae leaned in and whispered in his ear, still pulling him from our table. He kept his eyes glued to mine, and I waved as he was escorted back to his seat.

"What an asshole," I said, turning back to Nadra.

She was frozen in her seat with bulging eyes and a gaping mouth. "What just happened?" she whispered.

I shrugged.

"He, like, hates you," she said. "I thought he was going to kill you right here at the table."

I waved her off and sipped my chilled wine. "I was ready. I would have taken him out first." I'd never understand the southern prince. I combed through all of the run-ins we'd had. Nothing made sense. But then the words of my prophecy played like a song in my memory. Maybe he knew somehow. But no, he couldn't. Aibell would have mentioned it.

"Maybe we should go," I said, suddenly feeling a lot less confident. I looked across the congested room to see the prince's furious eyes watching me.

"Yeah. We should," she said, looking between me and the prince.

We left our half-empty glasses of wine at the table and squeezed our way through the crowd when the door opened again.

Nadra gasped and turned toward me.

Fuck. I knew this was what I needed to happen, but the look on her harrowed face was devastating. He had come again. It was a different female tonight, but the handsy fae from the night before had come back. The minute she mentioned the masquerade, I'd realized why he looked familiar. Her married lover apparently had many other lovers. I wasn't sure why she was surprised, but she certainly was.

I began to pull her toward the door, but she wouldn't budge. Her eyes were locked on Odir, and he didn't seem to care at all that she had seen him.

"Did you know?" she asked. "Did you know he was seeing someone else?"

"Nadra, no. I did see him here last night, but I didn't know it was him until you reminded me what he looked like earlier. I didn't know how to tell you."

She dropped my hand and stomped up to Odir. "Who is this?" she asked, gesturing toward his companion.

"Don't be that girl," he answered.

"You're a pig, Odir."

"You didn't think you were the only one, did you, love?" He reached out to touch her face, and she slapped his hand away. "You little bitch," he spat, pulling his fist back to punch her.

I was there in an instant. I shoved her behind me, blocking his arm mid-swing.

He tried to push past me to get to her.

Big mistake.

I kneed him in the crotch and, as he doubled over, I cranked my arm back and punched that fucker in his face. The boisterous room had gone silent, and I could feel the intense stares as I watched him hit the floor. I turned, grabbed Nadra's shaking hand, noted the prince's careful expression, and dragged her out the door.

She sobbed the entire way home. I didn't know how to comfort her. *Peopling* was just not in my skill set. I opened the door to her mother's store, and she flew past her and ran up the steep stairs, sobbing.

"It is done, then?" her mother asked.

I dipped my head. I wished I had thought of a better way, but to be fair, I hadn't even planned this. Nadra was devastated, but the guy was every bit the pig she said he was, and in the long run, she would be happier.

"I'll have your gown ready in the morning. It is nearly finished," she said, pointing to an empty corner.

"Would you make me something else?"

"What do you need, dear?" she asked.

I explained to her what I had in mind, and her smile grew.

"You are your father's daughter," she said. "I'll need a bit more time to finish it."

I shrugged. "It will be worth the wait, I'm sure."

"Yes," she answered. "It will."

CHAPTER 41

Temir

he winding tunnels were a dark maze of musty slime and broken rock as I followed close behind Roe while the lantern lit the walls closing in around us.

"Are you sure this is right?" I asked for the third time.

"Aye. I'm sure." He pointed to the carved phoenix on the wall of the tunnel.

The tumultuous ground was slippery and cracked, and several times I had to duck to keep my head below the tunnel ceiling. The deeper and deeper we went, the heavier the air became. "No wonder the king has no idea this is happening. A troll couldn't find his way through here."

I thought of Bolgan, the council member, squeezing through the tunnels and smiled for the first time in days. There had been an investigation on Thane's mysterious death, and Evin was brought in to confirm Thane had died by magic. Which helped me more than hurt me because no one knew my secret. No one would ever know. The king was more vicious than ever as he yelled and stormed through the castle day after day. He barely acknowledged the murder of Oleonis, but you would have thought Thane was his blood brother. I hadn't considered what his death would do to the king. I don't think I'd thought about the repercussions at all.

More lesser fae servants had died than ever before, and I was genuinely concerned for Iva and Roe. I'd begged them to leave, but they refused. Staying in the castle meant they could report to the rebellion, a role they were hopelessly committed to.

"It's just ahead, milord," Roe's voice echoed.

"Roe, for the thousandth time, please stop calling me that."

"Force of habit," he answered.

Eventually, the darkness ahead flickered with soft golden light as the sound of water dripped in the distance and the smell of oil burned from the lanterns.

We stepped into a large, cavernous room with slick stone floors and jagged walls. It smelled of musk and stagnant water but was filled with more lesser fae than I had ever seen together in one place. They moved in silence, whispering.

"Why are they so quiet?" I asked Roe.

"Voices carry and fae ears are powerful."

I nodded as I followed him into the packed crowd.

"Roe," a timbered voice called across the room.

All eyes turned to the male and then to Roe and finally to me. Several of them pulled back, some glared at me, and someone even threw a sharp rock, hitting me in the arm. I kept my horns down and followed Roe to the male. I had expected this. They knew who I was, and they had seen me at the king's side for years and years.

The voices grew until the fae in charge held up his hand. I wasn't sure if he had magic, but instantly the room silenced. He had more control than the king. "Come, Roe," he said. "Bring Temir."

Roe grabbed my hand and pulled me through the gathering to the front of the hollowed cave.

"Welcome to the rebellion," the male said. He stood the same height as I did—much taller than most in the room—with a satyr's curled horns and coarse hair. His powerful eyes studied me for several minutes. "We have watched you for a long time, Temir. Why have you chosen to come to the rebellion?"

That was the easiest and most difficult question he could have asked me.

"Among the high fae, I am an anomaly, but among the lesser fae, I am worse. I watched a fae that was like a father to me die because of the king. I intended to leave this place behind, but now I know I have to do something more. I have to be a part of something bigger. I can provide you access to the information gathered in the council meetings. The king keeps me close by. I can give you this information also. I believe I can be a valuable resource to you, if you choose to use me."

The male looked at me and then turned to face the room. "You heard him. Roe will vouch for his loyalty."

Roe stepped forward, removing his crimson hat. "Temir is the same as you 'n me," he started. "The only difference is his magic saved him from the king's hatred. But Temir has never been anything but nice to Iva 'n me. We've been beaten; most of you heard Iva's story of when she was held down and burned with that fire poker for not shutting a door all the way. But Temir's never let us lift a finger in his rooms. You've heard of his kindness to the lad in the stables. He's a good fae 'n we need him."

The crowd murmured.

"What happened to Oleonis?" someone hollered.

"He was murdered. I don't know all the details, but the king had him killed."

"Why?" another asked.

"I could never explain why the king does what he does."

"What's your magic?" someone asked.

The fact that I had magic was common knowledge. It hadn't surprised anyone when Roe said it, but I had never revealed it to anyone by my own choice. The rebellion needed to trust me, though, and I needed to trust them. "If I show you, it must remain here. The king does not allow anyone to know what I am able to do. If word spreads, he will kill me." I paused, scanning the room. "You there," I said, pointing to a small fae male with a broken and bandaged wing. "Please, come forward."

He turned to the slender female at his side, and she nodded to him. He reluctantly hobbled forward.

"What is your name?" I asked him.

"Rabrhe," he answered.

"I see that your wing is broken."

He dropped his head to the ground and gulped. "I'll never fly again. They've taken it from me." His voice shook.

"May I?" I asked, reaching a hand toward him.

He nodded.

I removed the bandage and placed my hands on the front and backside of his broken wing, closed my eyes and called my magic forward, moving it through his veins and to the tips.

The entire crowd went eerily still as I stepped back.

"Please, tell me if you can fly now."

He batted his wings flawlessly and lifted from the ground. He dropped right back down and fell to his knees in tears.

The female ran to him pulling him into her arms. "You are saved, Rabrhe. You are saved. Thank you," she said, looking up to me.

"Can you fix my leg?" someone asked.

"Please. One moment," the leader of the rebellion said. "Are there any that would refuse Temir joining the rebellion. You must speak now."

The room remained still and quiet. I knew several wanted to deny me. But I also knew what my power would mean for them.

He nodded. "Welcome to the rebellion. If you would, please," he said, pointing to the male with the broken leg.

"If everyone that has an injury could please move into a line, I will do what I can."

The room shuffled around, letting the injured come forward.

I moved down the line as relief and smiles followed behind. And so it began. I had joined the rebellion, and for the first time in my life, I felt like the magic within me was a gift.

CHAPTER
42

Ara

"N early done, dear," Nadra's mother said. "Just spin to the left a bit."

I did as I was told, though I had been standing on the ivory pedestal in her dainty shop for over an hour.

"You remember what I told you?" she asked, pulling a long thread at the hem of the gown.

"If anyone touches me, your magic will fade, and I'll be visible."

"Yes. It is lucky you move like a dancer."

"Or a fighter," I countered.

"Or a fighter," she repeated. "Turn."

I spun again.

"There," she said, stepping away.

"Can you see me?"

"Of course I can see you. It is my magic after all."

"Right. How's Nadra today?" I finally asked, searching for a reflection in the mirror.

"She will be fine, dear. I will see to that. Now get going. I can't imagine sneaking into the castle is going to be a quick trip."

"No, it isn't," I agreed, hopping down. "Thanks for this." I gestured to the gown. It really was a lovely robin's egg color of satin with layers of creamy lace. It was such a shame no one would see it.

She moved until she was standing before me again. She reached a hand to grasp my shoulder and pulled away at the last minute studying me carefully. Stunned, I watched her as pride filled her eyes. At her own work, I was sure. Until she shook her head.

"Since the day I met you when you were this tall," she said, holding her hand to her own waist, "I knew you were going to do something significant in this world. You were never a stagnant child. Never aloof to the world around you. I've seen you a handful of times since then and I still get the same felling. Just be careful, Ara. Alewyn would sooner chew you up and spit you out than accept whatever change you intend to bring upon it."

I pressed my lips together, unsure of how to respond to the familiarity from Nadra's mother.

Opening my mouth to speak, she interrupted me. "I should have your other order done in a day or two."

I considered her words. I imagined my father standing here and what he would say. This was the day that would change everything. I'd seen the carnage of the high fae in this world. Maybe only a taste of it, but enough. I thought I could get away with just seeking truth. Attaining the knowledge of who I was meant to be. But with each day that passed, each crime I'd witnessed, I think I knew. I wasn't raised to be someone that could sit on the sidelines while half the world suffered. I was my father's daughter, with the strength and loyalty of my mother. This was my destiny. All of it. No matter what I'd find in that book, nothing would be the same from this point forward. The world needed change. And somehow, the world needed me to. It was time to embrace the truth I'd known for a while now. I had to take a stand. And that started with my prophecy.

The golden bell to the shop rang as I exited and danced around the people in the busy streets. In theory, this would be a piece of cake, but now the logistics seemed a little more complicated. I jumped to the left and then the right. I'd never realized how much fae avoided each other until they couldn't see me and didn't know to shift to the side. Eventually, I abandoned the cramped sidewalks and traveled down the middle of the cobbled street. Surprisingly, that was the safest option.

I had been eyeing the prominent castle from my elevated room during my entire stay in the city. I knew I would make it over the drawbridge easily enough during the daytime. The portcullis was opened and shut frequently, so I stood to the side and waited for the guard to open the iron gate. I crossed the bailey and made my way to the keep. I climbed all the stairs and was surprised to see more than the traditional four guards. I didn't linger, slipping inside behind a high fae lady of the court.

So far so good. I stood in the middle of the castle foyer and my heart skipped a beat as I looked down the hallway where I had been taken prisoner. I hoped the queen was nowhere around. I hoped her hunters were not here, either. In fact, I hoped I'd killed them all.

I shook my head and reminded myself to stay focused. I had come all this way and needed to stay on track. I tried my best to weave through the people in the halls as I went.

"I think I'll wear green next time," a court lady said to another as I slipped past them.

I walked up and down the gilded halls trying to find the elusive library. I'd only ever heard of it. I wasn't sure where it would be. Though the halls weren't packed, I had to step carefully and not even breathe as I passed the scattered court.

A massive troll with musty clothes bounded down the narrow hallway, and I had to smash myself against a window hoping he would miss me. He did, but only just.

The gossip in the hallways could entertain someone for days.

"Her husband found her in the king's bed, and rather than killing her, they say he joined them," a male murmured to another.

I found a set of stairs, made my way up them and rounded a corner on a pair of lovers naked and panting against the pearled wall. I blushed passing them. She was screaming his name and some other colorful words I added to my vocabulary. I covered a snicker with my hands and kept going. Only in a faerie castle.

"He was dead as can be. Just lying there," I heard a winged servant say to another.

"A human? Are you sure? We haven't had a human in the Marsh Court castle for at least a hundred years."

This one caught my attention. First, because I knew that to be false. Surely everyone knew there was a human here during Beltane. And second, because it dawned on me that he could have been the human they were talking about. He had died, though, and that stung. I hadn't known him, but I knew he had a family. One who had probably mourned him long before he passed.

"Do you think they will actually go through with it?"

"If they do, we are all in trouble."

Another group of gossiping fae took up the entire hallway, and I had to stand and wait for them to move. I couldn't slip through on either side without risking being touched, so I stood there for ages as they discussed King Autus's betrothal to Morwena.

After several hours of searching and catching up on everything that had ever happened in the history of Alewyn, I finally found the royal library. I stepped inside and into a different world. The cathedral-sized room was lined from floor to towering ceiling with more tomes than I had ever seen. Court goers meandered, turning aged pages in their careful hands as they read. Aisle after aisle of the perfect records filled the laden space. It smelled of tattered pages and bound leather, and the magic in the air was as thick as fresh honey. For ages, I had listened to my mother dream about coming here. I hoped she was with me now. I breathed in the familiar scent of tattered pages and glued spines.

If there was one thing my parents disagreed over, it was books. While my father would agree they were important, my mother would argue that the right book could save the world, but a sword would never do so. I didn't think a single book or sword would ever save our damaged world, but what did I know?

Unfortunately, I had no idea what sort of organization the books were in. Nothing seemed to be labeled. I couldn't ask the female behind the cramped desk, so I was stuck searching. I walked up and down the towering stacks, letting my fingers run along the raised edges of the books.

The only thing I knew for sure was that I was looking for an old book. Fae could live for a long time. My father was over seven hundred years old. I would need to find books that preceded him by hundreds of generations. I was probably looking for something that dated all the way back to when the elven race of ancient times ruled all of Alewyn, before the Iron Wars, before the four kingdoms, and possibly even before generalized civilization in the world—as civilized as the folk could be, anyway.

All books were charmed for preservation, but I had to believe this book would still have deep signs of age. I walked up and down the stacks, scanning. Some of the books high above would need a ladder, which meant I'd have to carefully maneuver one during the night if I couldn't find it below.

I stopped mid-stride as I ran across a book I wasn't looking for. I searched the aisles to make sure I was alone, pulled it from the tightly packed shelf, opened the book and found the word "magic" written in firm, bold lettering. I jammed it into the front of my dress and checked once more for prying eyes. Still alone.

As the number of fae in the library grew, I quickened my pace as much as I could while still searching. The library was a treasure trove of novels, and people traveled far to come here, but I'd hoped it would be mostly empty since Nadra had said the king wasn't allowing anyone but the court into the castle. I was wrong.

"Catch me, Myck!" a boy yelled as he rounded the corner giggling.

I sprung back, but thought for sure he rubbed against the tail of fabric that trailed me. He didn't. I knew in theory Nadra's mother had created a luxurious gown, so if the charm was broken, I would still fit in, but it made avoiding people slightly more difficult in tight spaces. It wouldn't have been an issue, but the southern prince was staying here, and I had no clue where Morwena was.

"Mavy, be quiet," an older boy chastised as he stomped past, chasing the younger. "The crones will steal you away."

I smiled at the threat. I'd heard that one many, many times in my childhood.

I covered about a quarter of the stately library by nightfall. I realized the farther back I went, the more daunting the varied titles became, and I found some withered books along the way, so I decided to go all the way to the back and work my way forward, instead. The robust female who worked in the library passed me with a gleaming lantern several times, and had I not known better, I swore she could sense me. Something misplaced in her perfect organization.

As I moved down another row of books, my heart pounded uncontrollably. My palms sweated. I couldn't explain it, but I could feel the pull like a tug on my breath. I was close. Possibly a world away from Nealla, but finally, the answer was close. Attainable. I reached for the leather-bound book that called to me, and the minute my fingers touched the aged spine, a jolt of electricity moved through me. She knew I sought her. She waited. There was darkness deep within the fragile pages, and though I was drawn to sit right there on the floor and find her within the book, I couldn't. I needed to get out of the castle.

Again, I stuffed the book into the front of my dress. I took a deep breath, letting pent up tension release from my heavy shoulders. I only had to make it out of the castle and this final task would be done. I was so close I could taste it. I knew now more than ever that this was the path I was supposed to follow. This was why my parents had fought so hard to protect me.

I rounded the corner, lost in my own thoughts, and gasped as I sunk back into the aisle I had come from. He was here. I closed my eyes and tried to calm my beating heart. I was safe. The prince couldn't see me. I was fine. This was fine.

"Hello, you," he breathed into my sensitive ear, scaring me half to death. "Nice dress, though I prefer the one from last night so much more."

"Stay the hell away from me," I bit out.

"It seems you're the one that has the problem staying away."

"Then let me go," I said behind clenched teeth.

He scoffed. "You have no idea what you're asking." He reached to grab me, and I jumped back.

How could I have been so foolish? Of *course* he could see me. It was a charm. Magic. He was royal. He could see through the magic easily. Shit. "Keep your fucking hands off of me."

He smirked, and I tried not to notice my heart's response to it. His guards rounded the corner. "Get her," he commanded.

They looked at him like he'd grown another head.

"Oh, right," he said, taking a casual step toward me.

Again, I moved back, but he was faster. He grabbed me around the waist and pulled me toward him. The charm melted from the gown. I heard the guard's reaction but couldn't look at them. Couldn't pull my eyes from Prince Fancy Pants. I couldn't even move. His captivating face was inches from my own. His breath caressed my lips. I was someplace in between heated pleasure and icy rage, and the fine line between the two held me locked in his steady arms.

"Now," he said softer than I expected, "you can take her."

They came around the sides of me and took my arms. Fenlas held me for several long seconds, eyes locked with mine, until finally he stepped away.

"I will kill you," I breathed.

"I'm looking forward to it."

The prince's guards pulled me toward the doors of the library. There was no way I was doing this again. I tried to yank free, but they held tight.

"Oh, she's a feisty one, Greeve. Fen's in trouble," the sandy-haired, mouthy one laughed.

I glared at him, and he snapped his stupid mouth shut and looked forward. The dark-haired one faced forward and kept silent. The smarter one. Still, I fought them. I flipped myself backward, thinking the surprise alone would do it, but no.

The mouthy one chuckled. "We will never get her all the way to Fen's room fighting like this. She'll cause a scene."

"You're damn right I will."

My chest tightened and my palms sweated. The only thing keeping me from yelling at the top of my lungs was the fear of Morwena finding out I was in the castle.

The two guards looked to each other, and the stoic one nodded.

Then the world went dark and I could feel myself whisking through the castle on a fluid breeze. I screamed, but no sound came out. I could still feel the firm hands on mine. I pushed against them as we continued to travel on the wind. I had absolutely no idea what was happening. Before

I could even begin to grasp it, we landed in the biggest bedroom I had ever seen.

"Sorry, Princess," the chatty one said as he shut and locked the door behind them.

Damn it.

End of Book One

Chaos and Destiny

&

Fate and Flame

Control can either be lost or taken.

Ara finds herself locked in the prince's rooms and she wants answers.
All of them. But when she doesn't like what she hears, she storms out
and begins another journey. Only this time, she's got a prince and his
lackeys on her tail and none of them know how to take no for an
answer.

Temir is done. With the king. With the hatred. With it all. As the
newest member of the rebellion, he has to prove himself useful,
navigate a devastating loss, and somehow find a way to help Gaea
through her own grief. But when King Autus sends him on a
dangerous mission, all bets are off.

King Tolero has lived for thousands of years, but the last fifty have
been the longest and hardest. Losing your mate, and thus half of your
soul, can devour you from within. But when his kingdom is under
attack, and his son is gone, he's forced to take control and let the beast
within him loose once more.

One Prophecy. One Rebel. One King. Absolute Chaos.

Chaos and Destiny

FAE RISING

2

CONTROL CAN EITHER
BE LOST OR TAKEN.

MIRANDA LYN

Acknowledgements

First of all, to the readers, thank you. Sometimes it's so hard to pick up a book and give the author the power to carry you away. It's even harder on a debut novel, so if you are still here reading these final words, my heart is smiling. I love to chat about this story and these characters. Drop me a line on social media. I'll be waiting. If you want to support me, please leave a review. Simply stating that you liked it can go a long way. Also, sorry for that cliff hanger! No part of this series was ever meant for just one book, but I promise it will be worth the ride.

To my husband, who has always supported every one of my crazy dreams, thank you. I don't think either of us knew the journey this adventure would take us on, but aren't those the best kind? You've always been right there for me and you're everything I never knew I needed.

To my girls, my little dreamers, thank you for giving me the time to write this story and for listening to me ramble about it for months. I hope you take this lesson and flourish. Follow your dreams, girls. Every. One. Of. Them.

To Tristopher, you've changed my life. Sharing your sparks of creativity created a wildfire and I'll never find the words to thank you for always being there, always answering the questions and mostly for loving this story. Someday, we will find Richard.

To Jess, the one that read every single word... we did it! Thank you for loving my characters from the moment they were scattered words in my mind. Thank you for losing sleep with me and laughing with me and crying with me. While the readers are just getting started, you and I will always have Atlas and we will always know... Oleo knew.

To Tiffaney, thank you for reading the rough draft and still asking for more. You've always been there no matter what is going on in your life and I'm forever grateful for that. I didn't grow up knowing what it meant to have a sister, but I've navigated adulthood semi successfully because you've been here to guide me when I've needed you most.

To Michael, a million thank yous for your unwavering faith in me and all your work on the website. You've always been my biggest fan and I'll always be yours. You're the best nerd I know and since you're also my brother that's kind of a compliment, but don't let it go to your head. I'm not sure how much bigger those ears can get.

To the BRA ladies, thank you so much for always being right there to support me, make me laugh, and weigh in on all the decisions. I'm so glad I found you all along this journey.

And finally, to my street team, the ladies that hyped this book so much alongside me, loved these characters, and begged for book two, thank-you. They say that it takes a village to raise and child, well this is my book baby and you are all my village. Thank you.

About the Author

Blood and Promise is the debut novel for Miranda Lyn. She grew up smack dab in the middle of the United States with nothing to do but dream up stories of fantastical creatures and powerful heroines. Now married with three children of her own, an idea sparked a buried passion within her to follow a dream and teach her children that anything is possible if you're willing to work hard for it. Be sure to follow me!

Instagram: https://www.instagram.com/authormirandalyn/

Facebook: https://www.facebook.com/authormirandalyn/

Twitter: https://twitter.com/AuthorMirandaL

Check out our website for extras, character art and exclusive content. www.faerising.com

Also, click here to sign up for the mailing list and get access to more exclusive content and giveaways!

https://www.faerising.com/subscribe

Printed in Great Britain
by Amazon